FRANCES PARKINSON KEYES
REVEALS THE INTRICATE PATTERNS
OF EUROPEAN DIPLOMACY AND
AMERICAN POLITICS

FAITH MARLOWE
Born of a great tradition, she dared to defy
a startled Europe.

CHRISTIAN MARLOWE
Faith's loving father knew Washington well
and loved it too much for an
unscrupulous wife.

RUDOLF VON HOHENLOHE
The dashing baron seemed the perfect match
for his woman of destiny.

SAM DUDLEY
He showed Faith a new world of simple
things, as well as a world of grandeur.

SEBASTIAN DE CERRENO
The gallant nobleman compelled Faith
toward her great challenge.

Avon Books by Frances Parkinson Keyes

ALSO THE HILLS

CRESCENT CARNIVAL

THE RIVER ROAD

HONOR BRIGHT

BLUE CAMELLIA

DINNER AT ANTOINE'S

CAME A CAVALIER

THE SAFE BRIDGE

SENATOR MARLOWE'S DAUGHTER

ALL THAT GLITTERS

THE CAREER OF DAVID NOBLE

VICTORINE

THE GREAT TRADITION

PARTS UNKNOWN

STEAMBOAT GOTHIC

JOY STREET

THE ROYAL BOX

QUEEN ANNE'S LACE

FIELDING'S FOLLY

ONCE ON ESPLANADE

Frances Parkinson Keyes

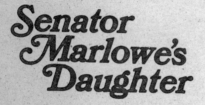

Senator Marlowe's Daughter

AVON
PUBLISHERS OF
DISCUS • CAMELOT • BARD

TO
Mary Gray

Whose faith in me never faltered throughout those years of novitiate which but for
her would not have culminated in dedication.

AVON BOOKS
A division of
The Hearst Corporation
959 Eighth Avenue
New York, New York 10019

First Avon Printing, December, 1961
Eighth Printing, August, 1970

AVON TRADEMARK REG. U.S. PAT. OFF. AND
FOREIGN COUNTRIES, REGISTERED TRADEMARK—
MARCA REGISTRADA, HECHO EN CHICAGO, U.S.A.

Printed in the U.S.A.

AUTHOR'S NOTE

Charles Morgan, in presenting "The Fountain" to the public, felt impelled to explain that in designating a great landowner of the Netherlands by a name typically Dutch, he had done so in order to give an illusion of reality to his story, and not because the character he had created bore any resemblance to the actual scions of an illustrious family. I feel that I should make a similar statement. For centuries, there have been von Hohenlohes in Germany and de Cerrenos in Spain, and the men bearing these names have been noble in every sense of the word. But as far as I am aware, none of them has had a career remotely resembling that of Rudolf von Hohenlohe or the Sebastian de Cerreno of my imagination. If I have wandered at times from the field of fiction to the field of fact in my portrayal of these personages, I have done so unconsciously and involuntarily.

F. P. K

CONTENTS

Senator Marlowe's Daughter

PART I

Flossie

Chapter I

FAITH MARLOWE sat on the dim, winding stairway, her plump, square little hands clasped tightly over her breast, her sturdy little shoulders braced against the heavy mahogany banisters. It was very dark in the hallway, so dark that she could hardly see the portraits of her grandfather, Christian Marlowe, who had been one of the outstanding figures in Buchanan's cabinet, and of her grandmother, the first Faith Marlowe, though she was standing directly beneath them, beside the tall clock which had been both made and owned by an earlier Christian Marlowe, before the Revolution, and which the cabinet officer had brought with him when he came to Washington. The gold frames of the portraits glittered, and this glitter penetrated the dust and the dusk, even though the painted canvasses which they enclosed were shrouded in gloom; and the brass balls with which the clock was surmounted glittered too. There was something comforting to Faith in their faint gleam, something steadying too, in the regular rhythmic ticking that tapped firmly across the hysterical tones of her mother's voice, as this rose, first in a shriek, and then in a wail, and then in a shriek again, from the closed library below.

"I don't care who hears me! I won't be quiet! I simply won't put up with it any longer! You keep telling me to be calm, and to be patient, and to control myself, until I am so sick of hearing you say all that over and over again, in your stiff, cold, New England way, that I feel as if I should scream just at the sound of your voice! I'd like to know if I *haven't* been patient! I guess any outsider who knew all the facts would say I had! I've scrimped and saved, and gone without company and clothes, and everything that a young, pretty woman likes to have, so that you could 'uphold' those silly old traditions of yours that you think are so holy, and go on with the stupid, tiresome 'career' that you consider

11

so ultra important. And what has all my sacrifice amounted to, I'd like to know? It's been bad enough all winter, trying to pretend that it didn't matter that you had been defeated, that the humiliation of having a husband who was a 'lame duck' didn't amount to anything! But I have struggled and smiled, and been nice to all the right people, hoping you would get an appointment of some sort—and you would have, if you had any guts at all! You could have gone straight to the President, and *made* him offer you *something*. But, oh no, you settled back and sulked and waited to be sent for—as if that old fish, Read, ever *sent* for anyone! And now you sit there placidly and tell me you propose to sell this house, and go back to the farm, and *vegetate* for the rest of your life! Well, Christian Marlowe, I can tell you this much—if you go to the farm, you go alone!"

"Faith loves it there." A man's voice, the voice of a man who was tired, and hopeless, and beaten, rose for a moment, ineffectually.

"Faith!" Flossie was shrieking again now. "Do you think I'd let her be buried there? What chance would she ever have, I'd like to know, of making anything of her life? Going to some little hick public school and marrying some country bumpkin! Well, I guess I can do better for her than that! I guess I've got money enough of my own, in spite of all I've squandered on you, to take her along with me! She's pretty enough and smart enough to bother with! If she was a horrid sniveling little nuisance, like some children—ugly and whiny and stupid—I'd be glad enough to leave her with you—it would serve you right! But Faith has got the goods to make a success of herself, and when she does I intend to be right there to cash in!"

An involuntary shudder of repugnance and premonition shook the child's solid little frame. She had not meant to be guilty of eavesdropping. She had spent a rather blank afternoon in her own room, playing with her two dolls, Clarissa and Rose, upon whom she usually lavished a good deal of maternal solicitude, but who had somehow seemed unsatisfying on this sultry, ominous day that was so unseasonably hot. So she had waited patiently until she heard the big clock on the stairway strike five, because it was tacitly understood between her father and herself that at five o'clock every evening she might come to the library, and that he would read aloud to her. Even Flossie, much as she resented this "waste of time"—a period which her husband might better have spent, in her opinion, making "worthwhile" calls with her—had come to take it for granted, and seldom intruded when Faith and Christian were thus preoccupied. So,

12

in starting down the stairs, the little girl had done so with a sense of complete security and happiness. It was her mother's voice that had halted her, first in surprise and then in horror. For a moment she had been so transfixed that she had not been able to go on. But now, aware that it was dishonorable to listen, she walked slowly down the stairs, across the hall, and out of doors, trying resolutely to close her ears to the shrill bitter tones that pierced her consciousness.

She did not know just where to go or what to do. Flossie did not consider it the "thing" for little girls to go out alone, but she could not afford to keep a governess, and she was far too engrossed with her ladies' lunches, and her "official" teas, to take Faith out herself. Indeed, she often left the house as soon as she had dressed after sipping the coffee which she drank in bed much later than Christian and Faith ate their breakfast, and played cards for two hours before luncheon. Christian took Faith to school on his way to the Capitol, and as he was busy in the "Chamber" when it was time for her to return, she walked back with two older girls who lived on lower Sixteenth Street. Then she had only Lafayette Square to cross diagonally, before she reached the tall, flat, narrow brownstone house with its black walnut front door, which had been such a center of distinction and elegance when Christian Marlowe, the cabinet officer, had lived there, but which his son, Christian Marlowe, the senator, continued to occupy only because he could not afford to move to a more fashionable part of the town.

Since Lafayette Square was the only place where she did not feel strange and ill at ease when she was unaccompanied Faith decided not to venture beyond it. She sat down on a bench, from which she could see her own house, her hands still clasped, her plump legs sticking straight out in front of her, and tried to think things over. It was hard for her to do this, partly because she felt so confused and bewildered and partly because it was so hot and noisy in the Square. The trees about her were drooping under dusty leaves which looked heavy with the heat, although it was only April; a few shabby and antiquated victorias drawn by dejected horses and driven by dejected coachmen were wheeling mournfully past, a few bicycles, noisily though listlessly propelled, lurched aimlessly along; men and women sprawled about in various stages of disorder and discomfort; fretful children hurled themselves against their parents' knees; and wailing babies twisted and turned in their crumpled carriages. Only the White House, remote and stately beyond the growth of trees and shrubbery, loomed clean and cool and lovely in the midst of all this squalor. Faith had been to the

13

White House several times. Her father had taken her in to shake hands with the President, Hillary J. Read, during the brief period before the public receptions, when members of both Houses of Congress were privileged to present constituents and relatives; and once Mrs. Read, who had three little sons of her own, had given a children's party in the East Room, to which the "younger official set" had been invited, and to which Faith had gone, as overawed as she was over-befrilled and beribboned. It would be difficult to say whether she had been more uncomfortable at the unaccustomed grandeur with which she was surrounded, or over the fact that she was the only little girl present who was not dressed in simple smocked silk or sheer embroidered muslin; but Flossie's taste ran to furbelows, and Faith submitted to it even though she suffered under it. Besides these memorable occasions, there were others of lesser importance: the annual Easter egg rolling and the annual reception to the Children of the American Revolution, for instance. But on the whole the White House was inaccessible, though Faith realized that her mother's vaulting ambition had stretched to its very portals before the political fortunes of the Marlowe family had begun to tumble.

"You know my husband's father missed the Presidential nomination by a *hair's breadth*"—Faith could just remember the mincing boast—"it was his short-sighted stand on the slavery question that was his undoing, but we feel *most* confident that Senator Marlowe will sweep everything before him at the next National Convention." Senator Marlowe had not swept anything before him, he had instead been swept aside himself. And since they could not go to the White House, since—it appeared from what Faith had involuntarily overheard—they could not even keep the shabby, gloomy, heavily comfortable house on Lafayette Square, why should they not all go contentedly together to the farm, why should Mamma hate it so? It was sweet and quiet and peaceful there, never hot and humid and dirty and noisy, as Washington seemed that night. In front of the solid old homestead there were lilac bushes which would soon be in bloom, as well as the apple trees in the orchard, and the place would be pervaded with their fragrance. There were calves and chickens and colts and lambs and baby pigs—a little girl could have all those delightful live creatures to play with out of doors, instead of being shut up in one small stuffy room with Clarissa and Rose. And Uncle Ephraim, who managed the farm which he and his brother Christian had inherited jointly, and lived there all the time, was so very kind and understanding, always realizing that

14

children like to go for the cows and ride on hayloads, while his wife, Aunt Emmeline, made such nice cookies, and always had a stone jar full of them, ready and waiting, on the pantry shelf behind the big pans where the smooth rich cream was set to rise.

Yes, certainly, the farm was a lovely place, Faith thought, and they might all be very happy there, if Mamma could think of it that way. Was there anything, Faith wondered, that she herself could say that would change her mother's viewpoint? Daddy had tried, of course, and failed. It was strange and sad that Daddy tried so hard and and failed so often—not only as far as Mamma was concerned, but as far as everybody and everything was concerned.

It had begun to grow dark. The fretful children and wailing babies had worn themselves out and were quieter now; the hot, tired men and women did not look quite so repulsive in the dusk; a little breeze began to stir the drooping leaves of the shrubbery; a light, suddenly snapped on at the entrance of the White House, shed its effulgent radiance on its classic columns clustered about the portico. Something tugged at Faith's heartstrings. It *would* be hard to leave Washington, even to go to the farm; never to gaze at the slender shaft of the Monument shining white against the blue sky that it seemed to pierce; never to take the boat down the river to Mount Vernon; never to hire one of the sagging old victorias and drive slowly to the Zoo; never to watch, enthralled, the money being made at the Bureau of Engraving and Printing; never to go down to Daddy's office, and listen to the fascinating tap-tap of the typewriters and admire the neatly piled bulletins and pamphlets. Faith had seen and done all these things with Daddy, and the memory of them was precious to her; she had not realized before how blank a future would be that did not include them. But it would be blank to Daddy too, for such sights and deeds had been his familiar pleasure ever since he was a little boy and went about with *his* Daddy—and his mother too, because, apparently, Grandmother Faith had not been as busy with other people as Mamma always was, and loved to roam around the Capital with her husband and their children. How selfish she, Faith, had been not to think more about Daddy and less about herself! She must go to him and comfort him. By now Mamma's outburst would be over, and she would have rushed out of the library, sobbing hysterically and slamming the door after her, and have locked herself in her own room. Soberly and slowly, as Faith did most things, she climbed down from the dusty

15

bench and started toward the house. Just then she saw her father coming toward her in the dusk.

He seemed terribly tired. His shoulders sagged and his head was bent; his hair was hardly grayer than his pallid face; and in his eyes, which always looked so hurt and hunted and hopeless lately, there was an expression of fear as well. But this lifted as he caught sight of Faith. He hurried over to her and clutched her chubby hand, which was already outstretched toward his.

"I missed you," he said, and Faith could hear the trouble in his voice. "I looked at the clock and it was after five and you hadn't come. Your mother had—been in the library with me, and I didn't notice how late it was until after she had gone upstairs. Then I went to your room, and Clarissa and Rose were both lying asleep in their beds, but you were nowhere to be seen. I didn't like to—disturb your mother by asking if she knew where you were, so I started to hunt for you. It's taken me quite a long time to find you. I don't believe your mother would like you to come to the park and sit alone."

"I won't do it again, Daddy."

"No, darling, I don't believe you will."

He had sunk down on the bench from which she had just risen, covering his face with his hands. Even to his child's uncomprehending vision he was a spent and tragic figure. She climbed up beside him and put her arms around his neck.

"Do tell me what the trouble is, Daddy."

He made a sound that was less a groan than a sob.

"I can't explain, Faith. You wouldn't understand. I'm a failure. I've come to the end of everything."

She waited silently, sure that after a moment he would go on, and that even if she did not grasp the meaning of his words, it would comfort him to utter them.

"My father was a great man," he said at last, "and he had confidence in me. He expected me to follow in his footsteps. He knew that my brother, your Uncle Ephraim—would never have any taste or any talent for public life. But he thought that I had. And he did everything that he could to get me started. I *did* get started, before he died. I'm thankful that he didn't live to see that I couldn't go on."

Again Faith waited silently.

"I didn't do so badly, in the State Legislature. Or even in the House of Representatives. I think he'd have been pleased with my record that far. But I ought never to have tried to enter the Senate, even though I did get in the first time I ran. I'm not Senate-size, Faith. I can't complain of being beaten. I don't belong there."

"You belong to me, Daddy. We belong to each other."

The man groaned again.

"Well, I don't know, Faith. Your mother thinks you belong to her. And I don't know that it is right to separate a little girl from her mother. If you had been a boy——"

"I could try, Daddy, to be ever so much like a boy."

Christian Marlowe laughed bitterly. "And put Clarissa and Rose to bed every night?"

"I could give them up, if that would help."

He drew her to him, burying his bent head on her shoulder. "No, darling," he said brokenly, "it's sweet and lovely and—and like you to offer, but it wouldn't help. Nothing would help. I don't blame your mother. I don't want you to blame her. I am ever so much older than she is—I wasn't young any more when I married her, though I tried to pretend that I was because I—wanted her so. She was so pretty and soft looking. And I tried to give her everything she wanted. But I couldn't. I know now that I never can. So I want her to be free to find it somewhere else."

"Daddy," asked Faith suddenly, "is it—is it usual for senators to sit on park benches and cry?"

Christian Marlowe jerked himself up. "No," he said, almost harshly, "it isn't usual. But after all, I am not a senator any more, you know, Faith. I haven't been since the fourth of March. I never shall be again."

"You might be, mightn't you, if you tried ever and ever so hard?"

"I'm through trying. I've tried all I can. I've let go. I told you, Faith, you wouldn't understand. I'm a failure."

"And you are going to let Mamma go away? Wherever she wants to? And take me with her?"

"She is going to take you to Europe, Faith," the man said pathetically, "on a big boat. You'll like it. Children always love the sea. I know I did. My father went on a special mission to France and England, just before the Civil War, and we all went with him."

"But this will be different. You said only Mamma and I."

"Yes, darling. Only Mamma and you. I'm going back to the farm. You see you couldn't stay there. Mamma wants you to have a good education, to learn languages."

"I could learn other things, Daddy, at the farm, just as useful as languages maybe. . . . Aunt Emmeline would teach me to make cookies. And I could get the cows for Uncle Ephraim."

The man did not answer. Slowly and soberly the child climbed down from the bench a second time and confronted him.

"All right," she said, gulping a little, but on the whole with much more composure than he was displaying, "I'm awfully sorry you're so sure you are a failure, Daddy, because I don't feel sure at all. I mean I don't feel sure that you *have* to be. And I'm sorry, if you are bound to be a failure that you won't take me to the farm with you, because I love it there and I love you and we could be ever so happy. But if I have to go to Europe with Mamma, and help her to try to be free, and learn languages, I guess I can. I guess I'll go in the house now and wake up Clarissa and Rose and pack their things. I want them to be all ready, so that Mamma won't say it's too much trouble to take them along. And I guess I can stand it, in Europe, just as long as she can. But some day——"

She had planted herself squarely in front of him. Through the dim light he could see her huge smoldering eyes glowing in the round rosy face that had suddenly become transfigured with purpose; her red-gold hair, sleekly parted and tightly braided as it was, escaped in springing tendrils of vivid color over her smooth brow and flat little ears. For the first time he realized that Flossie's kitten-like prettiness, fused with the dark distinction inherited from the first Faith Marlowe, had combined to produce elements of potential beauty and vitality in his daughter, the existence of which he had never dreamed before. Too startled to interrupt her, he heard her mutely to the end of what she was determined to say.

"Some day," Faith went on, drawing herself up tautly to her full height, "I'm coming back to Washington! If Grandfather Marlowe had confidence in you, and you haven't followed in his footsteps, the way he meant you should, *I guess I can do it* instead! If he was a great man, I guess I can be a great woman! Anyway I'm going to try! Anyway I'm going to pretend that I'm *not* beaten, every time I know I am! Anyway I'm not going to let go! Anyway—Some way ... I tell you I'm coming back!"

Chapter II

FLOSSIE had already begun to pack when Christian and Faith returned to the house. Two huge battered trunks, one rectangular, the other surmounted by a dome-shaped cover, stood in the upper hallway, and Flossie was rushing back and forth between her own room and these trunks, flinging wraps and dresses and underwear, negligees and hats, parasols and fans and shoes into them. Billows of pink tulle which had lost its first crispness, the froth of soiled lace ruffles, the rustle of stiff silk that was stained and spotted in places, scarves and shawls which she had dropped in her haste, trailed elegantly, if mustily, across the floor; two straight-backed chairs of carved black walnut, upholstered in horse-hair, stood piled high with heavily boned corsets, starched petticoats, chemises and nightgowns trimmed with Hamburg edging and "run through" with wash-ribbon which had never been washed, and a tumbled collection of unmended silk stockings. Faith, climbing the stairs on the way to her own room, tripped on some of the fallen finery, just as her mother emerged from her chamber with another armful of it.

"You clumsy child! Don't you know that is lace, real Duchesse, you're trampling over! Do watch where you're going!!"

"I'm sorry, Mamma. There isn't much light."

"No, there certainly isn't—with this horrible old gas I've had to put up with when everyone else is getting electricity! But we are going where there will be plenty! I suppose that your father has told you? Well, you needn't try to argue, or sulk, or take his side! Where is he?"

"He's in the library."

"You'd think he would come and *help* me! But of course he won't think of lifting a finger! And Lily's getting dinner, and was awfully cross when I suggested that she might help. It's Ella's day out, and Lily has to cook and wait on table both to-night, so she thinks she's just about killed. Your father doesn't realize what I've suffered trying to run this huge inconvenient house with only two servants. And servants, what they are nowadays—impertinent and thieving and everything else, and asking more and more exorbitant wages all the time! Lily had the impudence to say that if I wanted a lady's maid I'd better get one! And Ella wants a raise to four dollars a week! Well, they think I am just going over to New York for a little trip—they haven't any idea that in a day or two they will be hunting for jobs, with no reference from the lady of the house where they worked last! I get some satisfaction out of that anyway."

"Perhaps I can help you, Mamma."

"No, you couldn't. You'd only get under foot. But you'd better try to pack your own trunk—you'll have to learn

19

sooner or later and it might as well be now! I'm almost distracted with all *I've* got to do without looking for your clothes too! I'm not coming down to dinner—wouldn't sit opposite your father after the horrible scene I've had with him if I starved to death. But when you have finished the great hearty meal that you always eat, and that was absolutely necessary to cook this hot weather, perhaps he might condescend to get that cowhide trunk that was his mother's out of the attic for you. And there's a carpetbag there too that you could take. We haven't any decent baggage, of course. I'll get some new trunks in Paris—and something stylish to put in them too—I certainly haven't a thing to wear, not a single thing!"

Flossie rushed ahead with almost incredible celerity. The following afternoon she and Faith took the train for New York, sitting cramped among the bandboxes and valises that were piled all around them. Flossie was very tired, and snapped at Faith every time the child spoke to her.

"Do be *quiet!* Can't you see how exhausted I am? And you sit there staring, with those two great dolls in your arms and ask questions! It's enough to drive me crazy. I don't *know* what is going to become of Lily and Ella, and I don't *know* who's going to have our house and furniture—and I don't *know* who's going to help your father move, and I care least of all about that. He might've come over to New York and seen us off! He would have if he had any regard for appearance—ladies go to Europe without their husbands all the time now, and no one thinks anything of it, if the gentlemen come down to the steamer, and tip the stewards, and ask for places at the captain's table, and kiss their wives goodbye, several times, right by the gangplank. You would think that was the *least* Christain Marlowe could do! But no, it would be a 'needless expense' to take the trip to New York—as if twenty-five dollars more or less would matter when he is bankrupt anyway!—and a 'hollow sham' to pretend that everything was all right when it isn't! Well, there won't be any more hollow shams! He needn't worry!"

Flossie's voice was not loud, but it was shrill and penetrating. Faith saw that their fellow travelers were looking at them curiously, and was almost certain that her mother had been overheard. She was acutely miserable. As they neared New York, however, Flossie spoke to her with pleasant animation.

"We'll take a hack and go over to the Murray Hill Hotel. It's very select, and I know there'll be some lovely rooms reserved for us there. I think it would be nice to have an early supper, right in our own little parlor, and then you can go right to bed. I know you're tired. Don't you think that would be nice, darling?"

Faith was very tired, and she thought it would be very nice. But even her weariness did not prevent her from being thrilled by the hack, and by the "suite" into which she and her mother were ushered by two laden bellboys. She admired the Nottingham lace curtains and red velvet "over-drapes" that shaded the long windows, the thick pile red carpet, the heavy plush furniture, the massive bed, the shining tin tub in the private bathroom which was actually all their own—not shared with anyone else at all. She got undressed, and took a lovely bath right away, and put on her best cambric nightgown, that buttoned close up to her round little throat, and her feather-stitched blue flannel wrapper; and then, already nodding with drowsiness, she ate the nice supper that Mamma had ordered, and said her prayers, and lying down on her side of the big bed, fell swiftly to sleep.

She was awakened several hours later, by the sound of voices in the next room—Mamma's voice and another, a man's voice. Faith's heart leaped with joy—so Daddy had come over after all, on some other train! He was there with them, and would take her place in the big bed, and she would sleep on the "lounge" with Clarissa and Rose; and before they sailed he would do all those important things that would keep anyone from knowing that their family was not just like other families. She jumped out of bed, and pattered across the room, without even waiting to put on her slippers, and threw open the door into the parlor which Mamma had closed after they had said good-night to each other. But, on the threshold, her cry of welcome was suddenly hushed. It was not very light in the parlor, because in spite of everything that Mamma had said about longing for electricity, she had turned on very little of it; so Faith could not see very well. But certainly the man who was sitting on the sofa beside Mamma, with his arm around her waist, was not Daddy. Daddy was tall and slim and pale and clean-shaven, and this man was short and heavy and bearded and ruddy. Stricken with disappointment and startled with the shock of surprise, Faith drew back, and tried to shut the door quietly and creep away to bed again.

But she was too late. Mamma and the strange man had both seen her. She thought they looked startled themselves, and rather provoked too, as if she had done a stupid thing in opening the door. Then the man laughed, very hard and loud, and after that Mamma laughed too, in a funny, strangely hysterical way, and rose from the sofa and walked over toward Faith.

She looked very pretty. She had on her pink chiffon negligee trimmed with lover's knots and wide creamy lace flounces, and in the dim light its lost freshness was not evident. She smelled of the heliotrope perfume that she used on great occasions. Her soft rounded white arms and throat were bare, and the lovely turn of her breast. Her beautiful auburn hair was loose and curly all around her face, her blue eyes were shining and her cheeks were very pink. She spoke sweetly to Faith and put her arm around her.

"What waked you up, darling? Did you have a bad dream?"

Faith was confused, and a little unhappy, in spite of the fact that Mamma's voice was so unusually sweet. She felt shy about saying she had thought she heard Daddy talking, when it had been the strange heavy man. Mamma seemed to guess what was wrong, and went on talking herself, very, very pleasantly.

"You remember your dear Uncle Nelson, don't you, darling? He lives here in New York, and he's very fond of you and Mamma. He's engaged our passage on the steamer for us, and he'll come to see us off, and get us fixed all comfy and cozy. He's a lawyer, and he's going to take care of Mamma's own money for her, and send us what we need, all the time we're in Europe. Won't that be nice?"

Again Faith said it would be very nice. She did not remember her dear Uncle Nelson, but she supposed that he must have come to visit them in Washington when she was too little to remember—she could remember when she was four, but not very well before that. She shook hands with him very gravely and politely, and then she kissed Mamma good-night again and went back to bed. She could hear Uncle Nelson and Mamma laughing after she had shut the door, and presently she fell asleep again.

Next morning Mamma went shopping and took Faith with her. Then Uncle Nelson met them and they all had lunch together at the Brevoort House. Afterwards Mamma said she thought Faith looked very tired and had better take a nap, while she and Uncle Nelson finished the shopping and went to his office to sign some papers. Faith had not taken naps for a long while, not since that dim period before she was four that she could not remember very well. But she went and lay down, docilely, on the big bed, with Rose and Clarissa on either side of her, and sure enough, she did go to sleep.

It was dark when she waked up, dark and thunderous

and hot. Presently it began to rain very hard, and there were vivid flashes of lightning. Faith was not a timid little girl, but somehow the storm seemed frightening. She wished there were someone in the Murray Hill Hotel whom she could ask to come and stay with her, since Mamma and Uncle Nelson had not returned, and it did not grow light again. Faith grew very hungry. She rang a bell, the way she had seen Mamma do it the night before, and a kind waiter brought her some supper, but afterwards he asked her to pay for it and she did not have any money. It was dreadful. He muttered something about speaking to the manager, and finally he came and took away the dishes, clattering them a great deal and not looking kind any more. After he had gone, Faith lay down because there was nothing else for her to do, and by and by she went to sleep again.

When she waked a second time, Mamma was rushing around the bedroom putting her toilet articles into her valise and Uncle Nelson was sitting in the parlor smoking a long black cigar and waiting for her to finish. They told Faith that the boat was going to sail at four in the morning, so that it would be best to go aboard that night. Bellboys came and gathered up all the bags again, and they got into a hack, more crowded than ever because Uncle Nelson took up so much room, and were jolted over rough cobblestones for a long time. At last they reached a strange place called a pier, where everyone was jostling one another all around, and there was a great deal of noise and confusion. It kept raining harder and harder, and they got very wet going up a queer inclined thing that was like a stairway only there were no stairs. They walked and walked through little narrow halls, and then the dark jabbering man who was guiding them, pulled back a red rep curtain in front of a little cubbyhole, and motioned them to go in.

"You said you wanted to economize on the steamer, Flossie," Uncle Nelson was saying, "so I engaged an inside cabin. In stormy weather you can't have the porthole open anyway, so you won't miss one. And of course, you'll be on deck most of the time, so it doesn't matter if there isn't any daylight. Is this all right?"

Flossie said it was all right, though her voice did not sound quite as pleasant as it had the night before. But Faith thought the cubbyhole was very interesting. There were two wide shelves, with railings, built against the wall, one above the other, made up like tiny narrow beds; and there was a tall shiny brown cabinet that unfastened in a miraculous

23

way to disclose a washstand. Beside this was a sponge-bag made of string, and over the sponge rack were a carafe and two tumblers with towels twisted in them. Near the door were four hooks, and a small flat stitched bag with scalloped edges. She admired everything very much.

"Get the kid into bed and we'll go up to the bar for a few minutes, Flossie," Uncle Nelson said in a low voice. Then he turned to Faith and patted her shoulder. "You're a cute kid," he remarked good-naturedly. "Here's a little present for you; I hope you'll like. Take good care of your Mamma, won't you?"

Faith promised that she would, and put up her face solemnly to be kissed; then she said if Mamma would undo the back buttons, she could put herself to bed all right. And after Mamma and Uncle Nelson had gone she opened the box that contained her present. There were several presents instead of one: a package of lemon drops; two books— "Elsie Dinsmore" and "What Katy Did"; stiff muslin bonnets for Rose and Clarissa, trimmed with Valenciennes lace; a little silver watch that really told time, fastened on a bow pin. Faith was delighted with them all, and stowed them safely away in the little hammock which swung beside her bunk. Then she cuddled down between the coarse white linen sheets, and laid her head on the hard little pillow and closed her eyes. But she could not go to sleep again. It was very hot in the cubbyhole, and light shone in from the corridor beyond in spite of the red rep curtain drawn across the doorway; and it was very noisy. Baggage bumped along on its way to other cubbyholes, and above excited, rapid ejaculations in an unknown tongue, rose and fell the voices of men and women who had come to see their friends off, and men and women who were going away.

"*Hello,* there, Tom! Are you with Jack and Mable? No, I haven't been able to locate them anywhere. Number seventeen is their stateroom and it's a daisy." . . . "Well, I *did* mean to bring some flowers, but I couldn't seem to get around to buying any, and I thought oranges would taste pretty good—they're such a rarity at this time of year." . . . "For God's sake, don't cry so, Helen, it isn't as though the boy were in his grave. Most mothers would be pretty proud of having their sons win a prize that would give them two years in Paris free even if they did waste the time studying art." "Know any French? Well, you better learn some P.D.Q. Most of these froggies don't speak a word of anything else. Look out there, *gersong,* you bumped into me with that trunk! *Prunnay gard!* I said, darn you!" . . . "Oh, I

24

wouldn't think of going to bed! We're going to make a night of it and watch the Goddess of Liberty receding in the dawn's early light before we turn in. Time enough to rest up to-morrow—we'll be deathly sick by then anyway!"

Christian Marlowe had read to Faith about the Goddess of Liberty and had shown her a picture of it. It would be fun, she thought, to see it herself. She would speak to Mamma about it. But the hot rackety night wore itself away, and still Flossie had not come back to the cubbyhole when Faith fell at last into troubled slumber.

She waked to find the boat moving. It was queer, like everything else—it was queer, just to think how many times she had fallen asleep and waked up again since she left Washington, each time to discover something different. The light was still shining in from the corridor, and Faith inspected her new little silver watch. It was half-past four.

Rather clumsily she climbed down from her bunk and looked for Mamma. Flossie had come in and lay, still dressed, in the berth below, breathing heavily. She did not look as pretty as she had two nights before, and the scent that enveloped her was not sweet like that of the heliotrope perfume. Her traveling costume was tumbled, and the pins were half falling out of her gorgeous hair. Her small plumed hat and small soiled gloves lay beside her reticule, and her small buttoned boots had tumbled sideways on the floor. Faith spoke to her softly and she muttered something and turned over. But she was not really roused.

Faith dressed herself as well as she could. She did not dare to wash, for fear that the sound of unfastening the miraculous washstand would waken Mamma, and she could not reach the back buttons or braid her own hair. But she put on her sailor hat and her mackintosh, and reached for Clarissa and Rose. Then she pushed aside the red rep curtains and went out into the corridor.

It was not crowded any more. Faith found her way, slowly but without mishap, to the deck. Only a few people, most of them in little clustering groups, stood looking out toward the dim skyline. None of them spoke to her; they were absorbed with their own friends and families, or with their thoughts. Entirely alone, she stood and gazed at the symbolic figure of freedom, looming large and gray through the rain and mist, vaguely conscious of its significance, at one and the same time stirred and comforted.

"I'm coming back," she whispered resolutely, "I'm coming back."

25

Chapter III

FLOSSIE was very seasick. A voluble stewardess who did not speak a word of English, helped her to undress and hung up her clothes; after that whenever Flossie rang, the stewardess came back and did necessary and disgusting things. But Flossie would not get up, not even long enough to have her berth straightened out, she would not try to take any nourishment, not even *café au lait* or bouillon, and she was much too ill to do anything for Faith, whom the stewardess more or less overlooked.

After she had watched the great statue out of sight, the little girl, subconsciously aware that she must try to take care of herself, had set about systematically to find her way around the boat. Now that the confusion of the night before had been eliminated, this was not difficult, and she met with unexpected coöperation from several quarters. When she reached the door of the dining saloon, she was kindly greeted in mixed but expressive language by the *maître d'hotel,* to whom Uncle Nelson had, it appeared, spoken about seats for her and *madame* and who guided her to one of the small rectangular tables running at right angles to the long one which extended, in a narrow imposing expanse, down the center of the *salle à manger.*

"This is *monsieur le docteur's table,*" he told her tactfully. "*Mademoiselle* will like it ver' well." And she was grateful to him for not making excuses about his failure to provide the more exalted places which Flossie had coveted. "*Madame votre mère* does not raise herself so early, *non? N'importe!* Here is *mademoiselle's garcon,* Jules, and he will give her *chocolat* and *petits pains,* and *monsieur le docteur* will be here for *déjeuner* at half-past twelve and dinner at half-past six. He is altogether amiable. He and Jules will see that *mademoiselle is soignée.*"

The hot stimulating drink and crisp hard rolls were very good, and Faith consumed them gratefully. She was a little surprised that no cereal was offered her, but she was rather relieved than otherwise at the omission. She had always disliked it, and had eaten it at home only because she had been so frequently assured that she would not grow nor have nice teeth if she did not. There was no one else at the table when she began her breakfast, but presently a tall, homely boy with freckles and sandy hair came in and sat down opposite her, regarding her with interest as he drank his own chocolate and ate his own rolls.

"Hello!" he said at length. "Are you all alone too?"

"Hello!" said Faith. "No, I'm with Mamma. But she's asleep."

"Oh!" said the tall boy and Faith thought it was strange that such a little word could sound so friendly. "Has anyone helped you to get your steamer chair?"

"Perhaps Uncle Nelson got it last night. I don't know."

"Well, when we finish breakfast we'll go up on deck and see. Don't hurry though, we've lots of time."

When the question of the steamer chair had been adjusted, very satisfactorily, thanks to the tall boy—for Uncle Nelson had not, it appeared, remembered about that—they sat down side by side and talked to each other. She told him that she was Faith Marlowe, that she had been named for her grandmother, and that the name came out of the Bible, in a place that her great-grandmother had loved. She quoted the verse to him proudly: "Stand therefore . . . having on the breastplate of righteousness; and your feet shod with the preparation of the gospel of peace; above all, taking the *shield of faith,* wherewith ye shall be able to quench all the fiery darts of the wicked." The boy told her that he was Sam Dudley, that he had not been named for anybody in particluar, and that he had never read the Bible much, but that he had won a prize and was going to Paris to study art. Then Faith remembered about the lady called Helen who had been crying in the corridor the night before because her son was leaving her, and guessed that this had been his mother, and that he had felt badly about leaving *her,* and must be lonely too; so she stayed with him all the morning, and they had ten o'clock bouillon, and a walk around the deck, and a game of shuffleboard together; and when the bugle blew for lunch Faith bounded off to get ready, fairly bursting with all the wonderful news that she could tell Mamma.

But Flossie did not wish to listen to it. She was very seasick and very sleepy, and she roused herself only long enough to scold.

"I think instead of enjoying yourself all morning on deck with a strange boy, you might have stayed here and tried to do something for me—shut up in this stuffy little cabin! Whatever possessed Nelson Cummings to let us be shoved off into a hole like this I cannot imagine! I shan't forget it either! If I hadn't spend so much on that suite at the Murray Hill Hotel, so that he would have a comfortable place

27

to sit when he came to call, I shouldn't have had to *mention* economy to him, and I guess he could have arranged something better than this if he had half tried. No, I can't braid your hair or do up your clothes for you. Goodness, can't you see how deathly sick I am?"

Faith went up to luncheon still wearing her mackintosh and sailor hat and feeling dreadfully dirty and disheveled. It made her self-conscious and wretched, and she did not say much when Sam Dudley and *monsieur le docteur* tried to engage her in conversation; and she ate without appetite the oily, highly seasoned food which Jules set in front of her with a flourish. There was a married couple, plump and beady-eyed and prosperous-looking, at the table now, who had two little girls about her own age with them—little girls who wore small dangly earrings, and neat cashmere dresses trimmed with rows of narrow velvet ribbon, and who drank red wine mixed with their water, and picked their teeth after they had finished their luncheon. Faith would have liked to suggest playing with them, and showing them Clarissa and Rose. But they stared at her shyly and wonderingly, as if they were surprised that she should be alone and untidy, and they spoke only to their father and mother, and in French.

Conscience-stricken that she should have neglected Mamma all the morning, Faith returned to the cubbyhole immediately after lunch, and spent the afternoon lying on her own bunk, eating lemon drops, reading "Elsie Dinsmore" and waiting for Flossie to speak to her. It was a terribly long afternoon, interrupted only by Flossie's spasms of sickness, when the stewardess, who kept growing less voluble and more glowery, came in and wiped things up and emptied other things. It had become very rough, and even in the inside cabin, the sound of the waves lashing the side of the boat, and of the wind howling and shrieking was very loud. Faith decided that she would rather go without her supper than face the neat little French girls again in her untidy condition. So she stayed very still and ate more and more lemon drops, hoping that these would keep her from being more hungry; but they did not, and all night long she kept waking up, feeling famished and hollow.

The next morning Flossie was still very sick and the storm was raging even more violently than it had the night before. But Faith had finished both the lemon drops and "Elsie Dinsmore," and she decided that the time had come to adopt desperate measures. She started out in search of Sam Dudley.

He was nowhere to be found. He had told her the number of his cabin, and she looked for him there; but it was tidy and vacant. She looked for him in the crowded salon, filled with miserable passengers in various stages of sea-sickness, and in the empty *salle à manger*, very formidable with long green baize covers on all the tables. She looked for him in all the corridors, which were permeated with a steamy, oily, dish-watery sort of smell. Then, wrenching open one of the closed doors that led to the flooded decks, she staggered out in the face of a gale which lashed about her and struck at her without mercy. For a moment she was not only bereft of breath but blinded; then beyond the menacing torrent of uncurbed waves and hissing foam she saw her friend standing spellbound in the shelter of a hatch-way, impervious to the whirling torrent about him, his face raised in rapt admiration at the savage splendor of the sea.

She called to him before striking out toward him. Her cry roused him from his absorption and he waved to her and gave her a welcoming call in return. Then, startled by a sense of impending danger, he forged his way forward over the sluiced surface that separated them. He was just in time. Faith had been whirled off her feet, and slid across the slip-pery deck straight into the sucking maw of an onrushing breaker. As it surged back, it bore her violently away with it. Sam, springing swiftly after her, caught her by the cape of her mackintosh just as she was being swept across the shaking railing into the furious turbulent ocean.

Holding her with one arm and shielding her with the oth-er, he dragged her back to the comparative safety of the companionway. From there he had only a little space to cross before he could reach the door leading to the salon. It was only a moment, actually, before he set her down, drenched and dripping, beyond the zone of danger; but it seemed to him like eternity. And appalled at the narrow-ness of her escape, he spoke, when he managed to speak to her at all, sharply and sternly.

"What do you mean by going out on deck a day like this?" he asked. "Don't you know that it's forbidden?— *Fermez cette porte à clef!*" he added savagely to a terrified-looking steward who had appeared with the tardiness charac-teristic of his kind in an emergency. "*Voulez vous laisser noyer cette petite?*"

"You were out there," gulped Faith.

"Good God! I'm trying to be an artist! I was getting a glorious idea for a picture!"

"Well," said Faith, "I had a good reason too. I was trying to find you to ask if you had ever done up back buttons or fixed a little girl's hair."

29

Sam Dudley stared at her, petrified with astonishment. Faith gathered up courage to go on.

"I haven't been dressed really since I left New York, or had my braids combed out. I can't do it myself, and Mamma is so terribly sick, and the stewardess——"

Seizing her by the shoulders, Sam strode down two flights of stairs and along the narrow corridor leading toward her stateroom. Marthe, the glowering stewardess, happened to be standing in the passage, her arms folded, gossiping with Jacques, the steward who shared her labors. Sam accosted her with the fluency and eloquence which many persons, normally tongued-tied when they attempt to speak a foreign language, achieve when they are angry. Faith could not understand a word he said; but in spite of his pronunciation— the product of a small rural high school in Ohio—Marthe understood him perfectly. She answered him obsequiously, and her manner toward Faith changed suddenly and completely. She led the little girl away to a bathroom, the existence of which Faith had not even guessed before; and while Faith sat soaking in a tub of steaming water, the stewardess went into the dingy little cabin and rummaged through the cowhide trunk until she found fresh underwear and a creased but clean cashmere dress. Returning, she gave vent to exclamations of admiration as she dried the child with a huge shaggy towel.

"*Bon dieu, que tu es jolie! Je ne l' avais pas remarqué! Quel peau! Quels yeux! Quels cheveux magnifiques!*"

Even though Faith did not know what Marthe was saying, it was easy to get the purport of it. For as Marthe combed out the red-gold curls which hung about the child like a veil of glory, she kept spreading them over her hand as if she loved not only the color but the feeling of them. When she had finished brushing them, they looked as if they had been burnished; and instead of plaiting them in a tight long braid, she left them hanging loose around Faith's head and shoulders. Then, giving her a swift sidelong glance, she smiled as if she were pleased with a sudden thought that she had had and exclaimed, "*Attends! un tout petit moment!*" and whisked out of the bathroom. When she returned, almost immediately, she brought Sam with her; and Sam, for the second time within an hour, exclaimed, "Good God!" as he looked at Faith.

"I am very clean now," said Faith.

"I should think you were! You shine like a statuette made of ivory and copper. Good God!"

"I don't think that is a polite way to keep talking about God," said Faith.

"Listen, kid—would you be cold, do you think, if I wrapped you up—partly—in a blanket—and made a picture of you? It wouldn't take long."

"Without my Ferris waist, or panties, or anything, you mean?"

"Yes, just hair."

"Would you like to?"

"Would I like to? Good G——"

"All right," interrupted Faith.

Sam spoke to Marthe, authoritatively again. It was clear, however, that he was not angry with her any more, but highly pleased; and Marthe had ceased to glower and had recovered her volubility—a smiling expansive sort of volubility. Sam picked Faith up in his arms, and carried her, still enfolded in the shaggy towel, to his cabin; and Marthe, beaming blandly, followed them. Then she took Faith in her lap while Sam dug out paper and pencils and brushes and a big drawing board; and it was she who, two hours later, leaned over and touched him on the shoulder, saying in a voice charged with sympathy, *"Monsieur, la petite est très fatiguée."*

Sam dropped his tools abruptly. "What a thoughtless brute I am!" he exclaimed. "All in, baby? Well, I can finish alone now. You've been a perfect model in every way.— Here," he went on, pressing something hard and round and shining into Marthe's hand, "take her away and feed her. And keep quiet about this. . . . I don't want all hands and the cook crowing around asking to see the sketches. . . . You too, Baby. . . ."

"Yes," said Faith, wearily but exultantly. She was very happy because she had been able to do something to please Sam, who was so kind to her, and because she had made a friend of Marthe, who she realized, was going to be attentive to her for the rest of the voyage; and because Mamma had been so unresponsive when she tried to confide in her before, she had no particluar desire to tell the story of her day's adventures; in fact, she really felt that she would rather hug the unshared memory of them to her heart. She was glad, however, when she returned to the stateroom, clean and clothed, and replete with delicious food, to find Flossie no longer huddled up in a wretched little heap, but reclining gracefully against her pillows, looking amiable and cordial.

"Well, darling, have you been having a nice time? Poor Mamma has been so dreadfully, dreadfully sick, that she hasn't been able to get any enjoyment out of the trip, but she's glad if you have. A ship is so *fascinating!* Oh, if there is a storm? *How thrilling!* Well, yes, it seemed rough, but

31

I feel so much better that I haven't minded it . . . and of course, in this horrid little hole I can't *see* anything! I believe I'll try to take a little nourishment, and if I keep it down, I might wash my face and brush my hair and have this bed made. The stewardess has been good to you, hasn't she? Well, of course, I knew you'd have every care, so I haven't worried about you."

The next morning Flossie was so much better that she suffered herself to be supported to her steamer chair, and solicitously enfolded in rugs, though the clear and sparkling weather that succeeded the storm rendered wrapping somewhat superfluous. She smiled dazzlingly on everyone who approached her, and engaged the occupants of adjacent chairs in sprightly conversation. By evening she had already formed a gratifying nucleus of new acquaintances, and within thirty-six hours she was the center of an admiring circle, several members of which, Faith thought, bore a strange general likeness to Uncle Nelson. She was also astonished at the substance of Flossie's remarks, when occasionally she happened to be present during the course of one of the sprightly conversations.

"*She is* pretty sweet, isn't she? Yes, she was eight last December—she is always *so* careful to say she is eight and a half! I suppose I shouldn't agree with you, but I *do* think she is usually pretty, and she is so intelligent. I feel I *must* give her every advantage, and languages are so important! Senator Marlowe is simply exhausted with the cares and responsibilities of office, so I urged him to take a good long rest at our country estate; but when he recovers of course he will join us in Paris. In fact, though I tell you this confidentially, he is expecting a foreign appointment at any moment, so naturally he must stay within easy reach of the White House, as there is no telling exactly when the President will send for you. Oh, yes, *very* intimate . . . you know his father was in Buchanan's cabinet, and . . . well, I am not sure, but possibly minister to Belgium or Holland . . . either would be acceptable to Senator Marlowe and to me."

Flossie was not greatly interested in Sam Dudley. Faith led him up to meet her mother, immediately after Flossie's first appearance on deck, and Sam sat down, balancing himself more or less precariously on the foot of her steamer chair, and grinned and joked. But Flossie found him unstimulating.

"I can't see why you've taken such a fancy to that great, lanky boy, Faith! He's homely as a hedge fence! I hear that his people are quite ordinary, and that he's never been out of Ohio before in his life, except when he came to New York to compete for this prize that he won. No one on the boat seems to know exactly what it is, so probably it doesn't amount to much anyway. If it had I don't see how an uncouth creature like this could have got it. Of course it's quite all right for you to amuse yourself with him if you want to—he seems to be a good-natured soul—but *I* don't want him under foot."

Faith was delighted at not having to share Sam with her mother. She spent practically all her time with him, and he sketched her for hours on end. Much of this sketching was done in his cabin, and on these occasions Marthe was always a helpful and enthusiastic witness. *Monsieur le docteur* also was let in on the secret, and when he had looked over some of Sam's sketches, he asked for permission to show them to the *commandant*. After that Sam and Faith were both invited up on the bridge, and Sam painted and painted and painted. The *commandant* was very kind, like *monsieur le docteur*, but more jolly, and Faith grew to be almost as fond of him as she was of Sam. Indeed, she would have been entirely happy, if she had not been troubled and puzzled by snatches of talk that drifted to her from time to time, and that seemed without a doubt to refer to Flossie and herself.

"Did you ever see a mother and daughter who looked so much alike and yet seemed so different? Of course it's partly because the child's eyes are brown and the mother's that sort of feline blue that usually goes with red hair, but there's something else—you feel the child's got brains and character and the mother's a gushing little fool. Well, I don't *know* just how harmless—the child talks about her 'Uncle Nelson' who came to see them off, but Flossie Spencer never had a brother. There was a Nelson Cummings who was an old beau of hers though. I used to know her slightly, in Chicago, before she was married, though evidently she's forgotten me. She was a cheap little flirt—no breeding or background whatever, and the Marlowe family felt terribly when Christian married her. She certainly has wrecked her husband's career. There are some things the public simply won't stand for in the wife of a man holding public office—and now I've heard it rumored that she's practically deserted him. Of course she blames him for his failure—yes, she has a little money of her own, not much, but enough to manage with, I guess. Her father was quite a prosperous druggist and she's an only child. . . . I don't believe a word about this talk of an appointment—the President would probably have been glad enough to give one to Christian Marlowe if it hadn't been for Flossie Marlowe, but naturally a man with a wife like that, or separated from his wife, is done for as far as a diplomatic position is concerned."

Faith longed to confide her worries to Sam; but her very anxiety made her reticent. As a matter of fact, she talked to him comparatively little; she was satisfied simply to be with him; and the thought that she would be separated from him when the voyage was over caused her to dread the time of landing. The disembarkment, when it finally came, late one windy evening, was even more horrible than she had feared. Flossie had declined Sam's suggestion that he might be of service in seeing her through the customs, evidently because she was counting upon someone else to do this; but at the crucial moment no one appeared with offers of help, and the confusion and congestion on the wharf at Le Havre were actually terrifying. When Flossie and Faith were finally shoved by a gesticulating blue-nosed porter into a second-class carriage, already over-crowded, the train was beginning to move; and it was not until after he had gone, cursing over the inadequacy of his tip, that Flossie discovered that one of the valises was missing. She seemed to hold Faith responsible for the loss, and railed at her until the little girl was numb with wretchedness, and the other passengers, who all happened to be French, were plainly aghast at her violence. Then whimpering in an effort to secure their sympathy, she leaned back against the stiff, solid seat, as if so limp with exhaustion she were about to faint. Int the dim and flickering light of the compartment they stared at her, with repugnance rather than compassion. Then two of them turned their heads somewhat noticeably away from her, and gazed out of the windows, though it was impossible, in the obscurity, to see anything; the others went to sleep and snored; and two others began an animated conversation on the Dreyfus case, as they ate *croquettes of chocolat Meunier* and drippy pears. The train limped and rattled on and on through an unfamiliar and gloomy countryside. It was a dark and desolate journey, unilluminated, for Faith, by the thought that a great and glittering city lay at the end of it. She felt that she had lost her only friend, and that she was a stranger in a strange land.

Chapter IV

FAITH's first impression of Paris was that it was a city where there was no place to live.

It was past midnight when the boat-train got in, and after

a scene in a station which was hardly less noisy and confusing and hideous than the scene on the wharf had been, she found herself wedged between the bags in a strange-shaped hack, the driver of which—portly, surly, and incomprehensible as to speech—kept taking her and Mamma to one hotel after another. When the hack came to a stop, Mamma would get out and go through a lighted doorway which seemed to promise welcome, only to come back after a moment saying that this hotel was full, that there was no room for them in it, and shrilly if incoherently indicating to the *cocher* that he must take them somewhere else. It was two o'clock in the morning before they finally found shelter; and by that time Flossie was muttering angrily words that were almost as incomprehensible to Faith as the *cocher's*.

"To look as though they didn't *want* me in their old hotels! As if I wasn't respectable just because I'm young and pretty and have noticeable hair! I never was so insulted in all my life! I guess they will hear of it from the consulate! I guess the consulate will resent this insolence!"

Faith always longed to ask afterwards what the consulate did to punish the unfriendly hotels; but Flossie never mentioned the matter again, so Faith hesitated to bring it up. The hotel which finally did take them in gave Faith a queer feeling. It was very cold and dingy and bedraggled and it was permeated with a smell of dust and damp, of stale food and bad plumbing. It was on a narrow little side street where long sinister shadows cast a perpetual gloom, and where passersby seemed to slink from corner to corner. She was relieved that they only stayed there a day. Flossie did go, promptly, to the consulate, taking Faith with her, and sending in Christian's card with her own; and presently a pleasant-looking, rather stout, rather shabby, man came out into the gloomy reception room, and said he was Mr. Atkinson, and that he would like to have them come into his private office. Then he told Flossie that his wife would call on her, and set a day for her to bring her little girl to lunch.

Mrs. Atkinson paid her visit that very afternoon. It was plain that she was trying to do her full duty by the wife of an ex-senator. She mentioned Sunday the twentieth, as a possible luncheon date; and she offered to go out with Flossie and Faith then and there to find another place for them to stay—"Because," she said in a curious tone of voice, "of course it is unthinkable that you should remain here. . . . I know a number of very nice *pensions*," she went on more brightly, "perhaps you would like one of those better than a hotel. Suppose we try the *Pension Lafitte* first of all?"

So thanks to Mrs. Atkinson, Flossie and Faith were installed without further delay in the *Pension Lafitte,* the respectability of which was unquestionable. It was a "good address"; and this address, fortunately for Faith, admitted—though in carefully limited quantities—both sun and air. The room into which she and Flossie were ushered by Mademoiselle Lafitte had three long windows, which opened—if they opened at all,—down their entire length, straight through the middle, by means of an arrangement of iron bars and knobs that were hard to turn; but drafts could be—and usually were—excluded not only by lace curtains and overdraperies of wool tapestry, but also by swinging blinds, which rolled up like rugs at the top of the windows, and came down, with the suddenness of an accordion being let out, if one released the string that was twisted around a hook. Outside the windows was a narrow iron balcony, upon which it was possible to stand, or even to sit, if one placed a small straight-backed chair sideways; and inside, the skillful arrangement of the furniture permitted an ordinary-sized room to be used to advantage both as a parlor and as a chamber. Two narrow beds of dark wood, surmounted by lace spreads and crimson satin *duvets,* stood end to end on one side; and at the foot of one of these, in front of a window, was a huge double washstand. The beds, the washstand, and the night tables were shut off from the rest of the room by two large folding screens; and beyond these screens were an *armoire à glace,* a writing table with a tassled cover, and a sofa and two chairs covered with dark and serviceable material. A gilt clock which did not go, flanked with two coy gilt shepherdesses, surmounted a black marble mantel beneath which a fire was seldom lighted; and on the wall, suspended by green cords, were steel engravings of French battlefields.

Flossie did not seem enthusiastic about the room in the beginning; but somewhat to Faith's surprise, she adapted herself to it and to conditions in the *Pension Lafitte* generally without much complaint and without apparent discomfort. She felt herself a person of importance in the *Pension,* and enjoyed her prestige. She occupied the best room, she had the most clothes, and she shrewdly suspected that she commanded the largest income of any of the *pensionnaires.* Moreover, Flossie having been introduced to the *pension* circle by Mrs. Atkinson, Mademoiselle Lafitte saw to it that this official backing became generally known. The Russian family whose clothes were so threadbare but who wore such handsome jewels and spoke such perfect English; the German Baroness who was so untidy in person and so gluttonous at table; the young Swiss bride and groom who were so primly in love with each other; the Swedish student who was such a misfit at the Sorbonne and so irreproachably courteous—Flossie felt sure that they were all impressed with her, that they were thrilled when she invited them to her room to drink sweet sticky wine and eat bonbons and *petits fours;* that they considered it a privilege to take her shopping and sight-seeing. In the evenings, when everyone gathered together for an hour after dinner in the salon and Mademoiselle Lafitte poured coffee, Flossie regaled an apparently appreciative audience with tales of Washington, of the preëminence in public affairs of the Marlowe family, and of her own intimacy with Mrs. Hillary J. Read, the charming wife of the President. She also told everyone—in confidence —about the expected diplomatic appointment, adding gaily that as soon as she was really settled in the American Legation at The Hague or Brussels—which ever it turned out to be—she should want all her friends who had been so kind to her in Paris to come and visit with her. When she was asked to the embassy to lunch she kept referring to the invitation beforehand. "I'm so *sorry* that I can't go to the Louvre with you Wednesday, Baroness von Thurn, but you see I'm lunching with our ambassador and his wife. Well, no, I've never met them personally before, but we have so *many* mutual friends that I feel as if I knew them well already—which of course I shall soon." No second invitation from the embassy arrived, except one for the big reception on the Fourth of July, to which all Americans were asked; but Flossie explained this to herself as well as to her fellow boarders by the fact that the Montgomerys went away early that season to their château on the Loire, and were in Paris only "off and on" after early May. Mrs. Atkinson continued to do her duty; she came from Salem, Massachusetts, and she always would do her duty, even in Paris. So Flossie, lacking the embassy, made much of the consulate in conversation, and by autumn she had succeeded in dismissing the Montgomerys from her mind almost as completely as they had dismissed her from theirs. There was really no ripple in her self-satisfaction. It was the little girl, actually, who minded much more than her mother the perpetual veal, the boiled skim milk, the pulpy prunes and pale blancmanges at the *Pension Lafitte*. She thirsted in vain for ice-water, and hungered for Aunt Emmeline's home-made bread. She never had the sense of being wholly clean washing always from a china bowl and never in a tub. She felt perpetually cramped and crowded in the confines of one close room, after the spaciousness of the house on Lafayette Square, and the one at the beloved farm. She missed her father unutterably, and aching for him as she did, she found no solace in the society of the *pensionnaires,* though they made much of her, for she was the only child in the pallid place. At the day school which Mrs. Atkinson had recommended, and in which Flossie had entered her without delay, she found no joyous companions, as she had in the friendly kindergarten to which she had gone in Washington. The little French girls with their black aprons and pierced ears were very polite to her; but they were aliens and she was a stranger in their midst. There were no rollicking recesses, no jolly games, no gymnastics with the windows flung wide open. She shared no whispered confidences and exchanged no small notes and gifts with the child who sat at the desk next to hers. She was never taken home boisterously, to share potluck at a family luncheon, or even invited to a child's party. Her teachers were kind and competent; she was taught thoroughly and with meticulous care, and she learned a great deal in an incredibly short time; before long she was chattering French without even being conscious that she had mastered it. But her fluency did not seem to make her any less a foreigner in spite as well as in fact than she had been before she acquired it.

After she had gone to bed at night she lay, very still and straight under the red satin *duvet,* with Clarissa on one side of her and Rose on the other, counting over the days of the week on her fingers. "Monday, Tuesday, Wednesday—three days to Thursday," or, "Tuesday, Wednesday—two days to Thursday," or, "Wednesday—one day to Thursday!" Then after Thursday she did the same thing with Friday, Saturday and Sunday. This was not primarily because Thursday and Sunday were holidays; she did not actually dislike her school; indeed, she rather missed it during the brief summer vacation when Flossie, who believed in alternately scrimping and splurging, "blew in" the money she had saved in the course of a three-month sojourn at the *Pension Lafitte* on a hasty "tour" of the Châteaux district, Normandy, Brittany, Provence, the French Alps, and the French Riviera, dragging Faith along with her from castle to mountaintop and from cathedral to casino. The little girl's mental horizon became so blurred, and her small body so weary during the course of this rushing about, that she was actually glad when Flossie, having spent all her surplus, returned to the *Pension Lafitte* for another period of economy and thrust Faith back into school again, tired of having her "everlastingly under foot." On the whole Faith thought school the lesser of two evils, if she must choose between that and a "tour." But she looked forward to Thursdays and Sundays because she saw Sam Dudley on those days. With

38

no coöperation from Flossie, and as a result of considerable perseverance, Sam had discovered that she and Faith were staying at the *Pension Lafitte;* and having obtained Flossie's careless consent to this program, he came regularly as clockwork to take the little girl out with him, regarding it as a matter of course that she would carry at least one of her dolls with her, and that she would need to retie the streamers of the wide hat she wore, which fastened under her chin, every block or so, while he stood patiently by, holding Clarissa or Rose, as the case might be. It was thanks to Sam that Faith made the discovery that the main characteristics of Paris were not noisy stations, or unfriendly hotels, or prim *pensions* or strange schools. She discovered that there were Punch and Judy shows in the Champs-Élysées and balloon-men in the Place de la Concorde, row boats in the Bois de Boulogne and push carts laden with daffodils and violets in the Place Vendôme, a toy shop called *Le Nain Bleu* on the Rue Saint Honoré and *pâtisseries* at almost every corner. She discovered that there was an Eiffel Tower to climb, and arcades to walk under, and merry-go-rounds to ride. But Sam, though he revealed all these delights to her, took it for granted that she would also derive enjoyment from the same pursuits and investigations that he enjoyed himself. It never occurred to him—as indeed there was no reason why it should—that she would not be happy if he elected to spend an entire afternoon sauntering along beside the bookstalls on the *Rive Gauche* or standing absorbed before the jewel-like windows of the *Sainte Chapelle*. He took her to see the Gobelin tapestries woven, to see the fountains playing in the gardens at Versailles, to see the lights of all Paris twinkling beneath the *Sacré Cœur* at Montmarte, to see "Ruy Blas" at the Comédie Française, and to hear midnight mass sung on Christmas eve at the Madeleine. He kept her sitting for hours on end before Giorgione's "Concert" and Leonardo's "Mona Lisa." She came to know the Louvre as well as she knew the old house on Lafayette Square and to love every corner of it; she came to love the third balcony in the Opera House and the gorgeous performances enacted beyond the glittering chandelier; she came to love the forest of Fontainebleau, and the fussy little boats that plied up and down the Seine. But best of all, she came to love Sam's studio—a great messy, friendly room in a ramshackle old house with a stone courtyard, situated in the shabbiest part of the students' quarter. Sam cooked and ate and slept and painted all in this one room; and often boon companions of his who lived in similar studios, drifted in casually to cook and eat and sleep and paint with him. It was a terribly untidy place, and where it did not look cluttered it looked threadbare; but it was permeated with the warmth of good fellowship, and youthful enthusiasm and youthful hope. There were glowing colors on the smeared canvasses that stood haphazardly about, a fire always smoldering on the upswept hearth, an abundance of coarse, hot food dished up bountifully at frequent if irregular intervals. There was even a great, fluffy, friendly cat, which sang like a tea kettle, and sat with its paws folded away beneath it, blinking and motionless for hours together. More than once, when Sam, who had no clock and whose watch seemed perpetually out of repair, guessed, by the gathering twilight, that it must be time for him to take Faith back to the *Pension Lafitte*, she pled with him to let her stay.

"Just to-night, Sam. I could leave early in the morning and still get to school on time. It's raining outdoors and it's so lovely and warm here. I promise I wouldn't be any bother."

"Gosh, Faith, I'd like to have you. But little girls don't belong in the Latin Quarter, except just for visits."

"Velasquez is asleep. I don't think it would be very kind to take him out of my lap and wake him up." Velasquez was the fluffy cat.

"Well, I must see if I can take him out of your lap *without* waking him up then."

These arguments grew more and more frequent. At last they began to prey upon Sam's mind.

"Look here, Faith, if you're going to fuss about going back to the *pension* every time I bring you here, I'll have to *stop* bringing you, that's all."

"Couldn't you stop taking me back instead? Couldn't you let me stay here all the time?"

She climbed up into his lap and pressed her face against his.

"You could teach me to cook," she urged. "And I can dust. It would really be a good thing if someone dusted here. Nobody does now, and Ella showed me how at home. I took care of the doll-house and the piano legs myself. I could be very helpful to you. I am sure if I had been here to help, you would have had a picture in the Salon this spring. You know how disappointed you were because you didn't. If I stayed you could paint me whenever you felt like it and by and by the Salon would take a picture of me."

"Don't you know bribery is a crime?" asked Sam, running his fingers through her hair.

"Yes," said Faith confusedly, "what is a crime?"

"Sometimes it's hard to tell exactly," admitted Sam. He

drew out her curls to their full length, bunched them up, drew them out again. "Wouldn't you be sorry to leave your Mamma?" he asked at last.

"Not very," replied Faith promptly. "Not really sorry, the way I was to leave Daddy."

"Does Senator Marlowe write you letters?"

"Oh, yes. From the farm. There are six new calves. And a little colt. And the mowing has just begun. There will be hay-rides." Her lips quivered.

"You could ask Mrs. Marlowe to send you back, Faith."

"No, I can't. Daddy didn't want to take me to the farm. I asked him."

"Then he must have wanted you to stay with your mother, Faith. And she would feel badly if you went away from her."

"I think she mostly wanted to take me away from Daddy. Because he was a failure. But she is so busy, really, she wouldn't miss me. She is busy now all the time with Mr. Lindstrom. Even busier than in the winter."

Sam winced a little. "Isn't Mr. Lindstrom going back to Sweden this summer?" he asked slowly. "The courses at the Sorbonne must be almost over for the summer."

"They are over. So he and Mamma have lots of time to spend together."

Sam winced again, harder this time. Then he set Faith on her feet, and got up, stretching his long legs.

"Come on," he said, "I'm not saying I'll ask your Mamma to let you stay here with me. But I *would* like to talk to her a little while to-night. And maybe——"

He never finished the sentence. He was very silent all the time they were on their way back to the *pension*, in the bus. Then when Sophie, the *bonne*, opened the door for them, she looked at them strangely, as if there were something the matter; and almost immediately they heard Flossie's voice, shrill and furious, piercing the stale air.

"You evil-minded, vulgar, old prude! Insinuating such things just because I was *kind* to a poor lonely boy, slaving away in a strange country! What if the door *was* locked? What if it *has* been locked before? If you weren't snooping and spying around at keyholes how would you *know* whether it was locked or not? Oh, the other boarders have complained, have they? Slandering me behind my back when I thought they were my friends! Well, you wouldn't have needed to ask me to leave! I'd have gone anyway just as soon as I could get my trunks packed. I've been planning for quite a while to take a complete tour of Switzerland, and then go to Dresden for the winter. I guess I realize I

41

owe it to Faith, to give her a chance to learn German. I have the address of a *Pension Schneider* that is *really* select! And just you try to collect one cent of money from me and see what happens to you. I'll sue *you!* And I'll see that the consulate knows of this! You've told Mrs. Atkinson already that you were going to speak to me and she *approved* of it? Well, I guess *she'll* get an earful from the White House. When her smug husband's been sent to Mongolia or some such place I guess she will wish she had done a little less approving! I never was so insulted in all my life!"

Faith clutched Sam's hand tightly, raising imploring eyes to his. She knew, without taking another step forward, that when they reached the closely curtained, carefully screened room that she and Flossie had occupied for so many months, she would find Mademoiselle Lafitte looking dignified and final, and Flossie looking disheveled and outraged, and Mr. Lindstrom standing mutely by, saying nothing and hanging his head. Then presently her mother's two big trunks, the box-shaped one and the dome-shaped one, and her own little trunk covered with cowhide would be trundled in, and she would be packing quietly and miserably while Flossie flew about tossing mountains of ruffled dresses and plumed hats and soiled negligees into heaped-up piles. She turned to Sam with one last appeal.

"Dear, darling Sam," she begged, "can't you save me this time too—the way you did on the boat?"

She heard Sam swallowing. She thought for one blessed moment, that perhaps he was going to take her back to the studio after all. But after the swallow came something that was like a laugh, only it wasn't much like it after all; it sounded so unhappy and so helpless.

"No, Faith, I can't this time," he said, "there isn't anything I can do. I haven't any money, or any influence—or —or anything—I'm only twenty-one myself. And anyway, little girls have to stay with their mothers."

He swallowed again, and tried to go on, speaking words of comfort and reassurance. Instead, he strangled, stifling the agonized exclamation that fought for utterance.

"I guess, perhaps, it would have been better if I had let you drown!"

PART II

Rudolf

Chapter V

THE casual onlooker might have supposed the tall fair young man sitting alone beside one of the little iron tables in front of Florian's to be English. He had the well-knit slenderness, the clear bright complexion, and the complete poise of manner which are generally—and rightly—regarded as attributes of British youth and British breeding. But the more experienced observer would have noticed that he was not typically English after all: His perfectly cut clothes were too closely molded to his wide-shouldered, slim-waisted figure, his hair and eyes—unsubdued by any tinge of brown and gray—were both a shade too striking for that. So such a shrewd observer would have proceeded to guess, and guess correctly, that he was an exemplary product of German aristocracy, whose military and scholastic training were only recently behind him, and who had been sent out to see something of the world before embarking on the career which had been carefully chosen for him.

He shifted the strap of the field glasses, which, enclosed in a beautifully polished leather case, was slung over his shoulder; straightened the position of the costly camera which he had set down in front of him; and took a tentative sip of a glass of beer which he had ordered. Then disdainfully, though calmly, he set it aside. It was already evident to him that there was no beer worthy of the name in Italy, although he had been there only twenty-four hours, and he was slightly impatient with himself for having ordered it more than once. And yet, what else should he order, at four o'clock on a summer afternoon? Coffee? It was too warm for that! An ice? Insipid and ridiculous refreshment for a vigorous male creature! A heady whisky and soda, or a sweet sticky *Strega*? He was content to leave the first to the Scotchman and the second to the Venetian! Unless he could get a real beverage—bitter and brown and clear and icy-cold, and crested with foam like the top of a wave—it would be almost better to go thirsty. He pulled a pipe out of his pocket, tapped it lightly against the sharp rim of the table, filled it with swift, expert fingers, and began to smoke.

A band which was stationed near the café and to which most of its patrons were listening with evident enjoyment, was playing trivial, tinkling arias of obvious melody; multitudes of iridescent, pampered pigeons fluttered and crowded obtrusively about; beyond the piazza the gorgeous intricate façade of San Marco glittered in the afternoon sun. The traveler, too well bred to be unintelligently critical, could not entirely suppress a pang of homesickness. It seemed futile to him to leave the land of Wagnerian music, of isolated, castle-crowned crags rising above laden vineyards, of restrained Gothic architecture, in order to hear Rigoletto, and scatter crumbs for pigeons, and gaze at gold mosaic. He sat looking at San Marco and thinking about the Cologne cathedral. From time to time, allowing both his vision and his thoughts to be diverted, he regarded the occupants of a table near his with an absorption which was saved from being a stare only by the skill with which he tempered it. He was quite evidently wondering whether he might venture to go over and speak to them.

The same question had been forcing itself upon his attention, intermittently but insistently, ever since his arrival in Venice the day before. When he had presented himself at the reception desk of the Hotel Superbo he had found the manager in a state of volubility exceeded only by his incoherence. At first this functionary had persisted in speaking only Italian, of which the traveler did not understand a syllable; and having been politely, but firmly, persuaded that they might find a common medium of speech in French, German, or English, whichever he preferred, the manager shrugged his shoulders, spread his hands and rolled his eyes. The *signor* was quite sure that he had written for reservations? The letter did not seem to be anywhere about! The manager fluttered a sheaf of papers back and forth on his desk with an air of increasing helplessness. Oh, the *signor* had *wired*, also? Well, wires... the manager's manner seemed intended to convey the impression that no telegraphic communication had ever been known to reach its destination. Still perfectly courteous and perfectly self-controlled, the young German was swinging on his heel and signaling to a porter to gather up his hand baggage, when a young girl, accompanied by an uncompromising-looking, middle-aged woman, who had also approached the manager's desk, addressed herself to that plenipotentiary with surprising effec-

44

tiveness. The eye-rolling and hand-spreading ceased abruptly; there was a final shrug, but it was one of resignation rather than of protestation. The girl, having finished, in Italian, what she had to say to the manager, began to speak in unfaltering, correct, and idiomatic German.

"It is unfortunate that you should find the mails and telegraph system so unreliable in Italy," she remarked, with a suspicion of a smile, "someone really ought to speak to the Minister of Communications. . . . So much depends on first impressions . . . and in Germany everything is so efficiently organized and run! It would be too bad if a really important, influential German had cause for complaint! . . . I have just been reminding the *signor* director," she went on more gravely, "that there is a very good room available, overlooking the Canal. It was reserved for a friend of ours, who expected to arrive today from Paris. But a wire has come in —yes it really came in quite promptly and safely—saying that he had been detained, that he wouldn't be here for at least a week. Apparently the *signor* director forgot about this cancellation. I am sure you will take the room—we looked it over ourselves because we wanted to be certain our friend would be pleased. There isn't much furniture in it, but it has an arched ceiling, and the mural decorations are simply superb."

She had disappeared, with a swift, friendly smile, before her beneficiary had completed the deep, formal bow with which he had accepted her intervention, before he had been able to achieve a graceful phrase expressing his gratitude. He was conducted, without further delay, to the room so providentially untenanted; and though he was not given to facile and spontaneous mirth, he laughed, as he shaved and bathed and changed, at the brief and vivid accuracy with which the young girl had described the somewhat overpowering apartment in which he found himself. An enormous bed, carefully shrouded in mosquito netting, dominated its vacant surroundings; for the rest, the room contained an inadequate wardrobe and still more inadequate washstand, a chilly-looking table with a mosaic top, and two very stiff straight-backed gold chairs. The lighting fixtures, made of the same twisted and tinted Venetian glass with which the numerous mirrors were framed, were placed at an elevation which would preclude any practical use of them; the elaborate and unrelieved parquetry of the floor shone with a glacial glitter; the walls, which appeared to be at least thirty feet high, were intersected by numerous doors, which were evidently supposed to be invisible, as the "mural decorations" were painted over them without interruption of design and subject, and there were only narrow slits in the surface of the plaster and unobtrusive door knobs to indicate their presence; while the vaulted dome which surmounted all this slendor was embellished with a fresco representing the ascension of a solid and satisfied-looking saint surrounded with phalanxes of plump pink cherubs.

Suddenly conscious that he would be late for the *table d'hôte* luncheon, and also that he was amazingly hungry, the young German descended to the dining room and fell upon the excellent *hors d'œuvres* that were placed before him with zest and thoroughness. It was not until he had devoured several substantial courses, not until he had scoured a heaped-up plate of *ravioli* clean, and washed down the *ravioli* with red *Lacrima Cristi,* that he began to look about him with appreciative interest. It was, indeed, very late; the dining room was almost empty; but near the window, at some distance from where he was placed, the young girl who had so efficiently rescued him sat eating figs and almonds with healthful appetite and enjoyment, while the angular middle-aged lady who was with her tentatively fingered a peach that apparently did not really tempt her much.

Discreetly, he allowed his gaze to wander from one to the other. There was not the slightest resemblance between them; if there was relationship, he felt it must be very distant. Possibly the middle-aged lady was a *dame de compagnie,* though for some reason which he could not quite define he thought this doubtful. Her dress was as severe as her manner, and wholly lacking in elegance or distinction. She was colorless, correct, negative; but she was not negligible; she was unmistakably a gentlewoman. The girl was very different. Her face was shaded by a large black hat; it was impossible to see her features clearly. But underneath the hat there was a glimpse of gorgeous red-gold hair which was not wholly concealed, a glimpse of lambent skin. Her sheer black dress was simplicity itself; but it was exquisitely smart, and it revealed a lovely, graceful young throat and figure. There was something about her that he seemed to recognize, something vaguely familiar. Was it possible that he had met her? Certainly that seemed unlikely, for it was unthinkable that he could have forgotten so arresting a personality. Yet the impression that this was not the first time he had seen her persisted.

He was still trying to crystallize this impression when she passed him on her way out of the dining room. There was not even the suggestion of a pause as she went by his table; but she said *"Mahlzeit"* and smiled again, with that same friendly, illusive smile which seemed to reveal so much

46

human comprehension and sympathy, and which had so intrigued him as she stood speaking to him by the director's desk. Now it was slowly beginning to dawn on him that his failure to find Venice charming was based upon his failure to meet this charming girl. It was with this realization, and the need for thought preparatory to action which it entailed, that he had sat down beside one of Florian's insecure little painted iron tables and ordered beer; and it was with the consciousness that he was still unprepared to meet this situation adequately that he continued to hesitate, smoking, and watching the attractive young creature who was now so conveniently near him, and who this time had given no sign that she was aware of his proximity.

At last he could stand it no longer. He extinguished his pipe, placed two small silver coins beside the beer which he had spurned, and picked up his camera. Then he rose, his hat in his hand, and walked over to the adjacent table. He clicked his heels together, and bowed both to the radiant girl and to the severe-looking middle-aged lady; then he addressed the latter.

"May I venture to present myself, *Gnädige Frau?*" he asked in German, since this was the language in which the girl had spoken to him the morning before and he still felt uncertain as to her nationality. "My name is Rudolf von Hohenlohe, and I so greatly wish to thank the *Gnädiges Fraulein* for her pleasant and powerful intervention in my behalf yesterday." He bowed again and waited.

It was the girl who answered. "Mrs. Atkinson doesn't speak German," she said serenely, "but you speak English. I heard you trying it out, among other tongues, on our plausible but hypocritical director yesterday. He knew perfectly well that he had room for you, but he would have loved to brag all over Venice that his hotel was so crowded he was turning away even *noblessa*. Of course he saw the coronet on your baggage!"

"Perhaps," said Rudolf von Hohenlohe, rather formally. He bowed once more, and repeated the statement he had just made to Mrs. Atkinson, in English this time, with a Teutonic accent and Teutonic precision, but with complete grammatical accuracy. To his immense relief, the lady, though she regarded him with swift appraisal, appeared neither resentful at his intrusion nor critical of his temerity. She answered with less acidity than he had expected.

"I know Faith was very glad that she could help you," she replied, reservedly but agreeably, "and I am glad too. It is unpleasant to arrive alone in a strange place, and to find oneself without a habitation. I have had such an experience more than once myself. . . . Is this your first visit to Venice?"

"Yes, *Gnädige Frau*. My first experience in Italy in fact."

"Isn't it wonderful?" broke in the girl. "Don't you love to see the yellow sails at sunset and the moon coming up behind Santa Maria de la Salute? Don't you love the little arched bridges over the side canals that look like kittens with their backs up? Don't you love the big quiet stone *campos*? Don't you love the boats that anchor down where the Canal Grande and the Canal della Giudecca come into each other, with musicians on board who play and sing anything you like, for a few *soldi*, if you stop your gondola beside them and choose? Have you been through the Doges' Palace and the Accademia? Have you seen Titian's Ascension of the Virgin? Have you gone over to the Lido for a swim? Have you——"

"Remember that Baron von Hohenlohe arrived only yesterday, Faith," remarked Mrs. Atkinson, "and that he is not an American tourist. . . . My husband, John Atkinson of Salem, was in our consular service for many years," she went on, turning to Rudolf with something surprisingly like a twinkle in her eye, "and we had a good deal of experience with our compatriots who expected to see all Europe thoroughly in a week or so. Since you probably intend to proceed in a more leisurely manner, won't you sit down and have an ice with us? I am sure Faith intends to eat at least two before we go back to the hotel. Her capacity for ices is almost as great as her capacity for sight-seeing!"

Rudolf von Hohenlohe disposed of his camera, and this time of his field glasses as well, by unstrapping them and placing them on the pavement beside him. He forgot, or at least disregarded, his antipathy toward ices; and he was somehow unstartled by an intuitive feeling that Mrs. Atkinson had anticipated his desire to meet Faith and had been prepared to cope competently with his overtures toward acquaintance whenever he made these. Her next words, however, revealed a foundation more solid than any for which he had ventured to hope upon which to build a friendship.

"My husband was stationed in St. Petersburg some time ago," she said casually. "I remember that the German ambassador there, whom we had the honor of knowing rather well, was a Baron Rudolf von Hohenlohe. Possibly he was a relative of yours?"

"He was my uncle, my father's younger brother. I was named for him!" exclaimed the young man, with greater enthusiasm than he had ever before disclosed in speaking of his godfather, for whom he had hitherto always felt a rather tepid affection. Now he saw this uncle in a new

48

light, as a liaison officer of priceless value between himself and Faith. He was "placed" already, as far as Mrs. Atkinson was concerned; and the fact that his position was, so to speak, ready-made for him, would save both time and trouble, though he would have been entirely willing to take a good deal of both to establish himself in her eyes. He only wished that he was equally enlightened concerning Faith's identity; but the discerning lady seemed to know what was passing in his mind.

"If you have no one here with you in Venice, perhaps it would be pleasant for you to join us sometimes," she went on. "Faith speaks such excellent Italian that it is a great advantage. She went to school for two years in Florence, but this is her first visit to Venice, and she is all enthusiasm. She and I are both alone in the world, so we have joined forces. We have invented a sort of cousinship. It is a happy arrangement for both of us. Her father was the late Senator Marlowe, of whom you have possibly heard, if you have ever been interested in following the course of American politics."

Rudolf inclined his head gravely. He had never heard of the late Senator Marlowe and he had never been interested in following the course of American politics, as he felt sure that Mrs. Atkinson was well aware. But he recognized the simplicity and skill with which she had made Faith's identity, and her own connection with Faith clear to him. Details could come later, and he felt confident that all in good time these would also be revealed in a satisfactory manner.

"Of course you have letters to the German consul here?" Mrs. Atkinson inquired. "He is a very eminent scholar— one of the greatest authorities in the world, I believe, on Byzantine art."

"That's probably the reason Baron von Hohenlohe hasn't delivered his letters," broke in Faith. "You haven't, have you? You've been *dreading* to see it with an eminent Byzantine scholar! You wanted to see it with someone young and amusing!" Suddenly she pushed back her third ice, half consumed, and rose, impetuously. Her sheer black dress obscured the radiance of her vitality and youth no more effectually than a sheath of black tissue paper could obscure the splendor of a *Gloire de Dijon* rose. Her wide black hat had somehow ceased to shade her face. It was revealed laughing, lambent, lovely, as Rudolf had guessed it to be at luncheon the day before. His first full view of it now showed it to be even more vibrant, even more enchanting than he had divined.

A little forking flame suddenly seemed to leap from his

heart and to creep, darting and quivering, through every nerve of his body, as Faith went on speaking. He had never felt anything like it before.

"Well, you *shall*. You and I are going to see it together. Aren't we, Cousin Sarah?"

"I shouldn't be at all surprised," said Mrs. Atkinson dryly.

Chapter VI

"BUT, Good God, I've come all the way from Paris to do those things with her myself!"

Sam Dudley shook back the long lock of sandy hair that always hung limply over his forehead. The gesture was not, in itself, a savage one; nevertheless he seemed to invest it with a certain ferocity; and he spoke not only fiercely but bitterly.

"I know, Sam. If you had only arrived when you first planned to——"

"Yes,—if I had only turned down a five thousand dollar commission from a Youngstown magnate with a letter of introduction from the governor of Ohio—damn his smug smirking face!"

"Sam!" expostulated Mrs. Atkinson mildly.

"Sorry, Cousin Sarah . . . but you know yourself, darned well, that I needed the money. I needed it badly. And I was thinking not only of this five thousand dollars, but of all the other five thousand dollars that might result from it. . . . 'My friend, Mr. Josiah H. Seabury of Youngstown, Ohio, has shown me the portrait recently painted by you which hangs behind the mantel in his back parlor, and with which he and his daughter, Mrs. Elmer R. Todd, are both eminently satisfied. It has occurred to me that you might paint a picture of my wife that I would like equally well. I am expecting to take my first trip to Europe this summer, accompanied by Mrs. Grimes, and upon receipt of a favorable reply from you, we will call at your studio immediately after our arrival in Paris and arrange for sittings. There will be no difficulty about financial arrangements. I may say in passing that I am the inventor of the Grimes solid porcelain bathtubs and lavatories now being installed extensively all over the United States. Very truly yours, Alonzo B. Grimes.'

. . . Can't you see the letter, Cousin Sarah, and flocks more like it?"

"Yes," admitted Mrs. Atkinson with a slight smile. "Did Mr. Seabury buy anything besides his portrait?"

"He's offered me a small fortune for 'Mary of Nazareth,'" said Sam abruptly, "he's a very devout Catholic, and he wants to give it to a convent in memory of a younger daughter who died and who had intended to become a nun. I am thinking over his offer. . . . I've let all the other pictures go. . . . I rather hoped to keep the 'Mary.' I know it's the best thing I've done. But painters have to eat and pay rent just like other people, and they rather enjoy shoving a little into the bank for—for the future." He broke off suddenly. "I worked like hell to polish off Josiah H. Seabury in short order. After all, I'm only a fortnight later than I said I'd be."

"A good deal can happen in a fortnight sometimes," said Mrs. Atkinson quietly.

"Well, suppose you tell me just how much *has* happened," snapped out Sam, with a little of his former ferocity. "I get to Venice, expecting of course that Faith will meet me at the station, and she doesn't because—as you explained, having come alone—she's gone over to the Lido for a swim with a Baron von Hohenlohe——"

"Not alone," interjected Mrs. Atkinson hastily. "The American consul's wife, Mrs. Saunders, and their daughter Harriet, a very nice girl who goes to Vassar——"

"Oh, yes!" exclaimed Sam sarcastically, "I can just imagine how much Baron von Hohenlohe would notice the very nice girl who goes to Vassar when Faith was along! Well, anyway, next I arrive at the hotel and get shoved off into a little gloomy back room, and when I complain the mechanical boy-doll who calls himself a manager informs me that the room he *meant* to give me has been turned over to the Baron von Hohenlohe at the *signorina's* request; and that he himself doesn't like to dispossess so important a member of the *haute noblesse* for a mere artist, or words to that effect—set to music and motion, you know. That man's eyes and shoulders must work with springs! And finally I sit down for a quiet cup of tea with you, and you begin, with the manner of leading up tactfully to some very dark and disagreeable disclosure, to tell me you are *so glad* that dear Faith, after all the hideous experiences the poor child has had, is beginning to forget, and to enjoy herself . . . and apparently the sole source of her forgetfulness and cause of her enjoyment is a tow-headed German off on the loose! I bet his coloring is more brilliant than his intellect.

51

I thought Faith had more sense! And . . . if you'll excuse me for saying so! . . . I thought you did!"

Mrs. Atkinson set down her cooling cup of tea on the mosaic top table beside her. "My dear Sam," she said quietly, "I must ask you to be more accurate in your remarks. Rudolf von Hohenlohe may not have brilliance. I am willing to admit the possibility. But he has breeding, which is better, and he looks something like a viking god—tailored and trained and educated, of course, but still with the unmistakable air of a young Siegfried. He's quite as magnificent in his appearance—though in a different way of course—as Faith is herself. I can understand perfectly why she should have been attracted to him immediately. But nothing could have been more respectful and more correct than his behavior—which is not surprising, considering his traditions and upbringing. He belongs to one of the greatest families in Germany."

"I didn't know there *were* any great families in Germany," said Sam gloomily.

"Well, your ignorance is appalling, then," retorted Mrs. Atkinson with unaccustomed heat. "If Faith should marry into such a family as that——"

"Marry! Good God, the child's hardly out of short dresses! Has this cradle-snatcher started in talking about marriage already?"

"I don't think he has to Faith. In fact I am reasonably sure of it. But he has to me. He's asked me if I would be willing to have him address her, providing he could obtain his family's approval and consent—and he intimated that he was going to cut his vacation short in order to go home and confer with his family——"

"So you told him you *would* be willing?"

"I—Sam, don't glare at me like that! I told him I thought Faith was too young. But he more or less wrung the admission from me that I didn't object to him personally. And I don't. I . . . I think he's rather nice. Wait until you see him yourself, Sam!"

"Oh, I'm perfectly crazy to see him!" exclaimed Sam brutally. "And I'd like to know just how much you've told this young Siegfried about Faith—about her mother, rather. I've always understood that god-like dynasties had rather an aversion to family skeletons."

"Flossie Marlowe is dead, Sam," said Mrs. Atkinson quietly. "If she were not, I admit that the situation would present serious complications. As it is, I do not believe they are insurmountable. I have made no effort to deceive Rudolf

52

von Hohenlohe. I have answered every question that he has asked me. Indeed, I have forestalled some that I thought he might ask me. I have told him that Faith is an orphan. I have told him that her parents separated when she was eight years old, and that since then she has never been back to the United States. I have told him that Flossie Marlowe was a vain, selfish, and silly woman, fond of admiration and given to—coquetry. I think I have made him realize, to a certain degree, what Faith's life was like for seven years—that she led a neglected existence in a succession of drab *pensions*, while her mother amused herself, and that the monotony of the years was broken only by hasty and superficial 'tours' embarked upon whenever her mother decided that she herself must have a change. I did not say that this decision was sometimes made for her. I did not tell him—just how Flossie died. I must, of course, eventually—I or some other friend of Faith's. It would not be fair—either to him or to Faith—to leave him uninformed indefinitely. Meanwhile I think, that without having had Flossie Marlowe forced into the foreground of his consciousness, he has been made perfectly well aware how greatly Faith must have suffered. And that Faith should have suffered seems to him so lamentable that he feels doubly anxious to assure her a future of unclouded happiness."

Sam did not answer. Mrs. Atkinson paused for a moment, as if gathering her forces, and then went on.

"I have told Rudolf von Hohenlohe," she said, "that I happened to be in Vienna when Flossie Marlowe died there, and that as Faith was left entirely alone at the time, and as I had known and loved her when she was a child, I asked her to stay with me, at least temporarily. I told him that I was a childless widow and that Faith had grown very dear to me—as dear as any daughter of my own could possibly have been. I told him that she would eventually inherit my little competency. I also told him of Faith's legacy from her father."

Again Sam did not answer, and again Mrs. Atkinson went on after a slight pause. "Since Flossie and Christian Marlowe are both dead," she remarked, "I see no harm in emphasizing the more desirable parent of the two. The fact that Flossie died, as she had lived, selfishly and sensationally, leaving an innocent young girl crushed and unprotected, need never loom as large on Rudolf von Hohenlohe's horizon as the fact that Christian Marlowe, a former senator of the United States, and the son of a distinguished member of Buchanan's cabinet, bequeathed to his daughter not only an honorable name, but a considerable fortune. Of course he should have had the will power and initiative to take Faith away from Flossie. But when I think of that lonely man assembling the rare books and documents he had inherited, and disposing of them cautiously and advantageously, so that he might provide for Faith's future I am almost inclined to forgive his weakness. It all seems so pitiful!—I believe the house on Lafayette Square brought in only enough to pay his debts and I do not suppose the farm is worth much, though Faith has a great deal of sentiment about it. She has been—or rather *had* been—planning to go back to the United States and spend next summer there. But those first editions of Poe and Hawthorne! Those Lincoln letters! Those paintings by Stuart and Copley!—and Christian didn't sell them all! He managed to save out enough so that Faith would not be entirely deprived of heirlooms! And besides, she has a certain income of ten thousand dollars a year, with the principal held in trust, so that it can never be squandered, as Flossie squandered her own money, or 'misappropriated'—that is the euphemistic term, isn't it?—as Nelson Cummings 'misappropriated' it for her!"

"Do you think the Wagnerian hero would want to live on his wife's money?"

"Of course not, Sam! You are perfectly absurd! But I think the fact that Faith has a dowry will enhance her desirability in the eyes of his family, less because the money would be helpful than because her possession of it would meet their standards of the fitness of things. A German *Braut* never goes to her husband empty-handed. And the money undoubtedly *would* be helpful. There are five children in all to be provided for—the two elder sons are officers in the army and that always means a large outlay—and one of the daughters is already engaged. I imagine that Rudolf will have to practice some economy in taking up that post in Madrid to which he has just been appointed—young diplomats, like young artists, have to eat and pay rent, remember!"

Sam grunted. His ferocity had quite obviously begun to subside. Mrs. Atkinson, recognizing that she no longer had explosiveness with which to deal, permitted herself to enlarge upon another aspect of the situation.

"You haven't seen Faith in a long time," she reminded him. "You'll be surprised at the change in her. She was such a serious, silent child! And then, after her mother's death, she was so tragically mute that I lived in constant terror that something would snap inside of her, that she would have a complete nervous breakdown. If she hadn't possessed wonderful strength of character and something more than that—a real reserve of spiritual fortitude on which to draw, some sort of inner exaltation—she would have, of course. Remember her finding Flossie as she did——"

"I try not to remember it. I'd rather not be reminded of it," said Sam with a return of savageness.

"I know . . . and when she finally discovered that she could turn to me with confidence she began to—unfold. Very slowly, certainly. But it happened. Almost like a flower. At first the only difference was that she was less withdrawn, less self-protective and reserved. Then gradually I realized that she had succeeded—in partly forgetting. That she had begun to be happy—for the first time in her life—with me."

"Look here," said Sam, with sudden gentleness, "don't you go getting the idea I don't understand all you've done for Faith. You—you saved her."

"She saved herself, Sam. But I *was there*. Thank God! And, after that she began to be happy, to eat and sleep and think normally again. Then just recently the unfolding ceased to be gradual. It came with a rush. Of course she is at the most formative period of her life. And now, Sam, there's beginning to be something radiant about her. She's—she's joyous! And oh, Sam, she's the loveliest thing to look at you ever saw!"

Sam cleared his throat. "I don't doubt it," he said, still gently, but with a slight tinge of sarcasm, "which makes me all the more receptive to the idea of seeing her myself. When had she intended to come back from the Lido? Because she's had time, practically, to swim the Adriatic since I arrived, and still there isn't the slightest sign of her. I have no doubt that the consul's wife and the nice Vassar girl are perfect chaperones, and the high-born viking so correct that he wouldn't touch Faith by tying up her shoe string if it came undone, and all that, but it's nearly eight o'clock. And I got in at half-past two. If you don't mind, I think I'll wade over to the Lido myself and see if I can find her. . . . Anything I can do for you before I go?"

He reached for the electric switch. A pale, apologetic gleam emanated from the fanciful lighting fixtures, sending a faint illumination over the stiff, little twilit salon. But before he could put his purpose of departure into effect, the painted doorway was suddenly flung open and slammed shut; and Faith, a swift blur of gray and gold, rushed across the parquet flooring.

"Darling Sam!" she cried, throwing her arms around his neck. "Oh, I *am* so glad to see you! How wonderful you look! How wonderful that *you're here!* How's Velasquez?

Have you moved to the new studio? Did you get millions out of the magnate man? I know you put a terrible *steely* look into his portrait! Has he taken it away from Paris already? I hope not because I'm crazy to see it. I did feel dreadfully not to meet you at the station, Sam, and to be so long getting here. We'll make up for it to-morrow. But your wire came late, and Mrs. Saunders and Harriet couldn't seem to change their plan at the last moment, and go another day instead, and Rudolf and I had planned on the swim—and oh, I forgot—Sam, this is my new friend, Rudolf von Hohenlohe."

Sam had caught the girl to him with a hungry hug. Now, deliberately, he extricated himself from their mutual embrace, set her gently aside, and stepped forward. As he did so, his eyes met those of a very tall, very fair young man, who stood erectly and proudly, but unobstrusively, beside the painted doorway which Faith had flung open and slammed shut—eyes in the clear blue depths of which even Sam's searching glance could unfathom nothing but sincerity and steadfastness.

Chapter VII

THE afternoon had not been one of unclouded happiness for Rudolf von Hohenlohe.

This, he admitted to himself, was not Faith's fault. Faith had seemed even more entrancing than ever, from the moment when she met him in the reception hall of the hotel, dressed in trim gray flannel, her bathing suit folded into a compact, smart little gray bag, to the moment when the expedition ended at the door of Mrs. Atkinson's salon. And certainly it had not been Mrs. Saunders' fault or Harriet's. Mrs. Saunders had been up very late the night before, and had betrayed her agreeably somnolent state even before they had all left the little steamer that chugged along between the Schiavoni and the Lido; and went sound asleep before she had been settled five minutes on the silver sands. While Harriet had decided at the last moment that she did not care to swim, that she would rather sit beside her mother and read the book on Comparative Philosophy which she had been "meaning to get to" all summer and which she had brought along with her. So when Faith stepped from the

Stabilimento dei Bagni, and put her hand in Rudolf's and waded out into the shallow water beside him before they took the final plunge into the breakers, he had her all to himself. And *Gott in Himmel,* but she was glorious!

He was still tingling with unaccustomed rapture when at last they strode, still side by side and hand in hand out of the water again and sank down, weary but invigorated, upon the beach. Mrs. Saunders continued to sleep profoundly. Harriet's absorption in her book had not abated. No other bathers were very near them. To all intents and purposes, Rudolf still had Faith entirely to himself.

"Someone ought to paint you as Lorelei," he said, watching the movement of her arms as she lifted them and ran her fingers back and forth through her hair, shaking it out and spreading it over her shoulders to dry.

> " *Die schöste Jungfrau sitzet*
> *Auf oben wunderbar—*
> *Ihr goldnes geschmeide blitzet*
> *Sie kammt ihr goldnes Haar!* "

he sang in a remarkably good tenor. "Or else as Aphrodite, rising from the sea foam," he added, thinking of Faith's lovely emergence from the crested wave.

"Of course!" she exclaimed enthusiastically, "just as Botticelli painted 'La Bella Simonetta'—Aphrodite, I mean, not Lorelei," she continued hastily, "but Lorelei would be good, too. I must speak to Sam about it. He'll be awfully grateful for the suggestion. It will make up to him for not meeting him—I can't help feeling so guilty," she went on, "about not meeting Sam."

"Sam?" asked Rudlolf, honestly puzzled and startled. To be sure, Faith had mentioned that she was expecting a visit from a friend, but this had escaped Rudolf's memory; and he had entirely forgotten the friend's name, and had never heard the nature of his profession.

"Yes. I told you about Sam Dudley. He is my very best and oldest friend. Even better and older than Cousin Sarah."

"You mean that he is an elderly gentleman?" asked Rudolf hopefully.

"No-o-o. Not so very elderly. He's about thirty. But he's very well preserved. When I said he was my oldest friend, though, I meant he had been my friend *longer* than anyone else."

"I see," said Rudolf less hopefully, "and he is a painter?"

"Yes. He is getting to be quite well known. Not famous, you know, but recognized."

"*So*," said Rudolf politely, but without evident pleasure, "and just what is it that he paints?"

"Well, he does some marine pictures. The first one of his that got into the *Salon* was called 'A Storm at Sea.' I liked it because I saw the storm myself. I was nearly drowned in it. Sam and I were on the same boat, and I went to look for him on deck, and a big wave almost swept me overboard. Sam saved me. So I have a personal interest in that picture. But it was very badly hung and the critics didn't particularly praise it. So mostly Sam paints me. The reason your idea about Aphrodite was so *especially* good, was because it would be a marine picture and a picture of me too! —The first time Sam really had a *succes fou* at the *Salon*— got a prize you know and all that—was with a painting he named 'Young Eve.' It was sold, afterwards, to a very rich and noble Austrian."

Something clicked quickly in Rudolf's brain. So *that* was it—the feeling that had persisted ever since he had first seen Faith that he had met her before! Of course! "Young Eve!" The prize picture of the Archduke Stefan's modern collection! Stefan had given a magnificent dinner after it had arrived in Vienna, to celebrate its arrival and to show it to all his friends! Rudolf had been at the dinner himself! He never would forget his first view of the painting, hung, for just that evening, before being taken into the art gallery, on the crimson brocade wall of the state dining room: the picture of an exquisite child, the color of her rosy flesh emerging with a shell-like smoothness and firmness from the gloom of a sylvan background, the serpent hardly more than a curving shadow behind her white feet, her dark eyes luminous with still unfulfilled promise, her wistful mouth innocently provocative, her hair falling like radiant rain over her bare shoulders. . . . Rudolf suddenly felt as if he had been shot. The "Young Eve"—Faith!

"Did—did you pose for that picture?" he asked, quickly and involuntarily.

"Of course. I have posed for all of them. I was in Paris the first year Sam was there, you see. And since then he has spent his vacation wherever I happened to be. I posed for 'Suzanna,' and 'Lady Godiva,' and I posed last year for 'Mary of Nazareth.' That is the best one of all. It has taken a gold medal at three expositions. Sam hasn't sold it yet. The noble Austrian wants that too, but Sam says he can't bear to part with it—that it represents so much. It is the Madonna, you know, when she was very young—before the annunciation."

The Madonna before the annunciation! Again Rudolf felt

that swift stinging pain. For Stefan, fulminating against the stubborn genius who had created it and would not sell it, had dragged him to admire it at the loan exposition in Munich where it occupied the place of honor. And Rudolf had stood spellbound before the slender, white-robed figure of grace and chastity, recognizing that it was delineated with an understanding and a tenderness with which he had never seen it interpreted before. The Holy Child was hardly a dream, as yet, to this future Mother, no prophetic vision of Calvary had risen before her tranquil gaze. She stood, with the slim halo curving above the sheer veil that framed her heart-shaped face and fell softly over her shoulders, half-concealing, half-revealing her shining hair and budding breast: virginity incarnate.

Rudolf tore his mind clear from the impression that he was still looking at the picture, and moistened his lips. "You —you posed for that also?" he inquired at length.

"Yes . . . a year ago last May—the month of Mary. We were at Lourdes. We hadn't decided yet what this year's subject should be . . . it's especially hard when the 'Mary' has been such a success—it would be dreadful to follow it with a failure! And now you give us this wonderful idea of Aphrodite!"

Rudolf made a great effort. "I have been trying to think, ever since I first saw you here, where I had seen you before," he said slowly. "Now I know. 'The noble Austrian' is a cousin of mine. He is the Archduke Stefan. I saw the 'Eve' at his house. And he took me to see the 'Mary' in Munich. He greatly desires to possess it."

"Oh, but you won't mind, will you, if Sam won't let him have it? Because I don't believe——"

"No," said Rudolf still speaking very slowly, "I shan't mind."

"Rudolf!" cried Faith with intuitive alarm. "You mind *something!* What is it? Didn't—didn't you like Sam's pictures?"

"They are great works of art," said Rudolf with reluctant reverence. "You have inspired a genius to rare creation, *liebe* Faith. But I must be sincere with you. I am happy about the 'Mary.' But I am not so happy about the 'Eve.' "

"Well," said Faith with relief, "of course, when Sam painted that he wasn't half the artist he is now—all the critics say he's made tremendous strides. Probably you'll be happier about all his future pictures, Aphrodite, for instance."

"It is unthinkable that he should paint you as Aphrodite!" exclaimed Rudolf with vehemence.

Faith felt baffled. She decided to change the subject, which

59

she realized was unwelcome without in the least understanding why. "Don't you think," she asked finally, "that we have talked about Sam enough for a while anyway? Don't you think we might talk—about something else?"

"I think," said Rudolf hesitatingly and painfully, "that we must not talk about anything else just now—that we must arouse the estimable *Frau* Saunders and interrupt *Fraulein* Harriet's progress in philosophy. *Es tut mir leid, Liebchen,* but it is time that we should go back to Venice."

.   .   .   .   .   .

There was, as Sam had seen in that first searching glance, nothing but sincerity and steadfastness, courage and beauty and honor in Rudolf von Hohenlohe's deep blue eyes. And when, very much later in the evening, he turned regretfully away from his little balcony and crossed his small room to answer a knock at his door, to find himself confronted again with the same steadfast look that had, at one and the same time, reassured him and sent him into the depths of despair, there were no reservations in the greeting he gave to their possessor.

"Why, come right along in!" he said cordially, "I thought you'd have hit the hay hours ago. I was outside baying the moon—like the proverbial hound, you know. I'm afraid I didn't hear you when you first knocked."

"If I do not intrude, I must a little with you talk," said Ruldolf von Hohenlohe very earnest.

They had been together with Faith and Mrs. Atkinson all through dinner and the early evening. This was the first time that Sam had heard the German speak unidiomatically. He pricked up his ears. Something must have happened to shake Rudolf's Teutonic poise, and the strain of it was beginning to tell upon him.

"Sure!" he said easily. "Smoke? Drink? I wish I could offer you something to sit on beside these alleged chairs. I think they must have come out of the Doges' torture chamber. But they're all I have."

"You must at once permit yourself into your own apartment to be moved," went on Rudolf, almost as if he had not heard. "I have the manager my opinion of him told."

"Wish I'd been there to hear it," replied Sam, grinning cheerfully, "but really, I'm all right here—more comfortable than I'd be with your mural decorations. Faith described them to me. I'm supposed to be an artist, you know, and I really feel they'd be more than I could bear."

"But I must insist. I must a point of it make."

"Why, of course, if you feel that way about it. . . . But you don't want me to move to-night, do you? My traps are all thrown around, and——"

"The morning will do," conceded Rudolf, "I must to-morrow leave in any case. I must at once my family see."

"Yes?" said Sam still speaking easily, "nothing wrong, I hope?"

"It is that I must permission ask to marry Faith."

The words were out. Sam braced himself to meet them. "If there's the slightest chance that Faith will have you," he said as quietly as he could, "with or without your family's consent, you're so rotten lucky that——"

"She will have me," said Rudolf very gravely. There was a moment of tense silence. Then his words came with a rush. "It is not as you must think. I did not importune her. I know she is very young. And, moreover, I wished to pay her the tribute of giving her the same formal courtship that I would have given to a German maiden. But last night as we stood together on the balcony looking out at the water, and the moon, and the palaces, and listening to the sound of the waves lapping against the stones, it was all so beautiful that suddenly I was overcome. I knelt at her feet. I laid my face against her white dress. I kissed her hand. She did not repulse me. And when at last I rose and looked at her, I knew that she was responsive to my feeling, though no word had been spoken between us. And knowing, how can I in honor wait to speak?"

"You can't," said Sam simply.

He was terribly moved. All the time that Rudolf had been speaking, Sam had felt the blur of unshed tears against his eyelids. And now that Rudolf stood silent before him, waiting for his verdict, he knew what it must be. Characteristically, he endeavored to hide an emotion quite as genuine as that which Rudolf had revealed.

"And as long as you're sure she loves you," he asked, almost testily, "what in hell's worrying you?"

"It is that my family may not consent."

"Well, tell your family to——"

"*Mein Freund*, you do not understand. It is because of this that I give you my confidence, that I ask your help. It is impossible that I should marry without my family's consent."

"You mean that it wouldn't be legal?"

"Legal, yes, that. But I could be stripped of rank, fortune, career."

"Well, Good God, wouldn't Faith be worth it to you? Because if she wouldn't——"

61

"To me, yes. *Tausend Mal*. It is only that I fear, by and by, that I might not be worth it to Faith. She has said to me that you are her oldest and best friend. You know her well, much better than I. Therefore I have come to ask you, if in your opinion, it would."

Again Sam felt that bitter blur of tears against his eyes. More and more he wished, dully, that Rudolf von Hohenlohe would not force him to greater and greater respect.

"Mrs. Atkinson has disclosed to me Faith's so unhappy childhood," Rudolf went on, "therefore doubly have I wished that as my *Braut* she might have joy. Is she not too proud to be completely happy if in her breast there is the thought that her husband's family has not welcomed her that she has cost him his position, his future?"

"But why *shouldn't* your family welcome her? Why should she cost you your position and your future? Just the opposite, I should think! She's a girl in a million!"

"That is true, but my family may not so see it; and it is not only with my family that I shall have to reckon. The foreign minister sometimes declines to permit junior diplomats to marry, because this is not in accord with his policy, unless the marriage is most suitable. And Faith has to-day told me," said Rudolf laboriously, "that—she posed to you for the 'Young Eve' which hangs in my cousin Stefan's art gallery. It is not presumable that my family and the foreign minister will feel that an artist's model should become the wife of a von Hohenlohe."

There was another tense silence. This time it was Sam who broke it.

"Not even," he said, trying to control his sudden fury, "if the model for 'Young Eve' was eight years old when she posed for it? Not even if the same model, when she was fifteen, inspired the 'Mary of Nazareth' which your exalted cousin would sell an ancestral castle to get? Not even though the man who painted both those pictures has built his whole world around that model for eight years?—By all means go and tell your family—and the foreign minister— that Faith Marlowe is my model," he went on, his anger gathering force in spite of his efforts to check it, "that she is the inspiration for everything I have ever done or been! That but for her I should still be a gawky, provincial fumbler! That but for you I might still hope that some day she would be my wife."

"*Mein Freund!* I must beg you to believe that I meant no disparagement of Faith! And that I did not guess——"

"Oh, no!" Sam raged on. "You did not guess! There are a hell of a lot of things you have not guessed! The Archduke Stefan is your cousin, is he? Then is your mother by chance an Austrian by birth? The Archduchess Victoria Luise? Was her first husband an Austrian too? Did she have a son by that marriage who was an officer in the Austrian army?"

"Yes," said Rudolf quickly. "Yes, that is all so. But what then?"

"An officer who committed suicide," Sam shouted, now entirely beside himself, "after killing his mistress because he found another man in her room at midnight? And went off leaving her lying there dead, for her child to find hours later, in a pool of blood? O, yes, I know there was a revolver in her hand, that the verdict was brought in for double suicide! But Flossie Spencer never would have had the guts to shoot herself! She was a rotten coward, just as just as she was a rotten quitter! Her husband made her give up his name when he divorced her for desertion—as he could have divorced her a dozen times for worse than that! But the woman you knew as Flossie Spencer was Faith Marlowe's *mother!* Go tell your family that! And at the same time tell Faith that your brother was her mother's murderer—and then find out, and be damned to you, whether you can get *her* to take *you!*"

PART III

Victoria

Chapter VIII

SAM DUDLEY was too healthy and normal a man to be subject to either futile introspection or to vain regrets. Nevertheless, he spent the months that elapsed between his arrival in Venice and his departure for the Straits of Magellan—where he eventually painted the greatest of all his marine pictures—remorsefully contrasting his own clumsiness and violence with the constancy of Faith, the steadfastness of Rudolf von Höhenlohe, and the finesse of the Archduchess Victoria Luise.

It was in vain that he argued with himself that sooner or later—sooner *better* than later—Rudolf and Faith would both have been bound to discover and forced to face the sordid and hideous tragedy which at one and the same time linked and divided them. That *he* should have been the one to reveal the blood-stained intrigue which formed the background of their romance, because he resented the possibility of an injustice to Faith and because he had been defrauded of his own heart's desire—this thought was bitter bread upon which to feed perpetually. It would have been better—far better—to starve.

The projectile which he had hurled at Rudolf von Hohenlohe recoiled against Sam almost instantaneously. For Rudolf, having already braced himself against shot, was, in measure, prepared against shell. And the first words that he spoke were charged, not with concern for himself, but with compassion for Faith.

"Das arme holde Madchen!" he cried with horror-stricken emotion.

"I ought to be drawn and quartered!" groaned Sam. Rudolf advanced and laid a firm arm around his shoulder.

"Let us try to steady each other a little, *nicht wahr?*" he said in a voice that was already under control and that was wholly untainted by hostility. "I have stepped in and robbed you of a treasure which you hoped to possess—that I feel sure you deserve to possess. This has been to you a great shock. I must be sincere and say that even if I had known you loved Faith, I should have tried to win her. Because I love her also. But I did not mean to steal. For this I must ask your forgiveness. Also if I have been indelicate of language in speaking of Faith as your model. And *mein Freund*, you have done right to tell me what you have. With a little less suddenness, if that had been possible, but perhaps it was not. And it is always better to face facts—when there are ugly facts to consider, it is not only better, it is necessary. That is one of my mother's maxims. And my mother is a very sagacious lady."

Sam, fumbling toward self-mastery, was aware that the German had already assumed command of the situation. There was no indication of either defeat or despair on his face, though its look of untested youth had been swept away from it.

"At present we can consider the situation from every angle at once," Rudolf went on earnestly, "instead of incompletely, as it would have been considered, if I had returned to Germany without knowing what you have just told me. Afterwards, even if matters had been once adjusted, further readjustment, of very painful character, would still have been necessary. Now perhaps, when I go to Germany, it may be without any story to tell, without any permission to ask; it may be with finality, not to return. As you have pointed out, Faith would be justified in declining to marry me, when she learns that my half-brother was her mother's lover. In the morning we must tell her—not tonight, for she is already sleeping peacefully. But to-morrow, *so bald wie möglich*—as soon as possible . . . we will of course inform *Frau* Atkinson that she may be prepared to give both counsel and comfort to Faith."

"Well, and what about you?" burst out Sam with involuntary admiration.

Rudolf von Hohenlohe did not even wince. "But, *mein Freund*, there can be no question of me," he replied steadily. "Even if it had been my own brother Hans—my father's eldest son whom I love with my very soul—instead of my half-brother Otto, for whom I must confess I cherished no love at all, whose ghost stood between me and Faith, can you suppose that I would hesitate? You who have known her so long? *Nein, Tausend Mal.* The first part of the decision lies with Faith. We must speak to her, we must give her time to consider . . . when, having considered, if by a miracle she finds that she does not abhor the thought of me, I must go to my mother. For I think the second part of the decision must lie with her. If by a second miracle, she finds that she does not abhor the thought of Faith, we must bring them together. With as little strain, with as little design, as possible. My mother, if she consents to the meeting, will know how to arrange it. She is a very great lady."

In the light of subsequent events, Sam discovered that he concurred completely with Rudolf's high estimate of the Archduchess Victoria Luise. A woman like her had never before come within the range of his limited vision. He had gone straight from a side street in Jonesville, Ohio, and his classmates at the Jonesville High School, to the Latin Quarter in Paris with its haphazard, hearty *camaraderie*. Though he had occasionally come into brief professional contact with personages of note, as in the case of Archduke Stefan, the characteristics of a "very great lady" and her *milieu* were as unfamiliar to him as those of an Eskimo inhabitant of Greenland. And the acquaintance of one was now to be forced upon him. What Rudolf and Faith had said to each other, the morning after Sam's arrival in Venice, he never knew exactly; for the first time in years, Faith did not turn to him with overflowing confidences. But he knew that she had declined to let her mother's ghost stand between her and Rudolf with as little hesitation as Rudolf had declined to let his brother's ghost stand between Faith and himself. For immediately after the conference Rudolf took a train for Germany, still looking white and stricken, but still completely composed; and within three days, Faith also looking white and stricken, but also completely composed, showed Sam a telegram saying that Rudolf would return the following afternoon accompanied by his mother.

Sam dreaded the descent of the Archduchess upon Venice with unspeakable apprehension; he visualized her as being stupid, opinionated, and heavy both mentally and physically; he felt sure she would extinguish the still unflickering flame of trustfulness which burned in Faith's breast; that she would snub and slight Sarah Atkinson; and that she would give him the impression that she regarded him as an insignificant artisan of a doubtful personal cleanliness. It did not matter much, of course, what she thought of him; but it mattered a good deal how she treated Sarah Atkinson; while upon her attitude toward Faith, all creation, just then, seemed to hinge. . . .

He recognized, that in spite of his worst forebodings, it devolved upon him to meet the Archduchess and her son at the station. Certainly it would not be suitable for Faith to go; and certainly it was unthinkable that Faith should be left behind alone while Mrs. Atkinson accompanied him. He therefore set off by himself on his errand of grim greeting; but at the station he found what appeared to be a delegation of welcome: the German consul and the Austrian consul, both of whom he knew by sight, were standing on the platform conversing agreeably with an imposing-looking ecclesiastic in gorgeous raiment whom Sam rightly guessed to be a bishop at the very least; and close beside them had forgathered a sizable group of personages whom he labeled mentally as "eminent citizens," and who—he was forced to admit to himself—looked very eminent indeed. As the train swung into sight, they hurriedly clustered around the steps of a private car, emblazoned with coronets, which was attached to the rear; and when two men servants in livery, a very trim maid carrying an enormous jewel box, and a discreetly dressed young woman with a distinctly secretarial air, had alighted and had placed themselves in positions ready to render immediate service, a pale, slender, dark-eyed lady of infinite elegance and distinction glided out upon the platform at the side of Rudolf von Hohenlohe.

Her appearance was the occasion of immediate acclamation. Such an expression of enthusiasm and admiration would, Sam reflected, have been accompanied in Jonesville by the strains of the local brass band and a speech by the mayor. Here the method was different, but the general effect was much the same. Sam, a stranger to all these dignitaries, felt forlornly superfluous. He endeavored to slip inconspicuously away. But before he could make good his escape, he was conscious of the striking nearness of Rudolf von Hohenlohe and the fascinating gaze of the lovely lady.

"This is the famous American painter, Samuel Dudley, *Mütterchen*," Rudolf was saying, "my great friend, of whom I have told thee." And the slim gloved hand which the consuls and the "eminent citizens" had all been kissing with such rapturous respect was extended in Sam's direction, accompanied by a glance of melting charm. Sam had never kissed a lady's hand in his life. But he did so now, discovering, with swift surprise, that it was a fairly simple act productive of a remarkable amount of pleasure. Before an instant had elapsed, the Archduchess, with adroit facility, had contrived to include him in her circle, to make him feel at ease and acquainted. Then he realized that with the gracious acceptance of an invitation here and there, but with the smiling statement that she preferred to remain *incognita* because she was taking a little holiday with her son, most of the dignitaries were being courteously dismissed; and when the Archduchess was actually installed in her waiting gondola, Sam further discovered that he was among the favored few from whom she had not separated herself. And three hours later, after she had rested, he found himself seated beside her at the perfect dinner that was being expertly served in the salon of an imposing suite which the hypocritical manager had discovered to be providentially vacant, the moment he had heard of the impending arrival in Venice of the Archduchess Victoria Luise.

No, decidedly, Sam considered, sipping his iced Asti, after his warmed Burgundy, he had never dreamed that "very great ladies," dowered like this one with such suavity, such tactful charm, such exquisite urbanity, really existed. He had thought of them—when he thought of them at all—as the product of the flighty brain of the "dime novelist"; and he visualized them, moreover, as vain and vapid, unredeemed by either intellectual or moral stamina. But the Archduchess, sitting at the head of the flower-banked table, was a vital as well as a distinguished figure. Her dark hair was piled high above her regal head; for pearls glistened against her delicate skin; her lace dress, folded softly away from her sloping shoulders, fell in filmy ripples on either side of her slim waist. And she was, Sam realized, neither vapid nor vain. She was very beautiful and very clever; she was also very kind. They were all immeasurably better off because she had joined them. He looked across the table at Faith, and suddenly, in his heart, rose an inarticulate prayer that God would bless Victoria Luise. For Faith was gazing at Rudolf's mother with an expression that revealed her serene consciousness that in relying upon this great and wise lady to help her she had not been mistaken, and that in trusting her future to those slim, jeweled, skillful hands she was secure against betrayal.

Victoria Luise, gathering up a large black lace fan and a small white lace handkerchief was signaling to her son, with a smile, that she was ready to leave the table. As she rose, she turned to Sam with an air of interpreting and granting unexpressed wishes. "I am sure that you and Rudolf will wish to confer a little without the supervision of ladies," she said lightly. "I shall then take Mrs. Atkinson and Faith with me to my boudoir to confer a little without the supervision of gentlemen. And as I am the least trifle fatigued after my journey, shall we say *auf wiedersehn* until to-morrow morning? I am depending that then you shall show me the most beautiful vistas of Venice!" Again she had given him her finger tips; again finding it the easy and natural thing to do, he had kissed them. Rudolf also had kissed her hand; then she had raised her dark head and he had bent his blond one, and she had kissed his brow, murmuring, *"Gute Nacht, lieber Sohn—schlaf schön!"* before, with a rhythmic, undulating grace she left the room, Mrs. Atkinson striding solemnly beside her, Faith guided by the pressure of an encircling arm.

For a time, across the current of Rudolf's reassuring words, Sam could hear their three voices from the room beyond; then, after an interval, he realized that he was hearing only two voices. Mrs. Atkinson had gone. Faith was alone with Victoria Luise. In the course of the next hour, every essential of her life would be decided. Not the details of course. But everything that really mattered. He flung down the cigarette which he had lighted from the one he had smoked before that, and rose abruptly.

"Look here," he muttered with embarrassed vehemence, "I'm going to my room. I simply can't sit here talking to you while I know that Faith's in there with your mother. I guess I feel about the same way I would if I'd taken her to be examined by a doctor—even if it was the best doctor in the world—and was outside in the waiting room looking at humorous magazines six months old and all dog-eared, while I wondered how much she was being hurt and watched the clock until the doctor came out to tell me either that she was all right or had got to have a major operation. Of course if I'd had your training I could have stuck it out and talked about the weather, or the Greek tragedians, or trigonomentry. You take scandals and suicides and murders and matrimony all in your stride, without showing how you feel about it, because you've been taught how. But I haven't. Good God, they don't breed or raise men like you in Jonesville, Ohio, or in the Latin Quarter! But even then you don't hold a candle to your mother. I'd bet my bottom dollar on her. When everything is all over but the shouting, and Faith has told me what's what, I'll come back and shake hands with you. And I've got a hunch that after that I'll want to get down on my four paws and lap the blacking off the Archduchess Victoria Luise's shoes."

Chapter IX

VICTORIA LUISE's great, frescoed bedroom was fragrant with massed flowers and lighted with tall candles. Where the

69

slim, multitudinous tapers which had supplemented the in-adequate but glaring bulbs of electricity, with their little, candy-colored twisted glass shades, had come from, was a mystery—nothing of the sort had been supplied to any of the other guests at the Hotel Superbo. The source of the luxurious *chaise longue*, banked with small, lace-covered cushions upon which Victoria Luise lay extended, was also a mystery. But there it was. All the rigid little gilt chairs had disappeared as if by magic, and in their stead, besides the *chaise longue,* were several low, comfortable *fauteuils,* in one of which, her hands pressed rather closely together, but her manner completely composed, Faith sat facing the Archduchess. Autographed pictures, in large silver frames, of the members of various princely families, had been scattered about; there was a small basket of luscious fruit on the bedside table; there was even a cheerful fire burning beneath the austere mantel. In the course of a few hours, the stiff, bare room had been transfigured. For the first time, Faith realized how completely the personality of a woman may dominated her habitation; and looking back-ward, almost subconsciously, remembered that Flossie's room had always been cluttered, musty and permeated with stale scent; while Sarah Atkinson's room always seemed to bear the evidence of recent scrubbing, meticulous order, and slight chilliness.

The sound of Victoria Luise's soft voice recalled her to the immediate surroundings.

"So now that we are comfortable, and alone, we may talk together, may we not, *liebes Kind?*" The Archduchess was asking, gently. "We have so much to say to each other, you and I, that it seemed better not to wait, even until to-morrow, to begin. Or so it has seemed to me. Do you feel as I do?"

"Yes," said Faith quietly.

"And shall we begin by discussing those subjects which are hardest to mention? Then we shall not have the thought of them, the dread of them, constantly before us. We may dismiss them from our minds. At least, I believe we may, if we both try very hard to see clearly and think clearly. And I know I can depend on you to do so."

"I will try," said Faith, still very quietly.

"I know you will, *liebes Kind.* And so shall I. And be-cause we will both try, we shall probably succeed. It is gen-erally thus. To show you how hard I am willing to try, I am going to make a confession to you, and then I am going to ask you a question, which I hope you can bring yourself

70

to answer. Come closer to me, Faith, and put your hand in mine. *So!* That will steady us."

Her slim, jeweled fingers, surprisingly strong, closed securely over Faith's warm, little hand. With their pressure, Faith's sense of stability deepened. She waited, without impatience or fear, for Victoria Luise to go on.

"I did not love my son, Otto, who killed your mother," the Archduchess said in a low voice which did not tremble. "He was an uncontrolled, vicious, and violent man. From boyhood—almost from babyhood—he showed traits of weakness and wickedness which wrung my heart. His death was a shock to me, a source of shame and scandal. But it was not a sorrow. Within a few weeks after it happened, I knew that it was a relief—a release. I have shown respect for death, even though I could not respect the dead. I have worn mourning, I have lived in seclusion, I have been silent. I have faced this stark and sordid tragedy with my head held high. But this has not been as hard for me as has been supposed, because I have not really grieved. I have never admitted to anyone before, not even to my husband, or to my children, what I have admitted to you. But it is true. This is my confession. I make it now because I believe it is your due. And having made it, I ask my question: Did you love your mother?"

"No," said Faith, drawing a long breath.

"She also made you very unhappy? After you had recovered from the horror of her murder—for I know it was that, not suicide—after the good *Frau* Atkinson had befriended you, your life became tranquil and lovely for the first time, did it not?"

"Yes," said Faith, drawing another long breath.

"Then should we, you and I, permit the shadow of this dreadful double death to darken our lives? Are we not both strong enough to go—hand in hand as we are now—out into the sunshine together?"

"Yes," cried Faith convulsively.

Suddenly, vehemently, she had begun to weep, with an abandonment which would have betrayed, even to a far less wise and compassionate woman than Victoria Luise, the fact that these were the first tears she had shed since she had faced the revelation of Otto's identity. Victoria Luise bent over her, and clasped the girl in her arms, drawing the bright, bowed head against her breast. For a long time, holding her so, gently, steadily, she did not speak. It was only when the deep, agonizing sobs had begun to spend themselves that she commenced, caressingly, to murmur words of comfort and endearment.

"We have passed it, *Liebchen*," she whispered, "that dangerous and difficult place in the road—that menace to our purpose together. We shall never need to turn back and look at it again. Forget that it ever existed, as I shall. For if we forget, you and I, the world will also forget. The world recalls only what the individual is so weak as to remember."

There was a long silence. Faith felt a final kiss of reassurance brushing her brow, a soft, fine, cool handkerchief slipped into her hand. Victoria Luise was freeing the girl gently from the embrace that had enfolded her.

"There is a carafe of water near the fruit at my bedside," she said gently, "go and pour yourself out a little, *liebe* Faith, and drink it, and bring me some also, if you will be so kind. And on my dressing table there is powder in a glass jar. We will feel better if we dust a little over our faces and straighten our hair. You shall hold a little swinging mirror for me, and then I will hold it for you. The woman who permits her emotions, of whatever sort, to disfigure her, even temporarily, wages a losing battle with life."

Beneath the seemingly simple restoratives Faith sensed the poise and breeding which prompted their offer. Victoria Luise was right: the time of tragedy, the time of tenseness, the time of abandonment had passed. Spontaneously, Faith settled herself on the foot of the *chaise longue*, brushing aside the violet draperies to make room for herself. Spontaneously, she reached out to take Victoria Luise's hand again of her own accord. The Archduchess smiled.

"You are not too tired, *liebes Kind*, to talk a little more?"

"I want to," said Faith impetuously. "I want to talk about another difficult thing. The thing that troubles Rudolf so much."

"You mean your relation to Sam?"

"My relation?" asked Faith in amazement. "Sam and I are not related! We are friends."

"I used the wrong word," said the Archduchess, quietly. "Purposely," she added after a moment, as if compelled to candor, "as a test."

"I don't understand," said Faith with growing bewilderment.

"I see that you do not, *liebes Kind*. But it is that which I had to find out, even at the risk of wounding you again. And since you do not understand—well, we have passed another obstacle. Suppose you take my word for it that this is so, and do not ask me to explain too much to-night, when it is growing late, and when we have both, already, been *très emotionées*. Suppose you trust me to talk to Rudolf on that point later on, telling you only, now, that you have nothing to dread on this score and venturing only one suggestion: that you should not, at least for the present, pose to Sam for the 'Aphrodite.' That you should persuade him, rather, to give Rudolf the 'Mary of Nazareth' that my son may place it where his eyes can rest on it constantly, and his thoughts dwell on all that it so exquisitely reveals."

She rose and walked over to the open window, resting her white arm on the deep embrasure and gazing reflectively out toward the quiet canal. When she spoke again it was with the manner of one whose thoughts were finding undirected release in speech, rather than as if she were addressing anyone.

"Is narrow-mindedness not a greater sin than unchastity, and prudery even worse than immodesty? *Sicherlich, Sicherlich!* And since this dear child has been guilty of no sin at all, surely I am strong enough to shield her from slinking scandalmongers."

She turned, and sitting down in one of the two great armchairs that stood on either side of a carved table, motioned to Faith to take the other.

"Let us now be most practical," she said earnestly, holding herself very erect. "You are extremely pretty, unusually intelligent, adequately educated and moderately wealthy. Your command of languages is remarkable and would be a real advantage if you should marry a diplomat. So would your little income, which, from what Rudolf has told me, is large enough to dress you suitably and still leave you enough over to take care of your other personal expenditures— your charities, your gifts, the wages of your own maid, perhaps even the upkeep of your carriage. This would be most helpful to Rudolf. He is a younger brother, as of course you know, and ours is not a wealthy family, though it is a very old one."

Faith, who in spite of a natural and youthful nonchalance about money matters had rather gathered from Mrs. Atkinson that an income of ten thousand dollars a year was sufficiently substantial to enable an entire family to live comfortably, even if not luxuriously, was amused that it could be regarded so casually. She said so, quite frankly. "But of course," she added, "I should like to use it in any way that would be most useful to Rudolf."

"I know you would, *liebe* Faith, and that would be as I have indicated—after you have purchased your trousseau. Since—if I understand the matter correctly—you are not able to touch your capital, it may be necessary for you to make economies to pay for that out of your income, as I suppose you have never had any general provision for a marriage outfit. I know, you see, that such is not the American custom."

"No," said Faith, still frankly, "it isn't and I haven't. But I can. I can begin right away. There is lovely linen right here in Venice. Cousin Sarah and I might start shopping tomorrow. We can draw up lists, the way we do for Christmas, and you can tell us whether the things I want to get would be suitable for a German *Braut*. . . . I should like them to be," she added, *"suitable*, but perhaps not exactly the *same* as a German girl would get. Because I'm not a German girl. I'm an American."

"You are quite right to feel that way about it," said Victoria Luise, smiling. "I will look at your lists, and I will make suggestions, but all the decisions shall rest with you. And there is no hurry. You can proceed gradually. Because, you know, in spite of all the obstacles we have passed, we must not make the mistake of regarding your betrothal to Rudolf as an accomplished fact. We must only look forward toward it hopefully as a glad possibility."

"Why?" asked Faith.

Victoria Luise smiled again. "I think Rudolf has told you that it is not always in accordance with the policy of our foreign minister to permit junior diplomats to marry," she said pleasantly, "and any apparent defiance of his rule is apt to cost a young man his career. But with tact and time, adjustments can often be made. . . . I am confident that they may be in this case. Especially as you are an American."

"Why?" asked Faith once more.

"Because at this moment, there is no country with which Germany is more eager to cement friendly and intimate relations. You see, *liebe* Faith, that I am talking to you as to a woman of perception and understanding, not as to a child."

"I know you are," said Faith, "that is the reason I like you so much . . . what does Germany want?"

"We shall probably find out within the next decade," replied Victoria Luise lightly, but rather as if dismissing the subject. "Meanwhile a personal element enters into this particular situation which is most felicitous. It seems that the present American Ambassador to Germany, Mr. Carolus Cavendish Castle, was a great friend of your father. I believe they attended some university—Harvard, is it not?—together, and that also, after your father became senator, Herr Castle still used to visit frequently at the house. He recalls you, as a little girl. Do you at all remember him?"

Faith considered a moment. "Is he very huge and glowery, but jolly underneath?" she inquired, at length. "Do his eyebrows and his stomach both stick out? Does he show dozens of teeth when he laughs, and knock off his glasses when he gets excited?"

Victoria Luise laughed. "I might have added that you have rather unusual powers of observation and description, when I was enumerating your talents," she said with amusement. "I see that you do remember His Excellency. I am glad, because he is going to write to you, and Mrs. Castle is going to write to Mrs. Atkinson, suggesting that you and she should come and pay a long visit at the Embassy after the season opens this winter in Berlin."

"Oh, but how wonderful!" exclaimed Faith. "Why, you arranged all this—just in those few days after Rudolf got home, and told you about me—before you started for Venice! Even before you knew whether you were going to like me! I don't see—it's simply too marvelous—and too kind!"

"I have tried to be helpful," said Victoria Luise earnestly, "so I have earned the right—have I not?—to ask you, in return, to be very patient, and to trust me a great deal. I will make a little holiday here in Venice, for a short time, and we shall all be happy together. Then I must go home again, and I think Rudolf must come with me. After that, he will go directly to his post in Spain. When you reach Berlin, he will be in Madrid. You will not see him again for some months. Naturally, you will write to him and he to you. But not love letters!"

"Just the kind of letters I write to Sam?" asked Faith obediently. "I mean, as nearly as possible," she amended candidly. "Because, of course, I *couldn't* make them quite the same."

"I am sure you will try your best to express yourself with reserve," said Victoria Luise, "but we cannot hope for entire success, in this or any other endeavor. However . . . for the next few months, you and Mrs. Atkinson will doubtless remain in Italy, unless, just before coming on to Berlin, you should chance to go to Paris to do a little shopping. You have natural taste and style, of course, but no one, however gifted in these directions, should fail to take advantage of the existence of *grands couturiers* when this is possible, as happily, it is in your case. . . . The Honorable Carolus Cavendish Castle will wish to take you at once to the Opera. His loge is, fortunately, very close to the Imperial Box, which is generally occupied nowadays. There is, as you have doubtless heard, a lovely young English singer who made her début last year and who has found favor in the most exalted circles—but that is beyond the point. I have every reason to believe that your pleasing appearance at the Opera will pave the way for your prompt presentation at Court, a presentation which would have been assured, sooner or later, in any case, for the gentleman who is 'very huge and glowery, but jolly underneath, and whose eyebrows and stomach both stick out a little' is very much *persona grata* with the Emperor."

"And if the Emperor likes me, too, then I can marry Rudolf?" asked Faith bluntly.

Victoria Luise leaned across the table and patted Faith lightly on the cheek. "*Gott sei dank,*" she said whimsically, "that Rudolf did not fall in love with a *Dumkopf.* You have guessed very quickly, *liebe* Faith. If the Emperor likes you, and I feel more and more convinced that he will, then Rudolf will come home from his post in the spring; and there will be a beautiful little wedding at the American Embassy in Berlin; and afterwards, a honeymoon spent at the *caseria* of our distant kinsman and close friend, Sebastian de Cerreno, near Granada, which is to say, near Paradise. With all this to hope for, can you be patient, my child, and docile?"

The expression in the girl's eyes as she looked at the Archduchess answered for her more clearly than any spoken words would have.

"There is, then, only one thing more that I must say to you before we tell each other 'good-night' and I send you away to sweet dreams."

The earnestness with which Victoria Luise had spoken a few moments earlier crept back into her voice, but this time it had a new vehemence, a greater depth.

"Rudolph loves you," she said, speaking very seriously. "He loves you sincerely. I believe he will love you steadfastly. He was ready to risk forfeiting much in the hope of marrying you. According to his lights, he will never fail you. He will be faithful to his marriage vows. Within the limits of his consciousness, he will be kind and just. But he does not understand you. He has already revealed that by his complete failure to see your beautiful friendship with Sam in its true light. And though you are much more intuitive than he, I doubt whether you will always understand him either. There will be barriers between you—barriers which would have been high enough in any case, because of fundamental racial differences, and which your divergent temperaments may render insuperable. For all your adaptability, you are intrinsically American. No matter how long you remain in Europe—and I doubt whether you will remain here without restiveness much longer—no matter how gracefully you appear to accept adoption by an alien country, no matter how many children of yours are born in foreign soil, you will never become really naturalized. And Rudolf, who is not

76

adaptable at all, is the very embodiment and essence of the Prussian spirit. There can be no question of his unswerving adherence and allegiance *to* Prussia. He himself *is* Prussia personified."

"I know," said Faith, "and I think it is very glorious. There is something about the Prussian spirit that glistens, just as the Prussian uniform does."

"It is radiant; but it is not pliant. I believe that because you were dazzled by it just now, you do not see how inflexible it is in fiber. By the time your eyes are accustomed to its glitter, you may be aware also of its rigidity."

"I may be aware of it; but I shall not be afraid of it."

"*Liebe* Faith, a woman can experience frustration without experiencing fear; and frustration wounds her pride and breaks her spirit. But it is not only this racial barrier which I see stretched across your pathway. There are, as I have just said, many others. Two natures are not necessarily antagonistic because they are diametrically different. Sometimes they merge and blend, producing harmony; sometimes they interlock, producing strength. But they seldom produce both harmony and strength, and I do not believe that yours and Rudolf's can either merge or interlock."

"Why?" asked Faith again. But this time Victoria Luise did not smile as she answered her.

"Because I know Rudolf's character so well that I cannot be blind to its deficiencies. I have already told you that I realize he lacks adaptability, while you do not. He also lacks gaiety and imagination and fire. He has shown great self-control in this recent crisis, but strangely enough he often shows himself lacking in that. And because I have seen him gripped by violent though transient anger, I believe he is capable of an overwhelming outburst of a still more powerful passion; but I do not think he is capable of one that is really great and long sustained. Marriage, as soon as it ceases to be a novelty to him, will not mean high ecstasy and enduring rapture. So I am afraid of this betrothal, even though I am helping to bring it about. Because I have already discovered that you do not lack gaiety or imagination or fire or the capacity of a really great and long-sustained passion. Because you will ultimately—although you are now too young to know it—not find fulfillment in a marriage unillumined by these qualities. Unconsciously, involuntarily, you will seek the high ecstasy, the overpowering rapture. And your search will be very brief, even if it is not forestalled. For both will be offered to you. By many men. By some one man whom you will love in a way you do not dream of now."

77

"What makes you think so?" asked Faith.

Her voice was still untroubled. It was not even eager. Her question was hardly more than a matter of form. It betrayed, completely, the misplaced self-confidence of untouched and untarnished youth. Victoria Luise answered with supreme gentleness.

"I do not think, my child. I know. I, too, gave my heart away—or thought I did—when I was sixteen. And afterwards, because I had done so, I was tempted to give my soul away. I am confessing to you again, you see. I have pledged you my assistance; but now I am begging you—for the sake of my son and for your own sake—not to accept this assistance! To give Rudolf up, voluntarily, and before it is too late! To keep yourself free for the great lover who is still sure to come!"

Again she leaned across the table, taking Faith's hands in hers. For the first time there were tears in her eyes. Afterwards Faith remembered, there was a quality of prayer in her entreaty, and at the time wondered why it had moved her so little. She answered with the same brevity, the same steadiness, which had marked every word she had spoken to Victoria Luise.

"I am sure that Rudolf loves me," she said, "and that I love him as much as he loves me. And you must not be afraid. I know he is very loyal. But I am very loyal too."

PART IV

Sebastian

Chapter X

FAITH VON HOHENLOHE lay very still and straight in the narrow lower berth of a compartment on the Paris-Madrid *train de luxe,* subconsciously, but not resentfully, aware of the rhythmic metallic clatter that the car made as it jerked and jolted its uneven way along over the rough roadbed of the narrow-gauge railway. She was so thankful to be able to lie down, even on a hard and sloping mattress, that the minor irritations of travel were almost forgotten in her sense of relief. The first lap of the journey—from Berlin to Paris —had been comparatively comfortable; but this had been a trying day, very hot and dusty, and the garden-like country-side of France, usually so fresh and lovely in her eyes, had been tarnished by the glare of a relentless sun. The French couple sitting opposite her in the day carriage had objected to the amount of her hand baggage, which, as they kept reiterating, crowded them badly. They had as much as she did, and there was no reason why she should have felt remorse over their alleged discomfort; but she did, and she kept trying to rearrange her belongings, holding her heavy gold-fitted dressing case on her lap until she was so cramped and stiff that she could not keep it there any longer. When she set it down again, as close to her feet as possible, the man who was her *vis-à-vis* looked at her with increased animosity, and hissed *"Allemande!"* in an audible aside to his wife. Faith noticed that he was wearing the ribbon of the Legion of Honor, and felt a distinct surprise that anyone who was worthy of such recognition and reward should be so dis-courteous. It seemed to her that the frontier, where, at Irun, she would be able to change into the *wagon-lit,* and escape from the atmosphere of hostility, would never be reached.

Over and over again she thought it must be nearly half-past ten, only to find that it was five, that it was a quarter-past six, that it was twenty minutes of eight. And of course there had been veal for dinner, thin sizzling slices of it, folded down between mounds of fried potatoes. Faith often wondered how any of the calves in Europe lived to grow up, veal was such an omnipresent item on *table d'hote* menus. She had never liked it, and now she had reached the point of almost choking over it when she tried to eat it.

Rudolf had minded all this far less than she had. He was not disappointed in the appearance of the French landscape, because he never admired it in any case; he thought veal was delicious; and the discourteous couple had not troubled him at all. He had responded to their first complaints reasonably and briefly, with formal politeness; after that he had paid no attention to them whatever, until the word *"Allemande"* had been hissed at Faith. Then he had levelled a look of such cool insolence at the offending speaker that Faith had felt something turn over inside her.... She had never guessed that Rudolf could look that way at anyone. She was really relieved when after a little apparently superficial conversation, which was carried on in English, and which she realized was actually designed to reveal to those who must inevitably hear it, that she was an American, he turned his head away and went peacefully to sleep, still sitting very upright, and still retaining his air of complete superiority to his would-be annoyers.

He was sleeping now, calmly and deeply, in the upper berth. Faith could hear, above the clatter of the jerky little train, the even sound of his breathing. It had taken her a long time to get to bed, for she felt too hot and untidy to lie down until she had sponged herself from head to foot in the small lavatory that opened out of the compartment; and she had achieved her bath slowly and with difficulty, owing to the lack of space and the rocking motion. Rudolf had assured himself that all her possessions were disposed as she would prefer them, and then, after kissing her with a fond, *"Schlaf schön, Traüm süss,"* had swung himself lithely into the upper berth. His own ablutions, previously performed, though meticulous, had not been extensive, and they had taken very little time. He had already sunk into a profound slumber when Faith came back into the compartment, pleasantly refreshed. She had smoothed all the tangles out of her curls, had brushed them indeed until her scalp tingled agreeably, and then she had braided them into two great plaits with a part between them which went all the way down the back, so that she would not have to lie on their bulk; and the resultant feeling of smoothness and firmness was delightful. She had also poured a little eau de cologne into the basin with the water, and after her bath, had dusted herself from head to foot with violet powder shaken from a ball-like puff. Even her sheer nightgown, laced-edged, monogrammed, delicately embroidered, and folded, like the rest of her linen, in sachets, was faintly fragrant. After feeling soiled and mussy for so many hours, the sense of so much sweet cleanliness was very welcome to Faith. The thought flashed through her mind that she would like to share it with Rudolf, that she woud like to have him see her as she was now, after looking at her all day in her crumpled traveling dress. But of course Rudolf would see her every night now, and besides he was asleep. It would be selfish as well as silly to disturb him. Moreover, once in her berth, she found that she was strangely thankful to be alone. From childhood, she had been accustomed to much mental and physical solitude. She was suddenly aware that she needed the feeling of respite which they afforded.

Completely relaxed, she began to turn over the events of the past months in orderly review in her mind. She liked to "think things over"; it helped her to regulate her life—though, ever since her meeting with Victoria Luise in Venice, it was, she admitted to herself, the Archduchess who had regulated it. And with what marvelous success! The progress of events had been as smooth as it was steady. There had first been the "little holiday" which Victoria Luise had spoken of "making," and which they had all spent so happily together. . . . All except Sam, who was, unfortunately, called back to Paris to paint another magnate, and who had caught the express at an hour's notice one day when she and Rudolf and Cousin Sarah had gone with the Archduchess to have tea at the Austrian Consulate. He had left only a little scribbled note behind him to say good-bye, and when she heard from him again, it was to tell her that he was starting for the Straits of Magellan to paint marine pictures —and she had so counted on having him at her wedding! But aside from this, there had been nothing to regret. Even the parting with Rudolf had not been very hard because his mother made it so easy; and afterwards, the letters he wrote her from Madrid had been so completely adequate, so loyal and loving in tone. They reached her with infallible regularity, all through those golden weeks of early autumn that she and Cousin Sarah spent in Italy, although their address changed constantly, for they went, without definite schedule, from Venice to Verona, from Verona to Padua, from Padua to Bologna, and from Bologna to Lucca. It seemed incredible that Rudolf should be able to foresee, with such exactitude, when he was writing a letter, where she would be when it reached its destination. But never once did he estimate time and distance incorrectly. Her love letter lay under a bunch of fresh flowers on her breakfast tray every morning.

She saw the little cities of Italy through a haze of happiness; but when she and Cousin Sarah finally turned their faces north, she awoke to new alertness as they approached Paris. She could not afford to have many dresses, if these were to come from *grandes maisons;* but she was determined that each one should be precisely right. She insisted on visiting a dozen or more establishments of the first order; and even then she wrote to Victoria Luise before making any final decision.

"I am sending you *croquis*," she said in the letter that accompanied the sketches. "You will see there are two *tailleurs,* one navy blue and one golden brown, and two three-piece velvet costumes for afternoon in the same shades. If I do not go into too many different tones, it will be less expensive—because of hats and shoes to match, I mean; but I would love to have the champagne-colored ribbed silk and the mauve voile for occasions when I would need to be *habillée* and still not in evening dress. The party frocks that are really *jeune-fille* are all made of such perishable materials that I have chosen three. The pink tulle is so very pale that it really is all right with my hair, and of course I did not have to hesitate over the pale green taffeta or the white chiffon. The emerald-colored evening wrap will go with all of these, and Cousin Sarah has given me a lovely set of furs, in advance, for my Christmas present, so I do not have to think of buying those. Will you please write and tell me if you approve of what I have chosen?"

Victoria Luise had not written. She had wired. "Everything charming congratulations your exquisite taste but double number evening dresses add riding habit tweeds and flannels for country eagerly awaiting to welcome you weekend Schönplatz before going Berlin hope you can arrive by nineteenth." So Faith had decided that she could do with less linen than a German *Braut,* and had gone steadily and joyfully on with her shopping, buying the extra dresses that Victoria Luise had suggested, and finally setting out for Schönplatz with everything neatly packed in beautiful new Vuitton luggage. Even for Schönplatz, Victoria Luise had prepared her, so that she was not overwhelmed when she arrived there. "Expect to see a very large house, *liebes Kind,* and acres and acres of woodland," the Archduchess had written. "I tell you this lest you should not realize how immense are many estates in Germany, for I believe you have not visited at one before. And it is necessary on such estates that there should be a great many retainers, and natural that the house servants should wear the livery of the family. The week-end party however, will be small, not more than twenty guests in all, and some whom I believe you will especially enjoy. If you do not know how to ride we will teach you—in fact I have chosen a pretty gentle horse for you—and there is no reason why you should hunt if you prefer not. My husband wishes me to extend his fond greetings to you and tell you how glad he will be to see you in our *Heimat*."

It was Rudolf's father that Faith had dreaded to meet above everyone else. She had pictured him as a rigid and relentless figure. Therefore this kindly message from him was doubly reassuring. And its sender was the first person to welcome her when she and Sarah alighted on the platform of the little station that served Schönplatz; a tall, erect man, with ruddy color and frosty blue eyes, who looked almost as young as his wife. He was dressed for hunting, with a tiny gay feather stuck in the dark velour hat that he lifted with a certain charming precision.

"*Frau* Atkinson? Permit that I should present myself. I am Hans von Hohenlohe. It joys me to see here my brother's friend. And this is Faith, *nicht wahr?* The *liebes Kind* of whom Luischen speaks with such affection. As it is on the platform a little cold, she waits in the carriage to embrace thee. *Nein—nein*—all these luggage the footman will see to. Not to disturb yourselves. Please. If you please. This way."

Since Rudolf's father was like that, what did it matter that they were instantly surrounded by servants in livery, that there were coronets on the carriage doors, that they drove through acres and acres of forest and finally reached a huge looming house which must contain at least fifty rooms? Faith was entranced with the one to which she was shown, with the huge white puff on the bed, with the comfortable ponderous furniture, with the huge porcelain stove in the corner, with the rosy-cheeked maid who stood curtseying and waiting to unpack for her. And when she had washed and put on the amber-colored cashmere which she had brought, because she felt instinctively that it would be just what she would wish to wear for tea at Schönplatz, there was a rap at her door, and a lovely young girl came in.

"I am Elsa, the youngest daughter," this girl told Faith in friendly fashion. "The others are all below—Hans, and Heinrich, and Marguerita and her *Braütigam,* Friedrich von Mitweld. That is all, except Rudolf—*es ist schade, nicht wahr,* that he is not here too? But we hope, the next time you come, he will be. The *Mütterchen* thought you would like to come down and meet our other guests. Your—how do you say—*Botschaft* and *Frau* Castle are here—that was the *Mütterchen's* idea, that it would be pleasant if you could meet them at Schönplatz before going to stay with them. Oh, and yes—one of the Imperial Princes, only he is incognito —you are not to reveal that you know who he is, though of course everyone is well aware."

There was, with one exception, nothing frightening about any of these persons, Faith discovered, when she went downstairs, her fingers locked in Elsa's. The members of Rudolf's family and the friends they had collected to spend the weekend at Schönplatz, were cordial, simple, and wholly unalarming, in spite of the fact that they referred casually to most of the reigning potentates of Europe by their first names and seemed immune to insecurity or discomfort of any sort. It was not that they "put on airs" about their positions. They appeared, rather, unconscious of any occasion for "putting on airs." Even the Imperial Prince, an amiable and rather chinless young man, very blond and very slim, whom everybody called Willie and whom Faith soon called Willie too, was untouched by any regal tinge. He was chiefly engaged in playing with a puppy's ears and responding blandly to humorous comments that were being made about his admiration for a beautiful young English singer, Gwendoline Lamar, in the intervals between gulping down enormous quantities of weak tea.

The one overpowering exception to the general characteristics of this group Faith almost instantly discovered in the person of Mrs. Carolus Cavendish Castle. This lady had spent most of her early life in Belford, a New England manufacturing town where her father had made shoes: such very good shoes, indeed, that his continually increasing trade soon overflowed the room put aside for it in the little house where he both lived and cobbled; and he set up a neat shop which was in turn succeeded by a factory of sizable dimensions. His one fair daughter, Annabelle, who had married an apprentice, inherited a very comfortable fortune, which she had all to herself, as her husband—slightly dizzy with unexpected success—had followed her father to a comparatively early grave. She was still young, and of a commanding appearance which revealed her temperament so completely as to be deceiving—and she shortly afterwards chose a second husband. She was profiting by her widowhood to make a grand tour, looking about her in a comprehensive manner which included much besides scenic wonders; and at Monte Carlo she encountered Carolus Cavendish Castle, who was several steps above her on the social ladder, and who opportunely for her had just exhausted his letter of credit. In spite of a certain amount of will-power of his own, he lacked the energy to combat Annabelle, and their marriage was not long delayed. With ripening years and an income which continued to increase by leaps and bounds—thanks to the steady demand for footwear—Annabelle was more and more conscious of the need for widened horizons; and responsive to her impetus, Carolus contributed one hundred thousand dollars of her money to the campaign fund of a Presidential candidate who, fortunately for Carolus as well as himself, proved to be the choice of the nation, and Carolus forthwith was appointed United States Ambassador to Germany.

He had been a big booming sort of boy, the adored son of rather shrinking and stingy parents, who had amazed Belford by suddenly "loosening up" and sending him to Exeter and Harvard to be educated. And big and booming he still remained, with a curious mixture of the belligerent and the benign in his make-up. He did not speak a word of German, he did not pretend to understand international affairs, he did not aspire to diplomatic distinction; but there was something very likeable about him, and he was as popular in Berlin as he had been in Belford; and Faith had talked with him for only two minutes when she was sure she was going to find him as genial a host on Unter den Linden as he had been a welcome guest on Lafayette Square.

But Mrs. Carolus Cavendish Castle was different. She was so very rigid that Faith quailed before her. Her eyes and her mouth both snapped, and she held herself very erect. She was very firmly corseted, and the bones which upheld her high-necked collar rose to her ears. Her dress had unquestionably been made by Worth—indeed, Faith recognized the model—but in some way Mrs. Carolus Cavendish Castle had contrived to rob its smooth lines of all their softness. It looked as if it had been stiffened throughout with buckram, and its steel beltbuckle was in the form of twisted, teethed dragons. Long hatpins protruded menacingly from either side of the rigid gray bows of her high-perched hat and a rigid gray pompadour bristled beneath this.

"It is simply appalling," she was saying in a cutting voice as Faith entered the drawing-room, "how many Americans are coming to Berlin nowadays. Really, if things keep up as they're going on now we'll have as many tourists as there are in London and Paris. Hardly a day passes that we don't feel forced—yes, really forced—to invite some wandering Westerner to lunch or dinner. I think senators and congressmen must keep form-letters ready to fill in for the benefit of all their restless friends who want to range through embassies. Even in summer there is very little respite. You know we took a small house in Rugen for a few months—as a *retreat*—and while we were there we had sixty visitors —for *meals,* I mean, and some of them actually seemed to feel we might ask them to spend a week-end or to stay even longer. Not that we did. There are some limits left, I hope. . . . Oh, really? So you are Faith, are you? Senator Marlowe's daughter?"

Mrs. Carolus Cavendish Castle raised a lorgnette which clicked open with a metallic sound as she did so. Faith, stunned by the thought that the woman to whose views on hospitality she had just been forced to listen was to be her hostess for the next few months, admitted her identity as briefly as possible. But before the Ambassadress could open her trap-like mouth again, Victoria Luise had interrupted.

"We all realize how heavy are the responsibilities of your position, dear Mrs. Castle," Faith heard this daughter of a hundred kings, saying suavely, "and have therefore been doubly thankful to realize that Faith will be able to lighten some of the burdens for you this coming winter. Not only with the aggressive tourists. But in so many other ways. She speaks such beautiful German! She is so *gemütlich* a person to have at hand! She has such gentleness and tact! But it is not well, is it, that a young maid should herself hear of her so great merits? . . . Willie, that puppy is not a dachshund. I do not wish its ears further elongated. And please do not drink any more tea. If you so overindulge you will lose your figure, then what will say your lovely nightingale?"

"I have been thinking," remarked the personage last addressed, calmly continuing to gulp and to pull, "that *Fräulein* Marlowe would naturally be wishing to attend the opera."

"Oh, yes," said Faith eagerly, remembering her conversation in Venice with Victoria Luise. "I——" But she was interrupted. Mrs. Carolus Cavendish Castle had by this time recovered herself. And though properly resentful of the *double entendre* in the remarks of the Archduchess, with which she meant to deal in due time, she was primarily bent, for the moment, on upholding the purity of the arts, even at the risk of putting royalty in its place.

"I shall see to it that your opportunities along those lines are not neglected," she said, addressing herself directly to Faith, "the opera, though underestimated by the ignorant, and abused by the vicious, is, properly regarded, a great educational and inspirational instrument."

86

"Willie will be the first to agree with you," said Friedrich von Mitweld, winking at the tea-drinker.

"I was referring to the superb art of Emmy Destinn," retorted Mrs. Carolus Cavendish Castle grimly. "I believe she is singing 'Aida' on Friday. I shall consider it my duty to take Faith to hear it that night."

"Oh, but I am sure," remarked the tea-drinker, putting down his cup at last, and transfixing Mrs. Castle with a glance that had swiftly assumed a strange authority, "that you will feel the same way about Wednesday—when Gwendoline Lamar will be singing in 'Romeo and Juliet.' Father and I will both be looking for you—and for your lovely guest. . . . You have been to see the dogs, *Fraülein* Faith? *Nicht?* Well then let us, you and Rita and Friedrich and I go for a so little walk to the kennels. I must restore this baby puppy to his mother."

So after all, the terror inspired by Mrs. Carolus Cavendish Castle had been of brief duration. Between them, Victoria Luise and "Willie" had swiftly assuaged it; before the house party was over Faith had entirely recovered from its effects; and before another week was over she had forgotten all about it. By this time she and Cousin Sarah were safely installed at the Embassy in their own pink and silver suite, with their own pink and silver maid; and Mrs. Castle was really not inhospitable after all; she talked about the burdens of her position because this made them seem more imposing; but Faith discovered that she really liked to have company! And they did go to "Romeo and Juliet": The Ambassador and Ambassadress, Cousin Sarah and Faith, a nice young man named "Dulcey" Mitchell who was second secretary of the Embassy, and another man, Mr. Caleb Hawks, who came from Hinsboro and was "just passing through Berlin." He was really exactly the sort of man to whom Mrs. Castle had referred in her terrorizing speech, but he was "something very important in pencils," and therefore commanded consideration. And Faith, who remembered going to visit him with her father when she was a little girl, was tremendously glad to see him again, and much more thrilled by his "home news" that "Dulcey's" *blasé* observations on the performance and condescending compliments.

The Castles' loge was very near the huge central box with the shining imperial crown surmounting its crimson draperies, and it was easy for Faith to observe the occupants of this box without in the least seeming to do so: there was a gray-haired lady with a sweet smile who was handsome without being beautiful, and elegant without being stylish, and who had on almost as much jewelry as Mrs. Castle—almost, but not quite, for Mrs. Castle knew exactly how glittering the American Ambassadress should be on such occasion, and her tiara, her necklace, her brooches, and her bracelets all bore witness to this important fact. There was a very alert-looking middle-aged man, whose mustache turned up and whose eyebrows turned up and whose very ears seemed to be pricked to attention—a man who gave the impression of being very tall, he held himself with such conspicuous and superb dignity, but who, compared to the three handsome blond young men beside him, was not really very tall after all.

The Ambassador nudged Faith. "Some family, eh?" He grunted as if personally responsible for its size and very pleased at his responsibility. "And just to think they have three more sons like those at home, not to mention the little princess, and she's the cutest kid you ever saw. Well, the throne in this country's safe, anyway, whatever happens anywhere else. I've got a rather uneasy hunch all of them aren't. Look at Spain, now, with that one poor sickly youngster."

"I know," agreed Faith, "but Rudolf likes the young King. He says everybody does."

"Well, and I guess what Rudolf says *goes* with you, doesn't it?" the Ambassador asked slyly, giving her another nudge.

"Of course. If it didn't I wouldn't want so much to marry him. Oh, Mr. Castle, do you—do you really think that I can make a good impression?"

She turned in her chair, her eyes looked imploringly into his. So she did not notice—though she heard about it afterwards—that almost simultaneously "Willie," whom she had scarcely recognized in his splendid uniform, had leaned over and whispered first to the brisk gentleman with the mustache, and then to the lady with the sweet smile, and that they had both glanced toward the Castles' loge. The next moment the house was rocking with applause, and a slim, vivid, dark-haired girl with her arms full of flowers, was taking curtain-calls, bowing in every direction, right, left, straight ahead of her—even directly toward that great crimson box that stood in the center of so many tiers and tiers of other boxes. Melody seemed to flow from her; her smile was radiant; her grace was permeated with magnetism.

"Now, if I looked like that!" Faith exclaimed with irrepressible envy.

"Well, if you looked like that, it wouldn't be Rudolf that would be your beau. It would be——"

The Ambassador checked himself, and Faith, without un-

88

derstanding why, felt as if a slight chill had passed over the sunshine of her happiness; but somehow she did, and she was immeasurably relieved when he went on again, a little hastily.

"Come, come now! You know you're not such a bad-looking girl yourself! That pink mosquito netting—oh, pink *tulle* is it?—you've got on is a sweet pretty dress too. Becoming. I like the way those little bunches of roses sort of pucker it together in places. And when it comes to hair, young lady, let me tell you Miss Gwendoline would swap hers for yours in a minute if she had the chance. Honestly! But we must stop gossiping and give her a hand. She deserves it, and besides, that's what everyone else is doing. Let me see how hard you can clap."

. . . . . .

"Yes—yes indeed. Her father was a great collector and connoisseur of the arts, and, as of course you know, a member of the United States Senate—the most important legislative body in the world. His untimely death was a tremendous loss both to American culture and American statesmanship. Dear little Faith has inherited a remarkable library and paintings and correspondence that are uniquely valuable. As to the *fortune*—modest, but tidy, modest, but tidy. The Marlowes have been so self-sacrificing in their country's cause that they perhaps fail to think enough of the purely material necessities of life. But now the Ambassador and I feel quite as if Faith were our own daughter—oh, absolutely—and we shall treat her as such financially, officially, in every way! Oh, certainly! I'm sure everyone understands that!"

Faith hardly recognized her own background as she saw it sketched by Mrs. Castle's commending hand. Every disadvantageous detail was rubbed out. Every item that enchanced her eligibility to enter the ranks of German nobility was thrown into sharp relief. Her present position was painted with bewildering brilliance. It dazzled her so that she could hardly believe in its reality. Early in the new year she wrote about it to Sam, and wholly failed to achieve the sort of letter she intended. Still she tried.

"Dear Sam"—she scribbled hastily one evening when she was supposed to be resting before going to a court ball— "You never could believe how easy it has all been. I thought at first that Mrs. Castle would be hard to live with and hurt my feelings, but she's wonderful. She makes things happen, not in the same sort of way that *Tante* Luise does, but still the results aren't awfully different. The person I had to impress liked me from the beginning and I've been heaps to the Palace. It's a good deal like any other big house when you get past the sentries and through the long dreary halls and the Porcelain Room and Queen Charlotte's Study and the pictures of Friedrich the Great when he was a child. After all that it begins to seem actually homelike and I love to go there. In fact I'm going to-night and looking forward to it a lot. I'm going to wear a pale green dress that made me think of you when I bought it, because it's the sort of dress Aphrodite would have worn if she'd worn any dress at all, I mean. Of course, I know she really wouldn't."

"Christmas was wonderful, the sidewalks covered with trees to sell, in every size and all smelling so good, and the shop windows full of the loveliest things and wakes singing 'Stille Nacht' in the snowy courtyards. We all spent Christmas Eve with *Tante* Luise, and that fortified us for the morrow, as it says in Shakespeare or the Bible or somewhere. She had a lovely tree, decorated with white and silver lilies and white candles. It was the most exquisite thing and I helped her to make the lilies from a pattern that looked like a paper doll yet you can't think how effective they were after they had been cut and folded into place. And while we were all dancing around the tree and opening presents and kissing each other and calling out *'Fröhliche Weinachten,'* who do you think should walk in? *Rudolf!* He had not let anyone know he had Christmas leave and there he was. Well, really it was too perfect."

"Christmas Day there was a big celebration at the Embassy, dinner for the members of the staff and their families and a reception afterwards for the American Colony, you'd never believe how many Americans want to colonize Germany. It was pretty exhausting and I certainly was thankful that Rudolf was there to take refuge with, sort of, in odd moments."

"And now there doesn't seem to be any reason at all why we shouldn't be engaged, of course we have been anyway ever since August. But now its going to be announced! Rudolf worries about my going to balls as it is, though why he should I can't imagine, because I sit with Cousin Sarah on one side of me and Aunt Annabelle on the other between every dance. My partner comes up looking simply gorgeous in his uniform and clicks his heels together and bows, and then we whirl off for a waltz, not reversing at all until I get much too dizzy to talk to him even if I wanted to. Then the music stops and he takes his arms away as quickly

90

as if he had been suddenly burnt or someone had touched an exposed nerve in his tooth, and restores me to Cousin Sarah and Aunt Annabelle, bowing and clicking again. But Rudolf says that even with a foolproof cast-iron system like this there are sometimes accidents, so now I have my ring, which is not a solitaire diamond in a Tiffany setting, like those I have seen American girls touring in Europe wearing, but pearls and rubies and emeralds all sunk together in heavy twisted gold, very huge and ancestral."

"I do wish you could be here for my wedding, Sam, for I feel sure that it's going to be beautiful and it would mean so much more to have you give me away than anyone else. No matter how much I love all my new friends there will never be anyone—not even Aunt Sarah—that I care for the way I do you. I know you told me that marine pictures are awfully important in the 'development of your versatility' and that you always wanted to go to the Straits of Magellan, in fact you said you'd take me there some day, and now I suppose you never will. But won't you come back to Europe, even if it's only for a week, and stay with us here at the Embassy, until I'm safely married?"

Faith had a very indistinct notion of the length of time it took for a letter to reach Patagonia from Berlin. Intermittently she wondered at Sam's silence. But there was a round of official life in which she had been caught up to absorb her time, and the assemblage of the all-important trousseau to absorb her thought. Mrs. Castle would not listen to Faith's suggestion that she did not need as much linen as a German *Braut*. She marched her to Mosse's and pounced upon the first clerk in sight with ferocity. He was a stalwart man with a powerful jaw who played the bass-drum in a brass band during his leisure hours; but he quailed before Mrs. Castle's onslaught. Then he collected himself and began to spread out table-cloths and coverlets, sheets and towels, with the air of a general reviewing his troops in the presence of his sovereign. The result was stupendous—so stupendous, that it accounted in large measure for the fact that Faith's worries were at first intermittent, and that she finally forgot them altogether.

Sam's answer was handed to her with a sheaf of other telegrams as she stood, draped in snowy satin, veiled in snowy lace, a myrtle wreath encircling her head, waiting to hear that the Honorable Carolus Cavendish Castle was ready to escort her to her wedding. She had slept in the pink and silver suite with Cousin Sarah for the last time. Her baggage, full of beautiful clothes and beautiful linen, was packed and strapped and labeled Madrid. Her bridal bouquet lay beside her on the bare dressing table stripped of its dainty bottles and brushes and boxes. Everything was ordered, composed, complete. Faith lifted the telegrams from the proffered silver tray without excitement.

"THIS IS A CONVICT COLONY CAN'T ESCAPE UNLESS I MAKE MONEY IN SHEEP"—she read uncomprehensively. Her gaze leaped forward to the signature, and she gave a little startled exclamation and went on reading. "SWELL SUNNY SEA AND SKY WONDERFUL COLOR BLUE PAINTING A LOT MARINE PICTURES ONLY BROUGHT THE MARY WITH ME FOR COMPANY HOPE RUDOLF FINDS THE APHRODITE I MISSED YOURS FOREVER —SAM."

. . . . . .

A strange thin light seemed to be filtering around the edges of the drawn green curtains of the compartment. Faith raised herself sharply on her elbow. Was it possible that it was dawn? That she had spent the entire night mentally reviewing the events of the past months? That she had not slept at all? Since there was nothing to worry or trouble her in her memories, how could they have absorbed her so completely? It seemed impossible, but it was true. Very softly and slowly, in order to run no risk of awakening Rudolf, who was still sleeping as profoundly as he had before she went to bed, she slipped from her berth and raising the green shade halfway, looked out of the window.

She had expected a beauty that would be almost blinding. Instead, she saw a bleak and barren landscape, gaunt, treeless, strewn with rocks. In the midst of its emptiness a monstrous building suddenly seemed to rise from nowhere, defiantly, against the sky that was already hot although as yet it was hardly tinged with sunlight. While she stood looking at it, repelled yet fascinated, she felt Rudolf's arm slip lightly around her waist, pressing her sheer soft nightgown against her flesh. He had awakened and descended from his own bed so quietly that she had not heard him.

"The Escorial," he said in answer to her questioning look. "A strange place built by a strange man, but something of the spirit of Spain lies concentrated there with him in his tomb. Some day I must take you to it. . . . We are less than an hour from Madrid, now, *Liebchen*. We must perhaps somewhat hasten with our preparations. You look a little tired. Have you then not rested well these two nights on the train when I have slept so soundly? And have you a kiss for me this morning?"

Chapter XI

DURING the first period of her acquaintance with the von Hohenlohes, Faith had been both bewildered and impressed when they talked to her about their relatives. They had been quite unconscious of the effect they were producing, not only in referring to cousins scattered over the entire face of Europe—cousins whose numbers, nationalities and names were alike confusing—but in revealing casually and often tardily that these cousins were members of reigning families, even if not actually rulers themselves. Gradually, however, she became less bewildered and impressed, and ceased to feel an active curiosity in them one way or another. Therefore, when Victoria Luise told her that their "great friend and distant kinsman, Sebastian de Cerreno" had a house near Granada that would be available for a honeymoon, Faith dismissed him from her mind, except as the generous owner of an ideal estate ideally situated; and it was not until Rudolf remarked, about fifteen minutes before the *train de luxe* was due in Madrid, that he supposed Sebastian would be at the station to meet them, that she felt enough interest in him to make any inquiries about him.

"Is he your cousin on your mother's side or your father's, Rudolf?"

"On *Mütterchen's*. You know of course that she is a Hapsburg. My *Tante* Sophia—my grandmother's half sister—was Sebastian's mother. His elder brothers and sisters have all died, except one, who has entered the church."

"Sebastian wasn't at the wedding, was he? I don't seem to remember him, but there were so many. . . ."

"No, Carlos and Carlota were the only Spanish cousins who came. Sebastian hardly ever leaves Spain. But he sent the *parure* of aquamarine you liked so much."

"The lovely necklace and bracelets and tiara and brooch all to match? But those were from the *Duque* and *Duquesa* of Something. Is he married?"

"Yes, he is married. He would have sent his wife's card too, of course. But it is very sad. She is the victim of a strange malady. She has not been herself for years."

"You mean—she is *insane?*"

"*Ach, liebe* Faith, do not use such harsh words. She is a nervous invalid. There are many such."

A little shiver of horror ran through Faith, the strange feeling that in the midst of pomp and circumstance she had inadvertently touched a whited sepulchre and found it cold and ghastly. She had to force herself to go on speaking.

"Oh—I will be very careful to remember—I shall not be likely to see her, shall I?"

"No indeed. She lives in retirement, in one of the family castles among the Pyrenees."

"In retirement? You mean? . . ."

"*Liebe* Faith, is it necessary to dwell on details? Be assured she is well cared for."

Faith, closing her mental vision to the thought of high barred windows and futile screaming, tried again.

"It must be very lonely, for Sebastian, unless he has children."

"There are no children. Fortunately, perhaps, lest they might have been strange too. Otherwise it is sad, for he is the last of that branch of the family who could have had descendants. But I do not think he is lonely. He has many diversions. He plays polo and sails a yacht better than anyone else in Spain. He is a famous whip. He has even bought one of those new horseless carriages and dashes about in it at the rate of twenty miles an hour. He raises bulls and mules, and celebrated vintage wines come from his estate. He owns one of the finest libraries in the world and half a dozen palaces, and he is very much in demand everywhere. Besides—no, I do not think Sebastian is lonely. Well! I do not know whether you will like him much or not. Sometimes he is most agreeable and at other times he seems to withdraw into himself. To those who do not know him he appears somewhat haughty and cynical. He may appear so to you."

The train had begun to slow down while Rudolf was still speaking. It had not fully come to a stop when Faith was aware of a slender man standing directly opposite the window of their compartment, as if he knew by instinct exactly where this would be. He was carrying a light cane, and was dressed in gray flannel rather nonchalantly worn. A panama hat of extraordinary whiteness and exquisitely fine weave shaded his forehead. As he lifted his hat, Faith saw that he was very dark, that the face was blade-like in its keenness and narrowness, and that a strange scar, disfiguring out of all proportion to its size, ran horizontally across his left cheek. His deep-set eyes met hers with penetrating directness and he did not smile at all. She felt herself flushing, and was annoyed that this should be so; but as Rudolf lowered the window and hailed his cousin she impulsively held out her hand too.

"Good-morning, Sebastian," she said gaily, "you *are* Sebastian, aren't you? I'm Faith, your new relative. I do hope you're going to like me."

"A los pies de usted," said Sebastian gravely, still looking at her with that piercing gaze. His formality chilled her a little, and she felt herself blushing more deeply still. Probably she should have waited and taken the tone of her greeting from him, she reflected, as he bent over her outstretched hand, barely brushing it with his lips, before turning to Rudolf as if fully conscious of him for the first time. *"Qué tal?"* he said agreeably, "was it a good trip? But need I ask? All trips are good in the *luna de mielo!* . . . Now for the bags. Those are really all? Well, Manuel will look after them and we can come straight to the carriage. I am driving you up to the house myself. I thought my mules might amuse the *Señora."*

There was a short interlude consumed by the necessary detail of arrival. When it was over, and they were clipping along in a smart open landeau, drawn by four very sleek and sprightly mules ornamented with bells and tassels, Rudolf answered the question Sebastian had asked on the station platform as if there had been no interruption.

"It was a good trip," he said speaking rather precisely, "cool and pleasant in Germany—a little warm coming through France. And we had very bourgeois traveling companions who were rude to Faith. French, of course."

"Oh, but not 'of course' *querido!* Be more just! However, it is certain that no Spaniard will be rude to her!" Sebastian turned halfway around from his driving seat, and waved the ribboned whip. "Are you interested in the landmarks of Madrid? That is the Royal Palace over there, and this is the Puerta del Sol through which we are passing on our way to the Castellana, the residential section where I am taking you now. No doubt next month when you come back from Granada you will be choosing a house of your own near that of my Cousin Carlota's—we are going there, for the moment, as my own great barracks are closed for the summer and look so stiff and empty. All the furniture is wrapped in winding sheets—the effect is quite tomb-like." For the first time he smiled a little, but Faith did not think his smile was merry, and it intensified the lines of the scar. She remembered that she herself had already thought of a tomb once that morning and now Sebastian was speaking of one. "I walked through all the apartments yesterday," he continued, "and could not find a single one that I thought was appropriate for a bridal chamber."

"Rudolf says that it is one of the most beautiful palaces in

Europe," remarked Faith with an effort. She had been enjoying the bells and the tassels of the sleek mules immensely, and the smart landeau and the dashing drive through the streets. But now her pleasure was blighted. Little creeping chills began to dart through her again.

"I hope you will agree with him," Sebastian answered formally, "when the season opens perhaps you will permit me to give a dinner in your honor and you will be able to judge. Meanwhile, I am sure you will be much happier at Carlota's. The express to Granada goes only three times a week, and as there is no good train to-day I have had the necessary reservations made on it for you to-morrow night. I know you are eager to be on your way, but we are delighted at the prospect of this interval. Carlota has a lovely garden, full of flowers and sunshine, and the room prepared for you—if it pleases you—overlooks this. It has quite wonderful Louis XV furniture in it. Red and gold. We like to impress the colors of the Spanish flag on our guests. . . . Oh, and a very sumptuous bathroom—I suppose someone has told you that there are no bathrooms in Spain?"

"Oh, *everyone*," rejoined Faith, her spirits rising once more, "but then they told me the same thing about Germany."

"And still you were persuaded to marry a German?"

"I didn't even have to be persuaded. I wanted to anyway."

Faith looked affectionately toward Rudolf and reached for his hand. But Rudolf happened to be gazing in the opposite direction at the moment, and noticed neither the gesture nor the glance. It was Sebastian instead who saw both. He smiled again, and this time Faith discovered that his smile could be charming after all.

"*Muy bien,*" he said, more gently than he had spoken before at all. "*Felicitaciones, Señora.*" He checked the mules, bringing them to a smooth stop, alighted, and forestalling his groom, opened the door of the landeau himself. "Would it please you to get out?" he asked. "*Esta es su casa.*"

Chapter XII

FAITH had met so many of Rudolf's relatives and so briefly, at her wedding, that she retained only a very hazy recollection of most of them. But his cousin Carlos and his cousin

Carlota, who were like nobody else in the world and uncommonly like each other, had made a real impression upon her, and she was glad to learn that she was going to their house and not to Sebastian's palace. They were twins, between whom a tremendous devotion existed. There was something bird-like in their appearance and manner; they were tiny, timid, and twittering; they moved their minute hands about unceasingly, they jerked their heads forward as they spoke, and they darted restlessly from place to place. In their youth, both had married according to the wishes of their parents, but without much feeling of ardor for their respective mates; both had been left widowed and childless at middle age—in fact a strange similarity shadowed their lives. In their early sixties, with a happiness they had not known since childhood, they established a joint *ménage*, and arranged to spend their last years, as they had spent the first years, joyfully together. Their house was a delightful place, permeated through and through with the spirit of their affection. Its heavy carved furniture and somber paintings were lightened by this; its marble floors and high walls were warmed by it; and Faith felt sure she would be content in it from the instant she set foot inside its grilled gate.

The twins were waiting for their guests in the garden and before the first greetings were over two grave but friendly servants appeared bearing trays laden with *café con leche* and sugar-coated rolls piled into snowy mounds, which they spread out on the little iron tables standing on the gravel underneath the oleander trees. Both coffee and rolls were consumed in enormous quantities, for fresh relays of each were constantly forthcoming; and a long time was squandered in the pleasant process of breakfasting. When at last Rudolf and Faith went up to their crimson and gold room with their "sumptuous" bath, Carlota accompanied them to be sure they were comfortably installed in it and then retired to take a short rest, being slightly fatigued after getting up unusually early and the excitement of welcoming the bridal pair. But Sebastian and Carlos continued to sit in the sunshine smoking innumerable cigarettes, the older man slightly garrulous, the younger one very silent. And when Faith came down again two hours later, after unpacking and bathing, they apparently had not stirred from the place where she had left them. They seemed completely enfolded by the fragrant languor of the garden.

"Rudolf has gone to the Chancery," she said a little shyly, in answer to their unspoken question. Neither of them had expressed the least surprise at seeing her alone. Nevertheless she realized that they were astonished at this, and that though the astonishment of Carlos was mild and undisturbing, the astonishment of Sebastian was mocking and sarcastic. "It was understood that he should put in to-day and to-morrow there, on his way to Granada," she went on. "You see he has been away nearly a week already, and work was accumulated, though he tried to leave everything cleared up before he left to be married."

"Rudolf," murmured Sebastian, rolling still another fresh cigarette between his slim, restless fingers, "would certainly leave everything cleared up before he was married. Not that he would have much to clear up. He is far too meticulous for that; but he would do it anyway. He is so different from the rest of us, who spring into matrimony irrespective of the encircling wreckage."

"You will give our new cousin a most unfavorable impression of Spaniards, if you talk such nonsense," said Don Carlos. He spoke gently, almost too gently, Faith felt, as if he were trying to shield her from something.

"I shall try not to judge them all by Sebastian," she remarked, serenely.

The two men glanced at each other. Then Don Carlos laughed, as gently as he had spoken, and Sebastian smiled again, not cynically, but charmingly, as he had when she had said she needed no persuasion to marry Rudolf.

"Touché!" he said lightly, "but after to-morrow, what then? What about the next few weeks? Is Rudolf to keep coming back and forth from Granada to make sure everything is in good order at the Chancery?"

"He is not to come back at all for an entire month. His only official duty will be to read the history of Spanish colonization, in Spanish, for three hours each day."

This time Sebastian put back his head and laughed outright.

"Is the history of Spanish colonization especially amusing?" Faith asked, still serenely.

"It is not. It is very dreadful and very glorious, like many other things connected with Spain. But the thought of any man reading about it for three hours a day on his honeymoon is irresistibly comic."

"Sebastian!" exclaimed Don Carlos in his tone of warning gentleness.

"Tio mio, admit that only a German mind, concentrated on system, culture and acquisition could ever conceive such a plan, much less carry it out."

"Rudolf has not actually carried it out yet," said Faith rather thoughtfully and Sebastian laughed again.

"I challenge you to see whether you can keep him from doing so!" he exclaimed.

"Perhaps," interrupted Don Carlos mildly, "if the Spanish mind had been capable of more concentration we might have retained in our possession those same colonies about which Rudolf intends to inform himself. It is also possible under similar circumstances that the War of 1898 might have been either averted or won."

"Perhaps," replied Sebastian, evidently without interest. "It is certainly much too hot to argue the question now. Though your words remind me of what I had temporarily forgotten: that we have an enemy in our midst. With the shadow of defeats still hanging so heavily over us and the wounds of conflict hardly healed we can scarcely call her anything else. Remember that the *Señora* is an American.

"She is Rudolf's wife," said Don Carlos speaking for the first time a little sharply and impatiently, as if he had borne with Sebastian's vagaries long enough.

"No doubt it is prudent that you should remind me of that," replied Sebastian, his voice sarcastic again, and the mocking smile which twisted his scar reappearing, "though to do myself justice, since nobody else is so disposed, I have been considering, while this more or less futile conversation has been going on, what we could do to make the day pass pleasantly for Rudolf's wife while Rudolf is at the Chancery. I know that *Tia* Carlota has invited in a few relatives for dinner—not more than ten or twelve—but that she purposely left the day free. Unfortunately she did not reckon with the irresistible attractions of the Chancery! She actually imagined that Rudolf would wish to have the day free to devote to the *Señora*. And here is the *Señora* left stranded and alone! We must find a way of helping her out. For since she is an American I am very sure of two things; first that she never takes siestas, and regards persons who do indulge in them, unless they are aged and infirm, as incorrigibly slothful; and second that her conscience troubles her if she does not begin intensive sight-seeing the instant she arrives in a strange city. Though she rather enjoys sitting here in the garden, idealizing you and dazzling me with her gifts of repartee, she really feels she ought to be galloping through the Prado, stopping only long enough in her haste to gaze soulfully at Murillo's 'Immaculate Conception.'"

"Will you take me to the gallery?" asked Faith almost angrily.

She was intensely annoyed. Sebastian with his scorn and sarcasm had rent the peace that lay over the old garden. He had ridiculed her wonderful Rudolf for being conscientious; he had goaded his gentle old uncle to rage; and his attitude toward her had been insufferable. At first she had thought that she might like him after all, in spite of Rudolf's warning. But his graciousness was so corroded by cynicism as to lose its beauty. Faith was not often easily ruffled, but she was ruffled now, and there was a taunt in her question as she asked it, because she felt sure that Sebastian would be bored by the Prado, but that all things considered he would not decline to accompany her there. She felt that it would serve him right. She resolved to spend endless hours rooted before the dullest picture she could find. His answer was a distinct shock.

"I am desolated. If I had been free, of course there is nothing I should have enjoyed quite so much, nothing that I should have considered such a privilege. Naturally I should have kept the day open if I had considered the Chancery. But I have a luncheon engagement. In fact I must hasten away to it now. That is why I am concerned as to how you will pass the day. For naturally *Tio* Carlos and *Tia* Carlota sleep all the afternoon."

"Are you lunching with the king?" asked Don Carlos sharply; and Faith understood that he felt only a royal summons could justify Sebastian's refusal to go out with her.

"I am lunching, since you insist upon asking, with Felicidad," Sebastian said slowly.

Something like a spark of enmity suddenly seemed to flare up between the two men. But it was over in a minute, and when Sebastian had taken his leave with elaborate courtesy, Don Carlos said gravely and a little hastily that he would take Faith to the Prado himself—should he send a servant for her hat and gloves? She did not in the least care about going and she recognized that for him it would be a real effort; but under the circumstances, it did not seem possible for her to decline. Once in the glorious museum she became quickly and deeply absorbed; and after luncheon, for which Rudolf did not return, she was only too glad to lie down, making up for her sleepless night by falling into a profound slumber from which she did not wake until early evening. When at last she drifted back into a state of blissful semi-consciousness, she saw that Rudolf was standing beside the gold and crimson bed, looking lovingly down at her.

"Who," she asked sleepily, putting up her face to be kissed, "is Felicidad? Is she another cousin?"

She felt Rudolf's arm grow quickly taut around her.

"Who has been talking to you about Felicidad?" he asked indignantly.

"Nobody. But Sebastian went to have lunch with her. He said it was very important. He told me that otherwise he would have been delighted to take me to the Prado, and Don Carlos seemed very upset about it, just as you do now. Is she—oh Rudolf—is Felicidad the poor lady who is 'strange?' "

"No," he said after a moment. "The name of the poor strange lady is—Dolores. Sebastian has been known to say more than once that she is well named, that she had indeed brought him nothing but sorrow. That this is why he must look for 'happiness' elsewhere. He has found it—at least temporarily—in the companionship of a little gutter-snipe whom he has succeeded in placing in the corps of the Royal Ballet.

Faith gave a little smothered exclamation.

"*Liebe* Faith," Rudolf said, almost as if he were asking her forgiveness for something. "I did not mean that you should ever hear of this. I meant always to shield you for the rest of your life from everything sordid and soiled. I know what your childhood, what your early girlhood before the good *Frau* Atkinson took charge of the you must have been! . . ."

"I always had Sam," interrupted Faith, with a rush of grateful memory.

"Yes," said Rudolf grudgingly, "you had Sam. We must be thankful for that. But—I did tell you, *Liebchen*, when you questioned me that Sebastian was not 'lonely,' that he had his diversions. But I hoped it would not be necessary to particularize, though I knew you were bound to hear soon, perhaps, to see for yourself that he is—a wastrel. If he did not have great wealth, great position, great gifts he—he would have sunk very low. He has also certain undependable elements of generosity. My mother is inclined to feel that perhaps some members of the family have been judged him too harshly. But I have never agreed with her, and I am thankful that she did not hear him, on your first day in Spain, decline a request of yours, because he was going to lunch with Felicidad Gomez!"

"And he will be coming here again to-night! He may even take me in to dinner! He sent me jewels for a wedding present and I shall have to wear them! We are going to spend our honeymoon in one of his houses!"

"That is all true. But I must beg you to be calm. You have every reason to feel affronted. But you must try to put it out of your mind. I cannot believe that Sebastian will often err in judgment and civility as he did to-day."

"He said himself that no one in Spain would be discourteous to me and then he was the very first—"

"*Liebe* Faith, you must compose yourself, you must be reasonable. I was angry too, as you doubtless saw, but I forced myself to self-control. I deplore Sebastian's conduct. But at the same time I beg you not to attach too much importance to it. Above all I beg you not to permit him to guess that you attach any importance to it whatsoever."

He pressed her hand, released it and rising, reached for the electric switch.

"It is unfortunate that I could not return for lunch," he said practically and without further trace of emotion. "The arrival of some important despatches forced me to remain at the Chancery. Otherwise we might have discussed this matter calmly before you had become so completely upset about it. We will now dismiss it from our minds, however. I am going to ring to have our tea served to us here at your bedside, that you may continue your rest—let me put some extra pillows behind you—so! While we take it we will talk of pleasanter subjects. There is still much time before it will be necessary for us to dress for dinner, even though I should like you to appear *en grande toilette*. For it would please me greatly that you should look your best to-night. I have brought you very proudly, Faith, into a very proud family."

Chapter XIII

FAITH had cause to be thankful both for her siesta and her tea, before, completely exhausted, she sank into her gold and crimson bed at three the following morning.

Dinner, *Tia* Carlota, had informed her, would be at ten o'clock. At first Faith thought that she had misunderstood, but when, striving to sound casual, she tried, by means of an indirect question, to confirm her impression, *Tia* Carlota had reiterated her original statement.

"Of course," she added by way of qualification, "we are never too much bound by time in Spain. My sister and brother-in-law, Mercedes and Pedro de Mantoña, for instance, are always rather unpunctual. And as for Sebastian, he is incorrigible. He thinks nothing of sauntering in more than an hour after the time fixed for a repast. Of course I should like to have you and Rudolf receive our guests with Carlos and myself. But if you are in the drawing-room by quarter after ten, I am sure you need feel no concern lest you will not be there to welcome them."

This was meant, Faith gathered, to be reassuring. So she waited until she and Rudolf were having tea together for an explanation for the lateness of the dinner hour.

"But that is not late," he protested, "at least not for Spain. If this had been a formal function, instead of a quiet family gathering, the hour set would have been a much later one."

"But when do Spaniards sleep?" asked Faith in bewilderment.

Rudolf shrugged his shoulders. "Oh, all the afternoon. And every now and then besides that. They are a naturally slumberous race, particularly during working hours. Perhaps that is why they think nothing of sitting up most of the night—it affords an excuse for somnolence the following day." He paused a moment, devastated a scrap of pastry in one bite and added, "Of course you understand, Faith, that I am saying this to you confidentially. Indeed, half-jestingly."

"You are very cautious," she said, pushing back her cup. "Naturally I know when you are talking to me in confidence. I am not as indiscreet as you seem to think. You do not need to keep warning me. And do Germans always explain their jokes?"

Rudolf glanced at her in calm astonishment, and then leaned across the table and took her hand, "You must still be very tired, *Liebchen*," he said gently. "I fear we made a mistake to come straight through from Berlin. We should have broken our journey by spending a day or two in Paris. But I could not endure the idea of wasting even a little of our so precious time at some noisy hotel in a city I have always detested."

"I have had a good long sleep this afternoon. I am not very tired any longer."

"Then is it that you are even more upset than I had supposed? Certainly else you would not speak to me in just that tone of voice—almost as if you were irritated with me. It is unfortunate that your first impressions of Spain—or rather of Spaniards—have not been more favorable. I should try to change these and not to confirm them. For with all its infirmities, Spain is a very noble land. After you learn to speak its language and become familiar with its customs you will discover this for yourself. I must engage a teacher for you in Granada. While I am studying the subject of colonization, you could make real progress in grammar. The Spanish verbs are rather complicated, and it is wise to become well grounded in them from the outset."

Faith drew her hand away. The gesture was not impatient, but it indicated a lack of response which was slightly disturbing to Rudolf. Nothing of the sort had previously marred their relationship.

"You aren't honestly thinking of studying while we are on our honeymoon?" she said. "Or asking me to? Not really? Please don't, Rudolf! Can't we have these few weeks all to ourselves? Just for—for loving?"

"But, *liebe* Faith! How can the effort to acquire helpful knowledge interfere with our love for each other?" He was genuinely troubled. He was also, Faith saw, entirely uncomprehending.

"You don't understand. It's—it's only that I'd like to be able to sit beside you and talk about foolish little intimate things for hours and hours without having to say to myself, 'Now I must stop telling Rudolf that I adore the color of his eyes, because it's time to go and conjugate verbs.' I believe I want to be rather slumberous myself. I think I'd like a sort of—Spanish summer after a German winter. I've always liked the expression 'slumberous, amorous, Spanish summers!' Though I've never quite known what it meant. Spaniards are—amorous as well as slumberous, aren't they?"

"Yes," said Rudolf. "Sebastian, for instance, could be so described. But the effect he has had on you does not seem to have been agreeable, to say the least!"

He also was tired and he was very close to anger again. The effort which he made toward restraint, after his curt retort, was visible. He came around the table and sat down on the bed, putting his arms about Faith.

"Dearest," he said tenderly, "you have not married a Spaniard. You have married a German. A German who loves you very dearly. You must know this, and since you cannot doubt it, will you not let him reveal it in his own way, instead of in a way that would be less natural to him, even though it seemed more romantic to you? You shall have your Spanish summer after your German winter. A winter which I know taxed your strength and patience, and put you to a test which you met magnificently. I hope and believe it will be a happy summer for you, at your German husband's side. I shall do my utmost to make it so. But meanwhile I must not neglect my work, for it in its own small way is designed to contribute to the strength and glory of the Fatherland. I must not permit you to tempt me to do so. On the contrary, I must beg you to spur me on to

104

it, after the manner of the ladies in the age of chivalry who encouraged the knights!"

Faith did not answer. Rudolf realized that he had still failed to strike a responsive chord. He tried again.

"Out of twenty-four hours in a day only three for study! All the rest for you! And even those three hours devoted to building up a career which will make me more worthy of you as well as of my country!" He hesitated, his consciousness shot through with a sudden suspicion. "You have not before to-day objected to this program, upon which we agreed long ago," he said slowly. "Why do you object to it now? What has happened to make you discontented with it?"

"I suppose," Faith replied rather reluctantly, "it was something Sebastian said. He made fun of it. He thought the idea of any man reading about colonization for three hours a day on his honeymoon was 'irresistibly comic.' He pointed out that 'only a German mind, concentrated on system, culture and acquisition, could conceive such a plan, much less carry it out.'"

"Oh!" said Rudolf, curtly again. "And though you have been almost hysterical in your display of aversion to Sebastian, still you have attached enough importance to his opinions to permit them to influence yours?"

"I hadn't thought it out before. Now I have. But I didn't mean to quarrel over it, only to explain how I felt. Please Rudolf—I'd rather not talk about it. Do we have to?"

Rudolf was aware that her detachment was becoming more and more complete. A subconscious fear that through such withdrawal the spiritual and physical unity of their marriage might be threatened suddenly surged through him. He drew her closer to him, almost fiercely.

"No," he said. "We are not obliged to discuss it further —either that or anything else. There is a time for everything, and this is not a time for talk, any more than it is a time for work. It is a time for love." There was a vibrancy in his voice of which Faith had not been previously aware, and slightly startled, she raised her eyes to his face. As she did so, he pressed his lips down hard against hers.

. . . . . .

Never before had he dominated her completely or possessed her entirely; the violence of his emotion overwhelmed her, and left her as drained of strength when it was over as she had been powerless of resistance while it lasted. She was still shaken by the shock of it when, three hours later, she descended with Rudolf at her side to the tapestried

105

drawing-room were *Tía* Carlota and *Tío* Carlos were waiting for them. In her agitation and exhaustion, she felt as if she had lost forever both her individuality and her independence. It did not seem as if she could be, even in outer attributes, the same person who had arrived blithely and light-heartedly in Madrid that morning. Surely, during the tense twilight which had merged so swiftly and mysteriously into rapacious darkness, Rudolf must have set his seal upon her in a way that would be visible to all the world. She was grateful for the dim light in the great room, for the soft shadows cast by the tall tapers in the branching silver candelabra; and she was immeasurably reassured when her hostess greeted her tranquilly and affectionately. Surely, if *Tía* Carlota had been conscious of any startling change, she would not have spoken with such kind composure.

"So you've decided to be punctual after all, *querida!* You are on time to a minute for our little gathering! And how lovely you look in your green and silver! I see that not even a May night in Madrid can impair your freshness! But observe that others have been punctual, too, in their eagerness to welcome you. Here are your *Tío* Pedro and your *Tía* Mercedes of whom I spoke to you this morning, slanderously telling you they were always tardy! And they are actually waiting for you!"

The *Duquesa* de Mantoña had none of the bird-like characteristics of her sister. Instead, she and the *Duque* were both ponderous and portly and both faintly mustached; and however little others might be feeling the heat, they were themselves visibly affected by it, for perspiration flattened their hair and streamed from their faces. Each was twirling a preposterously tiny fan in a futile though energetic effort to obtain relief; and they simultaneously closed these with little hissing sounds as they wiped their brows and smilingly advanced toward Faith. The *Duquesa* was wearing enormous garnets, set in heavy gold filigree, and voluminous *moiré antique* to match, neither of which tended to make her look cooler or slimmer; and across the *Duque's* ample chest so many orders and decorations were stretched that Faith involuntarily wondered why his heavy broadcloth and stiff linen did not sag under the weight of them. But she was caught up too quickly by the tide of their cordial volubility to give the elaborate medals more than a passing thought: Had she had a good journey? Was it very hot on the train? Had she seen anything of Madrid that day? Ah—the Prado—was it not *prodigioso?* Did she care to do a little shopping the next day on the Carrera de San Geronimo and perhaps visit the church of the same name, where King

106

Alfonso had been married to the English Princess Ena? Would she like to lunch at the Nuevo Club, just another small family gathering? The real fiestas, like the real sightseeing, must await her return from Granada and especially the autumn season. But they wished her to resolve her first week-end after she got back for a visit with them at Ventosilla, ten miles out of Toledo. They would send the landeau and the mules to meet her there. . . .

"Faith has already had her first ride behind our Spanish mules," interposed *Tia* Carlota. "Sebastian met her with his at the station this morning."

"Ah, then she has begun by seeing the finest in Spain! However, we will place the best we have at her disposal—Josefina, I did not see you when you came! And have you met our new cousin?"

Josefina, Inez, Francesca, Beatriz. Vicente, Tomas, Raimundo. The *conde* of this. The *princesa* of that. Who was whose brother? Who was whose aunt? Would she ever be able to keep those involved ranks and relationships straight? Would she ever be able to disentangle herself from so much complicated cordiality? Would these kinfolk ever stop talking to her and each other? Would they ever stop coming? No, not yet, for they were still one man short. Josefina had come alone. Faith had the vague impression that this cousin had been betrothed in her youth to a grandee who was banished, just before the time appointed for their wedding, for participating in a Carlist plot. And Josefina, who, if her *novio's* revolt had been kept secret until it was successful, might eventually have become Queen of Spain, had instead immured herself in a convent and had been prevented from taking final vows as a nun, only because the precarious state of her health precluded her from enduring the rigors of the order of her choice. Her only ornament was a huge silver crucifix and her somber draperies seemed more suited to a cloister than a hearth. She was evidently a very ill woman who had made a supreme effort to be present at this assembly; and her face was scarred with frustration as well as fever and beckoning death seemed to walk beside her.

Faith turned away from her shuddering. Would the missing man never come? It was Sebastian, of course, who was keeping them all waiting. Faith had thought in the morning that she never wished to see him again. And now she was actually longing for his arrival. At least he was not completely a stranger, and that gleaming blade-like quality of his would cut its way trenchantly through this stifling solidarity which was as alarming in its smiling as in its sinister aspects. She found herself watching the doorway at which the heavy brocaded curtains were silently drawn back for each new arrival—the doorway through which Sebastian would enter. She had not once looked at Rudolf since she came downstairs. To save her life she could not have done so.

It was after eleven o'clock when the curtains parted for the last time. For a whole hour the stream of Spanish, the turmoil of a tongue as unfamiliar as the men and women who spoke it, had reverberated in her tired ears. For a whole hour foreign faces and figures had advanced and receded before her dazzled eyes. Now at last someone was coming toward her whom she knew; someone who would speak to her in English.

He was all in white, except for a scarlet sash tied tight around his slender waist and the vivid ribbon on which the Order of the Golden Fleece—the only decoration he was wearing—was suspended around his neck. His garments fitted as if they had been molded to him, and there was something glistening in their spotlessness. His appearance was as striking as it was exotic. No doubt he had meant that it should be. No doubt he had planned and executed a theatrical entrance, all the more dramatic because it was so long delayed. But it had lost nothing of its intended effect through premeditation. There was something electrical in the atmosphere as he crossed the polished floor with silent grace and greeted everyone of the relatives with deferential affection. When at last he paused before Faith, he spoke to her very softly.

"I come, *Señora*," he said, raising her hand to his lips, "asking your forgiveness less for being so late to-night—though this in itself is unpardonable—than for leaving you as I did this morning. I hope you will believe in the sincerity of my repentance. I also hope that it is not too late for me to make atonement for it."

Whether Faith actually answered him she was never quite able to remember. Her impression was that she did not. For she was instantly aware that whereas no one else had noticed anything anomalous about her, Sebastian's rapid penetrating glance had pierced the brittle veneer of self-control with which she was striving to conceal her emotional and physical exhaustion; and the consciousness of his swift discernment was so startling that for a moment she was incapable of speech. By the time she had collected herself, Sebastian had given a quick order to a passing servant and was addressing her again.

"Shall we not sit down?" he suggested, "I think there will still be a few minutes before we go into the dining room.

108

Spanish dinners are long as well as late, and I fear this one will be still another tax on your strength, which has been so greatly overtaxed, and so variously, already to-day. Manuel is going to bring us some sherry and I hope you will do me the honor of drinking a glass of it with me. I believe you will agree that it is not only delicious as a beverage, but most effective as a stimulant. Of course I should not extol its merits, but I take a natural pride in this particular product as it is an unusually good vintage, and comes from one of my own properties."

A decanter surrounded by tiny goblets and filled with amber-colored liquid was already being presented on a silver tray. Sebastian motioned to the servant to set it down, "I will pour it out myself, Manuel," he stood smiling at the old man, "and you might leave it here. I am hoping to persuade the *Señora* to sample it more than once." He lifted the decanter, and the wine flowed down with a thick rich gurgle. *"Salud, Señora!"* he said, passing her a brimming glass and raising his own ceremoniously. "Tell me if you think I have over-praised this."

"It is very good," said Faith slowly. Her hand was shaking a little, and she found it hard to hold the goblet steady; but she had recovered her voice and spoke quite calmly. "It tastes differently from any sherry I have ever had before, and I do not think it is quite the same color."

"You are right. It is much paler—paler and more powerful—than the inferior sherry that is used for export. You are going to have some more, aren't you—just to prove to me that you like it? And this time you must pour it and say *'Salud!'* to me."

The animating fluid was streaming through her veins, flooding her tired body and brain with refreshment. When she had emptied her goblet a second time she found out she could smile at him without an effort.

"You can't imagine how much better I feel," she said gratefully.

"I must try to continue the cure. *Tia* Carlota has been good enough to say that I might sit beside you at dinner. And after dinner there is always the garden. It will be very late before the party is over. By the time you return to Rudolf I hope you will be entirely restored."

Manuel was looping back the portières that hung between the drawing-room and the dining room. Beyond, Faith could see a long table, massed with flowers and glittering with glass and china. The relatives, who, momentarily, seemed to have forgotten her as completely as she had forgotten them, suddenly surged forward again, talking excitedly. Rudolf was not in sight. He seemed to have been swallowed up some-where in their midst. Sebastian rose and offered Faith his arm.

"The wedding feast," he murmured with a return of irony, "at which the bridegroom tarrieth. Shall you and I go into it together, *Señora?*"

Chapter XIV

FAITH woke reluctantly, with a sensation of one who has slept a long, long while, but still feels so incompletely refreshed as to wish to slumber on indefinitely; she also woke to the consciousness of the emptiness which pervades a room when one of two persons who share it is absent. Half opening her eyes, she saw that a meticulously folded note had been neatly pinned to the pillow beside her own; and reaching for it, she drowsily read the message that Rudolf had left for her.

"*Liebe* Faith . . ." it ran:

"It is time for me to leave for the Chancery, and you are sleeping so soundly and still looking so tired—though so lovely!—that I cannot bear to wake you, even to kiss you good-bye, although I long to do so. I also wish to talk to you a little, for I am very troubled. And now I fear I shall have no chance to be alone with you to-day, since the Mantoñas have made so many plans so that you will be kept busy until it is time for us to take our train for Granada. My aunt's maid, Angelina, will bring you coffee when you ring, and she will let *Tia* Carlota know, whether you still wish to visit the shops on the Carrera do San Geronimo, or whether you would rather rest until luncheon-time, when we shall all be meeting at the Nuevo Club. Please feel free to do just as you would prefer. Angelina understands French, so you will have no trouble in talking with her. Devotedly, Rudolf."

The small enameled watch, which Mr. and Mrs. Castle had given her for an engagement present, lay on the bedside-table. Faith pulled at its long jeweled chain, swung it in front of her, and sat bolt upright, rubbing her eyes, unable to believe that she had seen the hour correctly. Then she shook it and held it to her ear, thinking that possibly she had forgotten to wind it when she went to bed; for certainly

110

its tiny gold hands were pointing to quarter before one. But it was ticking away with a cheerful little gallop, and dismayed lest she should be late for luncheon, she laid it quickly down and rang for Angelina.

The afternoon was almost over by the time the copious repast at the Nuevo Club was finished. How was it possible, Faith wondered for anyone to do justice to so many and such abundant courses in such warm weather? The multitudinous *hors d'œuvres* alone would have made up an ample midday meal; and they were followed by an omelet, a fillet of beef, cauliflower, broiled chicken, green salad, *meringues chantilly*, and a variety of luscious fruits. But the assembled relatives ate their way from the beginning to the end of the menu with leisurely relish, and then sat sipping their strong coffee and rich liqueurs for an additional half-hour before they dispersed for their siestas. Even though Angelina helped her, it was necessary for Faith to hurry with her packing; and then came leave-takings at the station as protracted and elaborate as if she and Rudolf had been leaving for a two-year sojourn in China, instead of a fortnight's stay at a family house in Granada. The relatives, refreshed by sleep, reappeared *en masse*. In spite of the lateness with which they had finished lunch, their first concern seemed to be to provide more food for the journey: a large hamper, from which a cold fowl, long sticks of bread, a large cheese wrapped in silver-foil, and several slim bottles of wine, could be seen protruding beneath the folded napkin which covered its contents, was stowed into a rack by Manuel under the twittering direction of *Tia* Carlota. *Tio* Carlos seemed to feel that this snack would prove inadequate; so to reinforce it he had brought chocolates in an enormous and gaudy box, which was ornamented with glazed pictures, highly colored, of a bull-fight, and tied with red and yellow ribbons. Even Josefina had an offering of plums, which she whispered to Faith were known to have special miraculous value as nourishment, since they grew in the garden of the convent of Our Lady of Perpetual Sorrows —and came from the same trees as those which had been the sole sustenance, during a long period of abstinence, of a nun who had later been canonized. To offset the somewhat overwhelming effect of the plums. *Tio* Pedro lumbered down the platform staggering under the weight of a great sheaf of humorous periodicals and risqué novels which he had bought from an itinerant vender; and unperturbed by the fact that since Faith did not understand Spanish she would be unable to appreciate either the subtle witticisms of *Buen Humor* or the somewhat salacious stories of his favorite romancer, he presented these to her with puffing pride. The billowing bundle of *Tia* Mercedes proved to be filled with down cushions; and the crackling cornucopias of stiff white paper which Inez and Francesca thrust into Faith's hands contained huge bouquets of purplish-pink roses pressed together as closely as tinned-sardines; while the temperature, which was soaring well above ninety, had not deterred other members of the family from coming equipped with travel rugs.

It was not until the fussy little train, with a pompousness out of all proportion to its size, had tooted its way out of the station, past the low row of upturned faces, and the indefatigable hands throwing kisses and waving handker-chiefs, that Faith was actually alone with Rudolf. It was evident that he had something on his mind, and that what-ever this was, he was at one and the same time anxious to unburden himself of it and hesitant about how best to do so. But he could hardly be blamed for feeling that the stiff and stuffy little compartment, unconducive to physical ease, was not an ideal setting for intimate revelations. Besides, she was not only aloof, as she had been the afternoon before; she seemed actually to be on her guard against him; and her absorption in the gifts which had been showered upon her seemed entirely out of relation to their value, fitness, or usefulness. His tentative endeavors to converse with her and to caress her proved equally unsuccessful; and the fact that the conductor seemed bent on intruding at most inopportune moments did not help his cause. Finally, with characteristic Teutonic patience, he decided to bide his time.

His second attempt at an exchange of confidence had a happier ending. Though still silent and undemonstrative the following morning, Faith seemed less on the defensive; and her delight in the old vine-covered *casita,* which they reached shortly before noon, was instantaneous and unre-strained. Indeed, her mood had become more melting from the moment they left the train and started on their drive through the radiant Andalusian countryside. A stocky, swarthy, servant of expansive geniality, named Felipe, had met them in Granada; and as he pointed out the landmarks of interest along the dusty highway with a beaming smile, Faith responded to him with mounting enthusiasm. By the time they came in sight of the gardens and orchards en-circled by the olive groves and vineyards of the *caseria,* which was completely hidden from the highway by a tall blank wall, intersected only by one immense iron-hinged wooden door, she was sparkling with spontaneous admira-tion.

112

"Why didn't you tell me how beautiful it all was, Rudolf? I never saw such roses! Or such box-hedges—big and bushy enough to lie down and go to sleep on! I think I will some sunny day! What kind of trees are those? Pomegranate? Not really? I thought that pomegranates only grew in the Bible. I mean, I thought they were sort of mythical and symbolical like frankincense and jasper and things like that! And these are *real!* We can have pomegranates with cream and sugar for breakfast!"

"They are not usually eaten that way," said Rudolf practically. "In any case this is not the season for them, and they are rather acid. I doubt if you will care for them. And surely you know that Granada is a literal translation of the word pomegranate, so it is quite logical to expect to find this fruit in the vicinity of the city."

"I'm terribly afraid I'm not as logical as you are, Rudolf. Anyway nobody told me about the literal translation. And I *do* care for them. I think it's wonderful that they exist; And, oh, what a lovely, lovely little house!"

She leaped down from the creaking old carriage before either Rudolf or Felipe could stretch out a detaining or assisting hand. The next instant she was standing in the paved patio, tilting her head to look up at the shining sapphire sky, and then bending over to trail her fingers through the water that bubbled about the small stone figure of a chubby cherub, standing on a stone cockle-shell in the middle of the central fountain.

"So patios with fountains are real too!" she exclaimed. "We can sit here in the evenings and look up at the stars, can't we? And we can have a little table brought out and set in the corner and eat our meals here."

"We can have our luncheons and dinners here if you choose. It is cool and pleasant for that. But I think you may like the tower best for breakfast and tea. It is not hot there early in the morning, and the sunsets are very beautiful. Besides there is a fine view of the Sierra Nevadas and the *vega.*"

"Is there a tower, too? I didn't notice it, I was so busy looking at roses and pomegranates and box. Can we go and see it right away?"

She rushed indoors and came again to a happy halt. What wonderful old furniture! There was nothing in *Tia* Carlota's house half so beautiful as those high-backed black and gold chairs, those tall dark screens painted with flowers and scenes of Granada, those crimson velvet chests studded with metal! But how did it happen that there were Venetian glass chandeliers in an Andalusian house? Now the red-tiled floors—those were more like what she had expected to find at the *caseria!* Only she had not realized they would be so spotless and shining. How charming to have the bedrooms all opening into a *galeria* around the patio! Were they to put their clothes in those inlaid *bagueños* instead of bureaus? Was it all right for a Protestant to use a *prie-dieu?* She had always thought she would adore it. And was there a library in the *tower?* Whoever would have thought of putting one there! Yet it was an ideal place after all. And what a heavenly open terrace that was above it, looking out on all those green plains and white mountains beyond the groves and orchards.

"Of course we must have our morning coffee and afternoon tea here!" she agreed ecstatically. "It's marvelous. Do you remember the story about the householder who planted a vineyard, and hedged it round about, and digged a wine-press in it, and built a tower? We are just like him! I haven't seen the wine-press yet, but I am sure we have one."

"Yes," said Rudolf amiably, "we have." He was infinitely relieved at Faith's change in mood. "I think you will find it very interesting to go and visit the *bodega,* where the great barrels containing the wine made on the place are kept.— But I do not seem to remember the story of which you speak."

"It's in the Bible, like the pomegranates and the jasper. Grandmother Faith used to read it to me when I was very little. I was named for her, you know, and I was very fond of her. It's strange that I remember her so well, but I do. I remember what she looked like and everything she taught me. Besides, after she died, Daddy used to read to me the same way she did, in the afternoon before my supper, in Washington and at the farm, too. He never let anything interfere with our time together."

She leaned her arms on the parapet, and resting her chin on them went on talking with Rudolf while she continued to gaze away from him toward the distant Sierras.

"I've never been back since mamma first brought me to Europe nine years ago," she said slowly. That's along while to be away from home. Do you think perhaps the next time you have leave we might go there? I had been planning to, you know, when I met you."

"But *liebe* Faith," Rudolf reminded her, "Germany is your Fatherland now."

"No, it isn't, she contradicted quickly. Then seeing his pained expression she added, "Of course I admire Germany, and I understand, because you have explained it all to me so clearly, that when a girl gets married her husband's country becomes hers legally. But it doesn't seem that way to me. It seems to me that the place where you are born is really home. It seems to me that's the place you always want to go back to most. Of course just now I wouldn't want to be anywhere but here. It's like a fairy tale, isn't it? Much more beautiful than anything I've ever seen before. But just the same, it would never mean quite as much to me as home does."

"Perhaps some day I shall be appointed to Washington," said Rudolf. "It is coming to be considered quite an important place, though formerly, of course, it was looked upon as a rather undesirable post. Diplomatically, I mean. Residentially I am sure it is an agreeable city."

Having dismissed the capital of the United States courteously and concisely from their conversation, he felt the announcement that luncheon was ready to be extremely opportune. He did not wish to argue with Faith again; he feared that more differences of opinion might cast another blighting shadow over her radiant spirit. Therefore, the bulky form of Catalina, Felipe's wife, looming up before them with timely tidings about *almuerzo*, was extremely welcome. Faith, who had been too transported to take off her hat or wash her hands, went blithely off to do both, admitting that now she thought of it, she was really very hungry; and she did full justice to Catalina's oily omelet, to the fish which had been brought over the mountains from Malaga during the night, to the olives and figs which had been grown on the *caseria*. After luncheon she very sensibly raised no objection when Rudolf remarked that he would rest for a little while in the library before beginning his work there, while she took her siesta; and when she rejoined him, several hours later, on the terrace, she told him, with a touch of pride indicative of budding housewifeliness, that, instead of taking a nap, she had unpacked and arranged their belongs while he was studying, and that she had also been through the kitchen and larder with Catalina.

"I do like a little friendly house like this so much better than a big formal one," she said. "And just two or three nice old servants instead of rows of footmen and flunkies—Did you know that the water for our baths was all pumped up by hand from cisterns in back of our patio? Catalina showed them to me with very graphic signs, so that I knew that she wanted us to use as much water as we pleased. And, oh— I've had my first Spanish lesson! I pointed to things, and Catalina laughed and told me what their names were. It was great fun. I can almost order a meal already." She began to check words off on her fingers: *"pan-vino-sopa-huevos-carne-pescado-legumbres, dulce-queso-frutas.* There now!"

Rudolf smiled, but did not answer instantly.

"Your cue is to say *'Muy bien'* and whatever the Spanish word is for darling."

"There are all sorts of extravagant phrases," Rudolf answered. "Spaniards are no more given to restraint of expression than of behavior. I should prefer to go on calling you *Liebchen.*"

"But you might at least tell me what some of the extravagant phrases are. I am sure it is part of my education."

"Dulce amiga, vida mia, alma de mi alma, are a few of the more conservative ones," Rudolf said a little grudgingly and with a touch of sarcasm. "But I do not think, as I just said, that I shall become addicted to any of them. However, I am very pleased that you have spent your time so profitably. And is it not pleasant here now?"

"Pleasant! Oh, Rudolf, you know it is divine! Listen to those church bells ringing! Look at that color in the sky and on the mountains!"

With the first spontaneous sign of affection that she had made since they arrived in Spain, she linked her arm through his; and they stood in silence for a few minutes, while the silvery sound of the angelus echoed across the *vega,* and the radiant rose of the sunset spread like a flame across the horizon. Encouraged by her gesture, and by a sense of encircling benignity, Rudolf laid his cheek against Faith's, and was unaccountably thrilled when she turned and kissed him. Moreover, her next words filled him with satisfaction.

"I have been waiting for a chance to tell you," she said, with a slight hesitancy which seemed to spring less from embarrassment than from a desire to speak tactfully, "that I have been thinking about those three hours a day that you want to set aside for study, and I think you are right about them. I do not care much for siestas and I shall be glad to try and learn Spanish while you are working out theories of colonization. I think if we separate for three hours after lunch to do this we will enjoy our tea on the terrace all the more afterwards. I am sorry if I have seemed unreasonable."

"I felt sure, *liebe* Faith, that when you thought the matter over you would agree with me," Rudolf said in a pleased tone of voice. "I know I can always depend on your good sense."

"And before we go downstairs to get ready for dinner," Faith went on serenely, as if in natural sequence to her remarks on the acquisition of knowledge, "perhaps I ought to tell you—so that you won't be surprised—that when I unpacked I put our things in separate rooms. We have so much space here, all to ourselves, that it seemed too bad not to use it. For dressing you know. And for times when we don't want to disturb each other."

Rudolf stared at her in amazement, his complacence completely wrecked.

"But, *liebe* Faith! Nothing could disturb me so much as the knowledge that you would ever think of doing such a thing! And without consulting me at all!"

He was visibly appalled. Faith's color deepened a little, but she showed no other sign of concern.

"I did not mean to hurt your feelings. But I thought perhaps we both might be more comfortable that way. When you think it over perhaps you will agree with me, just as I agreed with you after I had thought over the study period."

"I want to talk to you very seriously, Faith," said Rudolf with great gravity.

"Yes. You said so in the note you pinned on the pillow. And I could see, on the train, that you kept thinking about it. I pretended not to notice because it did not seem to me like a good time. But this is a very good time."

Her candor was disconcerting. Rudolf was actually less self-possessed than she as he attempted to go on. His embarrassment made him abrupt.

"I was very glad that Sebastian did not come to the luncheon at the Nuevo Club," he said without preamble, "or return to *Tia* Carlota's house at all yesterday. I have not forgiven him for upsetting you so completely."

"He did upset me at first, in the morning. But I think that was partly because he is so different from any man I have ever seen before. Much more—more complex. He bewildered me. I felt that he was naturally clever and charming and at the same time that he was bent on proving himself cynical and cruel. But in the evening he did not upset me at all. He was wonderfully kind and understanding. I felt as if I had known him all my life. I did not expect to see him again yesterday. He explained to me that he would not be able to come to the Nuevo Club because he would be lunching as usual with Felicidad. He said she had grown to depend upon having him for luncheon almost every day, and he did not like to disappoint her, especially since he had so many evening engagements. He spoke about her so naturally and frankly that I did not seem shocked at all. He said that dancers were paid very little and would hardly be able to live unless they had *protectores*. He told me he thought

117

I would enjoy seeing her on the stage next winter, she is so light and gay and graceful, and he says she has a lovely laugh—that's what attracted him to her at first. A lovely laugh and a very sweet sunny disposition."

"Oh!" said Rudolf again abruptly, "and after he had put you at your ease, partly by talking to you about his latest mistress and partly by the equally unpardonable means of giving you some very strong sherry to drink, you did not by any chance talk with him intimately, did you? About our personal and private relations? Or subjects which should never be discussed except between a husband and wife?"

The startled surprise with which Faith gazed at him was all the reply Rudolf needed. Nevertheless, after a moment of mute astonishment she answered him so quietly that he did not suspect he had wounded her to the quick by his question.

"I was very tired when we went down to dinner, Rudolf. And then—after a while—I became dizzy. Everything had been strange and confusing to me all day and the strangeness and confusion kept getting worse and worse. There seemed to be no end to them. When Sebastian came into the drawing-room he seemed to guess exactly how I was feeling the minute he looked at me. That was when he sent for the sherry. I had two glasses and afterwards I felt ever so much better. Until I did he kept telling me funny stories and by and by I talked too. That is, part of the time. But I didn't discuss anything with him to speak of. Naturally nothing private or intimate. We didn't even keep up a regular conversation. It didn't seem necessary. It wasn't awkward when there were silences, the way it is with most people. It was friendly. I don't know that I'm explaining very well, because I've never felt exactly that way before. Not even with Sam. But I hope I've made you understand what it was like, if you wanted to know.—What made you ask?"

"Because," said Rudolf, "Sebastian upset me quite as much in the evening as he upset you in the morning. When the ladies went back into the drawing-room after dinner, he maneuvered to get me away from the other men, at one of those little tin-tables in the garden. He had Manuel, who simply feeds out of his hand, bring coffee and liqueurs to us there, and kept on bringing them, so that I could not get up and escape from him without a discourtesy so flagrant that it would be evident to everybody. He asked preposterous questions, and made preposterous comments on my answers. His effrontery is surpassed only by his indelicacy."

"What sort of questions do you mean?" inquired Faith.

118

"He asked me how old you were."

"But Rudolf, that is a perfectly natural question!"

"It depends on who asks it, and how. When I told him, seventeen, he remarked that even in Latin countries a girl was hardly considered marriageable at that age any longer, which is of course a great distortion of fact."

"Is it?" said Faith.

"You must know that it is. Early marriages are the rule rather than the exception in all Latin countries, especially in Spain."

"Was his—his wife very young when she was married?"

"I believe so. Yes. She was. Both of them were, in fact. I know that they have been married more than ten years, and Sebastian is only just past thirty now."

"Then can't you understand why he should have a special reason for feeling that early marriages are unwise? Remember how unhappy he has been!"

"I remember how profligate he has been!" exclaimed Rudolf bitterly. "You seem determined to find excuses for Sebastian, Faith! But even so, I do not believe you would contend that his next remarks were excusable."

Rudolf paused.

"What did he say?" inquired Faith.

She asked the question with interest and without eagerness. Nevertheless Rudolf seemed to feel that there was no reason why she should have asked it at all, in spite of the fact that he had invited it.

"If you must know, he insisted upon talking about marriage as an institution. He said that Catholics were taught it was a sacrament, and that even Lutherans talked about 'holy matrimony.' And then, he remarked mockingly, that the former were apt to convert it into bondage, and the latter into—legalized violence."

"Oh!" cried Faith aghast, "how terrible that he should feel he is in bondage!"

"Faith! I am appalled by your lack of subtlety! What do Sebastian's remarks about bondage—if they were really sincere—amount to compared to—his other expression? Don't you realize what he meant?"

Faith did not answer immediately, and when she did she spoke rather stumblingly. "I am sorry that I seemed so stupid," she said slowly. "But I honestly didn't realize—right away—"

"I am sorry to make you do so. But in view of Sebastian's hideous behavior I do not see how I can help it. He declined to be diverted, and he kept looking at me as if I were some kind of a violent criminal, instead of a loving

119

bridegroom. I finally decided that he must be either intoxicated, or temporarily deranged, or else that you must have said something to him which betrayed—that the consummation of our marriage had been forced upon you."

There was a long silence. It was Faith who finally broke it. "I do believe that Sebastian knew exactly what happened," she said at last in a low voice. "I thought so the minute he looked at me when he came into the drawing-room. It was uncanny, almost as if he were clairvoyant. But of course I did not say anything at all. How could I? I mean, even if I had dreamed of doing such a thing? It would have been impossible. I was too—overwhelmed."

"But Faith," asked Rudolf desperately, "didn't you guess at all—? I know that young maidens are kept in innocence, but didn't you have any idea—?" His bitterness had spent itself, and there was deep solicitude in his troubled voice.

There was another long silence, and when Faith spoke again it was evident that she had been considering carefully beforehand what she was going to say, that she was resolutely trying to be not only calm but just and truthful.

"It is very hard to explain, Rudolf. I knew of course that married persons slept in the same room. But it is all so vague and—indefinite to a girl. She senses that there is something. But something so mysterious and secret that it is—sacramental. Unless it is just the opposite. Unless it—seems shameful. I had begun to realize before my mother died that there was a—a sort of close relationship between her and certain men. But I never tried to find out exactly what it was. I tried *not* to find out! I felt so—so smirched by it all the time that I couldn't bear to. Afterwards—after she died—I was stunned for a while, I suppose. Anyway, I didn't think about any—any mysteries again for a long time. And then I met you, and suddenly the world seemed like a different place. Instead of being numb and wretched I was so happy and excited I didn't know what to do. I thought you were the most wonderful person on earth. Oh!—much more than a *person*—a radiant St. Michael! Driving away dragons! Bringing salvation and strength! Surrounded by All Angels!"

"*Liebe* Faith, in one way I am glad that you thought of me like that. I am thankful that I seemed to bring you deliverance and joy. But in another way I am sorry. For I am not a saint, and it did not occur to me that you thought of me in that light."

"Oh, Rudolf, I would give anything if I could make you understand! When I said I thought of you as a saint, I didn't mean that I didn't think of you as a human too! St. Michael was a very *masculine* sort of a saint anyway, wasn't he? What I am trying to explain is that I worshipped you so and trusted you so that when I did begin to wonder a little about—about mysteries again, I didn't worry over them. I felt sure they *would* be sacramental, since they were to be part of my life with you. I didn't even want anyone— any outsider—to spoil them for me by telling me too much about them beforehand. I wanted you to do that yourself. Cousin Sarah did try to have a 'little talk' with me the week before we were married. I could see that she thought she ought to. But I wouldn't let her. I stopped her by telling her that I wanted to leave everything in your hands. I told her I cared for you too much to doubt in your gentleness and your tenderness—and your loving kindness."

Suddenly she clasped her hands together and gave a little dry sob.

"That is what has made me so unhappy. It is not what you did. I—I understand about that now. It is the way you did it. You are usually so calm, and all at once you were—violent. It was *all* so sudden! You did not prepare me at all. If you had I am sure you would not have needed to use force. You did not caress me; you—compelled me. You were not gentle or tender and kind. You were not even loving, though the only thing you said to me was that it was a time for love. Oh, Rudolf, why—why did it have to be like that?"

She had broken into uncontrollable weeping. Rudolf bent over her and drew her toward him.

"Liebchen," he said tenderly, "my dearest Faith, don't— don't! I do understand everything now, but you must try to be understanding, too! I did mean to be very patient—to wait until we reached here. But I wanted you so much, and I felt that you were drawing away from me, not growing closer to me—that is why I lost my self-control! And I could not guess how far you had relied on my intuition and my guidance. Please, darling, tell me that you forgive me! I promise you that it will never be like that again."

She was not actually struggling against him, but still he was conscious of no real yielding to his embrace. In his real and deep concern lest he should again fail in gentleness he made no effort to hold her closely, and presently she raised a tear-stained face to his.

"What is it going to be like?" she asked.

He hesitated, torn between the passion that was surging through him again, and the insidious fear that if he erred a second time he might lose her altogether.

"You told me, when you first came up on the terrace,

that you had separated our belongings," he said gravely. "I shall not ask you to place them together again. And when I knock at the door of your room, I will not come in unless you tell me that I may. I give you my word of honor."

The glory of the sunset had long since disappeared, the moon had not yet risen. But the dark sky was jeweled with stars, the terrace luminous. Rudolf could see the tense expression of Faith's face changing, almost before he was aware that she was relaxing in his arms. He took courage.

"But I shall come to it hoping you will be more generous to me than I deserve," he said softly.

. . . . . .

Nevertheless, after he had parted from her that night in the *galeria* his hammering heart failed him. It was very late. Even at the *caseria* dinner never took place until after nine; and it had been delayed because he and Faith had remained so long on the terrace, where neither Felipe nor Catalina—who had a romantic regard for the exigencies of a honeymoon—had intruded upon them. Then the dinner—served in a corner of the patio, as Faith had desired—had lasted a long time; and after that they had sat, with Faith's head against his shoulder, listening to the bubbling fountain. Finally she had said it was bedtime and they had gone upstairs together. Yes, it was very late. He reached for his bedside candle to blow it out. Just then he heard Faith calling him.

He swung open the heavy door that divided the room which she had chosen for her own from his. The metal lamp suspended from the high ceiling had been extinguished; but through the long window leading out to the *galeria*, moonlight rushed in with a stream of radiance, flooding the smooth-tiled floor and high white walls with its light. In the great carved bed, set in an arched recess under a small high window, Faith lay beneath a golden coverlet, her shining hair falling over the snowy pillows, the sheer lace of her nightgown only half veiling her soft breast. As Rudolf came up to her she held out her hands.

"You didn't knock," she said softly. "You didn't give me a chance to be generous. Won't you?"

PART V

Gabriel

Chapter XV

A SENSUOUS quietude enfolded the *caseria*. Serene days, permeated with tranquillity and warmth, drifted fragrantly away into one translucent twilight after another. And with the descent of night, the little vine-clad house lay hushed and hidden in the embrace of poignant darkness.

Through Faith's sudden self-abandonment, Rudolf had been transported to rapturous regions of which he had never even dreamed before; and having attained them, the fear that this abandonment might not be lasting served as another spur to his stimulated senses. But she had done far more than yield to the urgency of his desire; she had surrendered to the principle that passion was his perogative; and in doing so she had made herself wholly his. The aftermath of her supreme submission was a languor so insidious that she found she could not prevail against it; and she succumbed to it utterly. But it was a languor that enhanced her radiance, and Rudolf found her more irresistible than ever. The "slumberous, amorous summer" for which Faith had pled so artlessly had become a reality, and Rudolf, who had rebuked her for her unconscious expression of emotionalism, was himself discovering an emotional heaven.

For some time there were no intruders in his passionate paradise; and it was not until he inadvertently glanced at a small calendar in the library, so unobtrusively hung as to be hitherto overlooked, that he realized, with a shock of surprise, that he had been at the *caseria* almost a fortnight, and that in all this while he had not read a single word about Spanish colonization. He had been on his way to the terrace when he made his disturbing discovery, and feeling nearly as guilty as if he had deserted his regiment under fire, he tore himself away from Faith, the instant they had finished their coffee, with lingering and ardent embraces, but with a Spartan injunction that she was not to come near him again until luncheon-time.

Freed from his dominating and demanding presence, and with a conscience slightly troubled because of the sense of relief of which she was almost instantly aware, she went outdoors and began to divert herself aimlessly but agreeably. She watched an old man who had come out from Granada to take up the honey; she gathered and sampled a few persimmons; she transplanted a palm for the mere pleasure of moving it from one place to another. When the heat of the mounting sun drove her back into the house, she filled twenty vases with the flowers she had picked, and then she settled herself contentedly in her bedroom, sorting and mending the folded piles of freshly washed garments which Catalina had laid there. She was accustomed to keeping her own clothing in order; and she was glad to sit down now peacefully in a low chair, to weave together a tear in a fine silk stocking and close up a rip in a French seam. When Catalina burst in upon her, visibly and volubly excited, and gesticulating frantially toward the drawing-room, Faith faintly resented the interruption to her tidy occupation. She could disentangle nothing definite from the servant's agitated exclamations about *Su Eminencia*. So when she reached the *salita* she was surprised to find herself confronted by a tall purple-clad figure of great distinction, who rose at her approach and came forward with an air of benign dignity.

"I have been hoping that you and your husband would come to see me," he said in excellent English, "but since you have not, I have come to see you instead, for I wished very much to welcome you into the family. I learned from my brother, of course, when you and your husband came here."

"I am very glad to see you," said Faith cordially and sincerely. Her visitor was indeed apparently very eminent; he was, moreover, kindly and gracious also, and though she could not instantly identify the likeness, he bore a certain softened but striking resemblance to someone whom she had seen already. "But I am afraid I do not know who you are."

"My name is Gabriel de Cerreno. I am Sebastian's elder brother—much older, for I am nearly old enough to be his father. But we are devoted to each other, in spite of the difference in our ages and—pursuits. Indeed we always write to each other every day when we are separated, as we unfortunately are much of the time. We have both lost so much that we are united by an unusually close tie. Our

124

parents and their other children have all died and we are the only remaining members of our immediate circle."

"I am sorry that you have lost so much," said Faith sympathetically. "I remember now when Rudolf first spoke to me about Sebastian he told me that there were only two brothers left out of a large family. He said that one of them had entered the church."

"Yes," said Gabriel, smiling a little, "I happen to be the Archbishop of Granada."

"Oh!" said Faith, "then I am afraid I should have kissed your ring or something like that, when I came into the drawing-room, instead of just shaking hands. But I do not know just how archbishops should be treated. I have never met one before. Are they anything like archduchesses? I should be relieved if you could say that they were, because my mother-in-law is an archduchess, and I am very fond of her."

"I do not wonder," replied Gabriel amiably, "she is one of the most charming women in Europe. She is also a devout Catholic, like all Hapsburgs. I should be pleased if you thought, in this instance, that there was a similarity between archbishops and archduchesses. In fact I should take it as a distinct compliment. As to the questions of ecclesiastical etiquette, do not let those disturb you. I am sure you will master them very quickly. Besides, I came to see you as a kinsman and not as an archbishop, though I should have been very glad if Rudolf had brought you with him to be received in audience, and to be given my Episcopal blessing. However, I am not surprised that he has not."

Gabriel smiled, and Faith thought there was actually a twinkle in his dark eyes, as if he were perfectly well aware how complete Rudolf's preoccupation had been since his marriage and precisely what form this had taken. She colored deeply, and the Archbishop, noticing her blush, continued speaking in a manner calculated to put her more at ease.

"Rudolf was, of course, baptized in the Church," he said smoothly, "as the children of mixed marriages always are. Perhaps you did not realize this."

"No," said Faith in genuine surprise. "I thought he was a Lutheran like his father."

"He is. He became one as soon as he was old enough to be confirmed. This was a great blow to Victoria Luise, but naturally she never mentions it. She is wise enough to know that piety is no excuse for tactlessness. In fact she and I have often agreed that Our Savior, who was a gentleman, would have been the last to tolerate ungraciousness from his followers. And certainly Victoria Luise was not to blame for Rudolf's defection, nor, to do Hans von Hohenlohe justice, do I think he was either. I have never known him to even contemplate a dishonorable act, in spite of great provocation. I am sure he put no pressure on the boy at all. I think it was merely that temperamentally, Rudolf was much more fitted to be a Lutheran than a Catholic. And, as a matter of fact, I have never felt as bitter about his apostasy as most of the lay members of the family. Sebastian, for instance, never neglects an opportunity to goad him to fury about it, though I have often pled with him not to do so."

Faith, remembering how Rudolf had recently been so goaded, and not all sure Sebastian had neglected to inform his brother of the episode, blushed more deeply still.

"I hope Rudolf does not imagine there would be the least awkwardness about his coming to the Palace," the Archbishop went on, with such an air of cordial composure that Faith ventured to hope her increasing confusion was not too evident. "Please assure him that there will not be—unless there is a prospect that I may give this assurance myself?"

"I am so sorry. Rudolf is studying the history of Spanish colonization. He gave strict orders that he was not to be disturbed. Of course he did not expect that we would have a caller. But still——"

"Oh, yes! I also learned from Sebastian about the proposed course of study. I would not have you interrupt it for the world. Besides, as a cleric, I think you are quite right to carry out Rudolf's orders literally. From the time of St. Paul, the Church has been teaching the Gospel of a wife's submission to her husband's every desire."

Faith was rapidly coming to the conclusion that it was futile to try to conceal anything from the penetrating intuition of these Cerrenos, that it would be much simpler to tell them whatever they wanted to know in the first place, than to have them find it out, adroitly, for themselves, in the end.

"This is the first morning that Rudolf has remembered to study," she said candidly. "But I do not think he will forget about it again. Instead I think he will study doubly hard to make up for the time he has lost.—And I *am* trying very hard to do just what he wants to have me about—about everything."

"I know you are, my child," said the Archbishop gently, "and as I have just said, I cannot, as a churchman, commend your conduct too highly. But as a relative I should like to see a little more of you. Particularly as I was predisposed in your favor by a very wonderful painting for which I believe you where the inspiration."

"You were predisposed in my favor!" reiterated Faith, with an astonishment in which thanksgiving was mingled. The wound which Rudolf had inflicted in Venice by his manifest abhorrence of the part she had played in Sam's career had never entirely closed. Now she suddenly felt, as she gazed gratefully at Gabriel, that it had been miraculously healed.

"Of course. 'Mary of Nazareth' is one of the most supreme pictures of modern times. In achieving it, Samuel Dudley has made a great contribution to religion as well as to art. I am sorry he has felt, so far, that he could not part with it. You may remember that the exhibition at Seville was one of those at which it won a gold medal. It was the hope of many of us then that we might retain it in Spain."

"Sam took it with him to the Straits of Magellan," said Faith in a burst of confidence, "to keep him company. I got a cable from him about it on my wedding day. He said he hoped Rudolf would find the Aphrodite he missed. The next picture was to have been Aphrodite, you see."

"I see," said the Archbishop gravely. "I am not surprised that he took the 'Mary' with him, and I am sure it will be a source of inspiration to him, as many other holy paintings have been to many other great and rather lonely men. In fact, that splendid canvas which he has just shipped back to Europe—'Magellan Passing the Straits' I believe it is called —discloses how rapidly his genius continues to develop. It is much more than a superb marine picture. It is a revelation of the indomitable courage which drove Magellan forward and crowned him with conquest. This has never been so vividly depicted before."

"Oh!" exclaimed Faith impulsively, "you don't know how happy it makes me feel to have you talk like this! It is so long since anyone has spoken to me about Sam! And I have missed him so much!—Did you ever meet him?"

"Yes," said Gabriel with an accent of genuine admiration. "When he was in Seville I went over there on purpose to do so. But I was one of so many that doubtless he did not remember me and did not attach enough importance to our meeting to tell you about it. But I hope that he will return to Spain and that when he does he will be my guest. He will be coming, you know, one of these days, to paint you again."

"As Aphrodite?" asked Faith doubtfully.

The Archbishop smiled. "No," he said, "I do not think that Sam will ever paint the Aphrodite. Instead, as he meant to infer when he cabled you, he purposely left the way clear for Rudolf, as far as Aphrodite was concerned, and Rudolf has not had the genius to visualize her as Sam would have done—or to make others visualize her. His method has inevitably been very different. Personally, however I have no regrets because Sam will not paint that particular picture, though I realize he might have rivaled Botticelli if he had achieved it; because I think he will paint a picture of you instead that will prove to be another divinely lovely manifestation of Mary."

"What sort of a manifestation?" asked Faith eagerly.

"I may be able to tell you before you leave Granada," replied Gabriel, looking at her intently for a moment and then appearing to dismiss the subject. "But meanwhile you must tell me—are you contented here? Are Felipe and Catalina doing everything they should and can for your comfort? Are you enjoying the *caseria*?"

"Yes. I am contented," Faith said quietly. Then she went on, with rising enthusiasm, "Felipe and Catalina are simply wonderful. I never knew servants could be so capable and thoughtful and friendly. I am learning a great deal about housekeeping from them. And some Spanish, too!" she added with a little laugh. "Though I must get a grammar and start studying it more systematically.—And I adore the *caseria*. I think it is the most beautiful place I ever saw. Rudolf is amused because I keep telling him I am sure that some fairy must have laid a spell on it. But I really mean it. It seems as if I could feel the magic. You don't think I am silly, do you?" she asked a little anxiously.

"No my child, I do not think you are silly. I think you are very wise," Gabriel said slowly. "Probably the house *has* magical—or shall we say miraculous?—properties. Perhaps instead of being spellbound by a fairy, it has been blessed by an angel." He seemed absorbed in reflexion for a moment and then continued slowly, "Be that as it may, since you feel as you do about *caseria*, I wonder if you would not like to have it—for your very own, I mean? So that you would be free to come at any time? I think it would please Sebastian greatly if you would let him give it to you, if you would let him make a reality of the phrase we Spanish constantly use. '*Esta es su casa.*' He has half a dozen other houses, you know, all much more pretentious than this one; he would never miss it. And besides, he is naturally generous. There is nothing that makes him so happy as to bestow presents right and left. Persons who themselves feel—bereft, for one reason or another, are often like that. I do not know how I should carry on all my charities without his help. He tells me, mockingly, that I pour water through a sieve in trying to help the

128

poor, and then he sends me a thousand pesetas so that I may do so more freely."

"And do you think he would like to give me the *caseria?* Really and truly?"

"I am very sure of it," said Gabriel gravely.

He watched her searchingly as she turned the matter over in her mind. Certainly she was touched. Certainly she was pleased. And yet he was almost positive that she was going to decline the gift. He did not, however, guess the reason for this until she spoke.

"Sebastian won't think I'm ungrateful, will he?" she inquired. "I do love it—and I should like to feel free to come here whenever I can.—Perhaps he'd let me do that anyway. But I'd really rather not own it. Because, if I did, it would be a sort of home. And I have a home already. I haven't seen it in a long time. For—for rather sad reasons. But now I want very much to go there for a visit as soon as Rudolf can take me. And some day I want to go back there to live. It isn't very clear to me just how I ever can, but I am hoping for it somehow just the same."

"I see," said Gabriel, understandingly, as he had spoken when she was talking about Sam.

"You wouldn't think my house was pretty at all," Faith went on, encouraged to further comment by his obvious interest. "It isn't at all an important house. It's made of wood. It's painted white and it has green blinds. Inside the ceilings are very low, and there are lots of fireplaces, and there is white panelling in the parlor. It all smells very clean.— There is a walk made of cobblestones leading up to the front door, which isn't very large, and has a big brass knocker in the middle. There are lilac bushes and maple trees in the yard around the house, and a lane leading down to the river in the back. It's on a farm, near a little New England village, and further off there are big meadows and mountains. My great-great-grandfather had two sons, and when he settled in the upper Connecticut Valley, he built two houses, so that the sons would each have one after he died. There have been only two Marlowes—men I mean—in every generation since then, just as you and Sebastian are the only Cerrenos. My Uncle Ephraim lives in one of the houses. The other belonged to my father. When he died he— gave it to me. So I'd rather not have anyone else give me a house."

"I see," said Gabriel a third time.

"I know you would," Faith answered. She had enjoyed Gabriel's visit immeasurably; and as she began to be afraid that he might soon think of leaving she realized that she would be sorry to have him go.

"I suppose archbishops are rather busy," she said artlessly. "So it was very good of you to come and see me at all, but now that you are here I have been wondering if you could not spare the time to stay for luncheon? Rudolf will come down from the library for that, and then you could see him too."

The Archbishop rose, gathering the purple folds of his robe about him. "That is a great inducement," he said, and again Faith was conscious that his eyes were twinkling. "But I am having guests myself for luncheon, so I am afraid that I must go back to the Palace. Before I leave, however, I want you to kneel down and receive my blessing. I will show you just what to do—it is very simple. And I have been wondering—as I said before, I should like very much to see more of you as a relative. You say you know nothing of ecclesiastical procedure, and since you seem to be really interested in it—would you care to learn something about it? In connection with Church History perhaps? It might be a good way for you to study Spanish."

"Do you mean you would come here and give me lessons?" cried Faith delightedly.

"No—I did not mean just that. You are right in supposing that archbishops are rather busy. I could not arrange to leave the Palace every day or even to teach you myself, though I should be only too happy to supervise the schedule. But I could send my carriage here for you if it could not conveniently be arranged to have Felipe drive you back and forth from Granada. As I remember, the only vehicle on the place is rather decrepit. And one of my secretaries—the elder one—is a very learned scholar. I am sure he would prove a satisfactory instructor. Suppose you talk the matter over with Rudolf. You can send me a note by Felipe when he goes in to market tomorrow telling me what your husband thinks of our plan. Of course we would time the lessons to coincide with his periods of research, and I promise there shall be no proselyting. If he approves, we might begin our work on Wednesday."

"That would be wonderful!" exclaimed Faith.

The sweetness and solemnity of Gabriel's blessing made a deep impression upon her. When she rose from her knees, after he had pronounced it, she stood looking steadily up into his face, her reluctance to have him leave her increasing every moment. He laid the hand which she had so recently kissed lightly on her shoulder.

"I should not be surprised if some day you became a good

130

Catholic yourself," he said quietly. "But Catholic or not, the goodness is there anyway.—Is there any message you would care to send Sebastian by me?"

"Of course there is! When you write him give him my best regards. And tell him now kind I thought it was of him to offer me the *caseria*. I suppose that was his suggestion."

The Archbishop was already preparing to get into his imposing carriage, beside which Felipe and Catalina were devoutly kneeling. He turned back and smiled at Faith once more.

"Yes," he said. "It was Sebastian's suggestion. I will let him know that you were touched by it, even though you did not accept it. But it will not be necessary for me to write him to that effect. He arrived three days ago to make me a prolonged visit."

Chapter XVI

WHEN Rudolf rejoined Faith for luncheon, he commended her discretion in leaving him undisturbed, and at the same time expressed genuine regret that he had not been at leisure to welcome Gabriel.

"There is no one among our Spanish kinfolk whom I respect and admire so much," he said, speaking almost enthusiastically. "Of course it is impossible not to be exceedingly fond of *Tio* Carlos and *Tia* Carlota. But they are simple souls. They are not of the same caliber as Gabriel. It is surprising how much alike he and Sebastian are, and yet how different. Many of their characteristics are almost identical; but the qualities which are distorted in Sebastian are beatified in Gabriel. Yes, certainly, I should have taken you to present you to him before this. You have made this fortnight a period of such delight for me, *Liebchen*, that I must atone for my self-indulgence by extra diligence from now on. I feel I must study not only between lunch and tea-time, according to our original plan, but all the morning too, as I did to-day."

"That would not leave us a great deal of time together, for a bride and groom," observed Faith thoughtfully, though not resentfully.

"We will still have the late afternoons and evenings. I can count on relaxation with you when my day's work is over. I can always look forward to finding you waiting for me on the terrace; and to long rapturous hours afterwards."

Catalina, having placed a basket of nectarines on the table, had vanished, with timely tact. She had enjoyed several honeymoons, of one sort or another, herself; and she recognized certain symptoms in Rudolf's manner which led her to believe that he was impatiently awaiting her departure from the patio to take Faith on his lap. Her surmise had been entirely accurate. She had hardly disappeared when he lifted his bride into his arms.

"*Liebe* Faith," he said fervently, "I cannot tell you how happy you have made me. I will confess to you now, that during that dreadful day in Madrid—and until you called me to your bedside the first night we were here—I was—very anxious. Besides, even while we were betrothed, I could not help having some moments of uneasiness—much as I loved you—lest we should not always be of accord. I had heard that American maidens were headstrong and willful; but no German *Braut* could have been more docile than you have proven. And besides, you are so serene and sweet! Anything that any man could hope and long to find in his wife I have found in you! I know I am blessed beyond measure in my possession of you."

Faith lay quiescent in his embrace for a moment; then she gently freed one of her imprisoned arms, and began to stroke the locked hands clasped around her waist. "I am glad that I have made you happy after all," she said earnestly. "I can understand that you must have been worried for fear I might not. And it encourages me very much to have you say I am turning out to be just the sort of wife you wanted. I have tried to be, and I will keep on trying.— Gabriel encouraged me this morning, too. He really seemed —to approve of me and to like me.—By the way, he asked me if I would care to come to the Palace and take lessons in Church History and things like that. I was very informal about welcoming him when he arrived. I didn't understand who he was when Catalina told me, and even if a had, I wouldn't have known exactly what to do with an archbishop. But instead of being haughty and hurting my feelings, he made this kind suggestion. He told me to talk the matter over with you and let him know the decision. He said he had an elderly secretary who he was sure would be helpful to me. And he said my lessons would come at the same time with your research, so that they would not separate us at all, and to be sure to tell you there would be no proselyting."

Rudolf did not appear to hesitate at all. "The elderly secretary of whom he spoke must be Father Constantino," he said approvingly. "Yes, he is a very learned scholar. I fear we are rather too apt, in Germany, to dismiss all Spaniards from our minds as illiterate, or nearly so. I do not believe you could have a better teacher. It is immaterial whether you learn Church History; but it is very important that you should learn Spanish, and the proper etiquette to observe in your contacts with personages of ecclesiastic rank, many of whom, in Spain, are incidentally also members of the nobility as well. I will write to Gabriel at once asking when I may go with you to the Palace for an audience, and when he sets a time we will take advantage of his offer and accept it."

"Gabriel told me that Sebastian had just arrived to make him a long visit," went on Faith, wondering why it seemed so hard to impart this information casually, and at the same time why she felt she would be guilty of duplicity if she did not. Rudolf, however, heard the news without attention, much less acrimony.

"Sebastian often makes the Palace his headquarters while he is amusing himself in this vicinity," he remarked absently. "He has a great many friends about here. So have I, for that matter. Some of them will doubtless be calling upon us before long, and naturally we shall have to return their visits."

His mind seemed centered on an exchange of courtesies rather than on the propinquity of Sebastian. Without actually dragging the matter into the conversation Faith did not see how she could refer to his offer of the *caseria* as a gift, much less do this with nonchalance.

"I shall be very glad to have your friends come here whenever they can," she said cordially. "Are they all Spanish?"

"Nearly all. But you did not have a great deal of trouble in talking with Gabriel, did you?" asked Rudolf, with one of his rare excursions into pleasantry.

Faith laughed. "Where did he learn to speak such English, Rudolf? He and—and Sebastian?"

"At Eton," said Rudolf, rather dryly. "Their father was the Spanish Ambassador to Great Britain for ten years. Incidentally they both have degrees from Oxford. In fact I believe Gabriel has two or three degrees from various institutions. He was always scholarly as well as devout, and since his uncle was the Papal Secretary of State, it was doubly logical that he should turn to religion as a vocation. But his parents were averse to his taking irrevocable vows until it seemed certain that the family name would be carried on by Sebastian. Having lost several sons in infancy they were naturally anxious on that score."

"And now the name is not to be carried on after all!"

"No. As I said before, in one way it is perhaps fortunate, while in another it is certainly a pity. Especially as Sebastian is very fond of children. He would have liked to have them, not only as descendants but as companions. It is one of those strange contradictions of character which sometimes occur. No one, to meet Sebastian casually, would dream that he had such a leaning. But he actually dotes on babies. He is like a different person when he is in the presence of a little child."

Rudolf's complacency had reached a stage where he was ready to make favorable comments on almost anyone. He was gratified by the benign visit of Gabriel. The sunny stillness of the patio was very soothing. He was replete with excellent food and even more excellent wine. And his wife, relaxed and responsive, was seated on his knees. Faith, aware of his contentment, decided to take advantage of it by asking a question to allay her curiosity on a point which hitherto had not been clarified for her.

"Rudolf," she asked without undue emphasis, "you have never happened to tell me how Sebastian's face was so badly cut. That is a queer scar on his cheek. Is there dueling in Spain as there is in Germany?"

"Yes, there is some dueling in Spain. Not much. But Sebastian's scar did not come from a duel."

"What did it come from?"

"*Liebe* Faith, why are you so inquisitive? This is not the first time you have so shown yourself. It seems to me almost your only fault. But since you are so insistent I will tell you what you want to know. In one of the periods when her malady took the form of frenzy, Dolores attacked Sebastian. It was before her condition was really recognized as—insanity. Up to that time she had simply been considered—very hysterical. No precautions had been taken against violence on her part. But she suddenly snatched up a jeweled dagger—a beautiful heirloom that was lying on a table among other treasures—and hurled herself against him. Gabriel was in the room when it happened. If he had not been Sebastian would doubtless have been killed. There was no forewarning of her maniacal mood, and Sebastian had no time to defend himself. In any case he could not have used force against her. She was his wife, even though she was a madwoman."

Rudolf did not look at Faith as he set her on her feet. He was resentful because she had insisted on hearing this frightful story about which he had been so discreetly silent; he felt she had unsettled the serenity of the afternoon by her

134

urgency. She was probably shocked and startled now, for which he was sorry, but it was her own fault. He hoped she would interpret his withdrawal as an unspoken reprimand. After all, she was very young and she still had a great deal to learn about finesse. He must make every endeavor to teach her for her own sake as well as his.

"I am now going to write to Gabriel," he said almost formally, "and give the note to Felipe to take into Granada at once. After that I shall return to the library. I have found a book there on the rights of neutral nations which is very absorbing. I think I shall supplement my studies on colonization by reading this work also, and perhaps preparing a report on what I have read. I will see you again at tea-time."

"Very well," Faith answered levelly. A sudden unexpected quality of maturity in her voice arrested him. He turned and saw that instead of appearing abashed by his reproof, she looked slightly scornful; and apparently she had not been frightened by his gruesome chronicle, for her expression was strangely self-reliant.

"Of course I will not ask you questions if you do not like to have me, Rudolf," she went on in the same even tone. "But I do not see how we can be really intimate unless I do— unless we ask *each other* questions. I do not see what good it will do us to come close to each other in the way you want unless we come close to each other in *every* way. Of course there will be barriers between us, no matter how hard I try to please you, if you make me feel that you are bored or annoyed by subjects which interest me. We can talk just about what interests you, but that will not change my thoughts. And anyway, I am glad I know at last how Sebastian got his scar. Also that he would not use force against his wife in any case. Even if she were a madwoman."

Chapter XVII

RUDOLF sat, staring at the closely printed pages of the very absorbing book on the rights of neutral nations. From time to time he turned one of its leaves mechanically; but he had not succeeded in making out any kind of résumé of the contents, though a plump pad and several neatly sharpened pencils, which he had placed on the desk in preparation for his important task, lay within easy reach of his long fingers. At last he shoved back his chair with an exclamation of impatience and strode across the room. For some moments he stood glaring out at the beautiful *vega*, his hands thrust savagely into his pockets, his shoulders sagging. Then he recrossed the library, flung open the heavy door, and called loudly to Catalina.

He was obliged to repeat his summons three times before he heard her willing but heavy footsteps approaching. His irritability increased with every second that marked her delay. When at last she presented herself before him, puffing and panting, he spoke to her with unprecedented sharpness.

"Is it necessary for me to wait indefinitely when I wish to give an order?"

"*Disculpe, Señor Barón.* I was preparing the tea. I set down the kettle and hastened the instant I heard the *Señor Barón* call. But to mount all these stairs—the *Señor Barón* understands that for this a *momentito* is required."

"It is about the tea that I wish to speak to you. Please tell your mistress that I shall be obliged to have mine here alone in the library. My work has not progressed as fast as it should. I cannot join her on the terrace."

In his exasperation, he thought he detected a shade of derision in Catalina's bland expression. He rapped out another curt question.

"Why do you look at me like that? Don't you understand me?"

"*Pero sí, Señor Barón.* I was only wondering how you could have your tea otherwise than alone, or how I could carry a message to the *Baronesa,* since she is gone?"

"Gone!" thundered Rudolf, terror as well as rage gripping him. "What do you mean?"

"I thought of course the *Señor Barón* knew," said Catalina unctuously and mendaciously, "that she went into Granada with Felipe. The *Señor Barón* perhaps recalls that he gave Felipe a note to deliver to His Eminence, the Archbishop?"

"Of course I recall it! What has that to do with the *Baronesa?*"

"After the *Señor Barón* had given Felipe the note, Felipe prepared with great dispatch to carry out the *Señor Barón's* wishes."

"With great dispatch!" barked Rudolf ironically. "*Gott in Himmel,* when was a Spaniard ever known to act with dispatch!"

"He had just finished harnessing Pepito into the cart," went on Catalina calmly and with thinly veiled contempt, "when the *Baronesa* came into the outer patio wearing a large white hat, and made signs to Felipe that she wished to accompany him. He made signs to her that he would get out the victoria, and harness Benito instead. She made signs that she would go in the cart, that he was not to molest himself. She laughed and climbed into the cart and took the reins herself. Felipe laughed and climbed up beside her. And *presto!* They were gone from the *caseria,* both laughing and both making si—"

"Stop talking to me about signs!—Do you mean to tell me that they have not returned yet?"

"Felipe returned more than two hours ago, *Señor Barón.* But the *Baronesa* did not return with him."

"Send Felipe to me this instant!" commanded Rudolf.

He began pacing up and down the library like a caged lion. Catalina's tale was simply preposterous. Faith had put on a large white hat, she had climbed into a rickety old cart and driven off behind an aged donkey into Granada, escorted only by an Andalusian peasant! And then she had remained behind in Granada under unimaginable conditions! The *Baronesa* von Hohenlohe, the wife of the Third Secretary of the German Embassy! In the most conservative section of the most conservative country in Europe! A section riddled with exalted families, many of them related to him, whose own womenkind had never been known to stir away from their patios in an undignified manner, who were always suitably accompanied, and who wore their delicate black mantillas drawn over their beautiful creamy brows to protect them from the vulgar gaze of the curious! The incredibility of Catalina's narrative was matched only by its monstrosity.

Felipe, when he finally arrived upon the scene, which was not until Rudolf had worked himself into a ferment, was quite as calm as Catalina had been. Who was he to attempt to prevent the *Baronesa* from doing as she pleased, especially as he of course supposed the *Señor Barón* to be fully informed of her purpose? Naturally he had not understood all her signs, but it was evident enough that she wanted to go into Granada for something. And fortunately everything had been explained to him all in good time. As they drew up in front of the Palace, a group of gentlemen were just emerging from the doorway, who had evidently been lunching with His Eminence. Indeed, His Eminence was among them. He had welcomed the *Baronesa* cordially, and with no sign of surprise. He had then read the note from the *Señor Barón,* he had spoken a little with the *Baronesa,* and finally he had told Felipe that she had decided as long as the *Barón* was so studiously occupied, to while away the period of his seclusion by doing a little sightseeing in Granada, which she had not visited at all, except to pass through it on the morning of her arrival at the station. His Eminence had also hastily written a little note, which Felipe had hesitated to deliver to the *Barón* for fear of disturbing him; but now that the *Barón* had sent for him, *mire!* Here it was!

Rudolf almost snatched the stiff little square of paper away from Felipe.

"Dear Rudolf"... he read:

"I too was sorry not to see you this morning, but I shall be glad to receive you and Faith in audience at ten to-morrow. We will plan then for her lessons. I am delighted to know that you approve of our tentative program. Meanwhile, since Faith had decided that she would like to see some landmarks this afternoon, I will arrange for this, and also for her safe return to the *caseria* later in the evening. Please do not be in the least anxious about her. Affectionately, Gabriel."

Felipe stood respectfully and patiently before Rudolf, fingering with joy the two coins which the Archbishop had given him, but taking the precaution of doing this very quietly, so that they should not jingle. He did not feel quite sure whether he was dismissed or not. The *Señor Barón* seemed to have forgotten all about him. At last he sighed, deeply and audibly, and then the *Barón* sent him off, with a gesture and an expression which the humblest hidalgo would never have used. Felipe shrugged his shoulders and went his way. He had been favorably impressed with the *Barón* at first, but he admired him less and less as time went on. It was a great pity, he and Catalina agreed, as they sat talking over the situation in the cool of the evening, that the *Baronesa*, who was not only *muy simpatica*, but, *preciosissima* as well, had not bestowed her lovely hand in marriage on some high-born Spaniard instead of on this abrupt and glowering German, who could hardly even be called a *caballero.*"

"We can only pray," said Catalina piously, "that since heaven has not blessed her with a Spanish husband, it may swiftly send her a Spanish lover, to whose ardent importunities she will speedily succumb, and thereby attain the bliss which she so well deserves."

"May it so please the Blessed Virgin!" ejaculated Felipe fervently.

· · · · · ·

It was nearly nine o'clock before Rudolf heard the sound

of horses' hoofs in the outer patio. His anger had burned itself out, for characteristically, his emotion had been as evanescent as it was intense, and he had spent several hours in searching self-scrutiny. He was intrinsically just, and the feeling that he had been unfair to Faith, kept steadily gaining ground in his consciousness. There was really no reason why she should not ask him questions, though it was unfortunate that in doing so she so often uncovered some family skeleton; but after all, it was not Faith's fault that there were so many skeletons in the family. He was even ready to admit, though the idea was novel to him, that a frank and habitual exchange of confidences might stabilize rather than shake the foundations of their marriage relationship. He knew that Faith respected his wishes and recognized his authority. Even her precipitant departure had not been, he began to realize, an attempt to escape on account of rebellion, any more than it had been a deliberate disregard of decorum. She had merely gone off, on the impulse of the moment, because she had no other outlet for her natural energy, because an opportunity presented itself for visiting a beautiful city, and she had been unaware of any reason why she should fail to take advantage of it. It was unfortunate that he had not himself suggested a sight-seeing expedition to Granada. But it had not even occurred to him to do so, primarily because his days at the *caseria* had been so saturated with sweetness that he had been oblivious to all the world that lay beyond its shielding walls. There was also another reason for his negligence; he had been to Granada so many times, in the course of numerous visits, that he was no more thrilled by the idea of a visit to the Alhambra than by the idea of a visit to the Palace at Charlottenburg. But then, Faith had been thrilled by a visit to the Palace at Charlottenburg. He should have remembered that. Yes, decidedly, he had been very short-sighted.

It was also unfortunate that he had betrayed his surprise at Faith's plunge to Catalina and Felipe. Gabriel, emerging from the Palace surrounded by dignitaries, had quite evidently not given the slightest indication that he thought there was anything the least extraordinary in being suddenly confronted by an unaccompanied young lady who jumped out of a donkey cart and hailed him with effusion. And yet, Gabriel must have been almost speechless with astonishment —well, probably not speechless, for the Cerrenos were never tongue-tied, but certainly very much astonished indeed. And he had welcomed her cordially, giving both the dignitaries and the servant rather the impression that he was hoping she might give him the honor of coming to see him about that time.—It was humiliating to admit himself outdone in delicacy by Gabriel on the very day when he had endeavored to teach his wife a lesson in tactfulness.

Having blundered so variously and so clumsily, how should he greet Faith on her return? And who would be with her when she did come along? Gabriel had assured him that she would be adequately cared for and his confidence in Gabriel was implicit, as he kept assuring himself. Yet a little forked flame of fear kept twisting through his body. Fear of what? Fear of whom? Why should he be afraid of anything or anybody as far as Faith was concerned, especially at a time when he was fortified by the might of Gabriel's pledged word? Yet was there not one person in the world against whom Gabriel's pledged word would not prevail? Would Jacob have denied anything to Benjamin? Why had he not thought of all that in the morning? How could he have been blind to the underlying motives of the Archbishop's visit, of his suggestion that Faith should go daily to the Palace? Why had he not recognized in Gabriel the emissary and tool of Sebastian, whom, in a sudden blinding flash, he saw revealed in his true and lurid colors? Sebastian, who wanted Faith for himself, who had followed her to Granada, who was planning, with diabolical cleverness, to get her through the connivance of his saintly brother? Sebastian, who had fascinated Faith as a snake fascinates a bird, so that he was never out of her thoughts? Sebastian, who was so lost to shame that he would not hesitate to defile a bridal-bed or to stage an intrigue on the altar steps?

Rudolf was as shaken with hatred and panic as he had been shaken with anger a few hours earlier. He knew that he should be ruled by reason, not swayed by suspicions—especially suspicions that were without substance, and which were an insult even to Sebastian, and almost a sacrilege as far as Gabriel and Faith were concerned. Yet some primitive instinct continued to kindle them. It was all he could do to steady himself against the insidious dread of the circumstances which would surround Faith's return. When he heard a horse's hoof clattering in the outer patio, he listened, breathlessly, for the voice which he felt sure he would presently hear too, rising and falling in response to Faith's—a cultured, liquid Spanish voice, as melodious as it was mocking.

He was aware instead of a nasal twang which grated across his consciousness as harshly as a rasping file. But its tones were music to his ears. He had never heard it before; and though he had no idea to whom it belonged one thing was certain: It did not belong to Sebastian. That, for the moment, was all that mattered. The nights were dark now, except for the twinkling stars, for the silvery young moon, which, a fortnight earlier, had flooded Faith's room with delicate luster, had mellowed to the ripe gold of maturity and sunk forever in luxuriant splendor; and in the patio of the fountain, where he had come at last to wait, were only the high, swinging lanterns of wrought iron and translucent ruby-colored glass for illumination. Rudolf could see nothing more than the indistinct outline of the two figures that were approaching. But dim as this outline was it showed that the man who was walking beside Faith though very heavy, was not much taller than she was. As they came nearer, Rudolf realized that though he was rather uncouth, he gave an immediate impression of strength; and when his features became vaguely visible, they were revealed as shrewd rather than stolid.

"Say, if that ain't a sweet pretty house!" were the first words which Rudolf heard him say clearly. "Cute, I call it!" The stranger paused, and drew a deep whistle of unconcealed admiration. "Just as cute as it can be!" he exclaimed.

"It's a magic house," said Faith happily.

"You don't say!" replied the stranger whistling again. "Well, I want to know!"

"I'm going to tell you all about it," Faith assured him, "but first I want to introduce my husband to you—Rudolf, this is Mr. Caleb Hawks of Hinsboro."

"Pleased to meet you," said Mr. Hawks, grasping Rudolf's hand heartily.

"Mr. Hawks is something very important in pencils, Rudolf," Faith went on. "I'm not sure just what, but I'm sure he'll explain it to you. He used to be a friend of my father's, and I knew him when I was a little girl. I met him again in Berlin, when I was visiting the Castles, and to-day again at Gabriel's. He's been touring Spain, and he'd been lunching at the Palace. He's going to have dinner with us."

"If you're sure it won't put out the hired girl any," said Mr. Hawks considerately.

Chapter XVIII

CATALINA'S dinner, and the wine from the *bodega*, which she poured out with an unusually lavish hand, were both excellent, and Mr. Hawks did full justice to them though Faith saw him looking vainly around for butter as the meal began.

"I'm sorry there is none," she said solicitously, "but the only kind we can get here is canned, and comes all the way from Denmark. It's horrible in this warm weather, so as Catalina cooks entirely with oil anyway, we don't use butter at all. We have jam for breakfast instead. And just think, Mr. Hawks! There are one hundred acres on the *caseria* and we haven't a single cow! Only goats! The people in the country here think goat's milk is much more healthful, and Rudolf has explained to me that it really is, because it doesn't carry tuberculosis. But of course the farmers aren't worrying about anything definite like that. It's just that goats are much easier to take care of than cows and much cheaper. And I simply love them. I think they are perfectly darling. There *is* one *caseria* though, not far from here, where there is one cow, and every now and then Catalina's nephew Timoteo, goes and brings us home some cow's milk in wine bottles. He brings us our drinking water too, from a spring, in earthen jars."

"Well, if that ain't all real peculiar," said Mr. Hawks, with interest. "I don't know but what I'd just as leave have the liquid that usually goes in the bottles though, as any milk, goats' *or* cows'.—Oh, thank you kindly, ma'am. I don't mind if I do."

Having quaffed deeply of the proffered beverage, Mr. Hawks smacked his lips, and turned to Rudolf with an access of affable garrulity.

"You could'da knocked me over with a feather," he said earnestly, though considering Mr. Hawks' bulk, it would have been difficult to visualize what sort of a feather would have effectually served this purpose, "when I saw Faith here jump out of that donkey cart and come racing up the steps. She didn't take in who I was, not right off. She'd only seen me once, of course—that is, since she was knee-high to a grasshopper—at that show Cal Castle took me to in Berlin; but I reccernized her right away. I knew her father and her grandfather both well, and looked up to them considerably, same as everyone did in our state. There was pretty general regret, I can tell ye, when this young lady come along, that she warn't a boy, so we could have another Marlowe in the seats of the mighty at Washington. But land! Christian Marlowe set his eye-teeth by her and I don't know as I blame him. I sure was glad to see her again. You know how 'tis Mr. Lowe, in these furrin' parts. You're so homesick all the time you keep your ears pricked for someone that comes

142

from God's country and speaks the King's English, same as you do."

"Rudolf's never had a chance to be homesick," interposed Faith. "He could take a train anytime, anywhere, in Europe and get off at any station; and when he looked up at the sign to find out where he was he'd be able to say to himself, 'Ach, this is the city where my grandfather's second cousin, Wilhelm, who married the Countess of Concertina is now living. He will be delighted to have me make him a little visit. I will then up the avenue walk until I reach his palace.'—But I know what you mean. I did it hundreds of times when I was a little girl. I shouldn't wonder if it were even worse for a little girl than a big man, especially if she had just two dolls for company, and spent lots of time in dingy little pensions, or got dragged around seeing Alps and things. Of course, after I went to live with Cousin Sarah, it was different. She had lots of nice consular friends. But I *do* know just what you mean."

"Not but what everyone's treated me fine," Mr. Hawks, who was eminently just, hastened to say. "Cal Castle now. I've known him ever since we was in first grade together. So when I decided to come to Europe, I went straight to Germany, on one of them fine new boats of yours. I give Cal the surprise of his life. He never figgered on my coming to Europe and neither had I, Mr. Lowe, and that's a fact. But Mrs. Hawks passed away last fall, and Myra, my only daughter's married. So my house was sort of quiet, as you might say, with no one in it but the hired girl and me. Of course I have my church—I'm a deacon in the First Congregational—and my lodge meetings—I belong to the Order of the Oriental Caribou and the Persian Panthers both. And then of course there's always politics. I've been on the city council in Hinsboro for fifteen years, and I kin run for mayor anytime I say the word. Mebbe I will when I go home. But all them associations don't take the place of your wife after thirty years. No sir, I was kinder lonely. So I thought I might as well come to Europe. Lots of people do. With Cal to turn to, I thought I'd get along all right. And I have. His wife was never one to hang the latch-string out, and she ain't changed, but neither has Cal. He's done mighty handsome by me himself, and he give me letters right and left besides. Everyone has been real hospitable. But of course you can't expect to eat every meal out in company. And in between times, I've wondered once in a while if it wouldn't have been better if I'd gone to stay with Myra for a spell. As I said, that's my daughter, Mr. Lowe, and I've got two of the cutest grandchildren! I never saw such kids! Smart

143

ain't no word for them! The things they get off! Just for instance——"

Mr. Hawks gave several examples of his grandchildren's precocious wit to which Rudolf listened with courtesy and Faith with real amusement.

"Oh, Mr. Hawks, that *was* smart! I don't wonder you hated to leave them. But I don't believe you'll be sorry you came to Europe in the end.—Don't you like Gabriel?"

"Don't I like him?" echoed Mr. Hawks solemnly. "Say, he's a prince."

"No," said Rudolf politely, "I'm sorry to contradict you, Mr. Hawks, but the Cerreno family has no more than ducal rank."

"Mr. Hawks only meant that Gabriel was a wonderful person," explained Faith, "and of course he is.—Was it Uncle Carolus that gave you a letter to him?"

"No, it was that handsome mother-in-law of yours," said Mr. Hawks, "but it was Cal gave me a letter to *her*. I don't know as I ever met a pleasanter-spoken woman, Mr. Lowe, than your mother, and that's a fact. But now, in Spain seems as if everyone was pleasant. Of course people are polite to you in other countries, but there's a difference. In France, for instance. You get the feeling that folks are sneering at you behind your back. And in Germany, well, you seem so downright dumb all the time. Not that anyone tells you you're dumb. But you get the idea. Here it's different. We've had a war with Spain a few years ago and cleaned them out of what little they had left on earth, and I ain't so sure we done right by 'em. It's a grand thing to talk about liberty and all that, but some of them Cubans are pretty slick. I've run into 'em considerable in my business. And it looks to me as if we'd got our own claws sunk pretty deep into the Philippines and Porto Rico. But be all that as it may, do you think I've met a single Spaniard that acted as if he had a grudge against me because I was an American? Not on your life! Hotel *conserges* and all, they've treated me like a member of the family. Even on the trains, all the passengers seem to want me to eat up half the victuals they're taking along with them to strengthen them for the journey. And land! They celebrate Thanksgiving every day! As for this here bishop—or whatever you call him— well, he certainly is a prince."

For a moment Mr. Hawks' enthusiasm rendered him inarticulate. Then, having drawn breath and shoveled a large portion of *pollo con arroz* into his mouth he continued.

"Say, you missed a treat not being with us today, Mr. Lowe, and that's a fact. I don't know as I ever seed a city

144

I admired more than Granada. Mebbe it wouldn't have suited Mrs. Hawks the way it is. She'd have wanted to houseclean it pretty thorough. She was a great one for having everything just poison neat. But a little dirt here and there never did anyone any real harm and never will. And it certainly is a sweet pretty place. The red geraniums kinder make me think of home. Mrs. Hawks would have liked them. They grow differently here from at home of course. More easy like, sorter tumbling over balconies instead of being set in tomato cans in the front parlor windows. But geraniums are cheery lookin', however you plant 'em."

"I have always thought they were very pretty flowers myself," said Rudolf politely. "Did the Archbishop take you to see the Capilla Real?"

"I should say he did!" exclaimed Mr. Hawks, warming to his subject. "I couldn't have told you its name if you hadn't helped me. But the Caterpillar Reel, that's the word. We looked at the tombs of Ferdinand and Isabella. And say, the Bishop pointed out a real peculiar thing. He said that the 'Catholic Kings'—that's the way he described 'em, though I would'a called Isabella a Queen myself—were both very wise, but that Isabella was wiser than Ferdinand. He said the man who carved them tombs wanted to make it plain, so he's got Isabella's head layin' on her pillow so's it makes a deep dent, but Ferdinand's is just as smooth as it can be. I guess women's rights ain't quite so new-fangled a notion as most people seem to think. I guess Isabella got hers or knew the reason why.—Say, Faith, do you think there's any more of that fricassee in the kitchen? It's real tasty, after all the fried veal I've choked down."

"Oh, isn't it awful!" exclaimed Faith. "Catalina, *un poco de pollo para el Señor, por* favor."

"Would you care to smoke?" asked Rudolf, still with extreme courtesy, and extending a coroneted cigarette case, as Mr. Hawks piled his plate high again.

"Well, Mr. Lowe, I don't mind if I do, but if it's all the same to you I believe I'll have one of my own."

Mr. Hawks' right hand, which was ornamented with a massive carbuncle sun in the deep claws of a heavy gold ring, sought his waistcoat pocket with the dexterity of long practice. He extracted from this an enormous black cigar, bit off the end of it, spat this to the ground, and, when he had scraped up the last morsel of chicken, stuck the cigar, tip-tilted and still un-lighted, in the corner of his mouth as he continued his narrative.

"After we had seen everything in the Caterpillar Reel, crowns and jewel boxes and all," he went on, "the Bishop

145

took us to another church where there was a sweet pretty saint over the altar all dressed up in silk and satin and diamonds fit to go to the Governor's Ball. I couldn't tell you the name of——"

"It is the Virgin of the Angustias," interposed Rudolf, "a very precious and ancient relic."

"That's the word," agreed Mr. Hawks heartily. "Say, it makes you feel differently about graven images, as the Bible calls 'em, to see some of these statues here in Spain, now don't it? As if they couldn't be such a symbol of sin after all, like we've always been taught. They're so downright handsome, as you may say, and then the way the folks all feel about them. Why it—gets you somehow. That church was full of the best appearing women you'd care to see anywhere, kneelin' in front of that statue, with them lace veils of their halfway over their faces, but not so far but what you can judge what their looks are. It tickles me to see them fan 'emselves and cross 'emselves at the same time. They're pious, all right. But they got a way with 'em just the same. I wouldn't look to find many maiden ladies in Spain."

"No," said Rudolf, "there are not many. Except for those who enter the church, they nearly all marry."

"Rudolf means except those who become nuns," said Faith, noticing Mr. Hawks' look of bewilderment. Certainly, his expression seemed to say, those ladies whom he had seen worshipping before the *Virgen de la Anguistias* had entered a church, and yet he could not bring himself to believe that they were all spinsters.

"Oh," exclaimed Mr. Hawks with relief. "Well, when we come out of this church, we went across the park. To see the——"

"The Paseo?" asked Rudolf helpfully.

"That's the word. The pretty ladies that had just been praying. Walkin' up and down. Enjoyin' 'emselves. Easy, like at a church supper at home. The Bishop had to leave us when we went to the park, and so did some of the rest of his company—a Cardinal, one of them was, from To*leed*o, if I understood right. He was a pleasant-spoken man, too. So the Bishop turned Faith and me over to that younger brother of his, and say, I certainly took a liking to him. I couldn't get the hang of his title and all, so I asked him what his first name was, and that was easy. There's a young marble cutter—we've got quite a few of them in my state— named Sebastian, lives right across the street from me in Hinsboro, whose mother was born in Spain herself—yes, sir, right here in Granada. It was him give me the idea of coming here. He ain't old enough to vote yet, but he does con-

146

siderable work for me among the furriners just the same. I'll always know just where he stands. I kin see he's goin' to be a stiddy supporter of mine. So I told this brother of the Bishop about my young Spanish friend at home, and asked him if it would be all right if I just called him Sebastian too. And what do you think he did? He said he'd been hoping I would, and by golly! He asked me what *my* first name was!"

"Sebastian is not without tact," conceded Rudolf.

"He asked me what I'd like to do next, and I said that if it was all the same to him I'd like to do a little shopping. I've been wanting to pick out a present for Myra, that's my married daughter you know, and it's kind of hard when you get into a store and just point, and someone starts spouting a stream of something you can't make head nor tail of. So Sebastian said of course, we'd go to an——"

"*Antiquario's,*" said Faith.

"That's the word. I didn't quite like the sound of it. I was kinder afraid it would be four-posters and things like that we've got rid of lately in Hinsboro. We have nice brass beds in almost every house now, Mr. Lowe, modern plumbing and steam heat too—Well, as I was saying, Sebastian took us to a store that looked outside as if it was just full of junk, but when we got in there, if he didn't ferret out some of the most elegant ornaments I ever clapped my eyes on. I bought Myra a breastpin which I bet will tickle her just to pieces. I never would'a found it if it hadn't been for Sebastian."

"I am very glad you have secured just what you wished as a gift for your daughter," Rudolf observed.

"And then," broke in Faith, "after we had been to the *antiquario's*—tell Rudolf what we did then!"

"Say, that was the greatest treat of all, warn't it? Sebastian asked us if we'd like to go to the gypsy quarter. Up on the——"

"The Sacro Monte——" prompted Faith excitedly.

"That's the word. You see, Mr. Lowe, we were just coming out of the store I told you about, when one of these gypsy fellows—dressed just like a postal card, if you'll believe it—come up and spoke to Sebastian. An old man, it was. They seemed real pleased to see each other."

"It was Mariano, the King of the Gypsies," exclaimed Faith, unable to restrain her enthusiasm for another moment, "He's an old dear. He has gray side-whiskers, and the most wonderful teeth. And, as Mr. Hawks says, he was in full regalia. Sebastian has known him ever since he was a little boy. He—Mariano, I mean—used to clip Sebastian's poodle. We all walked up the hill to the caves together. It was very steep and very dusty, but that was part of the fun, and the road had prickly pear hedges all along it. Mr. Hawks and I had never seen any before. Had we, Mr. Hawks? Or caves with people living in them?"

"There's more than prickly pears and caves I'd never seen before," chimed in Mr. Hawks. "Say, some of them gypsy dances—Well, I don't know as they'd go too well for entertainment at the Annual Church Supper. I don't know as I'll describe 'em too carefully in Hinsboro. Of course I'll tell Sebastian I seen 'em, I mean the marble-cutter Sebastian. But Lord! His mother's seen 'em too! And she's probably told him herself. I should think it would'da been kind'a a wrench for her to come away to a place like Hinsboro after she'd lived near the gypsy quarter in Granada. Well, they certainly are cute. The gypsy girls, I mean. But I kinda think the one that told fortunes was the cutest of all. And say, Mr. Lowe—what do you s'pose she told your wife?"

"I cannot imagine," said Rudolf rather formally.

"That's right, you can't. Not in a million years. Of course she strung Faith along with the usual stuff—Told her a tall dark man was going to enter her life, etc. Gypsies always pull that line, don't they? Of course that was bunk, because I don't know when I've seen a more light-complected feller than you are, Mr. Lowe. No offense, I hope. Honest, I mean it as a compliment. But that gypsy couldn't seem to let go of Faith. She clung onto her like a leech. And Sebastian, who was translating for us, said after he'd told us about the tall dark man—he told us that twice—that Chiquita —Chiquita was the name of this cute gypsy—thought Faith had the strangest hand she'd ever read."

"Indeed!" said Rudolf more formally still.

Mr. Hawks was unconscious of the increasing chill of the atmosphere. He pulled his tip-tilted cigar, now considerably chewed, out of his mouth at last, lighted it with a flourish, and leaned across the table, thumping it with his free hand.

"Chiquita told us," he said, his voice thumping too, "that she saw all kinds of terrible things hovering around Faith. Death, for instance—violent death! More than one kind! She made me think about that line I've heard somewhere, 'battle, murder and sudden——' "

"You must excuse me," said Rudolf, rising and drawing himself up very straight. "But this is fantastic. It is not seemly to dwell on a gypsy's raving."

"Well, they're weird," said Mr. Hawks, rising too, though with obvious reluctance, "but it kind'a gets you. It wasn't all this talk about death that got me so much though, as what Chiquita said about violence generally. 'Violent storms, violent conflicts, violent passions. Violence of every sort,' she kept repeating."

"Mr. Hawks! I am very sorry, but——"

"But in the end," persisted the unquenchable Mr. Hawks, "but in the end, Chiquita said, Faith would 'triumph.' She even said Faith would become famous! 'Very famous and great! In a way no woman ever has before!'" He fairly shouted the prophecy which Rudolf had not been able to silence. "*In a way no woman has before!*" Now, Mr. Lowe, I ask you! What do you suppose this cute gypsy meant when she said that?"

Chapter XIX

MR. HAWKS' visit which in the beginning, had seemed to Rudolf like a reprieve, seemed, long before it was finished, like a nuisance and an imposition.

The Yankee's enthusiasm over Granada reached its culmination in his detailed description of the visit to Sacro Monte, upon which he insisted on dwelling at length, in spite of Rudolf's every effort to divert him. When his excitement had finally spent itself, and Rudolf began to feel that there were reasonable grounds of hope for his imminent departure, he settled himself so securely in his chair that he gave the impression of being lashed to it, bit off the end of another cigar, and embarked on an exposition of the complicated and corrupt conditions of politics in Hinsboro, and the measures which, in his opinion, would remedy this.

To Rudolf's amazement, Faith, instead of being bored and puzzled by this recital, listened to it not only with rapt attention but with evident comprehension. The mysteries of "wards," "bosses," "machines," "gangs," "lobbying," and "plums," would, he should have supposed, be as tedious and baffling to her as they were to him. Instead, she drank in every word that Mr. Hawks spoke with avidity, and moreover revealed by her own questions and comments, and instinctive understanding of what he was saying that the actually startling. He was almost aggrieved at the facility with which his unsophisticated bride, whose naïveté was a source

149

of disturbance to him, mastered the intricacies of a maze which he himself could not disentangle.

It was when Mr. Hawks began a minute account of the career of an obscure young politician named Neal Conrad, a fellow member of his on the City Council of Hinsboro, that Rudolf, realizing he was growing sleepy, feared he would not be able to conceal his drowsiness. It was inconceivable to him that Faith could be really thrilled by hearing that this small town lawyer, without background or distinction, whom Mr. Hawks seemed to feel so certain would eventually become governor of his state and very likely "go even further," had a pretty young wife named Anne to whom everybody in Hinsboro had "taken a liking," though she was the product of a worthless farm "out back of Hamstead." But Faith was intrigued by Mr. Hawks' accounts of Anne's perfect housekeeping, and of her triumphs at fortnightly meetings of the Woman's Pansy Club. She was eager to hear all about the Conrads' "cute kids." She wished . . .

Rudolf gathered himself together with a start. So he *had* gone to sleep after all! Faith's light touch on his shoulder, gentle as it was, jerked him back with the suddenness of a shock from the somnolence into which he had drifted. Mr. Hawks was actually taking his leave, taking it sociably and slowly, but really taking it, and as a host, Rudolf had been remiss. He had not been on the alert to speed the parting guest with courtesy. Faith had been obliged to rouse him. Even if Mr. Hawks had remained oblivious to his negligence, Faith had not, and though Rudolf knew she would never refer to it, the fact that she was aware of it would always rankle. Besides, to-day of all days such a perception on her part was especially inopportune.

"Don't forget," Mr. Hawks was saying with heartiness, "that my latch-string's out and my spare-room bed's made up. Of course you'll be coming over soon to stay a spell at your own house, Faith, but it'd be convenient, mebbe, while you was getting settled and all, if you boarded out. —Well, Mr. Lowe, it certainly has been nice to meet you. I don't know when I've passed a pleasanter evening and that's a fact."

"But you'll come again, Mr. Hawks, before you leave Granada?" asked Faith hopefully. There was no possible doubt of it; she was almost pleading with this oaf to repeat his visit. It was with immense relief that Rudolf heard him declining her invitation.

"Say, I'd love to, Faith, and that's a fact. But I gotter get back. I don't like the look of things in Hinsboro, and they're liable to go from bad to worse unless I shove in somewheres. So I'll push along in the mornin'. But you'll be comin' to see me pretty soon. Don't you forget that."

He patted her on the arm. Rudolf saw that the gesture was meant to be encouraging, reassuring, even as well as affectionate. She put up her face and kissed him, as she might have kissed a favorite uncle from whom she was regretfully taking leave.

"Leopoldo and Leonardo will drive you to your hotel," she said, with the air of a chatelaine dealing with a social situation capably and with satisfaction, "and come back here at half-past nine to-morrow morning to take Rudolf and me into the Palace. Sebastian explained everything to them carefully. But of course Rudolf and I will come out to the carriage with you and see you safely in it before we say good-bye."

Beginning to wonder if he were, after all, thoroughly awake, Rudolf followed Faith and Mr. Hawks into the outer patio. In the dim light Felipe was revealed, sunk forward in a straight-backed chair and sleeping profoundly. A glistening new carriage, with red wheels and a ducal coronet emblazoned on its doors, to which a span of superb horses was attached, stood at the entrance. And on the driver's seat, in positions of comfortable relaxation, a coachman and a footman attired in gorgeous livery, were slumbering side by side. Faith waked first Felipe and then the man on the box, and Rudolf saw that she was doing it in much the same way that she had touched him, as unobtrusively as possible, instead of uttering the curt rebuke which they deserved for their lapse from alert attendance, and which a German *Hausfrau* would certainly have administered—though of course in the case of well-trained German servants no such a lapse would ever have occurred. He sensed too the joyous quality of the instant response to her summons—in some subtle way she had succeeded in making Felipe not only her respectful servant but her willing slave, in spite of her lack of aloofness and the gentleness of her rule. And it was evident that the mysterious new members of the retinue, whose sudden appearance on the scene was so far unexplained, were equally eager to meet her wishes with alacrity. She had proved *simpatica* to these humble Andalusians, and that she could not understand their language was of secondary importance, since she understood their psychology.

The dazzling carriage spun swiftly around, with Leopoldo cracking his beribboned whip, and Mr. Hawks waving his hat and cheering as it disappeared from sight; Felipe swung the heavy doors of the outer patio together, shot the iron bolts, and murmuring, *"Beunas noches, Señores,"* faded noise-lessly away, his lantern flickering like a firefly beside him. It was, Rudolf reflected with repugnance, like a scene in an opéra bouffe. For the first time, as Faith slipped her arm through his, though a little piercing thrill stabbed through his body as she pressed against him, it was he that with-drew himself from her.

"Perhaps you will be good enough to tell me the meaning of all this," he said formally.

"Mr. Hawks was a friend of my father's. We used to vis-it at his house when I was a little girl. And, as he told you, he is a friend of Mr. Castle's too. He was a very poor boy —almost a waif—I've heard him say himself that he was just a mongrel puppy that no one wanted around and that no one quite had the heart to put out of its misery. Isn't it wonderful that he has fought his way up to success?"

"It's no doubt commendable," said Rudolf stiffly, "but he is a very uncouth person. I was amazed to see you treat him as if he were a social equal."

"But Rudolf, he manufactures splendid pencils, and he is a great political power."

"In Hinsboro," said Rudolf contemptuously. "However, I do not suppose we are likely to see him again, so there is no reason why we should argue about him at this hour of the night. I should, however, like to have you tell me where this gaudy victoria which seems to be at your disposal has come from?"

"It goes with the *caseria,*" said Faith readily. "It was waiting for us when we came down from Sacro Monte. Se-bastian apologized for his oversight in not sending it out before. He had had so much on his mind, he said, that he entirely forgot it had gone into Granada for repairs, and had not been returned here before our arrival. He said there was really no excuse for such negligence on his part, and he was dreadfully chagrined over it, but that he hoped we would be charitable and forgive him."

"Faith!" exclaimed Rudolf in exasperation, "are you really such an ingenue? The two jackanapes on the box were probably supernumeraries on Gabriel's staff—he has so many retainers that he could easily spare any number at a moment's notice. But that carriage is brand-new. The paint on the coat-of-arms is not even dry yet. Sebastian must have contrived to buy and equip the victoria this very after-noon. I cannot imagine how or when—"

"He did not go with us to the Capilla Real," said Faith still readily, "he joined us later at the Paseo. If the carriage is really new perhaps he bought it while we were in the church."

"Of course he did! As an intimation that your behavior in visiting the Palace as you did was highly incorrect, but that if you were determined to run around the countryside unescorted, family pride demanded that at least you should do it with some show of dignity."

For a moment Faith stood very still. Then she spoke with a serenity which was somehow more disquieting to Rudolf than a sharp rejoinder would have been.

"I honestly do not believe that is the way Sebastian felt about my coming to the Palace, Rudolf. He and Gabriel both seemed very glad to see me. Perhaps they do not look at everything quite as you do. For instance, they liked Mr. Hawks, and you do not. But I do think possibly Sebastian suddenly realized—if he did buy the carriage this afternoon—that it would be convenient for us to have one here, especially since I am to go in to the Palace every day for lessons. You have said yourself that he is very generous— very generous, and when he wishes, very gracious. I think he felt that he was making a generous and gracious gesture in offering us the carriage."

Rudolf did not answer.

"Sebastian seemed much happier to-day than when we saw him in Madrid," Faith went on after a short pause, "something like a boy off on a vacation. Laughing himself and making the rest of us laugh too—just over trifles, but it was great fun. And he joined in the gypsy dances, and did them much better than any of the *gitanos* themselves, even the most intricate steps and movements, he is so lithe and quick. The gypsies seemed to adore having him with them, and he had a wonderful time himself. He kept scattering money around, and that was like a little boy too, a little boy squandering his allowance on candy and marbles. He gave gold pieces to Mariano and Chiquita and pesetas to the others, joking with them all the time and kissing them all good-bye when they went away. And I must show you what he bought for me at the *antiquario's*. He said that every bride who came to Granada should have Granada lace, and that every bride who came to Spain should have a fan, and a shawl and a mantilla and a high carved comb for pres-ents——"

"From her husband!"

"But Rudolf, we have been here two weeks and you have not even suggested buying any of them for me! Sebastian asked me whether you had, and when I said no, he told me he felt much better—that if a methodical German could be

153

capable of an inadvertence, a Spaniard who did not even
aspire to system might be forgiven one. Especially as he was
eager to make atonement."

"Did Sebastian mean that he was eager to atone for negligence on his own part or did he wish to infer that he was
eager to atone for it on mine?"

"Why—both, I suppose, in a way! Anyway, he bought
me the lace, and a fan, and the shawl, and the mantilla,
and the comb, and a few other trifles, besides arranging
about the carriage. Do come in and look at my lovely presents, Rudolf! I heaped them on the table in the *salita* when
I came home. I want to show them to you."

"I do not wish to see them," said Rudolf stiffly. "It is
very late and I am very tired. I have had a most fatiguing
day. I have not been frittering away my time with gypsies
and *antiquarios*. I have been doing constructive work."

"What did you construct?" inquired Faith with interest.

She asked the question affectionately. Unsuspicious of the
way in which he had actually spent his afternoon, she could
not guess how embarrassing it would be to him. The vagueness and brevity with which he answered hurt her self-
respect, already bruised, more deeply still. She felt not only a
worshipful pride but an intelligent concern in his career. It
wounded her to be treated as if she were prying into matters which were beyond her grasp and outside her sphere.
Besides, her joy over her new possessions was blighted because Rudolf would not share it. Evidently he was very tired
—tired and annoyed, though his vexation could not be deeply
disquieting to himself, for he was asleep before Faith was
ready for bed, as he had been on the train. But she knew
that now his desire was submerged in displeasure instead of
tenderness, for he had not even kissed her good-night; and
for the first time since they reached the *caseria*, there had
been no passionate prelude to slumber.

Lying wakeful beside him, her thoughts tumultuous, her
body tense, she knew that the night had marked a subtle
change in their relationship which was as ominous as it was
crucial—a change which would perhaps have been inevitable sooner or later in any case, but which had been
precipitated by forces which she could neither control nor
comprehend. Instead of finding peace in the respite from
her husband's urgency, she discovered in it new sources of
agitation. If this bond of the flesh, which she had at first
resisted and to which she had since succumbed so utterly,
weakened between them, what would hold her to him?
Only the loyalty she had so vaunted in Venice, for as was
so poignantly apparent, the mental and spiritual bonds be-

154

tween them were so fragile that they might snap at any moment!

Faith had dismissed the forebodings which had inspired Victoria Luise with such prophetic dread from her mind with the same serenity with which she had declined to be swayed by them; now suddenly they surged back into her throbbing consciousness. Were they already verging on fulfillment? A horror lest they were swept over her, for, with their onrush, the impediments to perfection in the communion of marriage, which she had so firmly believed existed only in the imagination of the Archduchess, rose relentlessly before her. She had felt wholly self-reliant that morning, when she had retorted to Rudolf's reproof with such level scorn. But the situation with which, in the daylight and sunshine, she had been so confident that she could cope, took on a sinister aspect in these dark watches. Certainly she* was frustrated, and distraught with perplexity, she wondered how she could make good her boast that she could face frustration without fear. For she was trembling, trembling before that menacing future which she saw must hold in store for her a succession of "insuperable barriers" which she had only just begun to glimpse. How could she contend that she was not afraid, when she was shaking from head to foot with terror, when her very teeth were chattering with it?

In her anguish, loneliness as well as fear engulfed her, and she yearned for the reassurance that comes with tangible tenderness. If she stretched out her arms to Rudolf, if he waked to find himself encircled with them, her head against his shoulder, her tears falling on his breast, surely he would divine the depth of her dependence on him, of the despair she would feel if he failed her! Surely he would comfort her through this desperate hour by convincing her that he cherished her for all time! Surely his sensibility to her need and her happiness must be greater than it appeared! Surely he could not be so alien to her in thought, in outlook and in standards as he had seemed increasingly ever since their marriage, and most of all throughout the portentous day that had terminated in this calamitous night! Surely there was somewhere between them a neutral ground on which they could meet without misunderstanding and without conflict, some pleasant place where peace prevailed! Surely since he had wanted her to be his wife so much that he had overcome obstacles that seemed unsurmountable before their marriage, he could overcome the obstacles that now arose, even if she could not! Surely since he had honored her by raising her to his high estate, by giving her his proud name, by taking her with him into the exalted sphere which was his natural habitat but which had not previously been hers, he would not withhold his confidence or fail in fostering solicitude!

She turned toward him, searching in the darkness for his hand, and when she had found it, locking her taut fingers between those which lay relaxed at his side. Almost instantly she felt a responsive pressure, light at first, but gradually growing firm and hard.

"Rudolf," she said breathlessly.

It seemed to her that her very soul cried out to him as she whispered his name. If he failed her in this supreme moment, she knew she would never call on him again.

He too had turned. She had crept so close to him that he did not even need to draw her to him, and his arms closed, like bands of steel, around her quivering body.

"I knew!" he murmured triumphantly. "I knew that if I waited you would ask my forgiveness. All day you have rebelled against my judgment and my authority; but I was sure that when you thought of your defiance through the long night, remembrance of it would distress and grieve you, that you would be repentant. *Liebe* Faith, I do forgive you, freely and fully! We will never speak of this defiance again, for I know you will never be guilty of it again! Hereafter you will always yield to my will!"

His voice, low as it was, vibrated with the same exultation that a Roman soldier might have felt after subduing a proud and beautiful Greek captive.

Chapter XX

IT was early nine o'clock before Rudolf woke the following morning. There was not time to have breakfast served on the terrace before starting into Granada. So he ordered Catalina to bring it immediately to Faith's room instead, and pending her somewhat leisurely interpretation of his command, bathed and shaved hastily, returning, with a dressing gown of dark corded silk knotted around him, to drink his coffee with his wife.

"It has just occurred to me," he said with a trace of concern in his voice, "that as Gabriel is receiving us in formal audience, you should wear a black dress of rather conservative cut. I do not suppose you own such a garment."

Faith, who had risen too, and was sitting in front of her toilet table brushing her hair, answered him calmly.

"Oh, yes, I have. Your mother told me that I should need one. It is made of that new material called georgette crêpe, and trimmed with fine tucks and little plaited ruffles. It is what the *grand couturiers* call *une petit robe très chic mais très discrète.*"

"I should prefer that you should not speak French to me, Faith, when you can avoid it."

"*Es ist ein sehr nettes Kleidchen,*" she said with equal tranquility.

"I am relieved. But as this is Spain, that is not all you require. You should wear a mantilla instead of a hat."

"Yes, I know. Well, as I told you last night, I have that too. I am so glad Sebastian thought of giving it to me yesterday.—Shall I pour out your coffee? We have not much time."

As she took her place beside him in the new victoria, her appearance was, he admitted to himself with satisfaction and complacency, highly conventional, and—he reflected with more satisfaction and less complacency—distractingly charming. The correct and exquisite dress had been cut by a master hand; it fitted Faith's budding figure like a sheath. Her hair shone like burnished gold through her filmy mantilla. Rudolf decided not to compliment her, lest it should give her an exaggerated idea of the attractions with which she had adorned adequacy.

"I have been giving Leopoldo and Leonardo a piece of my mind while I have been waiting for you to come out," he remarked instead. "I do not think they will ever go to sleep again while they are on duty."

"We must try to set them a good example," replied Faith.

He shot a furtive glance at her direction. Was she intimating that a master who went to sleep himself in the presence of a guest was hardly a pattern to hold up to a somnolent servant? But her fact and manner were so composed that he decided she must have been speaking at random; and the decorum and dignity with which she conducted herself throughout the audience gratified him intensely. No one, watching her as it progressed, could have devined that this was the first time that she had knelt before an enthroned ecclesiastic and kissed an Episcopal ring; and the grace with which she rose from her knees, and stood with slightly bent head and clasped hands before the Archbishop while he pronounced a few words of pastoral counsel was appealing. Even after Gabriel himself had signified that the audience was to close without further ceremony, by leaning forward and laying one hand lightly on her hair, smiling as he did so, she did not commit the blunder of glancing up too quickly with a responsive smile.

"I think," Gabriel said with the slight whimsicality which had drawn Faith to him the day before, "that it is time for us to resume the rôle of relatives.—Since you have broken in on your régime of study to-day in any case, Rudolf, why do you not take Faith for a short stroll through the Alhambra? It is always cool in the more sheltered chambers. Afterwards you might bring her back here for an early lunch with me, and when we have eaten, we will talk with Father Constantino about her schedule. I think, all in all, that would make a pleasant program."

Rudolf was half afraid that Faith would burst out with an impetuous acceptance before he could reply. He decided, if she did, that he would immediately decline for them both. But though he paused for a moment before speaking again, she pleased him by standing silent and motionless until he answered.

"Thank you. I know you understand how important it is that I should not neglect my work long or often, but as you say, I have already broken into my schedule for to-day. I shall be very pleased to remain. Especially as it is very important that Faith should also get started in her studies."

Except for the fact that Leopoldo and Leonardo were again discovered sound asleep on their box when he and Faith emerged from the Palace to visit the Alhambra, and once more when they left it for the *caseria*, nothing happened all day to mar Rudolf's complacency. He knew the history of the Alhambra thoroughly; and he expounded this to Faith all the time they were walking from the Court of the Lions to the Tower of the Two Sisters, and back again, while she listened with an attentive interest which was delightful. Their luncheon, at which Sebastian was not present, was most agreeable. Gabriel suavely explained that his brother had suddenly changed his plans and decided to visit his friend Don Jaime de los Rios, in Malaga, for a time, instead of remaining in Granada. He had gone off on horseback early that morning and no date had been set for his return—he would probably be gone several weeks. He had left greetings for Faith and Rudolf, and hoped they would excuse his absence. Rudolf said, very gravely, that they would be glad to do so, and turned his attention to Father Constantino, who had been included in Gabriel's invitation. It was evident from the priest's scholarly conversation, that he would make an ideal teacher for Faith; it was arranged that she should have a daily lesson at ten o'clock, and she was given some books to take home with her, so that she might begin to study without delay. Yes, it was all eminently satisfactory. Rudolf, returning to his tome on the right of neutral nations for a couple of hours before tea-time, found that he could not draw up the outline for his thesis competently and quickly, and because increasingly certain that the disturbing interlude of the day before had, after all, been a blessing in disguise, since it had been so beneficent in its results.

· · · · · ·

As the golden days flowed on, this sense of beatitude deepened. He was no longer dominated by the driving passion, which, during the first fortnight at the *caseria*, had proved so insatiable that he had begun to wonder whether it would ever be slaked. He had been like a ravenous man perpetually seeking repletion but perpetually rising, still unfilled, from a feast. Not until that supreme hour of exultation, when Faith had turned to him in the darkness, had he drunk deep enough from the fathomless cup of desire to drain it to its last drop. Now at last his senses had steadied themselves; intellect was no longer obscured by ecstasy; the student was no longer submerged in the sensualist. He was the master of his own mind and his own emotions, even as he was the master of his own house.

There were no further interruptions to his long hours of work in the library; a few more Spanish kinsfolk called, but when they did so before tea-time, Faith dealt with them alone and competently at the moment, and their visits were returned at his convenience; an exchange of dinner invitations did not disturb him, since he seldom cared to devote his evenings to research. His concentration bore rapid results; and a few days after he had dispatched his report to the German Embassy in Madrid, he came up on the terrace, where Faith was bending over her own books, holding a letter high above his head.

"I have good news, *liebe* Faith!" he exclaimed. "Felipe has just come in with the post, and in it is a communication from our Ambassador. He praises the thesis I sent him very highly—indeed he is so pleased with it that he suggests prolonging my stay here for an extra month, in order that I may continue my research undisturbed, along the same lines. You would be glad to remain at the *caseria*, would you not?"

"Very," said Faith closing her grammar. "And I am so glad, Rudolf, that the Ambassador is pleased with your report! I felt sure he would be!"

"But if we do stay on, it will be necessary for me to go to Madrid at once to receive further instructions and assist at a brief conference. Indeed, the Ambassador's letter is both a commendation and a summons. I have sent Felipe back to Granada to see if he can secure a compartment on the express to-morrow, and I have also given him a telegram to dispatch to *Tia* Carlota telling her to expect us, in case I obtain it."

"Do you really wish me to go with you?" Faith inquired.

"But certainly! Can you imagine that I would leave you here all alone? Why do you ask so strange a question, *Liebchen?*"

He saw that she hesitated for a moment before replying, and the idea that she was choosing her words carefully did not altogether please him.

"I thought that perhaps you would not think it was best that my lessons should be interrupted, merely because you had to go to Madrid. I know how eager you are that I should make progress."

"But you *are* making progress, wonderful progress! And the interruption would be for only a few days. Besides, you could take your books with you."

"I suppose I could," she said rather listlessly. Then, with increasing hesitation, she went on, "Really, Rudolf, I should not be lonely, staying here all by myself. I should enjoy it."

"You would enjoy a separation from me?"

"That is not just what I meant——"

"Then I cannot imagine what you did mean. And I should not enjoy a separation from you at all. Nor shall I consent to one."

"Very well," she said more listlessly still. "Perhaps I had better go and start packing then." She rose slowly, and as she did so, Rudolf noticed that she was very pale and that she swayed a little.

"Faith!" he exclaimed. "What is the matter with you? Are you ill?"

She reseated herself, stretching out her hands on either side of her as if for support.

"I think I must be," she said with evident effort, "I did not mean to bother you by telling you about it, Rudolf, but these last few days I have not felt at all well. That is why I would rather not take a long hot journey just now. This morning my head ached so that I could hardly see, and I was so dizzy during my lesson that I only half understood what Father Constantino was saying to me. When I started to leave the Palace I—I fainted. I never did before, and it

160

would have frightened me, rather, if Gabriel hadn't been so kind. Father Constantino called him at once, and when I came to myself, I was lying on a long divan in Gabriel's own study and he was leaning over to lay a cold cloth on my forehead. I never shall forget how good it felt or how gentle his hands were. Afterwards he gave me something cloudy to drink—aromatic ammonia in water I think he said it was—and sat beside me until I was better. It was nearly an hour before he would let me get up again, and then he came out to the *caseria* with me. He told me not to disturb you, because he knew you were studying."

"But Faith, I am much disturbed because you are not well! Of course if you are not able to travel—but I must go, and if you grew worse while I was away, what would you do?"

"I am sure Catalina would take splendid care of me. Gabriel told her, before he left, what had happened at the Palace, and she has been simply sweet to me all day. Sweeter than ever, I mean. Of course she is always a dear!"

Faith smiled faintly at the pleasant reminiscence of Catalina's attitude.

"Gabriel told Leopoldo and Leonardo too," she said, "and cautioned them that we must come out here 'with moderate velocity.' I love the way Spaniards express themselves, don't you, Rudolf? There is no end to their elegance of speech. Leopoldo is a dear too. When he was thoroughly awake— he was asleep, as usual, when Gabriel began to talk to him— he said '*Sanctissimma Maria!*' and kept on saying it, smiling to himself and walking the horse all the way to the *caseria*. —Did you know that he and Leonardo were twins, Rudolf?"

"No," said Rudolf, "I have had no occasion to be concerned with their relationship. But I am much concerned over your health. If you are not much better to-morrow morning, we will dismiss all thought of your going to Madrid, and I will hasten back here as quickly as I can. I shall miss you very much, *Liebchen*, if I am forced to leave you; but I do believe that Catalina will wait on you faithfully.—Did Gabriel speak of sending for a doctor?"

"He spoke of it; but he said he did not think it was necessary."

"He has probably seen such attacks before, as a result of the climate, and knows they are not serious."

"Probably," agreed Faith, "I am sure they do not amount to much."

·   ·   ·   ·   ·

But when morning came she was so much worse that it

was obvious she could not lift her head from her pillow, much less get up and prepare for a journey. She set aside her coffee with aversion, pressed her hands against her throbbing throat, and then sank into a state of stupor, from which she roused herself only occasionally and with evident effort. Felipe had secured the compartment, and Faith, though visibly disinclined to talk, agreed instantly if drowsily that Rudolf should not alter his plans on her account. The chances were that she would be all right again in a day or two.

"If you are not better in the morning," Rudolf said, "I should prefer that Felipe should fetch a doctor. I will send a note to Gabriel, telling him you are not able to come in to your lesson to-day, and asking him to recommend one."

"Very well," murmured Faith indifferently.

"Is there anything I can do for you before I leave?"

"No, thank you."

"Are you sure?"

"I should like a cold cloth on my head again. I have told Catalina to bring one. I do not seem to want anything else—just to be very quiet—not to move or think or speak."

She turned away and closed her eyes. She had not actually said, "I want to be alone," but her gesture revealed her unspoken wish.

"But Faith! I cannot go away without kissing you farewell!"

For a moment she did not stir. Then she lay back, both shoulders resting on her high pillow, her eyes still closed. Rudolf slid one arm underneath her to lift her to him, and with his free hand raised her face to the level of his own. She did not resist him at all; but there was no vitality in the pliancy of her body; and in spite of the molten heat of the day her lips and fingers were cold. As he laid her back on her pillows, he did so with a sensation of having embraced a statue, which, unlike Pygmalion, he had not succeeded in animating with his own ardor.

Really disquieted, he stood looking down at her uncertain whether to leave her after all. But her lethargy was so profound that she did not even seem to be aware of his presence; and at last, focusing his mind on the significance of the summons he had received, he went quietly out of the room and downstairs to his waiting carriage. In his anxiety, he even forgot to rebuke Leopoldo and Leonardo as he waked them. Felipe, who had carried down his bags for him and disposed them in the victoria, returned, after watching his master with apparent respect out of sight, and told Catalina of the omission, smiling broadly as he did so.

"His journey will be an atrocity in this heat," said Catalina with dark satisfaction, *"Madre de Dios!* When has there been so burning a day!"

"I fear that it will end in a storm. There are great clouds gathering."

"It would clear the air. But the thunder would disturb the *Baronesa* and the lightning might frighten her."

"I do not think so. She is a lady not easily frightened. But she needs sleep."

"Es verdad. What man ever let his wife sleep in peace during the *luna de mielo?"* asked Catalina contemptuously, as if in wholesale condemnation of the male race. "Now that she is rid—*gracios à Dios!*—of this German husband of hers, the *Baronesa* can have her sleep out. Afterwards she will feel better."

All through the torrid afternoon, Catalina plodded back and forth at frequent and regular intervals between the kitchen and Faith's bedroom, each time returning to inform Felipe that the *Baronesa* still slept, that so far she had not even stirred. But as the smoldering clouds, closing in over the brazen sky, plunged the *caseria* into premature darkness, Catalina reported a change.

"I carried a candle into her room, shielding it with my hand and looked at her closely. There is a little color in her face again and she has moved. She lies relaxed at least. This morning she frightened me, she was so still and white. She looked like a sheeted saint in a sepulcher."

Catalina interrupted herself to join Felipe in making the sign of the cross. As she did so, a bolt of lightning, followed by a terrific explosion, zig-zagged violently across the menacing heavens; and as if released by the flood-gates which it had torn open in its wild flight, torrential sheets of rain descended like an avalanche. The onrush of the elements had come with such swift frenzy, that though they had been waiting for it all day, Catalina and Felipe stood for an instant stupefied by it; and as a second crash of thunder rent the supercharged atmosphere and reverberated along the black horizon, the sound of a galloping horse coming closer and closer over the cobblestones rang out above the storm.

"Someone is going to try for shelter here!" shrieked Catalina. "Whoever it is, do not let him in! It might well be the devil himself, riding through the darkness!" She sank on her knees, under the shelter of the *galeria.* Felipe, no less terrified, crouched beside her. As the heavy knocker hammered against the door of the outer patio, and the shouting of a man rose above it, they hid their faces and screamed.

163

Then they were conscious that someone else was calling, calling calmly but imperiously.

In the first grip of their superstitious fright they had momentarily forgotten even the lady of their loyal devotion. Now, as they opened their eyes and looked across the patio, they saw, through the translucent rain, a shadowy white figure beckoning to them, and mistook it for an apparition. It was not until Faith had succeeded in making herself heard above the battering at the gate, the lashing water, and their own outcry, that they realized what it was.

"Felipe! Catalina!" she cried. "Shame on you! What do you mean by such behavior? Go at once and open the gate for your master! Do you not recognize Don Sebastian's voice?"

Chapter XXI

"Once, a long time ago, I went to visit a relative who was the Spanish Minister to Ecuador," Sebastian said. "We spent a good deal of our time at a country place not far from Quito, which had been put at his disposal by Ecuadorian friends. The Ecuadorians are great land lovers, just as we are. It is their Spanish heritage. Many of them have five or six estates, and spend most of their time in the country. This house where I stayed was built of pale blue stucco and had a red-tiled roof. It was long and rambling, with deep *galerias,* and it had frescos running along the outer walls, and a great bell that hung above the stone steps leading from one balcony to another. There were twenty rooms on each floor, all opening into each other with wide doors, and a splendid staircase. Really, it was charming. I was very happy there."

"It must have been beautiful.—What made you think of it just now?"

"I thought of the house because I thought of the garden, which was even more lovely."

"But, Sebastian, that is no answer at all! What made you think of the garden?"

"You did. Everything about the garden was beautiful: the little streams with rustic bridges curving over them, and the quiet pools where swans swam about, and the violets and orchids and the roses and forget-me-nots that bordered the

164

paths and extended in beds and clustered over the terraces. But the most beautiful thing of all in the garden was a waterfall that fell in smooth broad sheets over a background of lilies. It veiled them without concealing them." He paused for a moment and then said vibrantly, "When I came into the patio, and saw you on the *galeria*, with the rain streaming down between us, you looked to me like a lily shining behind a waterfall."

Faith did not answer at once. The storm was over, for it had spent itself almost as suddenly as it had descended, and she was seated opposite Sebastian at a little table which Catalina had placed near the fountain. She had told the old servant that she was sure Don Sebastian would want some tea as soon as he had shed his drenched garments and reclothed himself. And as she hastily dressed and wound up her hair, she was conscious of a craving for the steaming, fragrant drink herself. When she went downstairs again, and found that wine, cold ham and olives had been laid out beside a great loaf of bread, but there were no tea or biscuits in sight, she was disappointed and for a moment bewildered.

"I am sure I told Catalina tea," she said to Sebastian, who had entered the patio just then, his black hair still glistening with moisture, and clad in corduroy breeches, a soft white shirt open at the throat, and a wide red belt. "I don't know much Spanish yet, of course, but that is easy enough to say. And look what she has brought!"

Sebastian laughed. "I am afraid she was thinking of my taste rather than yours. The true Andalusian buys tea at a pharmacy, and uses it as a medicine for colds and colic! Catalina knows that I would always have ham and olives at six o'clock and wine at any hour rather than tea, if I were free to follow my preference. But of course you must have yours just the same. I hope you have usually been properly served?"

Faith assured him that she had. She thought it was rather touching, and told him so, that Catalina should have so instinctively reverted to her natural custom, in serving her real *patron*, that she had forgotten the habits of the temporary chatelaine of the *caseria*. But she drank her tea thirstily when it was finally brought to her and ate her biscuits with relish, listening with interest as she did so to the account Sebastian gave her of his visit to Malaga, while he consumed his ham and olives.

"It is a lovely city, *Señora*," he said. "And Jaime de los Rios, whom I visited there, has a delightful house. It is reached through a long avenue of royal palms, and there are innumerable great poinsettia trees and cutsard apples on the place, besides of course quantities of jasmine and roses and orange blossoms."

"I wish I could see it," said Faith eagerly.

"But you can, *Señora.* Any time you like. Jaime would be delighted to have you come there."

"Sebastian," asked Faith abruptly, "why do you always call me *Señora?* We are almost relatives, aren't we? Anyway, friends and 'kinsfolk' as you say here. All the other members of your family call me Faith. I have wondered why you don't?"

Sebastian hesitated. "Do you know the Spanish word for Faith?" he asked at length.

"No."

"It is Fidelidad."

"Fidelidad! Why, Sebastian, that sounds almost exactly like——"

"Felicidad. Yes. Now you see."

"But, Sebastian, the meaning is not at all the same!"

"Gabriel would tell you that it is. He believes that Faith and happiness are interwoven. But I have always known Felicidad to be without faith, and I doubt whether Fidelidad would grant me happiness."

His play on words confused her, and she sat silent for a moment. "But since we always talk in English," she suggested at length, "perhaps——"

"You really wish it?"

"Very much."

He reached across the small table, took her hand, and lifted it to his lips. *"A los pies de Usted,"* he said and stopped. "If I call you by your Christian name I shall claim the privilege of following the Spanish custom in such cases and using the term 'thou' also," he ended.

"Of course."

"A tus pies then. Do you know what it means?"

"Yes," said Faith readily. "It is a conventional expression of courtesy."

"Not when 'thou' is used. Then it has a more literal meaning. You know, Faith, do you not, that I am 'at your feet'?"

Something in his voice startled her a little, but when she looked at him, and saw the gentleness of his expression, she was reassured.

"You came over the road from Malaga to-day?" she asked, giving no direct answer to his question.

"Yes," he said following her lead without insistence. "I love to come over it, for it is one of the most picturesque in Spain. It takes you through high clefts in the mountains, and

166

deep gorges, which open into the fertile valleys where dates and grapes are cultivated. I stop along the way at the *ventorillos*—the roadhouses—for refreshment—when I am off on a holiday I always travel very simply. There is one *ventorillo* consisting of several arbors built up high on a hill, of which I am especially fond. I go there very often. To-day I lunched and rested there and found the whole place simply a mass of purple morning-glories."

"Oh, how gorgeous! Have you ever thought, Sebastian, that there is so much beauty in Spain—that it almost hurts?"

"Yes," he said softly, "very often.—Is it the beauty of Spain that has hurt you, Faith?"

Once more she looked at him with startled eyes, and once more was disarmed by the gentleness of his expression.

"What makes you think I have been hurt?" she asked, a shade too quickly. "I have not been well the last few days. But it is only the heat. I am always better toward evening, and this evening I am very much better. I have slept for hours and hours to-day, and I feel like a different person now."

"Faith, do you think I am blind? Can you imagine I will ever forget the look on your face when I entered the drawing-room that night in Madrid? Or when you came up Gabriel's steps that afternoon at Granada? Of course I know you have been hurt. But I do not think it has been the beauty of Spain that has hurt you. Is it?" And as she did not answer he went on, more gently still, "Will you not tell me about it, *querida?*"

"No," said Faith slowly. "There are some things we do not talk about to anyone."

"I have not offended you, have I? You must forgive me if I have. I do not mean to seem curious. It is only that I want to comfort you."

He took her hand again, this time without kissing it, and she let her fingers lie in his as she answered him.

"You do comfort me, Sebastian. And it is very easy for me to talk to you—so easy that perhaps I should be tempted to tell you secrets, whether it were right or not, if I did not have the feeling that you had guessed them all anyway! That makes it unnecessary, doesn't it—for me to say very much? Suppose you talk to me instead?"

It was then that he told her about the Ecuadorian garden. He was still holding the hand that he had taken when he asked her if he had offended her, and as he said, "You looked to me like a lily shining behind a waterfall!" he reached for the other hand also, and resting his elbows on the little table, leaned toward her above their interclasped fingers.

"But it was not only of a lily I thought," he said. "I thought of so many different manifestations of loveliness that I was confused. I thought of the Virgin in the Grotto at Lourdes, as I first saw her, very late one misty evening, when I was the only worshipper at her shrine. I thought of Juliet standing on her balcony, still unaware that Romeo was in her garden. I thought of Rapunzel of the golden hair. She let it down, do you remember——"

"Yes," exclaimed Faith excitedly. "Of course I remember! Oh, Sebastian, I am so glad that you read fairy tales! Because I believe that this is a magic house, and perhaps you can tell me if I am right. Is it?"

"I think it must be. Indeed, I have never doubted it," he said gravely.

"Tell me why you are so sure!"

"Because so many fairy stories have come true here."

"What kind of fairy stories, Sebastian?"

"Love stories. Shall I tell you about them, Faith?"

"You mean that people who have loved each other very much have been happy here together?"

"Yes. That is what I mean. One of my ancestors bought the *caseria* and built the *casita* for a——a lady he loved very much. A lady whom he could not marry."

"Why not?"

"He was married already. To a princess. They lived in the most beautiful palace in Seville, except the Alcázar. But they hated each other. It was here, in seclusion and simplicity, that he found real joy."

"And what finally happened?"

"Oh, finally the princess died. And he married the lady he loved. I told you it was a fairy story!"

A slight bitterness suddenly tinged his speech. But as if conscious that Faith was fascinated with the thought that he agreed with her about the magic qualities of the *caseria* he went on more lightly.

"Of course the family protested. But after all, it was necessary that he should have an heir, and the princess had never had any children, while the lady he loved had four."

"What was her name?"

"Doña Cecilia. Her three daughters, who were born before her marriage, entered convents. But fortunately her only son was legitimate. He was one of my great-grandfathers."

"And since then——"

"Since then the men of my family have always contrived to find sanctuary here with the women they have loved. It has been our refuge from the world, the flesh, and the devil."

168

"And you offered to give it to me!"

Faith's voice trembled as she spoke. Sebastian realized how deeply she was moved.

"I hoped very much that you would honor me by accepting it, *querida*. I was grieved when Gabriel told me you felt you could not, though I was interested and touched by the reason you gave for declining:—That you wanted to think of your own little house in America as your real home. But if you should ever reconsider, it would make me very happy. And you must not misunderstand what I have just told you. There is no stain of shame on the *caseria*. It has not been a bower for illicit intrigue. It has always been a sanctuary, as I said—it was a sanctuary for me to-day. It is true that Doña Cecilia was not married to my ancestor when he first brought her here. But she was not a light woman. She was a great lady. And my great-grandfather was the one love of her life, as she was of his. While in later years—" Sebastian stopped for a moment, and then went on very softly, "It was because my mother loved the place so much, Faith, that I wanted to give it to you, not merely lend it to you, as I have to so many others."

"Did—do you feel as if you could talk to me about her?"

"I feel that I cannot help talking to you about her. Her name was Christina, and no woman was ever better named. I think her spirit lives again in Gabriel. She and my father came here together when they were first married, and as long as she lived, after that, she never failed to spend part of every year here. Even when my father was Ambassador to England, it was here that they came for his leave of absense. My mother adorned any gathering, and was as much beloved in London as she was in Spain; but she was never dependent on courts and crowds for enjoyment; in fact she was happiest of all when she could live simply and in seclusion with her own family. I can remember, when I was a child, walking hand in hand with my father, beside the donkey on which she rode, when we went on little excursions together—I suppose you have been to the Carthusian Monastery?"

"No," said Faith, in a voice as hushed as his own.

"Really? I should have supposed—but never mind! Cartuja—the monastery—is only a mile from here. It has a very famous sacristy filled with chests and cupboards of inlaid tortoise shell, and mother-of-pearl, and ivory; and I never tired, when I was a little boy, of opening and shutting those countless glittering drawers. There is a statue of Saint Bruno in the church, which I loved. I know now that it is the work of the great artist, Alonso Canaso, but then I loved it

169

merely because Saint Bruno seemed to me such a very friendly saint."

"Tell me more," Faith urged as he paused.

"There is really nothing much to tell. It is just that I was so happy in those days and that I adored my mother so. On our way home from Cartuja, we sometimes stopped at the next *caseria* to this, where our olives were ground into oil, as we had no mill of our own. The mill was really very primitive. But to me it was intricate and exciting. And we were nearly always here for the harvest. We used to get up early in the morning to watch the grape-pickers at work. A great many extra helpers came in at that time, for we had only two old house servants here regularly, just as I do now. Nearly all the grapes were white, but there were always a few dark ones mixed in. I used to count the bunches of those. And I gorged myself on them so, as they came off the vines, that it is a wonder that I did not succumb from over-indulgence. I suppose the only reason I survived is because it is the good who die young!"

"Nonsense! You survived because your mother took good care of you, and watched you carefully to make sure that you really did not eat too much."

"*Querida,* you are right. No man ever had such a mother."

He sat so long seemingly absorbed in memories that Faith began to be afraid he would forget that he had not finished telling her about the harvest. But she did not like to break in on his pensive moods; and when he turned to her again, she was glad she had not, for she saw there were tears on his cheeks, though he took up his story calmly.

"Later in the day," he said, "the baskets, brimful, were brought up to the *casita*. Before the men emptied the grapes into the presses, they trod on them with their feet. It is a very old custom, and not at all dirty or unattractive as you might think. They washed themselves very thoroughly beforehand, and wore a special kind of sandals, called *alpargatas*. And of course they sang all the time they were working.—Some day, *querida,* would you like to see a harvest here?"

"Is it still like that? Could we watch the men trampling the grapes and listen to them singing?"

"Of course. And we could go to the Cartuja and the *caseria* of the olive mill—you on a donkey, and I walking beside you, and perhaps——"

He broke off abruptly.

"And perhaps what, Sebastian?"

"Nothing, *querida.*—Let us talk about Rapunzel again. You cannot think how instantly I thought of her when I

170

came into the patio and saw you standing, dressed all in white, with your hair falling over your shoulders. I had not seen you with it down before. But it looked exactly as I have been imagining it would ever since I met you. I am sure it is the most beautiful hair in all the world. I have been wondering—it is a great deal to ask, I know, but I have been wondering—if you would let me touch it?"

Without hesitation, Faith bent over. They were so close together that she could feel his breath on her face.

"I may touch it with my hand?"

"Isn't that what you wanted?"

He disengaged his fingers from hers, laid them lightly on her shining head, and then let them slip softly down on either side of the part which divided the glistening waves, until they met under her chin, tilting it up a little.

"Yes, that was what I wanted," he said slowly, "in part."

"In part?"

"I hoped—I suppose vainly—for a miracle. I hoped you would also let me touch it with my lips."

Their eyes were almost level with each other. Faith, gazing into his, saw through the dusk a wellspring of light rising in them. It reflected, though she did not know it, the wellspring of light in her own. As if in the clarity of two fountains swiftly mingled, her assent merged into his quest; and though the pressure of his lips against her brow was so light that the golden tendrils framing her forehead hardly quivered, almost instantaneously she became aware that they had both risen; that the table was no longer between them; that her arms were around his neck and his were around her waist; that her face was lifted and his bent; that his kiss no longer rested on her bowed head but on her upturned mouth; that all her being had been fused with his into a heavenly harmony.

How long they stood there, clasped against each other's hearts, Faith never knew. At last a tremor passed through Sebastian's frame, communicating itself to hers, and he released her, without abruptness and without haste, stooping to brush his hair against the hollow of her throat and letting his hand linger over hers. Then, as if he were fearful of breaking his spell unless he were silent, he stood looking at her with a dark luminous gaze of wonder.

"Sebastian!" she whispered breathlessly, "what have we done? What has happened to us?" Then as he still stood looking at her without speaking, "I did not know a kiss could be like that—so gentle and—so sweet!"

"Nor I," he answered simply, "I have kissed countless

women. But I have never kissed or been kissed like that before."

It did not seem to occur to him that Faith might shrink from the knowledge of the kisses that were so different from those which they had just exchanged. He spoke rather as if, after what had taken place, anything less than complete candor between them was unthinkable.

"But I do not understand—we were sitting on either side of the table and suddenly—was it you who moved or I?"

"We moved together, *querida,* impelled, at the same time, by the same force. What has happened is neither your doing nor mine. But the miracle for which I did not dare to hope has come to pass."

"And now—what are we going to do now?"

Sebastian smiled. Faith who had not seen his face radiant before, marveled that she had ever thought his face cynical and cruel for all its charm.

"I am not quite sure. I think perhaps we had better consult Gabriel, who is an authority on miracles. I am not. This is the first time I have ever caught a glimpse of one."

There was a ringing quality in his voice as unfamiliar as the light in his face. As he went on talking, it seemed to her that it became increasingly joyous.

"But I do not think we need to consult him immediately. Do you? At least not until we have sat down and talked the question over ourselves!"

He motioned toward the stone bench flanking the fountain; and when they had seated themselves, he put his arm behind her, without trying to draw her close to him, but as if he expected her to lean against him for comfort and support.

"Do you not think we might have dinner here, together, first?" he went on. "A little *fiesta,* all of our own, a sort of thanksgiving to celebrate the revelation of our miracle? That would give us time for a long discussion. And afterwards— The moon is beautiful to-night—Have you been to the Alhambra yet?"

"Yes," said Faith. "Gabriel suggested that Rudolf should take me there. We walked all through it one morning, and Rudolf told me its history. He——"

She stopped short. For the first time it came over her that Rudolf's absence had neither been questioned nor explained.

"Sebastian! We have both forgotten—about Rudolf! He was summoned to Madrid."

"Yes, I know," said Sebastian carelessly. "So he dragged you through the Alhambra in the burning sunshine and told you its history! It is just about what I should expect of him!

172

In a nation which describes sausages as delicatessen almost any incongruity may be looked for!"

"Sebastian!" said Faith severely, "I cannot let you speak in that way about Rudolf." She paused for a moment, and then went on, "I told you a little while ago that there were some things it was not loyal to discuss with anyone, and that anyway you guessed all my secrets, almost before I was conscious of them myself. But there is one thing that you do not seem to realize, and that I feel I ought to tell you: I wanted to marry Rudolf, just as much as he wanted to marry me. I thought, the moment I saw him, that he was a paragon. He looked to me as I think Saint Michael must have looked. He knows I felt that way about him. I have told him so."

"Oh!" said Sebastian with mild mockery, "You thought he looked like Saint Michael and you told him that! I can imagine how delighted he must have been! I think Rudolf has always rather pictured himself in that rôle, and to have you recognize him in the part must have been most gratifying to him. But now you have discovered that your idol's feet are clay, surely you may admit this—at least to me?"

"No," said Faith steadily.

He looked at her with unreluctant respect. "Very well," he said quietly. "I shall not again make the mistake of asking you to do so. But tell me, *querida*, when you met me—did I appear to you like a supernatural being also—the kind that is supposed to have cloven hoofs? I am sure Rudolf had prepared you for that by giving you a long list of my delinquencies."

Faith colored a little. "He was not very flattering," she said frankly, "but I am afraid I did not think—about delinquencies very long. Because almost immediately—as soon as I got over being angry with you for ridiculing Rudolf and for declining to take me to the Prado that first morning —I felt—so happy every time you came near me. I watched for you to come. It seemed to me as if I had been waiting for you always, and yet as if I had always known you. It is hard to keep delinquencies in mind when you feel like that about a person—as if you could not imagine what your life would be like if he did not have a part in it."

"Do not try to imagine," Sebastian, a slight huskiness blurring his ringing voice. "*Vida de mi vida*, can you guess what it means to have you say this to me? Oh, Faith—if I had only found you years ago."

"You have found me now," said Faith.

"Yes. I have found you now. That in itself should be miracle enough."

For a moment he seemed almost to forget her physical presence. She had to force herself to intrude on his silent immobility.

"You must let me finish what I started to say about Rudolf," she said resolutely. "Perhaps you do not know about the tragedy and the disgrace that lay between us. How much he was willing to forget and forgive in order to marry me."

"I know that his brother killed your mother," said Sebastian almost angrily. "The more such stories are hushed up the more they spread. But I should have said it was you who had a good deal to forgive and forget. I will not—ridicule Rudolf, since it pains you that I should do so. But neither will I permit you to speak as if he had condescended in marrying you."

"Perhaps we had better not talk about him any more just now," Faith said slowly, "except that I wish you would explain to me how you knew he had been summoned to Madrid."

"Does it matter? As far as that goes, how did you know I was calling to you through the storm?"

His savage look had melted in a smile. He seemed actually ready to jest with her, so unclouded did his happiness appear. But as he saw her face lose its serenity, his own became grave again.

"*Alma de mi alma,* do not look so startled! You dreamed about me, did you not, in your deep slumber? You thought that I was calling you? And then you woke and heard my voice at the gate? There is nothing alarming in that—It is strange, but lovely, like everything else about our miracle!" He rose, holding out his hands to help her to her feet. "It is getting late," he said. "Catalina has been a pattern of discretion. She has left us undisturbed for nearly three hours. But she will be wondering if we are never going to have our dinner. Shall we call to her to bring us candles, and go to prepare for it?" Then, before Faith could answer, he asked, as if a pleasing thought had suddenly occurred to him, "Tell me, Faith, if you have ever worn the relic I bought for you the day we went to the Sacro Monte together?"

"The beautiful rhinestone cross on the long shining chain, you mean?—No, not yet. I have been waiting to christen it on some great occasion."

"*Rhinestone!*" exclaimed Sebastian. Then catching himself up quickly, he went on, "Will you please me very much, *querida,* by going and putting it on now? With your loveliest dress? Or better still, by bringing the cross here, and letting me hang it around your neck, when, but for that, you are

174

ready for our fiesta? We will dine here in the patio—as neither of us has ever dined before! And later—after we have finished our feast—we will go to the Alhambra and walk together through the moonlight in Lindaraxa's Garden!"

Chapter XXII

IT was Gabriel de Cerreno's custom to celebrate mass very early every morning, as he had done when he was a young priest, instead of taking over a later service, as his age and rank would have warranted. But in spite of the fact that he was always up before dawn, he went to bed very late, even for a Spaniard. Long after Father Constantino and his other secretaries had gone their austere way to chaste and untroubled sleep, he sat in the sumptuous study adjoining his great tapestried chamber, reading by the light of a massive lamp, writing the family letters for which he had no leisure during the preoccupied day, and arranging and rearranging the priceless collection of medallions and crucifixes to which he was constantly adding, though they were already worthy of any metropolitan museum. It was his period of pleasure and relaxation, upon which only one person was privileged to intrude; and since this one person, at that time of the night, was apt to be very differently occupied, the period was almost always undisturbed. Gabriel looked forward to it with quiet anticipation, when his executive duties pressed down upon him, or when the misery of the souls and bodies committed to his pastoral care wrung his heart through some fresh example of suffering or sin with which, for all his skill and saintliness, he was unable to cope. In the tranquil and beautiful surroundings to which he retired, he recaptured the joy and quietude of spirit which so often deserted him through the troubled hours of the day, though even Father Constantino never guessed how much inner turmoil was concealed behind his calm and gracious countenance and bearing; and his hours of slumber, however brief, were permeated with peace, so that he always rose refreshed to face the "burden and heat" of another day.

He had laid aside Rudolf's letter, announcing Faith's continued indisposition and his own impending departure from Madrid, with a benevolent smile. Of course Rudolf had been right in responding immediately to his Ambassador's summons; his absorption in his career, combined with his capacity for unremitting work, would certainly assure his rapid rise, for his intellect, if not brilliant, was comprehensive at least as far as diplomacy was concerned, Gabriel added to himself, still smiling. As for Faith, the quieter she kept the better, until her "attack"—Gabriel smiled more deeply still at Rudolf's choice of words—was over. Certainly she did not need a doctor—in fact, he doubted whether she needed, or desired, anything, except to be let alone. The conviction that she did not, combined with the complexities of the cares which crowded in upon him throughout the thunderous afternoon, caused him to dismiss from his mind the tentative idea that he might drive out to see her during the cool of the evening; and when the storm burst with such unleashed fury, he went, earlier than was his custom, to the secluded apartments which no violence of the elements could invade.

His friend the Cardinal Archbishop of Toledo had brought, when he had made his recent visit, a new treasure for Gabriel's collection: a very ancient medallion from Arequipa, made of vegetable ivory framed in carved gumwood, and representing the Virgin kneeling with a lily clasped between the hands folded over her breast, before the Archangel of the Annunciation. "It is fitting that you should have this rather than I, Gabriel," the Cardinal had said with amiable innuendo, "not only because you collect such relics and I do not, but also because your parents saw fit to christen you as they did. The papal nuncio to Peru, who has just sent it in, assures me that it is a very rare piece. Certainly it is a very charming one." Enchanted with his offering, Gabriel had awaited an opportunity to study it circumstantially; and reëxamining it now, under the glow of the effulgent lamp, he was struck afresh with its ethereality. The disposition of the draperies flowing around the genuflected figure—the veil, the mantle, the robe—had been indicated with an unusual feeling for modesty and grace; the carving of the exquisite profile had the finesse of consummate art; even the fingers encircling the lily stems gave the illusion of delicacy. Enraptured by each new detail that his minute inspection revealed, Gabriel was reaching for a magnifying glass in order to discover these still more clearly, when an almost subconscious feeling that he was no longer alone caused him to glance swiftly up from the image that he held.

The damask portières hanging over the entrance to the outer corridor were certainly stirring. Gabriel was still uncertain whether this movement was not caused by the breeze, which, in spite of the sultriness of the night, drifted, from time to time, through the open windows, when he heard the door behind them close softly, and was aware that his brother was standing on his threshold.

"Sebastian!" he exclaimed, with an affection which masked his amazement. "When did you arrive? I had no idea you had left Malaga or thought of doing so. But it does not matter—as always, I am delighted to see you." He laid down the medallion, and went toward his brother, holding out his arms. *"Que tal?"* he said cordially.

Sebastian advanced a step or two, knelt to kiss Gabriel's ring, and then rising, laid first one cheek and then the other against the Archbishop's. "I came over the road from Malaga to-day," he said when they had embraced, "on horseback. I was caught in the storm a few miles outside Granada."

"But you took shelter? You borrowed clothing?" asked Gabriel, glancing at Sebastian's somewhat fantastic and informal costume. Sebastian appeared to be both unaware of what he was wearing, and indifferent to Gabriel's appraisal of it.

"Yes," he said slowly. "I may even say that I found sanctuary. At the *caseria.*"

There was a moment's silence. Gabriel, standing immobile, permitted his gaze to wander from Sebastian toward the enameled clock that stood on his desk, and then back again to his brother's face.

"The storm was over a little after six," he said at length. "If you have just left there, your visit was rather prolonged."

"Yes. It was rather prolonged. Though it seemed, while it lasted, as if the moments were flying by on wings. I have come to talk to you about it."

"Then suppose we sit down?" suggested Gabriel suavely. "We shall be more at our ease—not that I imagine, of course, that you have anything disturbing to say." And as Sebastian did not answer immediately he continued, "You might begin by telling me how you knew that Rudolf had left for Madrid."

"He sent Felipe to the station yesterday to secure reservations on the express and to wire *Tia* Carlota. It somehow occurred to Felipe to wire me at the same time. He has the unerring intuition of the perfect servant regarding his master's wishes.—Surely you did not have the naïveté to imagine, Gabriel, when you persuaded me to go to Malaga, that I would do so without arranging to return at the first opportune moment."

"I am afraid I did. I am afraid I made the mistake of assuming that you were a man of honor."

For an instant the shaft which Gabriel had released quivered between them; then it seemed to fall harmlessly to the ground. For Sebastian recoiled from it with less violence than Gabriel had expected.

"That is not just," he said, almost entreatingly. "It is true that I was determined to see Faith alone, to talk with her without interruption. After you dissuaded me from my first plan of seeing her here, when and as I could, on the reasonable ground that you could not permit the episcopal residence to shelter such hole-in-the-corner meetings, I knew I should have to find some other way to accomplish the ends I had in mind. I have done so—not in the way I should have preferred—you cannot suppose that I would choose to approach Faith through the medium of a servant. But as I could—desperate men use desperate measures. But nothing has happened in the course of my meeting with her which you could criticize, much less condemn."

"Suppose you tell me just what has happened," said Gabriel.

He still spoke with controlled courtesy; but Sebastian was aware of a slight sting in the suave suggestion.

"*Hermano mio*, is it necessary to speak to me in such a voice? Especially when I have come here for the express purpose of doing exactly that!"

"You cannot blame me for being anxious about Faith, all things considered."

"You priests are all alike," interrupted his brother, anger beginning to master him. "I came here to confide in you, to ask your help and guidance. And instead of giving me a chance to speak, you begin to denounce me. Anyone would think I had confessed to committing most of the deadly sins."

"It would not be the first time," said Gabriel levelly. "As I said before, I am still awaiting enlightenment as to what you have done."

"I have seen a miracle. It is the first time I have ever caught a glimpse of one," replied Sebastian swiftly, repeating the words he had spoken to Faith, "so I came to ask you to interpret it for me. I have always looked upon you as an authority on miracles. I see now that I was mistaken. You are only an authority on the commandments, especially the seventh, which in this instance does not concern me in the least, however much it may have done so in the past."

He flung himself, with a sort of furious grace, out of the great chair which Gabriel had drawn up for him beside the desk, facing the one in which the Archbishop himself was seated. Gabriel rose too, laying a constraining hand upon his brother's arm.

"Sit down," he commanded, "and control yourself. I cannot help you if you rage and rant." Then more gently, he added, "Forgive me, *querido*, if I have seemed harsh. Your unexpected appearance here at this time of night was, in itself, something of a shock. Your abrupt announcement that you had been alone with Faith for many hours was a still greater one. It cannot surprise you that my confidence in your trustworthiness where young and lovely women are concerned has been badly shaken, considering certain—episodes, shall we call them?—in the past. But I am relieved that in this instance I misjudged you, and repentant that I was too ready to pronounce judgment.—What was your miracle?"

"A revelation of faith."

"And how did she reveal herself?"

"First on her balcony. In the rain. She made me think, as I told her, of a lily shining behind a waterfall.—Do you remember our *quinta* in Ecuador?"

"Yes," said Gabriel thoughtfully, "I remember it very well, and I think your comparison is apt.—Well, and afterwards——"

"Afterwards she came downstairs and we had tea together. And later on we had dinner. That is to say, I had dinner, and succeeded in getting Faith to drink some champagne."

Gabriel moved slightly in his seat.

"I mean," said Sebastian hotly, "that champagne was the only thing that tasted good to her. She had been ill all day, and had eaten nothing except a few dry biscuits while I and ham and olives at six o'clock."

"And you urged champagne upon her when she had had no food for twenty-four hours?"

"Yes!" shouted Sebastian. "Of course I did! As a restorative of which she was in great need! You act as if you never heard of champagne except as an accessory to the seduction of a chorus girl! You, who serve it at ten o'clock in the morning to every visitor who enters your house!"

He was beside himself with fury. But his rage, instead of kindling a responsive spark in his brother's breast reassured him as no amount of argument would have done.

"*Querido*, again I must beg you to calm yourself. And again I must ask your forgiveness for misinterpreting what you were trying to tell me.—So you and Faith dined together, and sat for hours together in the starlight, talking mostly of rather insignificant things perhaps. Was that it?"

"Yes, that was it—How did you guess? I told her of our life at the *caseria*, yours and mine, when—our mother was alive. And later she told me of her own little home on a farm, to which she longs to return."

"And as you talked of these familiar things, all the secret places of your hearts were suddenly revealed to each other?"

"Yes. Yes. Yes."

Sebastian spoke with increasing intensity. His next words came swiftly.

"I had meant to take her with me to the Alhambra—to walk with her in Lindaxara's Garden, and beside the pool in the Patio de las Narangas, where you taught me to swim, when I was a child, Gabriel. But I could see that she was very tired. So though she would have gone with me eagerly, I dissuaded her from doing so. I had proposed the plan and yet in the end, it was I who insisted we must give it up— for to-night."

"And so you left her?"

"And so I left her—and came to you."

"Is that all?" asked Gabriel searchingly.

"All except for one thing, which is everything. We kissed each other. She told me afterwards that she had not known before a kiss could be so gentle and so sweet. Of course, I had not known it either."

For an instant, Sebastian bowed his head. When he raised it again and looked imploringly at his brother he saw that there was no censure in Gabriel's expression, but that he looked suddenly careworn and stricken.

"And so you came to me for help? *Hermano mio*, what can I do to help you?"

"You can release us from bondage. You can secure our freedom. You can give us to each other."

"*Probito*, what are you saying? Do you not know that it is only in the service of God that perfect freedom is found? And that only God could give you and Faith to each other?"

The tone in which he spoke the words robbed them of all effect of a pronouncement of dogma, and made them seem, instead, like the utterance of a powerless man wrung with anguish.

"You have enormous influence with the Rota—and if the Cardinal of Toledo also pled our cause as you could persuade him to do——"

"To annul your marriage? Or Faith's?"

"It would need to be both, would it not? I do not know. But I knew you could tell me."

Gabriel's lips moved, but he did not speak.

"Are there no grounds on which my marriage could be annulled?" Sebastian asked at last in a voice so low that Gabriel could hardly hear him.

"There may be. I am not sure. But it is possible," said Gabriel laboriously, "if you went to great lengths. You would have to abandon all reticence, to dwell on the pitiful condition of Dolores as if it were criminal——"

"Is attempted murder not a crime?" asked Sebastian quickly.

"Yes. If the attempt was intentional. You know in her case that it was not, that she had no idea what she was doing when she attacked you. You would have to swear that she did know what she was doing. Are you prepared for that, Sebastian?"

A terrible silence fell between them. It was Gabriel who finally broke it.

"Let us grant then, for the sake of argument," he said painfully, "that the annulment of your marriage could be achieved. What then?"

"The annulment of Faith's should be very easy. I have already told you I know she was coerced."

"Not into marriage. She married Rudolf not only willingly, but gladly. As for what may have taken place afterwards —I fear, Sebastian, that many marriages would be annulled if every bride to whom her husband's vehemence had been a shock sought and secured release from him."

"You would condone an act of violence merely because it is often committed?"

"Never. But since I am a man myself, I would recognize how much all men are in need of forgiveness—from God, from other men, and most of all, perhaps, from the women committed to their care. Our instinct fails us so frequently— Our understanding is so incomplete—Our desires drive us headlong into such excesses! So, as a man, I would not be too harsh or sweeping in the condemnation of any other man."

Gabriel's voice, as he went on speaking, gained in volume and power with every word he uttered. Sebastian, who had been totally unprepared for such a declamation, stared at his brother with a stupefaction which momentarily submerged all other sensations.

"How dramatic you are!" he said tauntingly, when at last he had recovered enough to talk. "I should not have supposed that you would be so well qualified to speak with conviction on men's sins of commission and omission toward women. But perhaps there have been—episodes shall we say?—in your life as well as mine!"

"It will not help your cause, Sebastian, to insult me."

"The insult came first from you."

Once more a poised dart quivered between them. This time it was Gabriel who turned it aside.

"Again I must ask your forgiveness, *hermano mio*," he

181

said. "I know there is no blot upon your past, whatever it may be, which can spread far enough to stain your love for Faith. That is a thing apart, the greatest thing that has ever come into your life or ever will. But I must beg you to believe that I know what I am saying when I tell you that Rudolf loves her too—as deeply, as sincerely, as intensely as you do. Because you have found him lacking in delicacy, you are making the great mistake in believing that he is lacking in devotion. It is a mistake that is unworthy of you."

Sebastian hesitated, but only for a moment. "Very well," he said evenly, "I will accept your apology—this once more. And let us grant—for the sake of argument, as you said a little while ago—that in his own way Rudolf may love Faith —a stupid and barbarous way, but let that pass. What difference does it make in any case, since she does not love him?"

"I admit that she has suffered a revulsion of feeling toward him which has caused her great anguish, which she has courageously tried to conceal. Part of the revulsion might have been avoided if Rudolf had not underestimated both her intelligence and her sensitiveness—I deplore his lack of discernment as much as you do. But another part of the revulsion was inevitable. Faith had not seen Rudolf as he really was, but as her dazzled imagination had pictured him. He was bound to topple from his pedestal. Her disillusionment has hurt her terribly; but when she recovers from the shock of it, I think she could adjust herself to realities without too much pain. For her lot would be cast in very pleasant places; and she was deeply attached to him, though certainly she did not love him in the sense you mean—in the sense of a woman recognizing her mate and yearning for him. She was too young, when she pledged herself to him, to know that such a radiant revelation, such unutterable longing, would ever come to her."

"She knows it now!"

"Subconsciously."

"No, instinctively."

"And do you think she will be swayed by her instincts? Or controlled by her sense of integrity?"

"I think—after to-night—that there is nothing I could ask of her that she would deny me!"

"And what," inquired Gabriel poignantly, "are you going to ask of her? That she should commit perjury also?"

"Perhaps in her case it might not be necessary. She is not a Catholic."

"And so?"

"And so, if she cannot obtain an annulment for coercion, she might obtain a divorce for something else."

"For instance?"

"I have not thought it out. But there must be something. And after the divorce was granted—surely the Church could rule, since her union had not been blessed by a priest, that it had been in a way irregular, that there was no impediment to another marriage—especially if she should become a Catholic."

Sebastian's statement was so concise that Gabriel guessed that it was meant to be tantalizing. But he did not betray his consciousness of his brother's strategy.

"She is not a Catholic yet, at all events," he said, almost as if declining to admit the potentiality. "And the Rota cannot be bribed by the prospect of a convert, as an ignorant servant can be bribed with money. But, as you say, the avenue of divorce is not closed to her. I cannot think of any pretext by which she could bring suit against Rudolf. It would, of course, be very simple to find one by which he could bring suit against her."

There was a calmness about Gabriel's expression that was ominous. Sebastian was instantly aware of this.

"What do you mean?" he said sharply.

"Since you do not object to perjury, since you are ready to go to any lengths yourself to secure your freedom, and to persuade Faith to do the same thing, you would not blame Rudolf too much, would you, if he should divorce Faith—for unfaithfulness, let us say?"

Sebastian stared at his brother in sudden and horrified revulsion. But before he could open his lips, the Archbishop went on speaking.

"I know, of course, as well as you do, that your visit to her to-day was entirely innocent. But do you think Felipe and Catalina are so sure? You have already confessed to Felipe's connivance, and there must be a record of the telegram on file. And apparently Catalina knew better than to intrude upon you all through those long hours while you were in the patio with Faith. If they were put on the witness stand against her, have you thought that someone else might bribe them—or terrorize them—into giving testimony that would be most incriminating? And since the question of paternity would necessarily be involved, the proceedings would be ugly as well as sensational. I cannot help wondering whether Faith would have the strength to survive them."

For a moment his penetrating glance swept over Sebastian's horror-stricken face. Then, apparently inadvertently, it fell on the medallion. He picked it up and turned it over slowly.

"I had meant," he said deliberately, "to go out and see Faith in the morning taking her this little image as a gift. It has just been presented to me by the Cardinal of Toledo for my collection, which of course it would adorn. But I felt there would be something almost symbolical in offering it to Faith—under the circumstances. Perhaps you will take it to her for me. Would you care to look at it? It is really very beautiful. I do not know when I have seen a more exquisite interpretation of the Annunciation."

Sebastian snatched the medallion from his brother's hand and threw it down on the table without looking at it. "What are you trying to say to me?" he asked hoarsely.

"But surely, Sebastian, you must have guessed—and guessed that she has not? Did it not dawn upon you that Faith is with child?"

Gabriel knew that he had shot his last bolt. The effort left him so completely spent that for a moment he felt as if he could not hold himself erect another second, as if he must succumb to the strain which had taxed him beyond the limits of his endurance. The keen distinction of his features became strangely blurred and his fine face looked old and sorrowful. But steadying himself with a supreme effort, he looked straight into Sebastian's eyes.

"When you see Faith with her baby," he said, and there was infinite compassion in his voice, "you will thank God on your knees, even in the desolation of your own childlessness, that you did not sin against her. And willingly or not, you will love her son better than anyone else on earth, except Faith herself. Better than you have ever loved me."

Suddenly, and with horrible mirthlessness, Sebastian laughed. But Gabriel made himself heard above his convulsive mockery.

"You think I do not know!" he cried triumphantly, "but I do! If I had not how could I have prevailed—against you, my dearly beloved brother—for Rudolf who should have been my son!"

PART VI

Hans Christian

Chapter XXIII

A VERY erect little boy, whose well-set head was covered with short ruddy curls which gave the effect of being impervious to both shears and smoothing, stood with his nose pressed against the window-pane, looking fixedly down toward the wide bleak street below him. His attitude evinced neither impatience nor weariness, but complete absorption and hopeful expectancy. He seemed oblivious both to the two other occupants of the large luxurious room to which his back was turned, and to the dismal drizzle of rain slanting across the façades of solid, but gloomy houses on the other side of the street, and descending to the dripping pavements. From time to time, an elderly lady of great elegance, whose dark, snow-flecked hair was wound in a superb coronet of braids above her white brow, looked up from her letter writing, to glance first at the child and then at the clock; but it was not until the soldierly looking man who had been reading the *Berliner Tageblatt* with a concentration which precluded interruption, threw down his paper exclaiming, "Surely the train is late!" that the lady laid aside her correspondence and spoke.

"Actually only a few minutes, I think—Hansel, darling, are you sure you are warm enough? It must be cold over by the window, and you have been there a long time already."

"I am very warm, thank you, grandmamma. But I think grandpapa is right. I think the train must be late."

The lady smiled, and rising, walked over to the window and put her arm around the child's shoulder.

"You have been happy here with me, while your mother has been gone, haven't you, Hansel?" she asked persuasively.

The child hesitated a moment, and then replied with evident sincerity but without enthusiasm.

"Yes. But it is not the same."

"What is not the same?"

"Nothing. Nothing is the same when my mother is away.

185

You are very pleasant, and it is kind of you to take me walking with you in the Langelinge and to ride in the flying carousel at Tivoli. But you do not invite me into your room when you are getting ready for a party, and let me choose which dress you will wear between those that have been laid out on the bed. You do not let me take the things out of the jewel box and put them back in different corners. You do not let me watch Hilda dressing your hair—and then, of course your hair is nice, and there is lots of it, but it does not shine like my mother's. You are not such a shining lady as she is anyway."

His grandmother laughed. "No, Hansel, I know I am not," she said regretfully. "And there are other ways also in which I am inadequate?"

"You smell very good, but it does not seem as if you were made on purpose to hold little boys, the way my mother is. She is soft in just the right places. I do not fit in when I try to cuddle up to you. And you never call me your precious treasure."

The lady laughed again, and this time the soldierly-looking man frowned slightly, and throwing down his paper joined his wife and grandson at the window. "Your mother indulges you a great deal, Hansel," he said with a touch of seriousness. "She is a very busy lady and you ought not to impose upon her. You are not a baby any more."

"I am quite big, I know. But mother says it will be a long time before I am too big to sit on her lap. She says she has to make me do, because she has not two or three real babies like Aunt Rita. And she is never too busy to hold me."

As if politely dismissing a closed subject, the child resumed his contemplation of the street, which, in spite of the endless stream of bicycles and carriages wheeling past, was, to all intents and purposes, empty as far as he was concerned. At last, as a pair of handsome bay horses attached to a smart brougham turned the corner above the house, he gave a sudden joyous shout, and tearing across the room, precipitated himself down the stairway, shouting more loudly and joyously with every step he covered in his headlong rush.

The sounds attendant upon the return of distinguished persons from a journey to their own well-regulated household merged with a child's voice. Doors opened and shut with prompt precision. One piece of hand-baggage after another thudded softly against a carpeted floor. There was an exchange of greetings—respectful on the one side, courteous but slightly aloof on the other—followed by questions and answers. Yes, everything had gone well while Their Excellencies had been away—the weather had been very bad, but what could one expect of Copenhagen in April? Had it been fine in Norway—ah, that was well! And the Herr Baron's cough, was it entirely gone? The large package from Worth's which the Frau Baronin had been expecting had come in—everything seemed to be quite in order, except that point-de-Venise instead of Duchesse lace had been used on the violet stain. The Herr Baron's secretary had been waiting for him in his study since nine o'clock. A number of dispatches had come in, and there was a message from the Palace to which the Herr Baron would probably wish to give immediate personal attention. Her Serene Highness and the Herr General were in the drawing-room—Would Their Excellencies like the coffee served there?

"Yes, and at once," a somewhat peremptory voice ordered. "I must get to my study without further delay—this lateness of the train is most upsetting.—Stop jumping over your mother and asking her questions, Hans Christian! How can she answer so many all at once?"

"I only want to know if she had a good time—and if the snow was very deep—and how many prizes she won— and whether she was the King and Queen of Norway, and if they were as nice as the King and Queen here—and if she will promise to read to me to-night——"

"My precious treasure! Of course I am going to read to you to-night! I had a lovely time—and the snow was 'way over my head—and I won two prizes, a second and a third, for skiing—and father and I had lunch with the King and Queen at Bygdo Konsgaar* and they are charming. Now— race me upstairs! I want to see grandmother and grandfather!"

There was another rush on the stairway, swifter and lighter than when the child had pelted down it alone; then the drawing-room curtains were flung aside, and he bounded into the apartment again, just in front of a young, graceful woman, wrapped in lustrous furs, who instantly caught him back to her in a close embrace.

"I am out of practice! I can't let you win like that!"

"Race me again!"

"Yes, darling, by and by—Oh, *Tante* Luise, I am so glad to see you!—Dear Father Hans, have you been comfortable and happy here with your namesake while Rudolf and I have been away?"

She turned impetuously first on one and then to the other,

* A suburban palace not far from Christiania.

presenting both cheeks to be kissed, her arms still around the child.

"We have been very happy and comfortable. Your household runs on velvet, and Hensel has been as good as gold. But it is pleasant to have you back again, *liebe* Faith.—As Hansel says, nothing seems quite the same when you are gone.—Are you by chance going to take off your wraps and linger here a little while? Not that I blame you for keeping on your coat, for it is beautiful! Did you get it in Christiania?"

"In Bergen. I never saw such furs as they have there! I knew you would admire it—that is why I didn't take it off downstairs—I wanted to show it to you right away. It fits nicely, doesn't it?"

She detached herself gently from the little boy, drew the coat still more closely around her slim waist, and turned slowly around so that the older lady could see it from all sides, before throwing it open to display a lining of rich brocade.

"Very. It is beautifully cut—and your figure does it entire justice!"

"Oh, but my figure is not a bit better than yours, even now, and you know it—I wish I could have seen you when you were my age, *Tante* Luise! But speaking of figures, the Queen of Norway has the smallest waist I ever saw.—Really, it is no bigger than that!" And she made a hoop of her hands.

"I see that Faith, as usual, is engaged in exaggeration—no woman could possibly have a waist of that size!—And is this a fashion show? Or are we eventually going to have some coffee?"

Rudolf von Hohenlohe's entrance into the drawing-room had been made far less precipitately than his wife's. His coat, although it was also new and handsome, had been surrendered to the ministrations of a footman immediately after his arrival; and he had retired to wash his hands and brush his hair before coming to the drawing-room to greet his parents. In spite of being extremely well-built, he gave the effect of a solidity that was beginning to verge on heaviness; and the seriousness of his expression did not relax as his son clambered up beside him on the sofa where he had seated himself with a certain precision of manner. He watched Faith without further comment, as she folded her furs over the back of a chair, took off her hat, and rather nonchalantly smoothed her hair and adjusted the white frills of the blouse she was wearing with her traveling suit. But if she were conscious of his unspoken but obvious criticism of her casual preparation for breakfast she gave no indication of this, as she took her place behind the shining service which the butler brought in and set down before her, just in time to forestall a second question as to when this might be expected.

"Oh—thanks so much, Johann!—You will have some coffee with us, won't you, *Tante* Luise?—Nonsense, Father Hans, that must have been nearly two hours ago!—Hansel, my precious treasure, do you want a *canard?*"

She dipped her lump of sugar into her own cup, and dropped it gaily into the eagerly opened little mouth close beside her elbow. Then as she drank her steaming coffee and ate her flaky crescents with evident relish, she began an enthusiastic account of her trip.

"It has been the greatest fun, from the very beginning— that is why I haven't written you more about it, *Tante* Luise! I wanted to tell you all about it, myself. In the first place, I think it is delightful to take a ferry at Elsinore—I looked everywhere for Hamlet's ghost! He was nowhere to be seen, but some dark night I am going back to look again! It was very smoky and foggy when we reached Christiania, but of course we went directly out of the city. Our Minister had sent Franz von Witzleben, the second secretary, to meet us and he was most helpful! He went out to the Voksenhollen Sanatorium with us, through the pine forests and snow. The air was glorious, so cold and bracing and windless, and the sunshine was simply dazzling! Our rooms were all ready for us, lovely ones with a view of the mountains and fiords, glorious too——"

"Glorious seems to be your favorite word, Faith," remarked Rudolf. "May I interrupt you to ask for another cup of coffee?"

"We have been breakfasting downstairs all the time we have been gone," Faith went on as she complied with his request. "There is no such luxury as coffee in bed at Voksenhollen unless one is really ill! That seems strange, doesn't it, for a health resort! But of course it is really not a sanatorium in the sense that we use the word, but a hotel where people go for rest and recuperation after an illness, just as Rudolf did.—His cough got better almost immediately, by the way.—You would never guess now that he had been so sick with bronchitis only a month ago! Everything was very simple. But it was the cleanest, pleasantest place you ever saw, and very attractive. The huge room where everyone sat was decorated with black rafters and quantities of carving, and there were comfortable little rooms adjoining it for reading and cards. I played almost as much bridge as I do here—while Rudolf was resting, of course."

"Did you enjoy the sports?" General von Hohenlohe asked, lighting his pipe and turning toward his son.

"I went for an hour's walk regularly every day. Holmenhollen made a good objective. There is an excellent inn there, a copy of a medieval dwelling house. I enjoyed lunching there occasionally—I cannot say too much in praise of Norwegian food. The skiing did not appeal to me. But Faith indulged in it. You doubtless heard her telling Hans Christian as soon as she arrived that she had won two cups."

"I asked her!" the child said quickly.

"Certainly you asked her, darling," his grandmother interposed smoothly. "Father knew that you did.—I am delighted to learn that the Voksenhollen experiment was so wonderful. You have had some diversion, too, have you not?"

"Yes, everyone was very kind. The Prime Minister invited us to dinner almost immediately—a state function given in honor of the King and Queen, who were most gracious. There were one hundred guests, a very distinguished company. There was a musical program after dinner, very well rendered, and the drive back to Voksenhollen afterwards in the moonlight was peaceful and agreeable—a pleasant contrast to the one going in, which was quite the opposite."

Rudolf paused significantly, and glanced at his mother with the air of one expecting to be questioned.

"I am so sorry. What happened to make it so?" she asked instantly.

"When Faith started dressing for dinner—at the last moment as usual—she found she had no long gloves with her. So she rushed off to the manageress, half hooked into a conspicuous petunia velvet dress. She failed in her attempt to borrow a pair of gloves at the sanatorium, so then she started telephoning into Christiania to one shop after another. It was just closing time, but at last an obliging establishment was persuaded to send a pair of gloves to the Prime Minister's residence. The episode was certainly very disquieting, besides involving a great deal of delay, so that the drive in town, as I said before, was something of an ordeal for me."

"Mother has such lovely arms, I should think everyone would be pleased to see her without gloves,' said Hansel, again speaking very quickly. "I am. I like to see her when she has nothing over them at all. And I am sure Uncle Sam does. I heard him saying, the last time he was here——"

Rudolf set down his cup, and turned abruptly toward his son, "Why are you not at your lessons?" he asked curtly.

"You should have been, long ago.—Tell your tutor for me that you are to work two hours this afternoon, to make up for the time you have lost this morning."

"But then mother and I will not have our walk in the Langelinge!"

"You should have thought of that instead of lounging around here! And I must be off myself. Will you excuse me, Mother? I am lamentably late."

"My dear! As if I would dream of detaining you!"

The Archduchess smiled affectionately at him. But as he left the room, accompanied by his father and propelling his protesting son in front of him, it was on her daughter-in-law that her glance rested; for with the child's unwilling departure, the buoyancy of Faith's expression seemed suddenly blighted.

"I am afraid Rudolf is not quite himself yet after all," Victoria Luise said gently. "It takes some time for the nerves to readjust themselves after an illness. I am sure you realize this, *liebe* Faith."

"Oh, perfectly, *Tante* Luise."

The Archduchess had risen, and as she spoke, she put her arm lovingly around her daughter-in-law's shoulder.

"Tell me, my darling," she went on, "if I am not indiscreet in asking, what impression the Councillor of the Italian Legation makes upon you? Is it a favorable one?"

Faith looked at her mother-in-law searchingly for a moment, but when she answered, it was with a nonchalance that was obviously unassumed.

"Guido Bonatelli?" she said after a moment. "Why, he has never made any impression on me at all! What made you think of him?"

"My dear, he is very much in evidence, and he is not without a certain fascination, if you care for the Italian manner. And I have somehow gathered—one senses these things rather than hears them—that he has been endeavoring to attract your attention for some time—that he has been delicately trying to indicate his hope that you would consent to an *amitié amoureuse.*"

"But *Tante* Luise, I do not think Guido Bonatelli is fascinating at all! I think he is a nuisance! I shall probably find half a dozen notes from him in my mail, and I shall tear them all up without even reading them—I read the first three he sent and they were all alike! You would never believe that a man would have so little to say, and say it with so little originality! If I were going to have an *amitié amoureuse,* at least I should want it to be amusing. And one with Guido Bonatelli would be too dreary for words!"

"Then you have thought, my dear, that you might like to have one? If not now, some time? If not with Bonatelli with someone else? Provided it were amusing?"

"Not really. It has occurred to me, of course. I suppose it does to most women, doesn't it, after—after a certain time? When their husbands are—very preoccupied, I mean? But it is just playing at love, isn't it? I have never wanted to do that, *Tante* Luise."

She returned her mother-in-law's caress as warmly as it had been given. Then, smoothing down the fur of the gorgeous garment which she had laid over her arm, she paused on the threshold and looked back at the Archduchess.

"Will you come in and see the new dresses that have arrived from Worth's?" she said. "Hilda is sure to have them spread out all over my room for me to look at as soon as I get there. I shall be only a few minutes in the kitchen, and I hope it will not take me long to go through my mail."

"I should love to see them. You have such exquisite taste—which reminds me that I should think petunia would be an ideal color for you. I am surprised that Rudolf cannot see that it is."

"Perhaps he is color-blind," Faith said lightly. "I thought, in Norway, that he was snow-blind. And often before this, that he was blind in other ways. But it does not trouble me any more because Rudolf does not like my clothes. He would always rather see me in a nice black dress made in Berlin.—Why are you so worried about me, darling, all of a sudden?"

"My dearest child! Why should you imagine that I am worried?"

"Because I can see that you are. Is it because I am so hopelessly American and still have so many rough corners left, in spite of all these years of association with your perfections? Or is it because Rudolf is so hopelessly Prussian, and just as inflexible, though not quite so glittering, as when you first warned me against him?"

"*Liebe* Faith, why do you talk such nonsense?"

"Because you began to talk nonsense yourself, *Tante* Luise! All because Rudolf was cross and critical, and you were afraid he forgot to get the enamels you surreptitiously told him to buy for me in Christiania! And because I have been playing too much bridge and doing too much skiing with Franz von Witzleben, and you think you must tactfully lead up to the tales that have been told you about that by sounding an Italian note first! And because I almost precipitated a diplomatic crisis between Norway and Germany by neglecting to take any long white gloves with me to a sanatorium! All this is unworthy of a lady of your fine balance, *Tante* Luise! And as to *amitié amoureuse,* you have nothing to fear—remember that Americans take their love affairs very seriously—more seriously than any other people in the world, except, perhaps, the Spaniards."

"What makes you think Spaniards take their love affairs seriously?" inquired Victoria Luise quickly.

"Oh, it was just a general impression—enhanced by some chance remarks of Gabriel de Cerreno's. Isn't it correct?"

"My dear, how should I know? After all, I have spent very little time in Spain."

Faith laughed, and drew the curtain back. "But after all, Gabriel has spent a good deal in Germany," she said, "so you have had an occasional opportunity to listen to his views. And you will admit that he speaks with conviction and authority. However, suppose we dismiss the subject of an *amitié amoureuse* for the present—I am really rather surprised that your Serene Highness should put the idea of one into my head! But if I should ever decide to have one after all, I shall certainly tell you about it before anyone else. I am sure you would have all kinds of helpful advice to give me."

Chapter XXIV

When Victoria Luise entered Faith's room two hours later, she found her daughter-in-law sitting in front of her desk, still occupied with the masses of correspondence which she was sorting and stacking into neat piles as she ran through it. Her bare feet were thrust into turquoise-blue mules, and a dressing gown of turquoise-blue satin was tied loosely over a flesh-colored slip banded with cream lace. Evidently she had just stepped out of her tub, for the aroma of bath salts still clung to her, and her freshly washed hair, still damp, hung in burnished masses all around her. As her mother-in-law approached, she put down the last letter she had opened, tilted back her head, and ran first her fingers and then her comb through the coppery cloud.

"I do not wonder that Sam's painting of 'Lorelei' took so many prizes," Victoria Luise said admiringly, placing her fingers on the shining tresses. "This seems to me more beautiful every year, Faith."

Faith sprang up, laughing and laying down her comb. "It is humorous, isn't it, that it was actually Rudolf who suggested that picture, considering how he hates it?" she said lightly. "The first time we went to the Lido together! Of course he did not guess he would ever be taken literally, or he would have bitten out his tongue first. Since then he has learned to beware of the true word spoken in jest—indeed of all jesting!—How nice of you to come, *Tante* Luise! I did not hear you until you were actually beside me. I find that the household still seems to function, and so do the mails—some of my letters this morning are especially interesting.—Where would you like to sit?"

"It does not matter, so long as I have a good vantage point from which to look at my surroundings. I never come into your room, Faith, without marveling at the exotic atmosphere you have captured and conveyed to this gray Danish city. Considering the comparatively short time that you were in Spain, it seems to me nothing short of miraculous that you should have been able to create for yourself so completely the setting of a Spanish princess."

She seated herself, her gaze wandering from the great bed of carved and gilded wood, the sumptuous hangings of mellow brocade, and the splendid somber pictures in their rich frames to the inlaid *escritorio* at which Faith was sitting.

"You were so ill all that summer in Granada," she went on wonderingly, "and you were hardly settled in Madrid the next autumn before you had to stop going out because you were so far *enceinte*. Then, when you returned from Schönplatz after Hansel's birth, apparently you continued to spend most of your time in his nursery—you had only just weaned him when Rudolf was promoted and transferred! And meanwhile you had posed for three pictures! I should have said you could hardly have known whether you were in Spain or Siberia! Yet you appear to have absorbed the very essence of Spain."

"Perhaps it is just because I actually saw so little of it that I wanted to bring a bit of it away with me," Faith said still lightly. "You must admit that my essence of Spain is very concentrated—all the rest of the house, even the drawing-room, is admirably Teutonic! It is only here that I have been guilty of self-indulgence. But I did fall a victim to the lure of Spanish *antiquarios* almost immediately—even before I began to be ill in Granada!—But to change the subject—or rather to revert to one that you indirectly brought up—I have a long letter from Sam. He says Cousin Sarah's rheumatism is becoming more and more troublesome. She thinks the Paris climate is very bad for her, and

194

I gathered that Sam believes she is secretly pining for Salem —not that the climate there is any better!"

"But, Faith, Sam would never leave Europe for any length of time now! And that joint ménage has been such a happy arrangement!"

"I know. But after all, Salem is home for Cousin Sarah. I know how she feels. Sam thinks he might at least take her over, and see her settled there among her old friends. And he could use it temporarily, as a base for more marine painting.—By the way, Sam also says that the Luxembourg is bent on acquiring the trilogy of which you first spoke."

"The trilogy?"

"Is it only three plays or three poems that can be called a trilogy? I am never sure. I thought it might refer to three paintings too. Perhaps I should have said the trinity—or is that merely a triple Divinity?"

"You mean all three of those pictures Sam painted while you were in Spain—'The Annunciation,' 'The Holy Mother' and 'The Flight into Egypt'?"

"Yes. It seems he has held out a long time. Of course it is obvious now that he will never part with 'Mary of Nazareth.' But I think he was greatly moved by Gabriel's entreating that he would permit either 'The Annunciation' or 'The Holy Mother," to be kept in Spain. Gabriel did not care much for 'The Flight.' But of course the series would have much less value if it were divided, and it is almost unheard-of for the Luxembourg to make such an offer. It is too bad it could not have been for 'The Lorelei' instead."

"Yes. But, even if that did take prizes, you know it is not comparable to 'The Trinity'—I really think we may use that definition. There are times when I understand Rudolf's dislike for 'The Lorelei,' even though I recognize its *allure*. And it seems strange that this should have been Sam's only interpretation of you since the Trinity."

"Dearest, do not sound so tragic! It was the *'Schiffer in kleinem Schiffe'* that went on the rocks, remember—not Lorelei! She just went on combing her hair!"

The telephone beside her tinkled. She picked it up and answered the call. Then, covering the mouthpiece for a moment she flashed a smile at her mother-in-law. "Speak of the devil!" she whispered mockingly, "as you did a little while ago!—Yes, this is the Baronin von Hohenlohe," she went on, uncovering the instrument again. "Yes, thank you, Bonatelli, most delightful. Yes, I did meet him. Yes, he did teach me how to ski. Yes, I like him very much. Yes, very much better. Yes, of course, at the Chancery. Yes, five or six of them.

195

No, I haven't read any of them yet. Yes, a great bouquet on the piano and another here on my desk, but I haven't looked at the cards that went with them, and of course I never guessed they were from you. Yes, very busy. Tea at the Citadel and the American Legation in the evening. Yes, this is the dinner the Madisons are giving in honor of the surgeon who has made such a stir. Oh, getting organized again. No, I don't see how I could. You know I always read to Hansel about that time. Yes, I found the invitation waiting for me here, but I don't know whether I shall accept. The Radens' house-parties are always delightful, but it is still so dreary in the country at this time of year. No, I shouldn't advise you to. I am really very busy, and my mother-in-law is with me. Yes, right here in my room. Yes, not for a long time yet I hope. I adore her and I am always desolate when she goes back to Berlin."

"But I must go, you know, *liebe* Faith, to-morrow," Victoria Luise said, looking at her daughter-in-law attentively as Faith replaced the telephone. "Rita's baby is due very soon now, and she was so ill when Luischen was born that I cannot help being anxious about her. Her children have come very close together, and her strength has been over-taxed. Just think! she was married after you were, and she has six!"

"I know, dearest, and I am very envious of her. I do realize how much she needs you, but I begrudge you to her. I wish you did not have to go away. I need you too."

"You will feel freer to accept the invitation to your house-party if I am not here."

"You are mistaken. I should feel much freer to go if you went with me. You see, when we are asked to the country, Rudolf always finds at the last moment that he must stay in town to catch up with some unusually important work. The first time we went to a Danish castle, it happened that the women all sat around after lunch making little sachets from the lavender which had just been brought in fresh from the garden, while the men played very languid golf. He has imagined ever since that this was typical of all house-parties. So now I go to them without him, not only with his approval, but at his express wish."

"Faith," asked her mother-in-law gently, "do you remember our first conversation together?"

"Do I remember it? Are you going to remind me that I promised to be very loyal?"

Her levity had suddenly deserted her, and her voice was edged with bitterness. Victoria Luise spoke more gently still.

196

"My dearest child, can you believe that I would gloat over the fulfillment of a prophecy which I have done my best to keep from coming true? And do you think you need to tell me that you are loyal, that it is only to me that you have shown your heart? But I will confess—though I would not do so when you first charged me with it—that I am very troubled. I cannot help seeing in you so much of the 'Lorelei' where a few years ago I saw only the 'Mary'."

"It is unfortunate that Rudolf has seen neither the one nor the other," said Faith, still bitterly.

"It is worse than unfortunate. It is tragic. Even though I am his mother, and love him dearly, I cannot defend him," said Victoria Luise. "My darling, I know how much deep disappointment, how much wounded pride, how much real heartache, underlies your apparent volatility. I know that your quest for pleasure rises from your failure to find happiness—that because of the intensity of your nature you seek out one outlet whenever you are denied another—even your perfect housekeeping is an indication of this. But you cannot wonder that I am anxious—as to just where this intensity may lead you.

"It is not going to lead me anywhere," said Faith. This time there was no bitterness in her voice. There was instead a hopelessness so profound that Victoria Luise looked at her in startled astonishment.

"My Darling, do not speak like that. Think of all you have —of the place you have made for yourself, of the wide-spread admiration that you have won, of the inspiration you have been to Sam, of the confidence and respect which you know Rudolf accords you, however imperfectly he reveals it!"

"Would that have been enough for you, when you were twenty-five?" Faith asked.

Victoria Luise had never heard Faith's voice tremble before. She steadied herself against the shock that this quivering note in it gave her now.

"My darling, have I not helped you at all?"

"You know that you have! You know you have helped me in every way that my own mother failed me! That I could not have loved you any more if you really had been my mother! But you have not answered my question!"

"It seems that I do not need to," said Victoria Luise quietly. "I see that in some way you have guessed that something in my own experience has taught me how perilous is the path of the young wife who feels she has ceased to be desirable to her husband and realizes how desirable she is to

197

other men. But I had a safeguard, and so have you—a lovely child whose very world you are." She saw the sudden tenderness that flooded Faith's face and pressed her advantage. "Thank God you have Hans Christian," she went on. "The namesake of your own father as well as Rudolf's. When a woman has a son she has a protection which is hard to penetrate. And if her own heart has never been touched, as in your case, she is doubly safe, for then there is no overpowering temptation lying in wait to engulf her."

The telephone rang again, and again Faith reached for it. This time, as soon as she had controlled her voice, there was real cordiality in it. But she was speaking in Spanish, and though Victoria Luise could not mistake Faith's tones, she could not understand Faith's words. It was a long time before her daughter-in-law turned to her again.

"That was Jaime de los Rios," she said. "It is delightful having him here as minister. He is really one of the most charming men in the world. He is very anxious to hear all our impressions of Norway, so I have invited him to lunch to-morrow. I do hope you will not leave before then, *Tante* Luise, for he especially asked after you. It seems that a treaty is about to be negotiated between Spain and Norway, and he himself will be covering the same ground that Rudolf and I have been over later on in the month. I did not gather just what the treaty was about but evidently it is very important, for King Alfonso is sending a special representative to confer with Jaime about it. He will be arriving almost any day now—in time to take part in the celebration at Odensee commemorating the one hundredth anniversary of the arrival of the Spanish troops on the Island Fijen." *

"How very interesting! Of course we will wait over to see Don Jaime. Did he mention whom the King had designated?"

Faith rose, smiling. "We almost forgot that we were going to look at my finery!" she said. "We grew so very earnest and intent—*très emotionées*, as you said the first time we talked together—and really over nothing! As you say, I have all sorts of blessings, and all sorts of safeguards. And I shall put you at the top of the list!—I told Hilda not to lay the dresses out until you came; after all they clutter up the room. I must ring for her, before she decides she is forgotten." Faith walked across to her golden bed, and pulled the

---

* This celebration actually took place a year after the signing of the treaty between Spain and Norway, and both events slightly earlier in the century than the period in which this story takes place.

brocaded rope hanging beside it. When the bell had ceased to tinkle she reverted to Victoria Luise's unanswered question. "Yes," she said, "the King has chosen his great friend, Sebastian de Cerreno. I wonder if he will have changed much? It is a long time since I have seen him."

Chapter XXV

"I am looking forward to this dinner very much," Faith said to Rudolf, as their brougham clipped smartly down Trondhjemsgade in the rain. "I had a nice little note from Mrs. Madison, besides the engraved invitation, telling me that it was being given in honor of a famous American surgeon and his wife—a Dr. and Mrs. Noble. They are passing through Denmark on a roundabout way home from Vienna. Dr. Noble was a delegate to some clinical congress there, I believe. *Tante* Luise said he made a great impression by an address he delivered about the removal of tumors on the brain—he has effected remarkable cures on persons who were supposed to be hopelessly insane—some of her relatives met him and wrote her about him. Besides, I was especially interested anyway, because I found a letter about them from Mr. Hawks waiting for me too. It seems Dr. Noble comes from Hamstead."

"From Hamstead!" echoed Rudolf. "A great surgeon!"

"Well, a cabinet officer and a senator came from there," Faith said whimsically. "Good sometimes does come out of Nazareth! You may be pleasantly surprised in him—or at least in his wife. She is half-French, a great heiress and very fascinating."

"I am not usually swept off my feet by the French, even the half-French," said Rudolf dryly. "How did Dr. Noble happen to meet anyone with all these enchanting qualifications in Hamstead?"

"You will have to ask yourself, Rudolf. Neither Mrs. Madison nor Mr. Hawks explained that part to me."

"I should hardly be guilty of prying personal questions."

"Well, perhaps the secret will come out of its own accord in course of time!—If you find that you do not actually dislike the Nobles, we might give a dinner for them ourselves."

Rudolf did not reply, and Faith realized that his silence

indicated that he was dubious as to the social qualifications of anyone introduced by Mr. Hawks. But to her immense relief and agreeable surprise, it was evident, long before the evening was over, that far from taking a dislike to the Nobles, he had not only been pleasantly, but greatly, impressed by them. And when she went to bed that night she slipped a little note under her mother-in-law's door which the Archduchess read the next morning with much amusement.

"Dearest" . . . it ran:

"I know you will be as thrilled as I am to hear that it is *Rudolf* who seems bent on an *amitié amoureuse!* Not that I believe it will do him much good, as I fear the lady in question, whose name is Jacqueline Noble, is hopelessly in love with her own husband. But at least Rudolf has taken a step in the right direction. The conquest was so immediate and overwhelming that I have asked the Nobles to waive formality and come to luncheon to-morrow. The Madisons —Mr. and Mrs. and Eleanor—are coming too, so with Jaime it ought to be a very pleasant little party.

Exuberantly,

FAITH"

"P. S.—I thought she was lovely myself. She is what the Spaniards call *encantadora.* She had on an American Beauty satin—which is apparently much less objectionable than petunia-colored velvet! But I must admit that no woman who is not at least half-French could look the way she did, whatever she wore."

"P. S. No. 2.—Of course it is all nonsense about Rudolf. He was much more excited by David Noble's conversation concerning tumors than by Jacqueline Noble's charms. And David Noble is exciting! He looks like a Sicilian brigand or something—very white teeth, very dark skin, very brilliant eyes—you know the type! And still he is wholly *homme du monde.* It was a great shock to Rudolf to discover that such a finished and arresting product could come from Hamstead. I am sure lots of ladies are willing to let David chop them into little pieces, just for the sake of being sewed together by him afterwards. Probably he creates brainstorms in order to cure them!"

"P. S. No. 3.—The Nobles are friends of Sam's too. They saw him in Paris just before they left for Vienna. And they think his work is wonderful."

This missive caused the Archduchess no uneasiness, and

indeed, she took her departure for Berlin with a lighter heart than she had anticipated. The luncheon had been a great success; and a considerable portion of the succeeding afternoon had been devoted to mapping out a program for which the Madisons and the von Hohenlohes were to be jointly responsible, and which was designed to make the Danish visit of the striking surgeon and his charming wife as agreeable and as comprehensive as possible. A strenuous schedule of sightseeing had been arranged—Victoria Luise had heard recurrently the words—Glyptotek—Thorvaldsen Museum—Rosenberg Palace—Royal Porcelain Factory—and there had been a good deal of discussion as to the best hours for visiting points of interest and the surest ways of saving time. The arrangements were eventually developed to include a supper at Froken Nimb's Tivoli Restaurant, an opera party, and several official appointments. And when the American Minister pulled out his watch with a startled exclamation at the time, it was obvious that he and not Rudolf had been the first to be conscious of neglected diplomatic duties. Evidently German efficiency and American energy had merged for once with mutually satisfactory results. It even seemed possible that an acquaintance had begun for which Faith and Rudolf might feel a common enthusiasm, and a friendship founded which might form a tie for Faith with the home she had not seen in so long.

"Faith always gives us a *déjeuner dinatoire*," Jaime de los Rios said as he bowed over the Archduchess' hand. "We have talked so long that it is almost tea-time, and we have eaten so much that we shall not be able to take any tea!"

"That is no hardship for an Andalusian!" Faith said quickly. "You know that you would much rather wait until six or seven, and then have wine and ham and bread and olives!"

"But I shall not be able to eat those either!" Jaime exclaimed in mock despair. "Meanwhile, will you permit me to escort you to the Palace, Faith—you have an appointment with the Crown Princess, have you not?"

There was real consternation in the cry with which Faith sprang to her feet. "You have saved me again, Jaime!" she exclaimed. "I had forgotten all about it, and if I had made another *faux pas* at the Palace I never should have been able to live it down!—Will you forgive me, dearest, if I fly and dress? And if I am not back in time to see you off at the station? It is not as if you were a Spaniard—you can take an overnight journey without a family assemblage!"

Faith cast a teasing look at Jaime de los Rios, embraced her mother-in-law lovingly and impetuously, and fled from the room. And she was still almost breathless from haste when, half an hour later, she entered the antechamber of the Crown Princess' apartments. There was not a single member of the royal family for whom she felt a more affectionate admiration; and yet she seemed fated to maladroitness in all her associations with this exalted lady. On the occasion of her first audience with Queen Luise, she had passed through several rooms, and at last had been received by Mademoiselle de Wimpfen, Her Majesty's lady-in-waiting, with whom she had talked for some time before her presentation to the Queen. She had taken it for granted that much the same procedure would be followed when she was received by the Crown Princess. But from the entrance hall she had been taken directly into a salon where she was pleasantly greeted by a tall dark young woman in mauve whom she had assumed to be another lady-in-waiting; and it was not until she had shaken the cordially extended hand instead of kissing it, taken a designated seat upon a tapestried sofa, and began chatting quite volubly, that she discovered she was in the presence of the Crown Princess herself!

The thought of this episode, and several others almost equally embarrassing, discomforted her intensely now, as she took her place among the diplomatic ladies who had already foregathered in the Princess' drawing-room. The circle was, she saw, with a swift glance of chagrin, already complete except for her; and there was an element in the atmosphere so alien to the tranquil stateliness with which the Palace was normally pervaded, that she felt bewildered as well as distressed. There was no stir of welcome as she slid into the chain; instead she was conscious of a suppressed, almost a stifled, murmur. It took little imagination to sense that this was critical if not actually hostile. The very chandelier, quivering icily over her head, had taken on a glacial aspect that chilled her. But the Crown Princess began to make her rounds almost immediately, talking for a few moments with the wife of each envoy as she did so; and as she paused before Faith, the amiability of her greeting seemed unusually marked. With characteristic volatility, Faith's depressed spirits began to rebound. But after the group had been dismissed, she felt a light touch on her arm, and was aware that Mrs. Madison was attempting to draw her inconspicuously aside.

"What happened to detain you?" the American Minister's wife asked in a low tone. "We *did* stay a long time after luncheon—it is so delightful at your house that it is always hard to tear ourselves away, and the Nobles were enjoying it immensely! But surely we left in ample time for you to dress!"

"Do you mean I was late? Really late?" asked Faith in consternation.

"My dear, we waited half an hour for you! Then the Crown Princess spoke to us all, and was about to leave the room, when a lady-in-waiting went up to her and whispered that you had just arrived. So we were asked to resume our places, and say nothing, in order that you might not be upset—the comedy was played through a second time for your benefit! Really, the Crown Princess is the personification of tact. But the wives of some of our husbands' colleagues are not. I heard the *doyenne* murmuring that only an American would be so *gauche!* You know how fond I am of you, Faith—I am sure you will not mind if I beg you to be more careful. Rudolf will be really angry if he hears about this, and one of our dear friends is almost certain to feel 'he ought to know' and tell him!"

The older woman's voice was gentle, almost playful, her manner affectionate; but in spite of the kindly *savoir faire* with which she tempered her reproof, Faith turned away from her with burning cheeks and brimming eyes. If she could only have fled from the Palace and walked briskly home, she could, she thought, have steadied herself; but she could hardly leave the Amalienborg Square on foot, even if the chilly drizzle of rain which was relentlessly descending had not made such a plan impracticable: her brougham was waiting in line for her and her costume, strikingly appropriate for a court reception, would have been unsuitably conspicuous on the street. She forced herself to take her turn at the entrance, and to keep up her end in the small talk with which she was surrounded, though conscious of the captiousness of the comment which would be unrestrained after her departure. But when she had bowed her last smiling farewell from the window of her carriage, she flung herself back in one corner of it with a recklessness that bordered on rebellion.

It was seldom that she chafed, even subconsciously, against the established order of her life; but now the incident which her tardiness had precipitated, had set her spirits seething. A sudden mutiny against the rigidity of her existence engulfed her. She saw herself rising, reclining, sleeping, walking, eating, drinking, speaking, moving, in accordance with inflexible rules, to which, despite her every effort, she failed to entirely conform. There was no challenge to a restless mind in such a rentless régime, no spaciousness for a soaring soul. If it were not for Hans Christian she would find some avenue of escape from the shackles of a system which seemed to deprive her so mercilessly of every essential liberty.

If it had not been for Hans Christian! But without this radiant child, whose loveliness was his legacy from the "slumberous amorous summer" to which he owed his being, what would liberty of life be worth to her? Was he not only the core of existence to her; but existence itself? Why should she rebel against the usuages which fettered her, when these were, after all, the symbols of a sphere where he was monarch? Her hour of humiliation was behind her, and she would rise above it as she had risen before; she would remember the Princess' tact, not the tattle of the diplomatic circle; and though she could not justify herself to Rudolf, she could bear his condemnation uncrushed, with candid apologies, and with the earnest assurance that she would not again fail to do him credit. The hour of revolt was passing too—had she not promised to be loyal? Loyal to a code as well as to a man? Could she be faithless to her own pledged word?

She straightened herself again in her dark corner, dried her eyes, and lifted her head. Then, conscious that her brougham had turned into Trondhjemsgade, she leaned forward, looking up toward the window where Hans Christian always stood to watch for her home-coming, the shade raised above his glowing hair, the light shining behind his erect little figure.

He was not visible; and as she approached her house, a swift stab of alarm, which went far deeper than momentary disappointment, smote her. Could anything have happened? Had he been taken suddenly ill? Could Rudolf, as he had so often threatened, have interfered with their precious twilight hour by imposing another lesson on his son? A dozen different fears assailed her as she mounted the steps. But as the front door was thrown open for her, she heard the familiar headlong rush on the stairway, and the next instant the little boy was locked in her arms.

"Hansel!" she cried, kneeling down and pressing her face against his. "You were not watching for me at the window! You frightened me! What happened?"

"I did watch, mother, a little while. But then a visitor came. He asked first for father, and Johann said that he was in the Chancery. And then for you, and Johann said you were at the Palace. And then for me, and Johann said I was in the drawing-room. So I came out to welcome him. That was why I was not at the window. He is very easy to talk to and I like him. He is a Spaniard, and he has been telling me about Spain—about bull fights and *ferias,* and the little Prince of the Asturias who looks like his beautiful English mother, and the young King who plays polo. He is a very pleasant man and his eyes crinkle when he smiles. He says he is a cousin of ours, and that he hopes you will be glad to see him."

"What is his name?" asked Faith, faintly and superfluously. For she knew that when she reached the top of the stairway, she would find Sebastian de Cerreno waiting there for her. She put her free hand on the banister to steady herself and stopped for a moment. But even as she did so, she was aware that Sebastian would span the years of their separation with some smiling syllable, and that his facile grace would smooth away all constraint from their meeting. She looked up and saw him standing above her; and as she met his eyes, her heart gave a sudden joyous leap, and she hastened toward him.

"Se bien venido, Sebastian!" she exclaimed. *"Esta es tu casa."*

"A tus pies, Fidelidad," he answered gravely, *"siempre."*

Chapter XXVI

There was something in the gesture with which Sebastian kissed Faith's outstretched hand which gave the illusion that he had knelt before he raised it to his lips. And as he released it, lingeringly, and spoke to her, she felt the quality of worship in his voice.

"Will you not come into the light where I can look at you?" he asked her gently.

"I do not need the light to see you have not changed at all!"

"No, not at all," he said, still very gravely. He did not stress his words, and yet the double meaning which he gave to them was unmistakable. "But you, Fidelidad, have changed immeasurably!"

She had passed swiftly on into the drawing-room, then, turning as swiftly, she had faced him. Hans Christian looked from one to the other anxiously.

"Mother says," he announced in a slightly troubled voice, "that she has no real elegance, like Mrs. Noble, who just came here, for instance. But I think she is lovely-looking, just the same, don't you?"

"I have always thought so, Hansel," Sebastian answered, looking down at the eager upturned little face, "and so has everyone else who has ever seen her. She is talking nonsense to you, *querido!*" He glanced quickly from the child to his mother, his narrow somber face illuminated with his smile. "Why do you trifle with your son's sense of values, Faith?" he asked lightly. "Can elegance compete with loveliness? And yet, as far as that goes, what could be more elegant than cream broadcloth and sables, worn with topazes? Your taste is unerring as it always was. But I was not prepared to find it so sophisticated!"

"I am not seventeen, you know, any longer. I am afraid the lily, shining behind the waterfall, has emerged!"

"A lily is still a lily, whether it is behind a waterfall—or not, Fidelidad—and its clarity is still more dazzling when this is not veiled . . . Are you not going to sit down so that Hansel and I may do so? And ring perhaps for some sherry, if there is any in this Teutonic household? And ask me when I arrived, and if I had a good journey, and how long I am going to stay, and so on—the usual conventionalities of welcome at least?"

Faith walked over to the bell and pulled it. "There is sherry," she said, "though I am afraid you will find it abominable compared with yours. And of course I am immensely interested in learning when you came, and so forth. I am sorry I did not ask you without being prompted. But I am remiss about conventionalities still—in fact, I have just been late at a royal reception. The knowledge of my guilt and the consciousness that the entire diplomatic corps is discussing me at this moment, combined with the surprise of seeing you several days before I expected, has made me more negligent than ever, I am afraid. . . . Sherry, please, Johann."

Sebastian seated himself quietly at the further end of the brocaded sofa on which she had flung herself down, drawing Hansel up between them, and keeping his arm around the boy's shoulder. "If the entire diplomatic corps is discussing you at this moment, Faith," he said calmly, "it is less because of your guilt, that because you are young and beautiful, and an heiress in your own right, and the daughter-in-law of an Imperial Archduchess, and a great favorite with the Danish Royal Family, as all Europe knows. Therefore women less favored by fortune must vent their jealousy in some way, and the unfortunate men who are fettered to them must pretend to agree with them. What do you expect? I see that I shall be obliged to continue reminding you that you have lost your sense of values!—As to my own insignificant program, I did arrive a day ahead of schedule—it is a plan I always follow whenever I can. It never fails to furnish me with exceptional opportunities. For instance, in this case, when I reached the Spanish Legation, I found that Jaime was at the Citadelet playing bridge, instead of waiting for me at the station accompanied by various other personages of rank, all eager to engulf me immediately with tiresome talk about treaties and commemorations. I was therefore free to walk out of the house again unhampered as soon as I had washed my hands.—Tell me how you like Denmark, Faith. Does everyone ride a bicycle? And does it always rain like this?"

"Nearly everyone and nearly always," she answered, smiling in spite of herself. "But there are exceptions and interludes." Her sense of inadequacy and tension had melted away, and the old impulse to talk with Sebastian discursively and confidentially surged over her. "And there are interludes in the country itself, just as there are in the rain. Most of the landscape is so trim and tidy that it all seems to be part of a neat pattern! I have kept hoping, ever since we came here, to see a fallen brick somewhere, or a woman with her hair tumbling down, or sunshine that really blazed——"

"The way it all is in Spain," said Sebastian encouragingly.

"Yes—and I know now I never shall! But in the midst of all this trimness, you suddenly come upon some of the most enchanting forests in the world. Those are the interludes. They are beech woods, and they are symphonies in emerald! The leaves are green and the tree trunks are green, and the sward is covered with green moss. Even the lights and shadows that flicker back and forth are green. And there are elements of magic in them; I am certain they are fairy forests!"

"Have you wandered in these fairy forests, Faith—since you left your magic house?"

"Not yet. But——"

"Mother says she is sure there are elves and gnomes and goblins in them," Hansel interrupted excitedly. "And some day she and I are going out to find them!"

"Will you take me with you?" Sebastian asked gravely.

"We would love to, wouldn't we, mother? I am sure Sebastian could help us find the fairies! You said that father couldn't find them, because he didn't believe in them, and so they hid. But you believe in them, don't you, Sebastian?"

"With all my heart. And I am glad, Hansel, that your mother still does so too—in spite of everything."

He glanced at her over the child's bright head, ruffling up the crisp unruly curls as he went on talking.

"And besides the fairy forests—what are Denmark's delights?"

"The country life is very pleasant," Faith hastened to say. "Almost all the people we know spend ten months of the year on their estates. There is a law which forces them to pay a huge tax if they sleep in the city more than sixty nights annually. Just think how funny it would seem to you, Sebastian, if every night you were in Madrid you had to say to yourself, 'Well, this is the thirty-ninth or the forty-second,' —or whatever it was—'there was only so many left before New Year's Day!' "

"It might teach me to spend them more prudently," he said with his old whimsicality, "if I could not be prodigal—prodigal with time of course I mean. You have no idea how austere I have become in other ways. It is all Gabriel can do to emulate me."

"Is Gabriel well?" Faith asked with affectionate solicitude.

"He is well. But he is not strong. He tires easily, and even minor cares rest heavily upon him. He has aged very rapidly these last years.—He sent his love to you, Faith, and said he hoped you would come and see him soon and bring Hans Christian."

"To Spain? To Granada? Oh, mother, can't we?"

"I wish we could, darling. But you know father does not like to have us leave him—and if we ever can go away, it must be to America."

"You have never been there yet—to the old New England homestead?"

"Never. But to-day, coming home from the Palace, I felt as if I could not wait any longer—to go home, Sebastian!"

"You may not have to wait much longer," he said soothingly, averting his gaze from the desperate look in her eyes. "Are you going to tell me more about this Danish country life which you say is so entrancing? I suppose its charm is not wholly confined to its efficacy against taxation?"

"No, it is really delightful. Most of the castles are very old, and have turrets and battlements and arches and courtyards and moats—especially moats. The life is very feudal in some ways; but in others it is very modern. There are splendid tennis courts and golf links, and everyone plays bridge and ping-pong at the house-parties. But a watchman goes poking around with a lantern at night, and calling, 'All's well.' "

"At inopportune moments?"

"Occasionally. But the Danes are very correct. It is only their foreign visitors who are sometimes inconvenienced. . . . At one castle there is a curious old slide that was formerly used to shoot prisoners down to a dark cell. It leads straight out of the kitchen—apparently that was another old custom! And still another is to place a carafe of champagne in front of every dinner guest, and this is drunk as if it were water —no one here considers it an important wine at all!"

"And do you think there is any hope that I may be asked to see something of Danish country life?"

"Any hope! Who is being ridiculous now, Sebastian? A grandee of Spain and the King's special envoy! You know you would be asked to a house-party every week-end, and to all sorts of other parties besides, even if——"

"Even if what, Fidelidad?"

"Even if you were not the most charming man in Europe. But you are!"

She spoke with a vehement sincerity that robbed her words of all coquetry. Sebastian answered her with a seriousness commensurable with her own.

"I shall try to be worthy of this conviction, Faith, not to swerve you from it."

"You and father will ask Sebastian to dinner when the King comes here, won't you, mother?" inquired Hansel, again feeling vaguely that a moment meet for intervention had come.

Faith smiled. "When the King dines at a Legation in Copenhagen," she told Sebastian, "the Minister stands at the front door to welcome him, with the footman holding a huge candelabrum on either side. Then royalty is 'lighted up the stairway.' That is another charming old custom. It made a great impression on Hansel when he watched it from a corner in the hall. So now he wishes you to see it!"

"I am very eager to see it," Sebastian assured the child. "But I hope I may dine with your mother, Hansel, without waiting until the King does also—Are you by any miracle free to-night, Faith?"

"No," she said regretfully, "I am never free." Then, conscious of her *double entendre*, she sprang quickly to her feet. "But I am sure Guido Bonatelli, at whose house we are dining, will insist on your joining the party, when he hears you have arrived. He is giving a dinner dance in fancy dress, and it will be very gay. Will you excuse me while I go and telephone to him?"

*   *   *   *   *

It was just eight o'clock when Rudolf von Hohenlohe knocked on his wife's door. He detested fancy-dress parties, and absolutely declined to appear in costume; but since Faith adored such festivities, his colleagues continued to invite him to them on her account. He also detested Guido Bonatelli; for though he held fast to the comfortable theory that a woman who had been married nearly ten years must necessarily have ceased to appear desirable to any man, he mentally characterized the Italian as a trivial idler, unentitled, except for the position he had unaccountably attained, to serious consideration from any other diplomat. In any case, therefore, he would have prepared grudgingly for this gala dinner; but his aversion to participating in the madcap revelry before him had been intensified a hundredfold by the tidings, which had just been brought to him, of Faith's tardiness at the Palace. If it had not been for the fact that a failure on his part to appear in public, and with her, on the evening after her lamentable breach of etiquette, would certainly be interpreted as a timorous and apologetic gesture, nothing would have persuaded him to leave his own house.

She flung the door open suddenly, and confronted him with a scintillating smile. She had put on a black dress of heavy corded silk, the low, square-cut bodice molded to her figure, the skirt a billowing mass of full and narrow ruffles edged with velvet ribbon. Over one shoulder was flung a heavy fringed shawl of black crêpe embroidered with brilliant and exotic flowers; there were roses clustered at one side of the high black comb that surmounted her head, and crimson slippers on her feet; a cascade of brilliants fell glitteringly from her ears, and around her neck, on a long dazzling chain, was hung a magnificent cross of splendid diamonds.

Rudolf stared at her with overwhelming stupefaction as she seized his arm, and began to propel him gently but urgently in the direction of the stairway. They had almost reached it before he recovered himself enough to draw away from her. And to his own amazement, the first words he spoke had nothing whatever to do with her recent lapse from decorum.

"Where did you get that pendant?" he demanded.

Faith laughed and slipped her hand through his arm again. "I don't remember exactly," she said blithely. "Somewhere in Granada at a musty *antiquario's,* the day I went to see the gypsies on the Sacro Monte. It has lain at the bottom of my jewel box, wrapped up in cotton wool, for years. But to-night I felt like getting it out again."

"It looks very valuable to me to have come from an *antiquario's,*" said Rudolf doubtfully. "Besides, I do not con-

210

sider that a cross is a suitable ornament to wear with a fancy-dress costume."

"But it is a Spanish costume! Remember that the Sevillian choir boys dance the quadrille at Easter-time in front of the high altar in the cathedral! . . . Do hurry, Rudolf, or we shall be late!"

"That would be quite in keeping with your conduct, earlier to-day," Rudolf said formally and without moving.

Faith stared at him in her turn and then laughed again. "Oh, you mean at the Palace?" she said nonchalantly. "I was very sorry—but I am sure the Crown Princess understood and made allowances. She is always so sweet! I really had forgotten all about it until you spoke—so much has happened since then that is far more important!"

Chapter XXVII

THE stir of admiration which Faith's Spanish costume elicited, as she made her belated appearance in Guido Bonatelli's drawing-room, was significant in both its immediate and subsequent results. The evening was not over when her host suggested that if she would wear such a dress and dance the tango at the forthcoming Charity Bazaar in which the Princess Marie was so deeply interested, she would have a *succes fou* herself besides benefiting the cause immeasurably. Before Faith could answer Rudolf interposed an objection.

"Faith does not know how to dance the tango."

"I should be delighted to teach her. I am sure she would be a very apt pupil."

Rudolf turned with amazement to Jacqueline Noble, from whom this startling offer had come. She gave him a ravishing smile.

"My mother was a professional dancer," she went on tranquilly. "I am supposed to have inherited a little of her talent. I have often coached the dancing for amateur theatricals."

That any woman should voluntarily make such a damaging announcement regarding her maternal parentage was inconceivable to Rudolf. He nearly gasped out loud in his surprise. But he managed to recover himself enough to give a conventional answer.

"You are most kind. But even if my wife could avail herself to your offer, she would be without a partner."

"How tiresome you are, Rudolf! Do you think I spent a year in Argentina futilely? Of course I can be her partner! If Mrs. Noble will so far honor me, we might give an exhibition dance now, to show you what a vivacious addition one would be to an evening of stodgy tableaux."

Sebastian detached himself nonchalantly from the group with which he was sitting, and approached the self-confessed social pariah with a look of bland beguilement. Dinner was over, and though the drawing-room floors were already cleared, there had been an agreeable period of lingering over coffee and liqueurs, and dancing had not yet begun. No moment could have been more propitious for a dramatic gesture.

Jaqueline's response was immediate. She was on her feet almost before Sebastian had finished speaking, and there was a moment's smiling conference about music. It appeared that an orchestra was prepared to rise to such an agreeable emergency; and almost instantly Sebastian had swung her into position, and they had begun to move forward in swift symmetrical unison.

She was wearing a Breton peasant costume entirely inappropriate to the rôle she had so precipitantly assumed; but for all that, she gave it an illusion of exotic grace and fascination which stamped her performance with unmistakable genius. When at last she glided back to her seat, it was amidst cries of "bravo!" and "encore!" and a tumult of clapping. As the applause finally died down again, Sebastian slid quietly into a place beside Faith.

"You see how easy it is, Fidelidad!"

"*Easy!* To dance like that! I am only just average, Sebastian, at dancing."

"Perhaps you need practice," he suggested. "Does Rudolf dance much?"

"He does not dance at all," she said, her voice slightly edged with vexation.

"Oh—I suppose he spends all his leisure at the bridge table."

"You know perfectly well, Sebastian, that Rudolf has no leisure. And he detests cards."

"It must be tragic," Sebastian murmured smoothly, "to have such limited tastes.—I suppose you can waltz, Faith, in spite of all this vaunted inexpertness of yours! Shall we try?"

They had not gone twice around the room before she knew that the question of the tango was settled. She felt not only as if she had melted into his arms but as if her very being had been merged into his.

"I tried to tell you how it would be," he said smilingly. "But you would not listen to me—I shall have to call you Thomasina, because you would not believe me until——"

"Sebastian! You must not be blasphemous!"

"I did not mean to be blasphemous," he answered gravely. "Shall we rest a little? You are very pale, *querida.*"

"I—I think that I am going to faint."

"You are not going to do anything of the sort. You are going to tell me where I can take you without running the risk of having you snatched away from me immediately, and then we are going to sit and talk together. I am sorry to seem so unresourceful myself, but you must remember that this is the first time that I have ever been in this house."

"Guido has a—little conservatory back of the dining room."

"How thoughtful of him! By the way, you were not considering him as a possible *cavaliere servente,* were you, Faith?"

Her answer was delayed until they found the flowery enclosure toward which she led the way, her heart still hammering; and after they had taken their places on the recessed window-seat, she made an indirect reply.

"You are the second person to put that idea into my mind!"

"And who was the first, Rudolf?"

"Rudolf!" she exclaimed almost contemptuously. "No—it was *Tante* Luise—only she spoke of an *amitié amoureuse* instead of a *cavaliere servente*—Rudolf is sure he is the only person who ever fell in love with me."

"Whoever—what?"

"Fell in love with me," she persisted, with a little nervous laugh. "He still thinks he did, you know, and that he is the only person who ever will."

"Have you taken much advantage of this convenient viewpoint?"

"I haven't taken any at all," she answered flushing. "I think you know that."

"I do know it. I only wanted to hear you say it."

"And now that I have said it, may I ask a question? It flashed through my mind when Jacqueline Noble said her mother was a dancer. What has become of Felicidad?"

"She has six children, twins among them," said Sebastian imperturbably. Then as Faith gave a startled exclamation, he glanced at her with an ironic gleam in his eye, and suddenly burst out laughing. *"Querida,* what a look! And how little I deserve it! The twins, unfortunately, are not mine—or any of their delightful little brothers and sisters. Felicidad

213

is married—very happily married—to one of the doorkeepers at the Royal Opera House in Madrid. I have seen her only once or twice in the last eight years, quite by chance and in the presence of this worthy functionary. I am afraid her dancing days are over. She must weigh one hundred and fifty pounds, and she is always nursing a baby or preparing to nurse one."

"Sebastian, you are incorrigible!" said Faith, joining in his laugh in spite of herself. "It is fortunate that you did not look for a *dulce amiga* in the ballet here—it is the finest one in Europe, except perhaps the imperial ballet at St. Petersburg; but the standard of morality for the girls is very strict. They are considered government employees and if they digress from the strait and narrow path, they are instantly dismissed."

"As you say, it is fortunate I do not live in Copenhagen," said Sebastian soberly. "I should constantly be haunted by the thought of the dismissals I had caused." Then as Faith laughed again, involuntarily, he added, "But I have really lost all interest in dancers, or thought I had. Your charming compatriot has rather revived it. Her bombshell about her mother was most refreshing! Who is she and where does she come from?"

"I only know that she is half-French—the French half was the dancer, I suppose!—and that her husband is a famous surgeon. He is delightful too."

"I thought so myself," said Sebastian idly. "I talked with him for some minutes after dinner, and found him most *simpatico*. What is his specialty?"

"He concentrates on mental cases. He has had a most remarkable success."

"What do you mean, mental cases?"

"It seems he has removed tumors from the brain, and cured persons who are supposed to be hopelessly insane—when it was not hereditary, I mean.—Sebastian, what is the matter? Have I said anything to hurt your feelings?"

He had risen with a smothered exclamation, swinging swiftly away from her. As he turned again, she saw that the expression on his face was almost savage.

"What are you telling me this for?" he asked harshly.

"But you asked me! I never thought—Sebastian—are you thinking—*that he might cure Dolores?*"

For a moment they stood staring at each other, shocked beyond utterance at the sudden insidious supposition that had darted through their mingled consciousness. Then Sebastian took Faith's hands in his and carried them to his breast.

"No," he said without a tremor in his voice, "I am not

thinking that. She is incurable. A dozen different doctors have pronounced her so. The greatest specialists in Europe. It is not possible that this American could succeed where they have failed. And it pains me, Fidelidad, to hear her name on your lips. Shall it be agreed between us that we will not speak of her again?"

He kissed her hands, released them, and offered her his arm. "I have not told you how much it pleases me to see you in Spanish dress," he said. "Except for that charming costume which the Icelandic Minister's wife is wearing, yours is certainly the most effective one here. And I am delighted that you have put on your cross of "*rhinestones*" to celebrate my arrival.—But we must go back to the ballroom, *querida*, before we are missed—in each other's company. Indiscretion is the thief of opportunity. And this time I do not intend that anyone—or anything—shall divert our destiny."

· · · · · ·

When the question of the charity ball and the tango was next raised, it was not by Sebastian. He left for Norway only a few days after his arrival in Copenhagen, accompanied by Jaime de los Rios, "to talk about treaties and look at cod," as he wrote Faith in a letter that was delivered to her with a big box of snowy flowers during the course of the afternoon following his depature. Meanwhile, besides making official calls, he had been playing tennis at the Citadelet and golf at the Eremitagen; and Faith had seen so little of him that she had begun to wonder to what lengths he proposed to carry his discretion. But there was a postscript to the letter saying, "This is the kind of lily that shone through the waterfall in Ecuador. I have hunted all over Copenhagen in the rain for it"; and she read and re-read her note with eyes that sparkled and then softened.

"If you will bring me some vases, Johann, I will arrange these lilies myself," she said as she glanced up at last, and saw, with a slight sensation of confusion, that the servant was still standing at her door.

"Pardon me, Excellency. I do not think Your Excellency heard me say that Dr. and Mrs. Noble are calling, and wish to know if it would be convenient for you to receive them."

She hastened down to the drawing-room, genuinely distressed because she had kept them waiting, and giving swift instructions as she went, that tea should be served at once, and that the Minister should be informed of their visit as soon as he returned from the Chancery. It was Jacqueline, who, after the first greetings had been exchanged, referred to the question of the tango.

"I have quite lost my heart to Don Sebastian," she said gaily. "He sent me some beautiful red roses the morning after Signor Bonatelli's dinner, with a note saying they were a thank-offering for the privilege of dancing with me. It is a pity Americans never learn to express themselves like that."

"I should not have thought that Dr. Noble was inexpressive," Faith answered, glancing at the surgeon, who was leaning back rolling a cigarette between his long dexterous fingers, and looking at his lovely wife with mingled amusement and affection.

"He has had some beneficial Gallic influence," laughed Jacqueline, "which has improved his technique immensely. But even so, he could never compete with your attractive Spanish cousin—he *is* your cousin, isn't he?"

"He is distantly related to my husband," said Faith, wishing that she would not blush, and conscious that for all the nonchalance of his manner, there was little that escaped David Noble's scrutiny.

"Oh—he rather conveyed the impression—he called on us yesterday at the Angleterre—that the connection was quite close; and I have heard several other persons refer to it in the same way. But I know how united most of the great European families feel!—At all events he is very hopeful that the exhibition dance of which we spoke should be featured at the Charity Bazaar. Apparently he is much interested in this—the Princess Marie received me on Friday, and told me he had sent her a thousand kroner for it. So I have come to say that if I could help you at all with your preparations, I should be delighted. I have agreed to do some Majorcan dances myself, that I learned from an old peasant when David and I once spent almond blossoming-time near Palma."

Faith hesitated. She was ashamed of the swift stab of jealousy which had pierced her at the thought that Sebastian had given roses to Jacqueline as well as lilies to her, and that he should have found time to call at the Angleterre when he had not darkened the door of the German Legation. But as his strategy became clearer to her, she could not help admiring it, and she was irresistibly tempted to take advantage of it.

"If you really feel that I should do credit to your teaching—" she began. But Jacqueline interrupted her.

"I am positive you would! When you are sitting or standing,

216

when you rise and walk, you are very graceful. But when you dance, you stiffen the least little bit. You seem a trifle unyielding. I think that is the only difficulty we need to overcome. You must relax when you are dancing with Don Sebastian, in the same way that you relax when you pose for Sam Dudley. You are wholly natural with him, and when you are wholly natural, you are wholly captivating!"

"If you keep on, Jacqueline, Baroness von Hohenlohe will think that you are the surgeon of the family. You are very analytical."

"But the analysis is accurate, isn't it, David? And I am sure the Baroness wants me to be frank! Besides, you have probably been analyzing us both while we have been talking, so you have no right to reprove me!"

She laughed again, and turned to Faith with increasing animation. "You have a great deal of dramatic instinct," she went on. "Caleb Hawks told me so first, and I have seen it for myself in Copenhagen. Of course Caleb didn't put it just that way. He said it was a pity you didn't have a chance to speechify for women's rights, or something like that, because if you did, you would be a 'rabble-rouser' and 'liven up any campaign considerable.' I think he cherishes a hope that some day you will do so yet. But for the moment, you certainly can't decline to dance the tango! Is eleven in the morning a convenient time for you to rehearse? The day after Don Sebastian returns from Norway? And—you do not mind another suggestion, do you? Leave off your stays! You must not barricade yourself with steel! You must be absolutely plastic in your partner's arms."

She spoke as if the matter were entirely settled, and began to fasten her furs and draw on her gloves. Faith's lips parted ever so slightly, and then she closed them again.

"I think Baroness von Hohenlohe has something to say in self-defense," suggested David.

Faith turned to him with an uncanny feeling of fear. If he has noticed even so ephemeral a movement as the one she had just made, she had been right in believing there was nothing which escaped his observation.

"No," she said falteringly. "I—I will dance the tango with Sebastian, since Mrs. Noble has so much confidence in me. She has made me understand already—how to do better. It was about something else that I wanted to speak to you, only I am not sure whether I ought to—partly because I do not know whether Sebastian would wish to have me, and partly because I realize that it is very incorrect to talk with a doctor about a professional matter when he is making a friendly visit."

"I hope you will talk with me about anything you wish," said David encouragingly. "That is, unless you really feel that Don Sebastian might prefer you do not."

He spoke with such sympathy and kindliness that Faith was disarmed. She locked and unlocked her fingers as she usually did when she was excited, but she began to unburden herself almost immediately.

"It is about a lady who is—a—relative of Sebastian," she said, her words coming with a rush. "He cannot bear to talk about her, it is all so tragic; but the night of Bonatelli's dinner, he asked me what your specialty was, and suddenly we—suddenly I—ever since then I have felt I must tell you about her, that I couldn't keep still. She has been—strange—for a great many years. She lives—in great retirement—in a castle in the Pyrenees. Once, when she was not watched very carefully, she even tried to kill her husband. But there is no insanity in her family. She is the only one who has ever been—as she is. And if she could get well—and—and have a child, it would—it would mean everything. Her husband is the last of his race."

"Is this lady Don Sebastian's wife, Faith?" David asked gently.

She looked at him in deep astonishment, too amazed to even notice that he had called her by her Christian name, and that he had spoken almost as tenderly as if he had been comforting a troubled child.

"How did you guess?" she asked impulsively.

"Doctors need to be skillful at surmise," he said more gently still, "since they are certain of so little! May I tell you what else I have guessed? That you are hesitating to say, for fear that I will misjudge Don Sebastian—though I assure you I should not!—that his memories of his life with this lady are so interwoven with bitter disappointment and horror and grief, that he shrinks from reviving them, even if there were a chance that she might be cured."

"Is there a chance?" exclaimed Faith.

"I cannot tell without seeing her. There might be—a possibility."

"And could you go to see her?"

"To Spain? It is a long journey."

He appeared to be turning the question over in his mind, watching Faith's expression covertly as he did so. At last he answered rather slowly.

"It would mean the postponement of work at home which is important. But if Don Sebastian asks me to go, I will not refuse."

"And if he didn't ask you? You couldn't go, could you, right away? Without even giving him a chance to ask you?"

"You mean, before you have a chance to regret that you have asked me?"

"I could give you a letter to Sebastian's brother, Gabriel," Faith said recklessly, disregarding David's question. "He is the Archbishop of Granada, and he is very powerful and very wise. He would arrange everything for you. No one would even find out until it was all over. Would you be afraid to—to act secretly?"

"I should not be afraid. But there is one contingency I do not think you have considered: you are thinking only of what would happen if this lady were cured. Sometimes patients die while a tumor is being removed, or as a result of the removal. If Don Sebastian's wife did not survive an operation upon which you had insisted—how would you feel then?"

There was infinite compassion in his voice, an understanding so profound that it seemed fathomless. He reached over and took one of her hands in his powerful flexible fingers.

"You are a very gallant lady," he said gravely. "I will do everything I can to serve you. But I do not think you have a right to exclude Don Sebastian from this great decision."

Chapter XXVIII

IF Rudolf von Hohenlohe had not been anxiously abstracted because of certain subtle developments on the map of Europe which he knew were portentous, he would have observed that Faith was unusually silent all the evening. The Radens were in town, and had arranged a large "Dutch treat" dinner at the Angleterre, with informal dancing afterwards, to which only intimate friends had been asked; and as a rule Faith was at her best on impromptu ocasions of this sort, which she enjoyed far better than those attended with more ceremony. But she sought Rudolf out of her own accord a little after midnight, and suggested that since they were free to leave whenever they pleased, they should go home.

"Are you ill?" he asked, complying with alacrity, but obviously astonished.

"No, I am like Queen Victoria. I am not amused."

"You are not in the least like Queen Victoria," said Rudolf literally. "If you are indisposed, why do you not say so?"

His manner did not invite confidences. And yet, as he bade her good-night, Faith asked him, a little hesitatingly, if he would not come into her room for a chat and a cigarette before he went to bed.

"A chat and a cigarette?" he echoed. "At this hour? When you have left a party before it was half over because you were too tired to stay until the end? You are not very consistent, Faith. Try to get a long sleep—tell Hilda not to let Hans Christian come bounding into your room early in the morning. You cannot reasonably expect to keep on burning the candle at both ends indefinitely. I hope you will feel much better to-morrow."

Even then she longed to detain him. It seemed to her that she could not shut herself in for the night alone with the burning problems which confronted her. She felt impelled to take his hand, to look candidly into his face, to talk to him without reservations. The very words she seemed constrained to speak were trembling on her lips. But as he continued to look at her with an expression of detachment which she felt amounted to indifference, she turned despondently away from him, and went slowly into her sumptuous Spanish room.

For hours after Hilda had been dismissed, Faith sat on the edge of her golden bed, her turquoise-colored dressing gown wrapped about her, locking and unlocking the slim hands toward which she looked down unseeingly.

David Noble had made a profound impression upon her: his intuition had startled her, his sympathy had touched her, his arguments had overpowered her. Yet now that she could count on his skill and his wisdom, she knew she still could not prevail in her purpose unless Sebastian could be induced to consent to it. She realized David had been right in dissuading her from her first wild project; yet how could she perfect another plan. And how could she withstand a passion to which, with every fiber of her quivering consciousness, she ardently responded? The barriers before which Sebastian once had bowed—were not there to restrain him any longer; and such safeguards as she did have were not strong enough to repel him. She had no sooner looked into his eyes than she had known he had come at last to claim her; and when he told her that no power on earth could thwart their destiny a second time, she felt he spoke the truth.

The sound of a striking clock roused her from her tumultuous reveries. The reluctant dawn of the late northern spring had not yet penetrated through the drawn draperies at her windows yet it was nearly morning, and she was no nearer a solution of her perplexities than she had been the night before. She let her aqua robe slip to the floor, and lay down at last in her bed, falling eventually into a troubled slumber; but she woke unrefreshed, and for the next few days, she went automatically through her engagements, only half-conscious as to how she filled them. Even after Sebastian's return from Norway and the resumption of their meetings, she seemed to make no headway toward clarity. As if he guessed her intention to reason and plead with him, he kept mockingly aloof from her; and his attitude, during their rehearsals together, was so impersonal that she was almost piqued. He could, apparently, dance with her indefinitely, and still remain as detached from her in feeling as he was close to her in person. His grace, his litheness, his dexterity, were all inimitable; but she never recaptured the sensation of ecstasy to which he had so swiftly stirred her on the night of Bonatelli's dance.

She and Rudolf were invited to the dinner at the Palace given in honor of the special envoy of the King of Spain; and she saw Sebastian's eyes resting appraisingly upon her; for a moment as she came into the great room where royalty received its guests. She was wearing the most superb of all her Paris dresses—a lustrous heavy white satin trimmed with rare Alençon lace and finished with a square-cut train two metres long; and she was wearing her diamond cross and earrings as ornaments. She was conscious that she was looking her very best; and yet when he finally came and spoke to her, which was not until after dinner, he made a rather cutting allusion to her appearance, and immediately afterwards began to speak of how extremely interesting he had found the court ceremonial.

"Very beautiful," he murmured glancing at her glistening gown and jewels, "but just a little glacial, Fidelidad. Are you impersonating Andersen's 'Snow Queen,' by any chance?"

"The court is in half-mourning, as you know," she answered, with a slight tinge of annoyance in her voice. "I had to wear black or lavender or white, and I happened to choose white, that is all."

"Oh—I am glad to learn you were not trying to chill me with the rather frosty quality of your crystalline inaccessibility.—This is a delightful function, is it not? I never saw a dining room more brilliantly lighted, and the effect of the concealed music is charming. I was really much impressed with the health-drinking. 'Skaal,' is a perfect word for a toast, and this custom of standing and looking your royal host straight in the eye as he lifts his glass and you lift yours, is most inspiring. As to those flowered headdresses the footmen wear, I could hardly refrain from asking for one as a souvenir!"

He drifted away from her leaving her vexed with him, and with herself that she should be so vexed; and again she longed to turn confidently to Rudolf. But Rudolf apparently noticed her ruffled temper now no more than he had noticed her silence a few nights earlier. Indeed, as the spring advanced, it seemed to Faith that his preoccupation in his work had never been so complete.

Before pledging herself irrevocably to the exhibition dance at the Charity Bazaar, Faith made very sure that he did not disapproved of it. The only objections which he raised were inconsequential.

"I should think Sebastian would be too busy with this impending treaty to take time for amateur theatricals," he said coolly. However, that is his affair. . . . I have always known he had a weakness for buffoonery. I suppose King Alfonso knows it too, and makes due allowances. No doubt with Mrs. Noble's help you will be able to give a reasonably good performance. Though I have never thought dancing was your forte."

"What have you thought that was, Rudolf?" Faith inquired.

He shrugged his shoulders without answering her, as he always did when he seemed to suspect her of seeking a compliment.

"I have learned that Jacqueline Noble's grandfather was Horace P. Huntington, the plutocrat-philanthropist," Faith went on after a moment—"You know, the man who endowed libraries and built hospitals all over the world. His only son died very soon after his marriage to Jacqueline's mother, who was a French *artiste;* and she died too. It was old Mr. Huntington who brought Jacqueline up. I thought you might like to know. You seemed interested when they first came."

"I have too many things on my mind, Faith, which are much more important to me than the background of the Nobles, to be unduly concerned about this. They seem to have settled down here rather indefinitely, and to be generally accepted."

He gathered up a sheaf of papers that were lying in front of him, and began to glance through them, Faith correctly interpreted the gesture as one of indirect dismissal. And

Rudolf did not refer to the bazaar again, in spite of the fact that he knew of her daily attendance at rehearsals, until she reminded him that it was about to take place.

"I do not see how I can possibly go to the theatricals. The despatches which came in late last night will require hours of attention."

"Oh, Rudolf—don't you care at all about seeing me dance?"

He was drinking his morning coffee, and as she spoke to him, he set down his cup with unconcealed irritation.

"How can you be so unreasonable!" he exclaimed. "I tell you about despatches upon which the fate of nations may hang, and you answer by asking if I do not care to see you dance! So I will say that I do not care in the least about seeing you dance. I think this whole affair is ridiculous!"

He went out leaving her chilled with the strange sensation that she had been repudiated as well as rebuked, that he did not care what she did or with whom, as long as he was not inconvenienced by it. At lunch-time he telephoned that he was too busy to leave the Chancery; and it was not until evening that he came to her room, and told her that he had just learned that the King and Queen were to attend the tableaux, and that therfore he would accompy her to the Concert Palais.

"I am sorry that you should be put to so much trouble, because of royalty," Faith said icily.

"They are very grateful to you for your participation in this Bazaar, Faith. . . . I have just learned also, that it was at his special request that you were put at the King's side for the *quadrille d'honneur* at the last court ball. That was a real compliment—both to you personally, and to your dancing."

"I should hardly have been there except by his request," said Faith with continued iciness. She realized that Rudolf regretted his rudeness, and that his attitude was conciliatory of intention; but she still felt congealed and wounded; and it was not until she had reached her dressing room behind the stage, where she found a professional waiting to help her with her make-up, that her naturally buoyant spirits commenced to rise again. An enormous bouquet of white lilacs and lilies, tied with long streamers of vari-colored ribbon, lay on her toilet table; and beside it stood a silver cooler filled with ice, into which a pint bottle of champagne had been plunged. When the professional had finished his work, she sat fingering her flowers and sipping her wine, crushing the bubbles with her lips before she swallowed them, and conscious that a welcome feeling of warmth was permeating her being.

"Are you ready? May I come in? Our cue will be called almost directly now."

She had not seen Sebastian once alone since the Bonatelli dinner, but now he had opened the door of her dressing room and glided inside almost before she could answer him. In the midst of the confusion that reigned, he had evidently contrived to slip away so unobtrusively that no one had seen him. And he confronted her now, slender and dazzling in his superb costume, a smile on his lips and a look in his eyes which she had never seen there before.

"Try to dance for once as if you were a gypsy instead of a snow maiden," he said quietly. As he spoke, he suddenly drew her toward him, one strong supple hand crushing her waist, the other lifting her face to the level of his. He had taken her completely by surprise. Nevertheless as his mouth closed ruthlessly down upon hers, she knew that she was already straining upward for his kiss.

. . . . .

She found him waiting for her the following afternoon when she came in from a long walk in the Langelinge with Hans Christian. She had been a prey to such surging restlessness all day that she had finally sought release from it in violent exercise, and she returned to the house grateful for the exhaustion which she hoped would drug her tingling senses. When she was greeted by Johann with the announcement that the *Duque* de Cerreno was in the drawing-room, she unconsciously tightened her hold on her little son's hand as she went up the stairs.

But for once Hans Christian did not wish to remain with her. Sebastian had sent him a huge box of tin soldiers, gorgeous in Spanish uniforms, and equipped with tents, cannons, horses, and other paraphernalia. He had just finished arranging these in the nursery, preparatory to beginning maneuvers, when his mother had summoned him to go out with her; and now he was eager to resume his interrupted operations. He darted into the drawing-room and flung his arms around Sebastian's neck, thanking him ecstatically for his present; he made an appointment to go and see the changing of the King's Guards the next day with his cousin; but he disregarded Faith's remonstrance as he bounded swiftly out of the room again, leaving her alone with her visitor, who kissed her hand with his usual formality.

"I have come to confer with you about an invitation I have received," Sebastian said quietly.

"Yes? I hope it is a pleasant one?"

"Very. Countess Raden has asked me to spend the week-end at Radensholm. In spite of your confident predictions, I have not been to many house-parties after all. I have been too much entangled with cod and commemorations. But I thought I might enjoy this one very much. Especially as I have somehow gathered that you were planning to spend Sunday in the country yourself."

Faith was silent.

"Is it possible that I was misinformed?"

"No. But I do not think it is best, Sebastian, that we should spend the week-end at Radensholm together."

"Together? You talk as if it were to be a *solitude à deux!* I understand that the Radens are to have at least a dozen guests. But I did think that possibly we might create an opportunity at their countryseat—which somehow seems to have eluded us in town—to discuss a project which I know you have very much at heart."

"I am not sure I understand what you mean, Sebastian."

"I think you do. I asked you not to refer to the subject again, and you have been most magnanimous in your avoidance of it. But I know you feel I should consent to an examination of Dolores by David Noble—to an operation if he advises it. If you can convince me that this should be done—and I am inclined to believe that you can when you are not in constant danger of being interrupted—I will make arrangements to leave for Spain with him next week."

Faith's heart gave a sudden bound for triumph. This was the first reference to Dolores which she had ever known Sebastian to make; and the fact that he had voluntarily brought up the difficult subject which two months earlier he had declined to discuss, seemed a tribute to her influence for which she had not dared to hope. Yet some indefinable instinct of caution made her wary.

"Have you talked with David about this yourself?"

"No. Because I felt I must first talk with you about it. After all, the results of the contemplated operation—whether these are beneficent or disastrous—will affect you more closely than anyone else except myself. You cannot be so naïve that you do not understand that!—but Dr. and Mrs. Noble are going to the house-party also, and when you and I have had our preliminary discussion, we will ask David Noble to confer with us. I have guessed of course that you have spoken with him already. Indeed I suspect you urged him to proceed without consulting me at all, and I am thankful that his judgment acted as a foil to your recklessness! Considering how you have tried to circumvent my authority, I think I am magnanimous to treat with you!"

He smiled disarmingly and engagingly. Faith, sensible at his generosity in the face of her contemplated interference with his life, and more and more touched by his deference to her, smiled faintly in return but did not answer. When Sebastian spoke again, she was conscious of the reassurance in his courteous and guarded voice.

"Are you mistrustful of me, Faith? After all these years? Have I forfeited your confidence? Merely because I talked to you once about destiny and kissed you as I did last night?"

"I am mistrustful of myself," she said with a sudden strangled sob. "I have tried so hard to do right all these years! And now—and now—I feel as if I were rushing toward a precipice! I did ask David to go secretly to Dolores, Sebastian, but only because I thought—I hoped—that if she could get well, you might be happy—after all—with her. I never thought that if she died your—your bondage would be over. And even if it were—you know that mine would not. There is not hope of—of freedom for me. None at all. And yet—"

"And yet—*querida?*"

"You know," she said, burying her face in her hands.

For a moment there was no sound in the room except her smothered weeping. When she raised her head in a desperate effort at self-command, she saw that Sebastian was bending over her and found herself leaning against his shoulder and looking straight into his eyes.

"Fidelidad," he said earnestly, "you must control yourself! Remember that at any moment someone may come into this room—Rudolf, Hansel, Johann, another visitor! It is precisely because it is impossible for us to talk here undisturbed that I am urging you to come to Radensholm! For it is imperative—for your sake as well as mine—that we should converse intimately together. Besides, despair like this is as unworthy of you as it is needless. You are not a helpless child anymore. David Noble calls you a 'gallant lady.' You are that, *querida,* but you are much more than that—you are a beloved woman. Are you not brave enough to face your fate?"

He laid his face swiftly against her wet cheek, kissed her eyelids, her throat, and at last, very gently, her lips.

"I have waited for you nearly eight years," he whispered.

"I have tried, *alma de mi alma*, never to fail you. I shall be waiting for you Saturday—at Radensholm. I know that you will not fail me."

Chapter XXIX

WHEN Faith reached the railroad station on Saturday morning, she found that a number of her fellow passengers on the tidy little train were also bound for Radensholm. Bonatelli hailed her as she went by the compartment in which he was already installed with the French Minister and Madame Marceau; and a group of Danish friends also sought to detain her. But David and Jacqueline Noble had promised to save a place for them. So she went down the narrow corridor until she caught sight of Jacqueline's unmistakable figure, silhouetted upon the window against which she stood looking out with interest and amusement at the crowded station platform.

"Faith! I am so glad to see you!" she exclaimed, turning quickly as David touched her arm to attract her attention. "And Hansel, too!—Good morning, Hilda!—And so the Minister found, as he feared, that he would not be able to get away?"

"Yes. Sunday is often his busiest day. He was very sorry."

"And Don Sebastian? I thought he was coming, but I have not seen him on the train."

"I believe he and Jaime went down yesterday or the day before. One of the first things I learned about Spaniards is that they are not 'too much bound by time,' and their interpretation of a week-end is often a period lasting from Thursday to Tuesday."

She spoke casually, but as usual when she was in his presence, she was conscious of David's discerning gaze, and almost as soon as baggage had been disposed, and wraps arranged, she leaned forward and spoke to him impulsively in French.

"Sebastian came to see me the other afternoon," she said, "and brought up the subject of—of his wife himself. I have never known him to do this before, and I was tremendously encouraged. He has promised to discuss the situation with me at greater length while we are in the country, and I feel very hopeful now that he will consent to an examination at least. Indeed, he spoke of starting for Spain with you next week, if you would be free to go."

"Of course. I have been waiting all this time on purpose."

"And aren't you delighted?"

"I am very glad you have made some progress with the plan which means so much to you. I hope the results will be everything you could wish for."

Faith wondered whether the slight formality of David's manner rose from his inability to speak French with real flexibility and fluency, in spite of his long acquaintance with it. Languages, she had heard him confess more than once, had always been a stumblingblock to him; and Jacqueline, bilingual herself, catered to his weakness. Since Hilda as well as Hansel understood English, Faith did not wish to shift to that and pursue the subject in their presence; so she changed the topic of conversation tactfully, and talked to the Nobles about Danish coöperative farming, and the characteristics of the pleasant and peaceful landscape through which they were passing.

They reached the ferry that was to take them from Zealand to Funen a little before noon; and the party all lunched merrily together on *smordrod*[1] *rodgrod*[2], and a variety of hot and hearty dishes while they paddled across the placid waters dividing the islands. As they piled into the train a second time, Bonatelli detained Faith with the plea that she would make a fourth at bridge with the Tesdorfs and himself; and she was deeply engrossed in a rubber-game, when the guard began shouting the name of the station at which they were to descend. During the ten-mile drive that followed, she forced herself to talk mechanically; but her heart had already begun to beat fast and her thoughts to wander. She was both relieved and disappointed because Sebastian had not come to the station with the Radens' two attractive sons, Valdemar and Gustav; and she found herself alternately dreading and longing for the moment, now inevitably near, when she would meet him. As the carriage swung in through the tessellated entrance to the castle grounds, she saw him standing in the family group at the doorway, with one or two other houseguests, waiting to welcome the additional arrivals. He was beside Dagmar, the Radens' only daughter; and for once, the tall fair girl, with her milk-and-roses complexion, and her ropes of honey-colored hair, was laughing and talking excitedly. Faith

---

1 Thick bread, heavily spread with butter and cold meat.

2 A mixture of red fruit juices and potato flour, chilled and molded, which is served with chopped almonds, sugar and cream, and is a favorite Danish sweet.

had never seen her smooth beautiful face alight with animation before; and the knowledge that Dagmar was already unofficially engaged to Erik, one of the guests at the house-party, did not suffice to allay the swift stab of jealousy that always pierced her when she saw Sebastian paying the casual and graceful court which was as natural to him as breathing. Even after the newcomers had been installed in their apartments and had foregathered for tea in the garden, he did not detach himself from Dagmar except to stroll over to Jacqueline and ask if she would feel inclined to play a little tennis later on; and he turned again to Jacqueline as soon as the dancing began after the choral singing that followed the late dinner. It was Jaime who suggested a walk through the orchards to Faith, and who, as they wandered back and forth in the mild dappled sunlight of late afternoon, pulling cherries from the trees and eating them as they meandered along, told her how favorable an impression her kinsman had made upon their hosts.

"He is as firmly entrenched as if he had been here a dozen times already. Not that Sebastian has seemed to press anything at all—but you know how easily he fits into any situation.—I believe there is a plan for swimming at six—are you in the mood for sea-bathing? The water is actually very warm, warmer than I have ever seen it here before.—Or would you rather go on through the kitchen gardens? I always enjoy looking at those myself. I have never seen such ornamental vegetables as there are in Denmark—the asparagus-bean intrigues me especially!—How delicious these cherries are! I never can decide whether I like best to eat them fresh off the trees like this, or to drink them in cordial form after dinner."

When Faith went back to her rooms, she found a small rectangular package wrapped in old gold brocade, and tied with heavy silk cord, lying on her desk. Hansel, who had had his supper, and was waiting impatiently for her to come and read to him, was consumed with curiosity to know what it contained; so she permitted him to untie it, rescuing the exquisitely bound book and the note that fluttered from it, as they fell from his impetuous little hands.

"Is it a book of fairy tales?" he asked eagerly, watching her turn over the leaves with lingering fingers.

"No, darling. It is a grown-up book. The name of it is 'The Forest Lovers.'"

"I am very sorry," he said with real disappointment, but he added, with never-failing thoughtfulness, "unless you are pleased with it, mother."

"Yes, darling, I am very pleased with it," she said, trying

to speak quietly, and putting her arm around him. But her eyes were devouring the written words before her. *"Alma de mi alma,"* she read. "I hope you will enjoy this exquisite romance, which I think is the loveliest of its kind in the English language. I have had it bound for you in the covers of a book once owned by my ancestors, Doña Cecilia, and I am wrapping it in a piece of one of her dresses. I have thought of sending it to you because I constantly feel in this country as if I might come across Isoult and Prosper walking down a forest path—surely it must have been in woods like these in Denmark that they found sanctuary in each other's arms! And in such woods also, for that matter, that Daphne must have evaded Apollo. Which are they going to mean to us, beloved—fulfillment or frustration? *A tus pies, siempre,* Sebastian."

The gift and the letter threw Faith into a tumult of excitement; but when the party broke up for the night, she had actually exchanged only a dozen words with Sebastian, except during the course of the one dance for which he had asked her. As they glided over the polished floor together, he expressed himself with being enchanted with the Palace: with the huge banqueting hall, all galleries and gilding: with the big kitchen where the fat old cook and eight rosy-cheeked scullery maids were bustling about; with the chapel, which, in spite of the "sterile atmosphere pervading all Catholic churches that have turned Lutheran" was really very fine; but especially with his own room, which, he told her, was hung in dark red damask and furnished in carved ebony; and from which he could look out of a bay window set in a wall three feet thick, at the most beautiful laburnum tree that he had ever seen.

"The Countess says that she always puts you in an isolated wing on the ground floor overlooking the moat, because you like to keep Hansel with you, and she is afraid he will disturb the other guests," he remarked. "I hope you are as comfortable there as I am. It sounds gloomy and remote to me."

"It is somber, but it is not gloomy," Faith answered. "There is something very regal about all the rooms here. Mine are different from yours, but they are just as magnificent. I do not object to isolation as long as I can have Hansel with me—If he slept with Hilda he would be so far away that I could not even look in on him the last thing at night without covering a quarter of a mile or so of corridor. I always kiss him in his sleep, the last thing before I go to bed myself; and I like to be able to comfort him when he has bad dreams—quite often he dreams. And in the morning we read Andersen's 'Fairy Tales' together before breakfast. Hansel feels an especial interest in those because the story-teller's name was Hans Christian too. I have thought that some day I would ask the Radens if we could not arrange to go from here to Odense to see the Andersen birthplace. I am sure Hansel would enjoy that immensely."

"I should think it might be managed very easily—we might make up a party and drive over to Odense for lunch," Sebastian said idly. "And you are not going to hurry off again on Monday, are you? Countess Raden has suggested that I should remain until Wednesday at least."

"But if you are going to start for Spain next week—" faltered Faith.

"Friday or Saturday would still be next week," said Sebastian rather absently. "I have been wandering about in the park here, Faith, and it is really charming—the little pavilions which are scattered through it are exquisite, and the beech woods are full of enchantment, just as you said. I hope some time we can manage a stroll through them together."

"I hope so," answered Faith, trying to suppress the agitation in her voice. "I was delighted with the book you sent me, Sebastian—the book and—and the note."

"I thought we might possibly read aloud together in the woods," Sebastian said, still absently. "It will attract no attention if we eventually wander off together, since we have not rushed off together. And I should like to see those regal rooms of yours, Faith. Will you show them to me some time?"

"If there is a chance," she whispered, with suddenly quickened pulses.

"Oh, there is sure to be! ... Is there no encore to this dance? What a pity!"

The vagueness with which he spoke was somehow more disquieting to Faith than urgency would have been, and on Sunday he still seemed entirely content to let matters drift along. The guests, clothed in riding habits, breakfasted downstairs with their hosts; some of them had already been out for an early morning canter; others left almost immediately for one; and those who had ridden before breakfast, fished before lunch. At noon, the women, all in white dresses, were seated at one side of the long table and the men on the other. The program for the afternoon was equally unstimulating, though it was suggested that the guests should improvise costumes, and come to dinner in fancy dress. Sebastian joined Faith and commented on the plan without much enthusiasm as they went out of the dining room.

"Amusements in Denmark are agreeable, but they lack diversity," he said, looking as if he were stifling a yawn. "There have been a dozen fancy-dress parties in Copenhagen lately, and yet we no sooner get into the country than another is incongruously proposed. I am totally unprepared for such an emergency. I suppose I shall have to devote the afternoon devising something that I can wear."

"You are usually resourceful, under provocation," said Faith demurely.

"Yes. But just at present you are provoked, not I," said Sebastian, resorting to the *double entendre* in which he always took such pleasure. "I really think I shall take a siesta before I do anything else. I enjoy the tranquility of my carvings and brocades and the view of my laburnum tree more than I do this ceaseless round of wholesome sports, interrupted only by tepid tea in the rose garden."

He shrugged his shoulders slightly and drifted away; and feeling almost annoyed with him, Faith went back to her own rooms, read with unwilling absorption the book he had sent her, and looked up from it with genuine amazement when Hilda appeared on the scene with the respectful suggestion that it was time the Frau Baronin dressed for dinner. But the process of preparing for the fancy-dress party intrigued her. She had forseen the contingency which had arisen; and she had brought with her to Radensholm a costume which she had kept laid away in a trunk, ever since it had been sent to her, together with certain other unique heirlooms, at the time of her father's death. It was the dress which her great-grandmother, the first Faith Marlowe, had worn for her New England marriage: a narrow-skirted, high-waisted, puffed-sleeved, white silk, absolutely devoid of ornament. Faith had tried it on when it had first arrived, and had discovered that it fitted her perfectly; but she had folded it away, with the mesh mitts, the low-heeled ankle ties, the embroidered handkerchief, the parchment fan, and the short lace-edged veil that went with it; feeling, for some indefinable reason, that the time had not yet come when she wished to wear it. She had shown it once to Victoria Luise, who had been entranced with it, and had even suggested that Faith might wear it to her own wedding, and prove that contrary to popular European belief, Americans had a heritage and a tradition. But Mrs. Carolus Cavendish Castle had been firmly in favor of Worth's latest lustrous creation, and had pronounced the yellowing grosgrain entirely unsuitable for a function which was to be virtually a court ceremony. Faith had been inclined to agree with her; she had a sentiment about her ancestral dress, but she thought lengths of shining splendor far more glamorous than this trainless example of early nineteenth-century severity. It was only recently that a belated reëxamination of it had convinced her that she had underestimated its effectiveness. There was actually something primly provocative about it.

As Hilda did up its fastenings now, while Hansel jumped up and down on the tapestried bed, squealing with admiration, Faith realized that she had never put on anything that became her more. She had chosen a short tight string of pearls for her ornament, and had bound her head with a wreath of small white roses, from which the sheer veil fell over her shoulders; the grace of her throat and the splendor of her hair had both been accentuated. She could not help being conscious also of the soft whiteness of her arms, revealed between the short sleeve and the short mitts, and of her neck and breast rising above the tuckered bodice; and she knew that the quaint cut of the close-fitting dress revealed the slender unconfined curves of her figure as no stiff modern dress could have done.

"I am glad Mrs. Noble gave me the idea of leaving off stays," she said casually to Hilda as she picked up her handkerchief and fan. "I should never have thought of doing it myself, but I feel like a different person without them. . . . Goodnight, Hansel darling. I will come in to kiss you the minute I can get back here after dinner."

"But I will be asleep then! Kiss me again now, mother! You are beautifuller than ever, and you smell so sweet!"

"Just once more, darling! But do not muss me up!"

She disengaged herself gently, running her fingers through his tangled curls in a lingering caress; then, as Hilda held open the door for her, curtseying with admiration as well as respect, she stepped swiftly out into the long corridor.

It was dimly illumined by bracket lamps projecting from the walls at long intervals from each other; but as she passed quickly and quietly along, she saw a flickering light ahead of her, and was aware of the watchman's swinging lantern. She had not realized that he began his rounds so early; but dinner was later than usual, because of the long forest drive which had been scheduled to follow the afternoon swim; and at lunch there had been some laughing comment to the effect that if such irregular hours continued, the guests would begin to imagine themselves in Spain instead of in Denmark! As she approached the sentinel, she saw that the somber color of the garments in which he was clad made of him a dim apparition hardly distinguishable from the encircling shadows; and interested afresh at the mysterious mediaevalism of this faithful figure, she paused to greet him with a cordial good-evening. As she did so, he lifted his lantern; and with a startled exclamation, she stepped back, shocked at the subtlety of the artifice with which she was confronted.

"Sebastian!" she gasped, "what are you doing here? And what do you mean—mean by putting on those clothes?"

"We were told to appear in costume, were we not?" he inquired imperturbably. "Without forewarning enough to prepare any? I was thankful to find a coöperative as well as a congenial spirit in the watchman. I roused him from his well-earned slumbers after my own siesta, and solicited his help. I fear that I should hardly have been as expansive myself under the same circumstances as he was."

Sebastian smiled, swinging his lantern slowly around until it made a circle of light about her. Then, in his turn, he gave a startled exclamation.

"*Madre de Dios!*" he whispered. "Where did you ever find such a dress and veil? You are the reincarnation of some seductively simple spirit!"

"I have had them a long time. They belonged to my great-grandmother—she wore them on her wedding day. I am impersonating a Puritan bride, Sebastian."

"A Puritan bride!" he echoed deliberately. "And what happens, Faith, when a Puritan and a pagan meet? Do they clash—or do they merge?"

"I—I do not know."

"But you expect to discover, Faith, do you not?"

She felt as if he must hear the quickened beating of her heart in the surrounding stillness. But she could not answer.

"Listen," he said swiftly, "after the dance is over to-night —a long time after—I will come down this corridor again. As I pass along, I will call out, 'All's well.' Then I will try the latch of your sitting-room door. If it is unlocked, I will go in. If it is not, I will go away. But if I find it fastened. I do not know to what desperate lengths I shall be driven afterwards."

"And if you do not find it fastened," she faltered, "will you promise to leave me to-night whenever I ask you to? To—to go to Spain before the week is over?"

"On my sacred word of honor! By the memory—of my mother!"

He looked at her impellingly. She bowed her head for an instant, and then raised her eyes.

"The door will be unlocked," she said breathlessly.

Chapter XXX

A PROFUNDITY of stillness engulfed the castle. The last echoing footfall had died away hours before; the last twinkling light in the corridor had been extinguished; and from the high chest in the corner where Faith had set a single candelabrum, shadows rather than radiance appeared to stream. Outside her window, the surface of the moat shone as smooth as black onyx under the summer stars. She had sunk down among the cushions in the deep embrasure of the window-seat, her hands locked in her lap, her breath coming fast. It seemed an eternity to her since she had stirred. And still she heard no signaling call, she was conscious of no impending presence.

She had laid aside her fan, taken off her mitts, and removed her wreath and veil. As she did so, she could not help tingling with reminiscent pleasure at the thought of the admiration her appearance had roused. The Puritan bride! Why had she never thought of that rôle before? It was infinitely more effective and unique, infinitely better suited to her, than that of a Spanish dancer, or that of an Empire belle. Perhaps some day Sam would paint her wearing this dress, and give the picture the title she had just coined . . .

Her thoughts reverted to the grandmother she had loved so dearly in her childhood, the daughter of the ancestress whom she had impersonated that night, for whom the little house she had once described so feelingly to Gabriel had been built. It had been the first Faith Marlowe's bridal home; and to her descendant's clarified vision the woman who had lived there suddenly seemed a bright and living reality. She felt that if next she could only cross the threshold of the old homestead again, she might almost see her ancestress standing there. . . .

"Two o'clock and all's well—"

The call suddenly reverberated through the silent corridor. Faith shrank back still further against the window frame, trembling all over. As she heard the sound of the lifting latch, she bowed her head and held her breath. Perhaps, hidden as she was, Sebastian would not see her. Perhaps he would think she had already gone to bed, weary with waiting for him. Then he would turn away again and she would not call him back. Perhaps. . . .

"Did it seem long to you, beloved? I did not dare come until the house was sunk in sleep."

He had crossed the room noiselessly, and was standing beside her. As she did not answer, he unfastened the long gray cloak in which he had been wrapped, and laid it quietly down on a chair. Then he sat down beside her in the wide-cushioned window-seat, sliding his arm around her waist.

"How beautiful it is here to-night!" he said throbbingly. "It makes me think of Francesca's window, at which she sat with Paolo. Have you ever been to Rimini, *querida?* Some day, we must go there together. Francesca's castle stands uncrumbling still. I believe her love made it imperishable."

"Was she not killed? She and Paolo both?" Faith asked stranglingly. "And were they not—very wicked?"

"Very wicked, *querida?* How can you say that when their names are glorified among those of the other great lovers of the ages—Romeo and Juliet, Abelard and Héloise, Jacob and Rachel, if you will!—Yes, they were killed—but then it was too late to harm them. They were one body and one spirit already."

She did not answer him. He laced his fingers between hers and pressed them.

"You do not need to say anything more to convince me that I should go to Dolores with David," he said softly. "In fact, I have told him to-day that I will start as soon as he is ready. The preparations should not take long. . . . I feel sure that by the end of the week.—Of course I shall wire to the Castello Viejo to expect us. David says that in Dolores' condition it may be difficult to examine her. But he is confident that within a few days he will be able to tell whether he thinks an operation is advisable. If he does, it can then take place immediately."

Faith neither stirred nor spoke.

"If Dolores dies," Sebastian went on without a tremor in his voice, "we shall have a situation to meet that will in some ways present more complications than if she lives. I have thought of several ways to meet it, and have dismissed them all as impracticable. For instance, for a time I thought I might ask you to return to the *caseria*, and live there with me—as Doña Celia lived with my ancestor. But I know you could not be happy in that way—there would be too many lingering memories centering in the *caseria*. Inevitably you would associate it—with your marriage. And inevitably you would seek a more active existence than you could have there. You are too brilliant to be long at rest deprived of stimulating contacts. It was the quality of your mind, *vida de mi vida*, that arrested me first of all. It was

236

only afterwards that I was conscious of your physical beauty. No other woman had ever drawn me to her in that way before.—Do you remember that first morning in Madrid?"

"I remember."

"Besides at Granada there is Gabriel—he is growing very frail, as I told you. It is unthinkable that he should be bowed down with grief because of us. And he would be— if you went to the *caseria* with me."

"Yes—it would be unthinkable that we should cause Gabriel grief."

"There might be other solutions—you might go to the United States, for instance, and I might follow you there. I have no doubt that somewhere, somehow—a divorce could be arranged for you—I find that in certain Western States that is very easy—and afterwards—we could marry. I would chafe under expatriation less than you under imprisonment, *querida!* I know myself as well as I know you. But this solution would mean scandal, with which I could not bear to have you sullied, and it would mean heartbreak too—for Victoria Luise, whom I know you love, for Samuel Dudley, who, I know, has always loved you. And—it would ruin Rudolf's career. That is what he cares most about, so I feel we should leave him that."

A shade of irony had momentarily crept into his tender tones. But almost instantly it faded away again.

"Therefore I suggest that we dismiss this problem from our minds—unless or until we are confronted with it. You would consent to another conference, would you not, if we were faced with the contingency which released me and not you?"

"Yes."

"You promise?"

"I promise."

The sense of reassurance that Faith had begun to feel revealed itself in her voice. She leaned unresistingly back against Sebastian's shoulder and waited for him to go on.

"Then we will only consider for the moment what is to happen—if Dolores recovers. And that, I feel, is the contingency we are far more likely to face. I believe you have the same feeling. Am I right?"

"Yes."

"I will not force myself upon Dolores. You would be the last to wish me to do that." He paused significantly, and then went on, "But if she recovers, and—and feels toward me as she once did, I will return to her—as her husband. That is what you think I ought to do, is it not, Faith?"

"Yes."

"If I had not known you, it would not be too hard," he said musingly, almost as if he were talking to himself. "I have not forgotten that she was once very beautiful—innocent and sweet and lovely."

"I know. I saw her picture once, at Jaime's house. He does not hide it when you are not there. It was seeing her picture, realizing what she must have been, what she still might be, that——"

He pressed her hand. "You have an understanding heart, Faith. But she is not like you. She is lovely, but she is not radiant. She is gentle, but she is not brilliant. And she is sweet, but she is not 'gallant.' There is no one like you, my darling, in all the world."

He bent his head again, and this time he kissed her lips. But even now, though there was infinite longing in his caress, there was no vehemence.

"If I go back to Dolores," he said at last, "I must not—we must not deceive her. I would be—all the world to her. It would take a long time before she could become readjusted, before she could grope her way back to security. I should have to help her constantly. She would not be absorbed in a life of her own from which she shut me out, as Rudolf is absorbed, and shuts you out. And she would be in time—we hope——"

"Yes," said Faith again, steadily.

"We shall be very hungry for each other, you and I, *querida*, in the years to come. And your life, Faith, will be even emptier than mine."

"Yes," she said once more. But now the steadiness was shaken.

"Since all this is so, may I say what is in my heart to say, darling? Without fear that you will be surprised or shocked?"

His voice melted into a poignant silence. She could not answer him in words. But she knew he no longer needed such an answer. For a moment his immobility and stillness were as profound as hers. Then, she was conscious, that as gently as he had taken her into his arms, he had released her, and that he was kneeling at her feet, his hands still clasping hers.

"It is not seduction, Faith, that I am seeking," he whispered. "It is not even largesse, or the assurance of a memory. It is—fulfillment. For you as well as for me. If I did not know you loved me——"

"You do know it."

"As much as I love you——"

"As much as you love me——"

238

"Then—then—I want to take you for my own, Fidelidad, to-night. . . ."

Very slowly she rose to her feet, drawing him with her. In the accustomed darkness, he could see his own infinite passion mirrored in the eyes she lifted fearlessly and unhesitatingly to his.

"I am your own," she whispered.

He was aware that her lips did not even tremble as they formed the words.

. . . . . .

Hans Christian wakened suddenly crying aloud in terror. He had had a horrible dream—a dream that the shining lady whom he adored was lost, and that he could not find her anywhere. He had seemed to see her standing close beside him, smiling down at him, wearing the white dress and veil in which she had looked so lovely. Then gradually she had faded away from him and disappeared.

He sprang up from his cot, and flung himself across the great carved bed that stood beside it, calling to his mother as he felt for her. The bed was empty.

He groped his way across the dark room, his teeth chattering. As his small fingers sought for the latch, they shook so that he could hardly find it. When they finally closed down on it, still shaking, he plunged forward and threw his slender weight against the massive door.

It opened slowly. On the great chest which stood in the corner beside it, three candles were guttering in their sockets. The light was very dim, and he could see nothing in the obscurity which engulfed the huge room. Yet instinctively he felt that it was not empty.

"Mother!" he cried again. "Where are you?"

His voice seemed to echo in the silence and shadows. Almost paralyzed with fright, he cried once more.

"Mother!" he called desperately. "Won't you answer me?"

Suddenly he rushed forward. As he did so, he saw a slim white figure detach itself from the encircling gloom, and come slowly toward him. Then Faith, still wearing her bridal dress, gathered him into her arms.

Chapter XXXI

JOHANN was sure that the Herr Baron must be overwhelmed with weariness. He had not left the Chancery until

239

midnight; and when he came home, he had gone straight to his study and fastened the door. At eight the following morning, Johann, distressed at finding that his master's bed had not been slept in when he went up with breakfast, knocked hesitatingly at the study door, and asked if there were nothing he could bring the Herr Baron or do for him. At first the answer had been negative and monosyllabic; but a little later the Minister had emerged, looking old and haggard, and had shaved, changed his linen, and drunk some coffee before starting back for the Chancery. Now it was evening again, and he was once more locked in the study.

It required all the courage the old servant could summon to intrude a second time. But if his master went on at this rate, without rest or food, he would certainly collapse. Besides, there was now an additional and imperative reason why the Herr Baron should be interrupted. Spurred on by the conviction that a crisis was impending, Johann rapped decisively.

This time there was no immediate answer of any sort. But Johann declined to be daunted by the lack of response to his summons, and at length he was rewarded. Rudolf crossed the room and opened the door himself, confronting the servant with a look of stern rebuke. But Johann forestalled him before he could speak.

"Pardon, Excellency. But the Frau Baronin is very anxious to see you."

"The Frau Baronin!" repeated Rudolf in astonishment. "Why, she is at Radensholm!"

"Pardon, Excellency. She returned to the Legation about three hours ago. And I do not think she is at all well."

"Has she gone to bed? Have you sent for a doctor?"

"She has not gone to bed, Excellency. She is packing."

"Packing!" exclaimed Rudolf, echoing what the servant had said a second time. "First you say she is not at all well, and next you say she is packing! What are you trying to tell me?"

"I am only telling Your Excellency what I have seen. The Frau Baronin is packing, and she is so pale that I am frightened. She looks as if she had not slept at all, and as if she had wept a great deal."

"Go and ask her if she will not come here," said Rudolf slowly, recrossing the room to his desk, and picking up one of the letters with which it was littered.

The force of habit was so strong that it did not occur to him that he might hasten to her instead of asking her to come to him. Nevertheless, he was intensely disturbed by

240

what Johann had told him, and the pressure of fatigue which was almost crushing him, seemed suddenly to be redoubled in weight. As he heard the door open and close again, he glanced up apprehensively. And when Faith came toward him, he saw that Johann's concern was not unfounded. Never, in all the years of their marriage, had he seen her look so badly.

"What is the matter, *liebe* Faith?" he asked with unwonted gentleness. "Have you been seeing ghosts?"

"Yes. That is just what has happened, Rudolf."

In spite of himself, he shivered. A week earlier he had had a letter from his mother saying that the White Lady of the Hapsburgs had been seen wandering in the palace of the Archduke Ferdinand. And now...he forced himself to speak quietly.

"Will you not sit down and tell me about it, if it will relieve you? I did not know that there were any traditional ghosts at Radensholm."

"It was not a traditional ghost of Radensholm that I saw. It was the ghost—of a little girl I used to know."

"Yes?" said Rudolf with constrained encouragement.

"She woke in a strange place and found that her mother was not in the bed beside her. So she got up, and opened the door into the next room, looking for her mother—"

"Her mother was not in the next room, either?"

"Yes. She was there. But she was not alone. And that night was the beginning of—hideous years that ended in—shameful disgrace and violent death. It was—a—tragic landmark. I had almost forgotten about it. But suddenly—dreadfully—it was recalled to me."

She covered her face with her hands and burst into abandoned weeping. Rudolf went over and laid his hand gently on her shoulder.

"*Liebe* Faith, you must not grieve so," he said kindly. "I am not sure that I understand just what you are trying to tell me, though I am inclined to think you are speaking symbolically—that something happened at Radensholm which caused you to feel as if you were seeing a ghost, though actually you did not.... Something that perhaps recalled a —a painful episode in your own sad childhood. I am distressed that you have been made unhappy, especially in surroundings which you have always enjoyed so much. But you never need to go back to Radensholm again, or see—anyone who was there, if you prefer not to do so. And no real harm has been done." Then, as she did not look up or make any effort to control herself, he asked with a self-command which required increasing effort, "I am right, am I not? No real harm has been done?"

She gave an exclamation which he recognized as one of anguish. "No!" she cried, shuddering, "no real harm has been done! But it might have been! It was—almost! It may be yet! Another time—"

She was trembling, he saw, from head to foot. Suddenly she dropped her hands, grasping at his, and looking up at him with tears down her cheeks.

"Rudolf," she said imploringly, "you must let me go away! At once. To-night. Do not stop to ask me any questions—now. Some day—some day after I come back again I will explain—everything you feel I ought to tell you. But not now. I—I couldn't. I—I can't."

"Of course you cannot," he said soothingly, "and there is no reason why you should. I do not need explanations from you, *liebe* Faith—now or at any other time. I have complete confidence in you." He hesitated, and then, almost awkwardly, he leaned over and kissed her. "I know that it seems to you that for a long time I have shown my affection for you very inadequately," he said in a strained voice. "I realize it myself. It—it is hard for me to be demonstrative. I am not naturally light-hearted or pleasure-loving; I have always been deliberate and reserved. And I am afraid I have begun to seem—almost stolid. Lately I have also been —very much preoccupied and worried. You have a right to feel that I have neglected you, that I have been cold and critical. I—I am very sorry. It would mean a great deal to me, Faith, if you could tell me that you forgive my shortcomings."

"If I would forgive your shortcomings!" she echoed, staring at him with stupefaction.

"Yes. If you are thinking of going away for a time, I shall not try to prevent you. I shall help you get ready—if I can—indeed, I meant to suggest to you myself, when you came back from Radensholm, that you should try to have a little change. But it would make me much happier if I could feel, after you have gone, that we had parted affectionately. Perhaps some day you will feel happier too— if this could be so."

There was an unfamiliar huskiness in his voice which she had never heard there before. It was mysteriously touching, and at the same time it was strangely steadying. Faith felt a sudden return of composure.

"You must not talk to me about—forgiveness, Rudolf,"

she said. "If we were to talk about that—there is much that I should have to ask you to forgive me."

"I do not believe there is anything," he said calmly. "Anything for which I am not to blame—directly or indirectly. You were very young when we were married. I was older, and I should have insisted that we should wait until you were more sure of your mind. For you were not in love with me—you imagined you were, but you were not. And I was very precipitate—very violent. I shocked you and—hurt you—and dominated you. If I had not done so, you might have learned to love me—instead of learning to love someone else."

"Rudolf!" she exclaimed aghast.

"Did you think I never guessed—because I never spoke of it? *Liebe* Faith, I have always known of your love for another man—and of your loyalty to me. Always known and always grieved. But again, I might have taught you to love me after all, if I had not shut myself away from you —if I had not been proud and resentful and bitter—if I had not made you feel that I did not love you—that all I cared for was the career to which I have given the intensive devotion I should have given to you."

"Rudolf, Rudolf, why didn't you say all this to me long ago?"

"God knows," he said gravely. "Perhaps because this is something I can understand—and so often I have not understood. Perhaps because I never could have said it—except in a moment such as this. But I hope you will remember, Faith, that I have said it now."

He turned away from her, obviously striving for composure. Moved as she was, she did not dare intrude upon his struggle for self-control. When at last he spoke to her again, it was in a voice which he was evidently determined to keep calm.

"I am sure you will be very sorry to hear," he said, "that I have had bad news while you have been away. My mother's cousin, the Archduke Francis Ferdinand, and his wife, were shot yesterday in Sarajevo by a Servian fanatic. It is very tragic. Of course the entire family has been plunged into mourning."

"Oh, Rudolf, how terrible! How terrible! Would—would it be any comfort to *Tante* Luise, do you think, if I should go to her?"

For a moment he did not answer, but stood, picking up one after the other, the papers that lay on his desk, and then putting them down again.

243

"When you spoke to me about going away, a few moments ago," he said at length, "did you have any definite plan—any thought of where you would like to go?"

"Yes. I want desperately to go home. Just for a little while, Rudolf, until I can—until I am—"

"Until you feel better," he said soothingly. "I understand, *liebe* Faith. I know you have wanted for a long time—to go home, and I have been wrong in thwarting this yearning of yours. Certainly, I shall not thwart it now, and I am sure my mother would not wish you to change your plans on her account. After all, Francis' death is a—a Hapsburg family matter, which does not concern you intimately. I know my mother would urge you, as I do, to—to go to America at once. As soon as you can secure passage."

"I have secured passage. On the *Frederick VIII.* It is sailing at midnight," she said breathlessly.

"At midnight! And it is past seven now!"

He looked toward the bronze clock on the mantel, and for a moment its loud relentless ticking was the only sound in the room. Then he spoke very gravely.

"That will not give you much time to get ready."

"But I am nearly ready now. There are only my own trunks to finish. Hilda had all her own clothes together before I came in here, and Hans Christian's——"

The paper which Rudolf was still holding suddenly fluttered from his hands. He bent over and picked it up.

"I had forgotten," he said slowly, "that you would be taking Hans Christian with you. But naturally—you would. Hans Christian and Hilda. Of course—that would be best."

"You—you will not be too lonely, will you, Rudolf, without Hans Christian until we come back? You never see very much of him really. And you will always have your work."

He laid down the despatch upon a pile of other documents, straightening them all as he did so, before he answered her.

"No, I shall not be too lonely. As you say, I shall have my work. I think it may take me to Germany before the summer is over—perhaps even to France. It would be very selfish of me to suggest that Hans Christian should stay here—he will be much happier with you."

Suddenly Rudolf looked toward Faith with a smile that was wholly strange to her.

"I have always been glad," he said, "that we named Hans Christian for his two grandfathers—for your father, Faith, as well as mine. Both have been men of a great tradition.

When he grows older he can choose—which tradition he prefers to follow, and by which of their names he would rather be known. It is not impossible that he would like to use your surname also, as many Germans use their mother's names. Hans von Hohenlohe or Christian Marlowe—it will not matter which! Both are noble!"

He came over and put his arm around her shoulder.

"That is another thing I want you to remember," he said. "If I should not happen—to be with you, and Hansel is confronted with a choice, do not forget that I should be proud to have him bear your father's name and yours."

"I will not forget. But of course, Rudolf, we would all make decisions as important as that together!"

"Of course," he answered reassuringly. Then, as if something of significance had occurred to him, he asked, "Did you not tell me, *liebe* Faith, that Sam was going to America this summer? To take Mrs. Atkinson to Salem? Perhaps you could persuade her to stay with you at your old home instead—she loves you dearly and it is a long time since she has seen much of you. And Sam—"

He paused and smiled again.

"I am very much ashamed when I recall how much I used to resent your association with Sam," he remarked "All jealousy is ignoble of course. But this was especially despicable. Sam is not only a great artist, *liebe* Faith, he is a great man. If you had married him, he would have shown himself far more deserving of you than I have been."

"Oh, no!" she exclaimed, moved almost past endurance. "Rudolf, you must not say such things!"

"I will not say them if they give you pain. But I may say, may I not, that I am thankful to know that you can count on Sam's devotions whatever happens? And that I hope some day—in some way—it may be rewarded?" He laid down the last of the despatches he had been arranging, and put his arm around her again. "If you are willing, *liebe* Faith, let us go now and have something to eat and drink," he said, "before we make ready to go to the pier. I have had a busy day, a—a rather hard one, and I know you have too. We will feel better, both of us, when we have broken bread and tasted wine. And we must drink together —to The Day!"

"To the day? What day?"

Rudolf lifted his head. His face, Faith saw, was illumined by a radiant light. There was about him that same magnificence which had so dazzled her when she had first seen him in Venice, and which she had not beheld for years.

But now there was an enraptured transfiguration as well. She caught her breath as she waited for him to answer.

"The Day of Glory!" he answered. "The Fatherland's and yours—and mine—and Hans Christian's!"

PART VII

Caleb Hawks

Chapter XXXII

THE return of Senator Marlowe's daughter to her native village was the cause of unbounded excitement in Hamstead.

This excitement began long before her actual appearance. A radiogram arrived for Ephraim Marlowe, and Sol Daniels, the depot master, who had never before taken such a message on the ticker, locked up the station at once, and walked over to the Marlowe farm with the scrawled sheet in his horny hand.

It was generally considered that Ephraim Marlowe had "married beneath him"; and with the passing years the aura of Marlowe glory which once surrounded him had grown more and more dim, as he sank comfortably to the social level from which Emmeline, his kindly but unlettered wife, had never risen. Sol found the elderly couple, who were growing feeble, and consequently "took things as easy as they could," in spite of their "ample means," eating their dinner of fried pork, boiled potatoes, fresh asparagus and strawberry shortcake in the kitchen; and he leaned back against the door leading into the shed to watch the effect which the startling news of which he was the conveyor would have upon them.

"I can't just make out your writing, Sol," Ephraim said screwing up his eyes. "I recall way back when we was in the sixth grade together, 'twas the worst in the class. Let's see. —'Arriving New York *Frederick VIII* Danish American Line, July 10, accompanied by son and maid. Stop. Please wire me Waldorf-Astoria whether convenient for us to stay with you while getting my house ready for long stay. Stop. Love, Faith.' Land of Goshen, Sol! It's from my niece!"

"Looks that way," agreed Sol noncommittally.

"I'm expecting my second cousin Mem Wilkins and his wife up from Lynn next week," Emmeline Marlowe said anxiously. "It's his annual vacation from the shoe factory.

I don't see how I could have any more company just now —not but what I'd hate to turn your niece from the door, Ephraim, but I haven't housecleaned the north chambers this spring, and I don't feel equal to doing it in this weather. There isn't any other place I could put her and her little boy and her hired girl. Like as not this girl's a foreigner too!"

She lowered a piece of shortcake to the plate from which she had just lifted the last stalk of asparagus to her mouth, but she did not attack it with any real relish. It was evident that she was deeply troubled.

"Emmeline's been having a lot of sick spells lately," Ephraim said in an explanatory voice to Sol. "We don't rightly know what ails her. We've been kind of biding our time 'til David got home to find out, instead of sending for a strange doctor. But land! It looks as if he was never coming. Now if he and Jacqueline was only at the Big House, they'd take Faith and her family in."

"Maybe Sylvia Gray c'd think what to do," said Sol, trying to be resourceful in an emergency. "She ain't never at a loss. I c'd take this—this telegram over to the Gray Farm and ask her. I'd just as leave."

"Sylvia Gray's just had another baby, and her first ain't more'n a year old," said Emmeline, still anxiously.

"Well, I guess I know that same's anyone," retorted Sol, stung by the unjust inference that he was not aware of everything that was going on in the neighborhood. "But she kinda takes babies in her stride, as you might say. And she always has plenty of help. I can't think of no one else, seeing as the Big House is closed. Mary Manning's willin', but she's got her hands full. And the other Mannings never find it convenient to have company. No criticism to you, Emmeline. They're fixed different."

"I know," said Emmeline. The anxiety in her voice was deeper than ever, and she had not eaten more than one or two mouthfuls of her shortcake. "It's a cryin' shame there ain't a hotel in Hamstead. Some public-minded citizen ought to put one up. I guess you can't do better, Sol, than to go over to Sylvia's and tell her what's upon us. If she can't help out, I'll get into those north rooms the first thing in the mornin'."

But Sylvia Gray, who had lived in New York most of her life, was not in the least disturbed by the radiogram. She had been a young widow with a tragic past behind her when she had come to Hamstead for refuge, and found love there as well. Seldom as she left the country nowadays, she had never cut herself off either from contacts from the city which had been her birthplace or with the world at large; and she received Sol's tidings with genuine enthusiasm.

"Faith Marlowe—the Baroness von Hohenlohe!" she exclaimed. "Coming to Hamstead! Isn't that wonderful, Sol? You know I've never seen her—why, I don't believe she's been here in twenty years, not since she was a very little girl—I must ask Austin.—You know she's been the inspiration of all Samuel Dudley's wonderful pictures.—I suppose he's the most famous living American painter now."

"Mebbe," said Sol, who had never neard of Samuel Dudley, and who had a poor opinion of artists, but who was nevertheless relieved, since he judged, and correctly, by the tone of Sylvia's voice, that the complications arising from Faith Marlowe's impending arrival were to be smoothed out.

"The tenth of July!" Sylvia went on. "Why, Sol, that is day after to-morrow! I'll send my Nora over to the Christian Marlowe house right away, if Uncle Ephraim will give me the keys, and I believe we can have it almost ready for her by the time she gets here, though naturally Austin and I will want her to stay with us while she's getting settled. I'll write out two telegrams for her, shall I, one signed with Aunt Emmeline's name and one with mine? Then you can get them off right away, and they'll be waiting for her at the Waldorf when she gets there. And Sol, I know someone else who would like to know about this—Mr. Caleb Hawks, the Mayor of Hinsboro, who was such a friend of Senator Marlowe. I'll telephone him and tell him the Baroness is coming. It wouldn't surprise me if he went on to meet her!"

By evening there was not a family in Hamstead which had not heard that Senator Marlowe's daughter was coming back there. Her expected arrival was the sole topic of conversation at every supper table. And Mrs. Elliot, the most indefatigable conversationalist of the village, voiced a general sentiment about her in her comments to her taciturn husband.

"I tell you, Joe, I can't pronounce that heathenish-sounding foreign name of hers and don't propose to try," she said with spirit. "I called her Faith when she was a baby, and I aim to call her Faith now. If she don't like it, she can lump it. She was a queer young 'un, mostly hair and eyes, and giving you a turn now and again, she'd say such peculiar things. Her mother wa'nt no better than she might have been, if you ask me."

"I didn't ask ye. I ain't got no need to," muttered Joe, who felt fully competent to recognize a light woman when he saw one.

"She turned up her nose at Hamstead," went on Mrs. Elliot, wholly undaunted. "Just as if Hamstead didn't turn up its nose good and plenty at *her!* It always seemed to me there was somethin' real strange about the way she died—we never heard no details, but it was awful sudden. And her father had about as much backbone as a jellyfish. He didn't put on airs—I'll say that for him. But, land! What did he have airs to put on about, come right down to it? I've heard tell that the United States Senate is 'the greatest legislative body in the world' whatever that may be. But it don't make me tremble none, and everybody knew Cris Marlowe never would have got into it nohow, if it hadn't been for his father. And he *was* high and mighty! He wasn't any too pleased when his own son, Ephraim, wanted to settle down and stay in Hamstead, same as the rest of us. And I bet you'll find Faith Marlowe's high and mighty too. Probably she wears a crown regular, and a red velvet dress trimmed with ermine. I understand that's the usual court cost*ume* in Europe. I shall go straight over to Sylvia's the moment Faith gets here and see for myself. But I ain't prepared to be a mite surprised."

Contrary to her expectations, Mrs. Elliot was very much surprised when she saw Faith. This was not so soon as she had expected, however. The German Consul-General had met Faith at the pier, having received a cable from Rudolf, advising him when she would arrive. He and his wife had insisted that she should stay with them in New York, instead of the Waldorf-Astoria, and had almost overwhelmed her with Teutonic hospitality. Mr. Caleb Hawks had also met her; and he in his turn had been insistent: she must, he told her with an emphasis which precluded argument, come and spend a few days at his house in Hinsboro. The latch-string was out and the spare-room bed was all made up, just as he had told her they would be. His housekeeper, Mrs. Mead, had made her currant jelly a whole week ahead of time in order to be free for the Marlowe visit; and she had her heart set on seeing what a Baroness looked like. Besides, Mrs. Neal Conrad—that nice young woman whose husband had been such a help on the City Council before he entered the State Legislature—was about to entertain the Fortnightly Bridge Club and she was counting on having Faith as her guest of honor. Mr. Hawks had practically promised. He knew Faith was anxious to get into her own house, and it was being made ready for her as fast as it could be. But it *had* been closed a long time, and there were a great many things to do to it. They could motor over to Hamstead every day if she liked; but as far as headquarters were concerned —well, she must make those with Mr. Hawks.

Faith acquiesced almost apathetically. She was eager to be at peace in her own house—if indeed peace were to be found any where. But she did not feel equal to arguing about the details of getting settled or even to deciding for herself where she should stay temporarily. She permitted herself to be installed in Mr. Hawks' spare room; and she went docilely to the bridge party the day after her arrival in Hinsboro. But she looked so pale and listless as she came up the front walk after this was over, that Mr. Hawks, who was sitting on his porch in his shirt-sleeves waiting for her, felt distressed.

"Didn't you have a good time at Anne's party?" he asked anxiously, feeling sure that something must be wrong, and yet unable to guess what this could be.

"Oh, yes. Everyone was very kind and cordial. And Mrs. Conrad is charming," said Faith. But she spoke without real enthusiasm, though she added with more interest, "Why doesn't her husband take her with him to Belford? I should think she would be an immense success there and a great help to him."

"Well, likely he may, some time. But it's cheaper for him, living the way he does in a single room at the Talmage Tavern than if he took his family along—there are two cute kids, Nancy and Junior too. Maybe you didn't see them."

"Oh, yes I did, and they are beautiful children. The little boy—*why* do they call him 'Junior'?—is the same one who came over this morning and asked Hansel to play baseball with him and his 'gang'; and he and his sister Nancy both helped pass salad and cake and sandwiches and candy and coffee and about a dozen other things. Why didn't you warn me, Uncle Caleb, that there would be a hearty meal served at half-past four in the afternoon, instead of tea? And that the women would all take their hats off? And that they would get up and mill around the room every time they finished playing four hands—they called it 'progressing,' but I never saw anything less like progress! And that no one played for money, or even breathed of such thing—I asked what the stakes were, and you should have seen the look I was given! But I won first prize—'two darling little guest towels.' I shouldn't have known what they were if the lady sitting next to me hadn't gushed over them!"

She sat down beside him on the steps, leaning wearily back against the railing, and clasping her hands over one knee. Caleb could see that there were dark circles under her eyes.

"I guess you hadn't better go to no more parties until

251

you get rested up a mite," he said solicitously. "Everyone is so crazy to meet you, and that's a fact, that I give in when Anne pestered me. But I see I done wrong to urge you and not to tell you more about how it would be—not that I know much about these women's affairs myself."

"Don't men and women ever go out together?"

"Well, yes, some—nights. But day times of course the men folks are busy, and naturally their tastes ain't the same as their wives' anyhow."

He thought he saw Faith wince, and the impression troubled him deeply. He wondered if anyone at the party had unintentionally hurt her feelings; but her next question had nothing to do with the meeting of the Fortnightly Bridge Club.

"Is there any special news? I haven't seen a paper all day."

"Why yes. The Democrats are aimin' to thrust Shaw down the throats of the American people again—there's a long piece about it here on the front page. But the voters won't never swallow him for another four years. Cotton's gone up two points—the market's kinda unstiddy. And there's a drought in Kansas—looks as if the wheat crop might be damaged. Here in Hinsboro the Marblecutters' Union is threatening to strike, and my friend Sebastian Perez, who lives across the street, is one of the ringleaders——"

"I meant, any foreign news. I couldn't help feeling, when I left Europe, that there might be—distrubances."

"Because that Duke, or whatever he was, got shot? Shucks, I wouldn't worry none about that!"

Again he saw Faith wince; but this time she did not answer him at all, and after a moment he went on, in an eager effort to say something that would please her, "Do you want we should get started for Hamstead in good season, Faith? We can have breakfast at six instead of seven, just as well as not, if you say so."

"I think seven will be early enough," she answered with a faint smile. "But I hate to trouble you to take me back and forth."

"Gosh, Faith, it ain't no trouble! It's a pleasure to have you here, and that's a fact. If I should get tied up at City Hall or the factory any time, I c'd send the hired man with you. He drives the otter real smooth and easy, though you wouldn't think it to look at him."

Involuntarily, Faith smiled again. Mr. Hawks' hired man, whose name was Silas Sims, had given her the impression of being mostly Adam's apple, red flannel undershirt, and

252

chewing tobacco. It was difficult for her to visualize him in the rôle of chauffeur, though he had been so kind to Hansel, who had tagged at his heels most of the day, that her heart was touched.

"I have been wondering," she said hesitatingly, "whether I couldn't buy an inexpensive automobile, and learn to run it myself. I've seen a number of women driving in Hinsboro. If I had a car of my own—I—I could get out in the hills alone once in a while."

"Why yes," agreed Mr. Hawks heartily. "I don't know about hills and such, but you could slip back and forth between Hamstead and Hinsboro in two shakes of a dead lamb's tail, and that 'ud be pleasant for ye. It's kinda quiet in Hamstead, Faith, and I look to see you find it sorta dull. I think a car 'ud be a real nice thing for you to have. I'll call up my friend Will Emery, that's agent here for several makes, and trades in second-hands too, and see what he's got to offer. About what was you thinking of paying?"

The deal was settled that very night. Before supper was over, Mr. Emery and his two sons, all driving different kinds of cars, were parked on Mr. Hawks' front lawn between the stone deer and the geranium urns; and the evening was spent in making trial trips around Hinsboro and its environs. Faith eventually decided on a neat little five-passenger Dodge, which had been used as a "demonstration car" and was consequently a great bargain; and as something did "come up" at the factory, it was agreed that Mr. Emery should accompany Faith to Hamstead the next morning, and thus begin the driving lessons without delay.

She "caught on," he told her, very quickly; and she found a real exhilaration in the new experience. Before she reached Hamstead she was feeling almost happy, for the first time since she could remember. The countryside through which she passed, fertile and verdant, the mountains rising steadfastly in the distance, the quiet river winding its undisturbed course through the meadows which sloped down toward it—all these gave her a sense of fulfillment and peace. And the sight of her own house, smaller, more weather-beaten, and more isolated than she remembered it, nevertheless stirred her to sudden joy. There was smoke curling up from the chimney and the front door stood wide open; and as she leaped out of the car, and ran up the cobblestone walk, a tall slender young woman came forward to meet her with a charming smile.

"Welcome home!" she said cordially. "I'm Sylvia Gray, one of your neighbors—I do hope we are going to see a

253

great deal of each other. Your Aunt Emmeline is rather busy with company, so she couldn't come over here, but she hopes you'll drop in to see her later in the day. My husband and I are counting on you to have dinner with us—by the way, dinner in Hamstead is at twelve! We hoped you'd stay with us while you were getting settled, but we realized that Mr. Hawks had a prior claim. Shall we go in and see how my family treasure, Nora, has been getting along? She and I have been working here together."

It was evident that between them, Sylvia Gray and Nora had done wonders. The house smelled of scrubbing and scouring, the windows shone, the carpets and mattresses were hanging on a line where a long lanky man was vigorously beating them. But Faith's first sensation, as she walked from room to room, was one of acute disappointment. She had not realized that Flossie had set her mark so unmistakably on the place. The wall papers were garish; the old paneling had been painted in all sorts of fantastic colors; the fireplaces had been closed up, and gilded coal scuttles and bunches of dried grass protruding from hand-painted jars, stood before them. There were embroidered sofa cushions, chenille hangings, "whatnots" and "knickknacks" everywhere, a clutter of oak and wicker furniture, a scattering of highly colored, sentimental pictures. Sylvia, watching Faith's expression as she finally sat down without comment on the "parlor couch," spoke impetuously.

"I didn't dare make any changes before you came. But I felt certain you'd wish to. I suppose you know that the barn and attic are crammed full of your grandmother's possessions that your mother stored away when she 'modernized' the house."

"No, I didn't know," said Faith slowly. "I'm very glad they weren't—destroyed. It would mean a great deal to me to—to live surrounded by them."

"I was sure you'd feel that way!" Sylvia exclaimed. "Would you care to have me go with you to see our local paper-hanger and carpenter and plumber? I'd be delighted to serve as a liaison officer! Only first I must rush home and feed my baby—won't you come with me—and meet the rest of the Grays before you go any further?"

It was just after the various calls which Sylvia suggested had been satisfactorily completed that Mrs. Elliot decided to make her first visit to Faith, who was by this time in the attic taking account of stock. Nora was in the back yard, helping the long lanky man, whose name proved to be Perley Stubbs, with the carpets and blankets, when a rap on the knocker reverberated through the silent rooms. And as her first attempt elicited no response, Mrs. Elliot redoubled her efforts with such deafening results that Faith dropped the footboard of a spool-bed which she was examining and rushed down the stairs to the front door herself.

By the time she reached it she was breathless with haste and exertion. She had tied a cheesecloth duster, capwise, securely over her hair, which was so abundant that any violent exercise was likely to loosen its heavy coils; and it was entirely concealed; while the white silk sports suit, immaculate when she had left Hinsboro that morning, was now covered with a liberal layer of the dust and cobwebs which for twenty years had lain undisturbed in the attic. Mrs. Elliot gazed at the disheveled figure before her with disapproving astonishment; and Faith's unembarrassed greeting, though cordial of intent, was not soothing in its effect.

"Good afternoon," she said pleasantly. "Were you looking for Nora? She is in the back yard."

"Looking for Nora!" snorted Mrs. Elliot with indignation. "I guess I've got better ways of passing the time of day than hunting up hired help! I was looking for—for the Bar —for her as was Faith Marlowe. If you're that German girl she's brung with her, you better go and tell her this minute that Mrs. Elliot's calling."

"Oh! I am so sorry! I am the Baroness von Hohenlohe. Won't you come in?"

"You could'da knocked me over with a feather," Mrs. Elliot said to her husband at supper time. "She war'nt any more embarrassed at being caught looking as if a cyclone had struck her than if she'd been sittin' in the front parlor doin' tattin'! An' even if she'd been clean, there war'nt nothin' remarkable about her clothes—many's the time I've seen a heap handsomer right in the front of Mr. Goldenburg's store in Wallacetown. No trimmin' at all. It's queer, though. She has a sort of way with 'er, come to see her close to. And she ain't bad lookin'. Nor stuck up. I was wrong there, Joe. 'Don't forget, Mrs. Elliot,' she says when I told her good-bye, 'that the next time you come over we'll have tea together! I'm so sorry there isn't any in the house yet!' She's aimin' to move in just as soon as she can, though she's going' to have the place all tore up. I thought myself the house was sweet pretty, the way Flossie had it fixed; but Faith's got different ideas, and of course a woman feels to do what she wants with her own house. Anyways, I shouldn't be a mite surprised if we liked her in Hamstead after all."

Chapter XXXIII

By the time Faith was settled in her own house, most of Hamstead, and a good deal of Hinsboro were inclined to agree with Mrs. Elliot.

As she turned the Dodge triumphantly back into Caleb Hawks' front yard for the first time, she was conscious of a tall dark man standing before the house across the street, who was regarding her fixedly. Something about his carriage and expression arrested her; and as she covertly returned his glance, she could not suppress a startled exclamation.

"You're doing fine," said Mr. Emery encouragingly. "Just take her out of gear and put on the brake. Then shut off the engine."

Faith did not correct his impression that she had been momentarily perplexed by the mechanism of her car. But when he had taken his contented departure, she linked her arm through Caleb's and drew him down the walk with her.

"Yes, everything is going splendidly," she said in answer to his solicitous look. "I'll tell you all about it at supper.... Is that your friend Sebastian Perez standing over there? I want to meet him."

"Well, look here, Faith," said Caleb under his breath, vainly endeavoring to stay their progress, "it's like this: me and Sebastian's been good friends for years, but now that he's leadin' this marblecutters' strike I told you about, it makes things kinda awkward, seein' as I'm the Mayor."

"It isn't going to be awkward," she said insistently. "If you'd rather not go with me, I'll go by myself. But I want to speak to him. He looks unhappy to me. Perhaps if he could find some outlet for whatever is troubling him, he wouldn't be so hard to deal with."

Her grave and courteous, *"Buenas tardes,"* had been pronounced before Caleb could collect himself to meet the situation into which he had been thrust. For a puzzled moment he stood silently on the sidewalk while Faith and Sebastian Perez apparently exchanged compliments. Then Caleb was conscious that the slight tension which at first had pervaded the air was beginning to pass. The Spaniard's serious face relaxed into a smile and he motioned toward the piazza. Faith turned reassuringly to Caleb.

"*Señor* Perez wants us to come up and have a glass of sherry with his mother and himself," she said. "That would be pleasant, wouldn't it? A glass of sherry before dinner is always so refreshing. His mother does not speak much English, he says. But of course she and I can talk together while you and he do."

It was nearly an hour later before Mrs. Mead, whose anxiety over the condition of her waiting supper was beginning to mount to a frenzy, and who was watching the course of events with a distracted eye from her kitchen window, saw Mr. Hawks and his guest begin a series of elaborate leave-takings from the marblecutter and his mother. Hansel had joined them and had been eating with avidity something offered him on a small silver dish, while the rest of the group sipped a shining liquid from tiny glasses that were filled and refilled. Mrs. Mead felt sure that whatever the substance was which Hansel was devouring, it would "spoil his supper"; but he sounded so happy about it as he finally came rushing back into the house, that her wounded feelings were almost immediately assuaged.

"It was nice to have *mazapan* again, wasn't it, mother?" he was saying enthusiastically, "I haven't had any in a long time. I like *Señora* Perez and her son very much, don't you? It is funny the son's name should be Sebastian, because he looks a little like our Sebastian, and *Señora* Perez comes from Granada too."

"Yes, dear. It is funny. And I do like *Señora* Perez and her son very much.—Have you washed your hands for supper?"

In spite of Mrs. Mead's anxiety, the "evening meal" did her great credit, and the strange sticky candy which the Perezes had given Hansel, and which he continued to devour, had not spoiled his supper after all. He did full justice to it. Besides, she could not remember when she had seen Mr. Hawks look so happy as he did now.

"I don't believe there's goin' to be a strike after all," he was saying in a voice of astonishment and pleasure. "From what Sebastian said to me just as as we wuz leavin', I gathered he wuz goin' to say a few words at the Union Meetin' this evenin' that 'ud call the whole thing off. It beats me, Faith, to know how you cud o' smoothed things out the way you did, just settin' on the front porch drinkin' sherry and talkin' to that poor little old lady. As far as I know, she ain't asked any American to her house before. Fact is, 'cept to go to church regular, and to work in her garding, she hardly stirs out at all. Spaniards is sort o' sober most of the time, I've noticed—they ain't forever lettin' off spirits and

257

steam, like the Eye-talians. But *Señora* Perez is soberer than most. She's sad lookin'. She acts to me like a person with some kind o' secret that's troublin' her."

"Yes," agreed Faith rather thoughtfully, "she does. But she isn't very old, Uncle Caleb—that is, not much over forty. I think you're wrong there."

"Sebastian can talk the King's English, same as I do," went on Caleb. He wondered, fleetingly, why Faith seemed interested in the subject of *Señora* Perez' age. Then he dismissed it as unimportant. "But I could see how it pleased him to talk Spanish to you. He's got a heap o' friends here— that's how he comes to have so much influence; but even among furriners he don't take his mother around much. I guess she ain't wanted to go. But she cottoned up to you like you wuz a long-lost daughter. I never seen her smile before —for the most part she looks like them grievin' dark-complected women mourners in the pictures I wuz druv into lookin' at in the Spanish art galleries. But she sure smiled at you, and say, she looks like a different woman when she does, don't she? All that tickled Sebastian most to pieces— that she liked you and that you liked her, I mean—well, I guess you've turned the trick for me, and no mistake. I see in Granada you had a way with you. But I wouldn't a guessed you worked so fast."

"I do really hope I've been helpful," Faith said earnestly. "But don't give me too much credit—probably the trouble wasn't serious anyway. And I was delighted to meet the Perez—the *Señora does* look like one of El Greco's or Ribera's Mater Dolorosas. How observing you are, Uncle Caleb! And—and her son reminds me of someone too."

"You mean that smooth, good-lookin' brother of the bishop's? Well say, Faith, I've kept thinkin' of it too! It can't be imagination if you thought of it straight off, same as I did!"

Caleb paused to pour some tea into his saucer and began to drink it down with a relish that was slightly impaired because he thought he saw Faith wince. But after a moment she went on speaking so calmly that he decided he had been mistaken.

"I told Sebastian Perez that when I am settled in Hamstead, I shall expect him to bring his mother over to have dinner with me," she said. "It seems good to me to talk about Granada, about the snow on the Sierras, and the wind blowing over the *vega,* and the gypsies on the Sacro Monte, and the *antiquarios*———"

Her voice trailed away, a little brokenly. But she smiled and recovered herself quickly.

"Speaking of dinner guests," she said, "I have been wondering if you wouldn't like to do a little entertaining while I am here? I know it is hard sometimes for bachelors and widowers to manage without a hostess. Yet of course all men who are in public life, as you are, realize that it is important, as well as pleasant, to bring congenial groups together. That was one of the first things Rudolf taught me after we were married." She hesitated, and Caleb thought that her lips were quivering; but after a moment she went on again, more gaily. "I think it would be delightful, for instance, to ask the Conrads here, don't you? And several of the ladies who were at the bridge party told me that their husbands were on the City Council. We might ask them to dinner too—the husbands and wives together I mean. Hilda could wait on table, but Mrs. Mead is such a wonderful cook that we ought to take advantage of her talents!"

Mrs. Mead, who, just at that juncture, was bearing in a steamed blueberry pudding on a yellow platter, felt a glow of gratification permeate her being as Faith looked at her. She was a wizened, wiry little woman, with a grim mouth and a small upstanding nose which sometimes quivered unexpectedly, like a rabbit's. It was generally thought in Hinsboro that she was a Tartar, and that the redoubtable Caleb himself trembled before her. But Faith had not trembled before her. She had enslaved her.

"Well now, I don't know but what it would be a good idea," Caleb agreed, covertly watching Mrs. Mead's reaction to this suggestion, "though I never give it much thought before. My wife wuz kindo' like your Aunt Emmeline: she took company hard, and that's a fact. She had to start in the attic and clean right through to the cellar, even if 'twas only a member of the family or the minister comin' in for Sunday dinner. And afterwards she wuz all tuckered out. And Myra took after her ma. So I got out of the way of askin' anyone in. But Mrs. Mead says Hilda's wonderful help. So mebbe between the two of 'em, they cud manage. Yes, I guess mebbe they cud. But *you* look pretty peaked to me, Faith, and I don't want you should get all wore out with company on top o' movin'."

"It won't wear me out. It will be a pleasure."

He realized that she was telling the truth; indeed, he dimly divined, that in spite of her evident weariness and anxiety, she was eager to be constantly and actively occupied. And the first little dinner having proved a great success in every way, he himself suggested that others should be given; and by the time Faith left Mr. Hawks' house for her own, she had established a foothold of friendliness in the little

259

city of her temporary sojourn. This foothold, however, was by no means based exclusively on her startling innovation of "entertaining at dinner"; she had also made a pleasing impression sitting beside Mr. Hawks in his prominent pew at the First Congregational Church, and an equally pleasing impression at the early Mass which she had impartially attended with Sebastian Perez and his mother. She had gone to the annual outing of the Persian Panthers and the annual entertainment of the Order of the Oriental Caribou. She had visited the pencil factory and the marble works, where she had caused a stir of real excitement among the employees, by talking naturally and fluently with them in alternating Spanish, Italian, and French. And she had also visited the day nursery which Mr. Hawks had built in memory of his wife, where her coming, accompanied by a shower of small gifts, had seemed like the apparition of a fairy godmother. When her little car was loaded for the last time with the miscellaneous objects which she was taking with her to Hamstead, and she was about to step into it herself, she found that Mr. Hawks' yard seemed suddenly swarming with the well-wishers who had come to bid her good-bye. Every rung of Hinsboro's social ladder was represented, from Neal Conrad's haughty and exclusive parents to Sebastian's "helper" at the marble works. Angelico Mendoza, who was accompanied by his wife and six children, the eldest of whom was eight years old; and the shouts and cheers which followed her as she swung past the stone deer and out into the street resounded long after she had vanished down the road leading to open country.

. . . . .

Meanwhile, the progress she had been making in Hamstead, though less spectacular, had been quite as steady. From the beginning, Sylvia and Austin Gray had recognized her as a kindred spirit; and where the Grays led, the rest of Hamstead always followed. The Manning, the Westons, the Griffins, and the Taylors, had all called almost as promptly as Mrs. Elliot. Aunt Emmeline and Uncle Ephraim had both "worried considerable" lest she should be "put out" with them because of their apparent inhospitality; but she had dwelt so tactfully on her pleasure at the opportunity of visiting Caleb Hawks, that their relief was great; and their hearts warmed at the genuine affection of her manner, even before she made a suggestion which caused them to gasp by its prodigality.

"I thought at first I might try to move into my house right away," she said. "Sylvia Gray's done such wonders with it that if I hadn't decided to make certain changes in it

260

there wouldn't be any reason why I shouldn't. But Uncle Caleb has urged me to stay with him for a fortnight at least, and I enjoy motoring back and forth—it's a delightful new experience for me, driving a car, and the country is so beautiful at this time of year! So I'll commute for the present, until I have two or three rooms in order at least. I'm going to have them all repapered and repainted, and use my grandmothers' furniture instead of my mother's, and I think it would be easier if everything I don't want were taken out of the house first of all. Don't you? Then I could start in from the beginning."

"You don't mean to say you aren't going to use any of them handsome brass beds and oak sets and elegant hangings, Faith!"

"I—thought I wouldn't. I really think there's enough furniture stored in the attic and barn to make the house look almost the way it did when it was first built. So I thought I'd give away everything that is in it now."

"Give it away!" exclaimed Emmeline and Ephraim in one breath.

"Yes. Perley Stubbs is going to find someone to help him and load everything into hay wagons early to-morrow morning. But I thought you could advise me what to do with it. There must be some needy families, right here in Hamstead, who would be glad of it. Of course if there aren't, I know there are lots of people in Hinsboro——"

Again Emmeline and Ephraim spoke simultaneously. There were indeed several families in Hamstead who would regard the gift of substantial and stylish furniture in the light of manna falling from heaven. Faith's aunt and uncle did not word their answer just that way; but Faith knew this was what they meant; and before dark the following evening she watched the last creaking, top-heavy hay wagon, laden with tinsel and trash, heave its way slowly out of sight.

She gave a deep sigh of overwhelming relief. The house was bare and empty; but she felt as if it had been thoroughly cleansed of Flossie and all that she had represented. Faith put her arm around Hansel's shoulder, and paused for a moment beside him on the wide granite doorstep in front of the disused south entrance, talking over her plans with him quite as seriously as if he had been a contemporary.

"This was the front door when the house was first built, Hansel," she said. "I think it would be pleasant to use it that way again, don't you? With a driveway curving up to it, and a garden stretching out in front of it toward Uncle Ephraim's house—that ugly old barn looming up belongs to you and me, so we can have it torn down, and build a new one in the back where it won't show. Then there'll be nothing but lovely lawns and trees and flowers between the two Marlowe places. The room on the right of the front door will be our library, facing the river and mountains, and the room back of it, the dining room, instead of the kitchen as it is now—when that huge fireplace and brick oven are unstopped, it will be charming."

"And will this be our drawing-room, on the left of the front door?"

"Yes, darling. Only here they call it a parlor. We'll have it very glistening, don't you think so? With all that paneling painted white and brasses shining in the fireplace, and beautiful old pictures in bold frames and polished mahogany furniture. Then back of the parlor, on the other side of the little passage, will be the kitchen."

"And upstairs, mother?"

"Well, upstairs, the large room over the library will be mine, with a big four-poster bed and flowered chintz hangings; and the one leading out of it will be yours. The other large front room will be our guest chamber, and back of it, Hilda's. And the two small rear bedrooms I thought we would make into bathrooms. That will give us all the space we need for now. But later on we could finish off part of the attic if we wanted to."

"Oh, mother, it will all be lovely! I like this little house! Do you think we can stay here a long time?"

"I think so, my precious treasure. I—I hope so."

"Only of course it isn't so nice for father to have us away as it is for us to be here. So perhaps we ought not to stay too long. We mustn't forget about father."

"No, darling, we mustn't forget about father. But he knew he was going to be very busy this summer, and he thought it was really best that we should come away. You know he told us so, when he said good-bye to us on the boat."

"I know he did, mother, but I didn't think he looked very happy when he said it, did you?"

"Not very, dear. But saying good-bye is always a little hard. Perhaps next summer father can be here with us. Perhaps he can have a vacation."

She tried to make her voice sound calm and convincing; but she knew that she had failed, even before she saw Hansel's eyes resting anxiously on her face.

"Father was all right when he wrote to you last, wasn't he, mother?" he asked in a troubled way.

"Yes, Hansel, right as rain! Why, you know that, dear—I

showed you the letter! Of course it was sad for him, going to his Cousin Francis' funeral, and he had been even busier than usual, but he is all right."

"Yes, mother, I suppose so."

She saw that she had not wholly reassured him; and to divert his thoughts, she changed the subject.

"I didn't tell you that in the same mail with father's last letter there was one from Uncle Sam too," she said. "Father had very thoughtfully written him that you and I had come here. Uncle Sam told me he felt he had better not leave France this summer after all, though he didn't tell me why. But Cousin Sarah is coming just the same—Uncle Sam is going to see her on her boat and leave her in charge of the ship's doctor and her stewardess, He hopes you and I will meet her in New York, and try to persuade her to come and visit us for a little while before she goes to Salem. She is going to sail from Havre the thirty-first. So we must hurry and have the house ready before she gets here."

Apparently, his mother's reasons for haste were manifold; she was constantly mentioning a new one. So Hansel felt gravely conscious that he should try to help her as much as he could, that he should not spend too much time with Junior Conrad and his "gang" in Hinsboro, or with Moses Manning the seraphic-looking small boy who had immediately tempted him to join in agreeable and diversified deviltry in Hamstead. He wished that his mother would sit down quietly every evening before supper, and read him fairy stories as she had always done before. But he stifled his disappointment of the abandonment of their tranquil hour, as he had stifled his sense that all was not well with his father, hopefully assuming that in course of time life would take on a more normal aspect again.

The speed with which Faith was plunging ahead with her program of remodeling and refurnishing was startling to Hamstead; but like Hansel, the village as a whole coöperated with her unquestioningly; and the results were remarkable. By the time she moved in the worst of the chaos was over, though Hansel was to sleep in Faith's bedroom for the present, and they were to eat in the library. And as they sat down for the first simple supper in their own house, Hansel was aware that a subtle change had already come over his mother. There was a quality of quietude in her voice which he had not heard in a long time, a repose of manner which he had sorely missed, a look of contentment in the gaze with which her eyes kept wandering over their surroundings. Hansel himself felt that these were beautiful, and understood her content. The paneling in this room was of hard pine, and scraped free from the disfiguring colors which had defaced it, there was a mellowness and warmth about it which blended richly with the russet-colored volumes extending from floor to ceiling. An ancient maple secretary stood between two windows, the wide shelf dividing the drawers beneath from the cabinet above already equipped with writing materials. Over the mantel, between two tall brass candlesticks, hung an impressive portrait of the first Christian Marlowe, clad in fine broadcloth and snowy linen. Braided rugs were scattered over the wide-boarded painted floor, and a wingback chair drawn comfortably up beside the scrubbed hearth, where a cheerful fire blazed gaily above the polished andirons; and near this stood a gate-legged table temporarily covered with a white cloth and set with sprigged china. Sylvia Gray had sent over a profusion of sweetpeas from her garden, and clear glass bowls filled with these were scattered about; while almost every dish which Hilda brought beamingly in was laden with some delicacy donated by a kindly and thoughtful neighbor: Aunt Emmeline had contributed feathery rolls, ruby-colored currant jelly, and tomato relish; Mary Manning, a chicken pie, cottage cheese, and the "makings" for a mixed salad; and Mrs. Elliot a chocolate layer cake. And when they had finished their little feast, Faith took their well-worn copy of Grimm's "Fairy Tales" from its new nook in the tall bookcase, and drawing Hansel down beside her, began to read, for the hundredth time, the story of Snow-White and Red-Rose.

A little later, she and Hansel went upstairs together. Among the treasures which the attic had yielded was a quaintly turned trundle bed of generous proportions. For the present, this was to be Hansel's; and he and Faith pulled it into place together. By mutual consent, they decided that it was cool enough to have a fire in the bedroom too—for late July it was unseasonably, though agreeably cool. And when they had prayed, side by side, they lay down, hand in hand, and fell asleep with the soft glow from the quiet flames flickering across their faces, and the summer moonlight streaming in through the many-paned windows.

Chapter XXXIV

THEY were still sleeping profoundly when Hilda came in the next morning, and set a big tray down on the four-poster.

264

It was very late, she told the Frau Baronin; and Perley Stubbs was insistently asking whether those old beams were really to be left in the dining-room ceiling. He would have to know before he went ahead with the queer rough wallpaper; and to his way of thinking, the huge fireplace with the Dutch oven beside it was "unsightly." Faith laughed, more merrily than she had done since Hansel could remember, and said she would be "right down"; but she did not hurry over her coffee and rolls for all that. It pleased Hansel to see her sitting propped up against big pillows again, with her hair tumbling over her shoulders, while she ate her breakfast, instead of hastening downstairs early to have it with Mr. Hawks; and he was rapturously grateful to Hilda for bringing up his milk and eggs, so that he would not be separated from his mother while he breakfasted himself. Indeed, he was not separated from her all day. He stayed with her while she reassured Perley Stubbs about the dining room, which was, after all, just the way she wanted it; and when that important point had been settled, she and Hansel went out to see how the demolition of the old barn was getting along, and Faith explained to him where the rosebeds and sun dial were to be in the garden. Late in the afternoon, she actually suggested that they should leave the scene of reconstruction, since everything seemed to be going along all right, and take a ride together; so they chugged off in the cheerful little Dodge, and poked their way over back roads until the deepening shadows warned them that it was time to go home.

Again, Faith had planned to go to bed as early as Hansel; but just as they were finishing their story, the sound of the knocker reverberated through the quiet house; and before Hilda could come trudging to answer the summons, Hansel had bounded off to the door himself. The next instant Faith heard a shout of welcome from the child; and mingled with it the compelling ring of David Noble's voice.

He had arrived early that afternoon, he said, advancing toward Faith as she sprang up in her turn. Yes, Jacqueline was well, but she was a little tired, so she was resting that evening, though she would drop in the next day without fail; meanwhile he had come to give Faith her love, and to see for himself whether there was anything he could do to help her. What wonders she had accomplished already, he said looking about him with appreciative enthusiasm. And someone had told him, he added laughing, that she was going to put a flower garden where the old barn had stood—he would never have believed that she was so practically, as well as so artistically, minded—she would not have to buy any fertilizer for years! He had also heard that she had both mercantile Hinsboro and agricultural Hamstead groveling at her feet, and that she had settled the marblecutters' strike. Yet—news traveled fast in this part of the world. But apparently she had been traveling fast herself!

He spoke almost banteringly, but Faith was conscious that his raillery had no depth; and his unpresaged appearance set her newly calmed senses quivering again. Where had he been since she had last seen him—at Radensholm—in another world? Was he the bearer of good or evil tidings —or of no tidings at all? It took a supreme effort of will for her to betray no impatience, to sit quietly smiling at his badinage, and to eventually, with apparent nonchalance, change the topic of conversation herself. She asked him to tell her about the Cottage Hospital which he and Jacqueline had built in Hamstead: would they take her to see it some day? Was he able to use it as a center for much of his own work? His versatility was amazing to her—she had already gleaned that he was regarded as the "family doctor" by everyone in the village, for whom a substitute was chosen only during his long unavoidable absences; yet in the world at large, he was recognized as one of the leading surgeons of the day.

Faith was beginning to find suspense intolerable, when Hansel, of his own accord, confessed that he was sleepy, and said that he would ask Hilda to help him roll out the trundle bed. The door had hardly closed behind him, when David assumed control of the situation.

"I knew you would be very anxious to hear everything I have to tell you," he said. "That is why I did not wait, even until to-morrow, to come to see you.—It seemed better not to try to write—better to Don Sebastian and better to me. Especially since you left Denmark so—unexpectedly, shall we say?"

He paused for a moment as if to give Faith an opportunity to speak. Then conscious of the imploring quality of the gaze she turned upon him, he went on swiftly.

"Don Sebastian was most insistent that I should tell you first of all," he said, "that he had never intended to bargain with you—to promise that if you would do one thing, he would do another. He said you would know what he meant when I told you that—of course I did not inquire. I only know that he had pledged you his word to go with me to Spain and that he kept it. According to his own code—and there are many worse—he is a very honorable gentleman."

He heard Faith give a dry and stifled sob, quickly smothered. But she continued to look at him imploringly and without speaking.

"We traveled directly through, from Copenhagen to Biarritz," David went on. "Jacqueline and a French doctor and nurse with whom I have worked before, and in whom I have a great deal of confidence, went with us. From Biarritz we motored through the Pyrenees to the Castello Viejo, which is a very splendid old stronghold—perhaps some day you would like to hear more about it. We reached there very late one night, and early the next morning I saw Doña Dolores. She was fortunately in an unusually quiet state and I was able to examine her almost immediately. Because I wished to proceed very cautiously, I contined to watch her for a time, but I was convinced from the beginning that I might take the chance of operating. After I had been at the Castillo Viejo four days I did so. The operation was entirely successful."

David laid a steadying hand on Faith's trembling arm. "I stayed on at the Castello Viejo for ten days after the operation had taken place," he continued. "When I went away, I left Norchais and Sœur Celestine—the French doctor and nurse of whom I spoke—in charge. They have kept me informed of the progress of events by wire. Sœur Celestine is still there—Doña Dolores has become very much attached to her, and besides, the period of convalescence will naturally be long. But Norchais had left. That means that the Duquesa is wholly out of danger."

"And—Sebastian?"

"Of course, Don Sebastian has remained also. Doña Dolores can hardly bear to have him out of her sight, and his devotion to her is supreme. She recognized him almost as soon as she had recovered from the anæsthetic, though imperfectly—at first she was under the impression that they were young lovers, then that they were just married—as a bride she must have been passionately attached to him. But before I left she understood the situation completely. And it was very moving—very wonderful—to see her when she understood.—You have given Sebastian's heritage of glory back to him, Faith. That is a great thing for a woman to do for—for a man."

"For the man she loves, you started to say!" Faith cried. "Oh, David, why didn't you say it! You have guessed from the beginning! And Rudolf guessed too, years ago, though I never knew it until the night I went away—the night I *ran* away! It was only a miracle that saved me from—from —if I had stayed——"

"I know, Faith, But you didn't stay. Don't give way like

267

this—it isn't worthy of you. Don't even say that I 'guessed,' that Rudolf 'guessed.' Say we understood."

He bent over her, one hand clasping hers, an arm about her shoulder. But he made no effort to check the frenzy of weeping to which she abandoned herself, realizing that the floodgates of long repression had opened at last, and that she could not be comforted until she had recovered from the overpowering storm of passion with which she was torn. At last, as her sobs became less and less intense, he spoke to her very gently.

"I know that you feel a chapter in your life is closed, Faith," he said, "a very poignant and precious chapter. Perhaps you will never turn the pages of one like it again. I am afraid you will never love another man in the sense that you have loved Don Sebastain, and—may I say it?—in the sense that he has loved you. For you have been the great love of his life, as truly as he has been yours. Never let yourself doubt that—either because of his past or because of his future. What he has felt for you is altogether alien both to trivial intrigue—and to pride of race. Can you understand that?"

"Yes. I—I have always understood that."

"Then it will be a great comfort to you. And do not forget that for every chapter which closes another always opens. I told you that you had given his heritage back to Don Sebastian. And I believe that after a long exile you are going to come into yours. Haven't you begun to be vaguely conscious of this already—reaching home? You always felt yourself a stranger in Europe—even in Spain, much as you loved it—if you hadn't, you would have accepted the *caseria* as a gift. But here you feel that you belong."

She looked up at him in surprise. He smiled and went on speaking without waiting for her to answer.

"Now that I have reminded you of this and told you everything vital there is to say about Doña Dolores," he said quietly, "I think perhaps I should prepare you for certain world conditions which are very unsettled and which may affect you."

"World conditions!" she repeated dazedly. "What do you mean by world conditions—that could affect me?"

"Have you never thought—never feared—that the murder in Sarajevo——"

"Yes!" she exclaimed. "I have! But I haven't heard anything. I've dreaded to read—I've hardly let myself think—David, what has happened?"

"Austria declared war on Servia to-day," he said with

forced calm. "Russia has been mobilizing for three days already. If there is a general upheaval almost anything may happen. France and England will probably throw in their forces with her."

"Throw in their forces with her! Against whom?"

"Against Austria—and—and possibly Germany, Faith."

This time she cried aloud. He saw that the anguish from which she had just recovered was again threatening to crush her in another form.

"I must go back!" she exclaimed wildly. "By the first boat! If Germany is going to be drawn in, this means that Rudolf—David, I deserted him—when he needed me most!"

"No, Faith. A strange coincidence took you away just as he was on the point of sending you in any case. I'm sure he does not feel that you deserted him. I'm sure he is thankful that you are safe from the storm—you and Hansel. He knows that nothing can harm either of you here. If you had stayed in Europe, he could not have been so certain."

David rose, and walked over toward the east window. Under the summer moon, the valley lay bathed in peace as with a benediction. It seemed impossible, looking out upon it, that anywhere in the world there could be war. But when he turned, there was a note of admonition in his voice.

"I imagine you will have some sort of a personal message before long," he said guardedly. "In the meantime, I advise you to read at least one reliable newspaper every day.—If you are sure there is nothing I can do for you here, I must go home now—that is, when I have told you one more piece of news."

"Is it—is it more bad news?"

"No, it is good news—that is, I believe you will think so. Jacqueline and I saw Sam in Paris as we passed through there on our way to Havre. He asked us if we would not bring Mrs. Atkinson back with us, so that she would not have to make the voyage alone, as she had planned. She is at the Big House with us now. I know that to-morrow you will wish to see her."

• • • • • •

For the next few days Faith went mechanically through the process of living. It seemed to her that she always heard her own voice as if it belonged to someone else, speaking from a great distance. She felt as if she were constantly listening for a sound which did not come and watching for someone who did not appear; and at last the tension became

269

so great that it seemed to her that it would be better to hear anything and see anybody than to live indefinitely in terrified and unrelieved suspense.

The sound which finally shattered the strained silence was only another rap on the knocker, no more violent than those of Mrs. Elliot and David Noble. But she intuitively knew that it was portentous as she flew to open the door; and when she saw herself confronted with the solid figure of Sol Daniels, the station master, she instinctively put out her hand, even before he spoke to her.

He was beaming broadly. Evidently he was swelled with a sense of self-importance that was extremely satisfactory to him. As he extended the two flimsy envelopes he held in his hand, he chuckled.

"I never took a radio message of'n the ticker 'til I got that one sayin' you was on your way here," he said delightedly. "And I figgered the kick I got out o' that would have to last me quite a spell. But land! If this afternoon two cables didn't come in from Yrrup within half an hour of each other. I hadn't got one of 'em half writ before I had to turn to on the other. You've shook this town up good an' plenty, Mrs. Er—um—Faith. Well, good-evenin' to ye."

"Good evening," said Faith, in the mechanical voice that seemed to belong to someone else.

She had torn open one of the yellow envelopes. The scrawled sentences on the limp pages which met her eyes contained the message against which she had been bracing herself.

"WAR DECLARED BETWEEN FRANCE AND GERMANY," she read. "FATHER HAS TAKEN COMMAND HIS TROOPS MY BROTHERS WITH THEIR REGIMENTS I HAVE RESIGNED FROM DIPLOMATIC SERVICE AND AM REJOINING ARMY. WILL COMMUNICATE WITH YOU OFTEN. ALL MY LOVE TO YOU AND HANSEL.

RUDOLF"

She sat down on the stone steps and leaned against the lintel of the door. The envelope which had contained the message fluttered to the ground. It was some moments before she even remembered that she was holding another. Without premonition of further shock, she opened it slowly.

"WAR DECLARED BETWEEN FRANCE AND GERMANY," she read again; and for a moment she wondered, stupidly, if Sol had brought her two copies of the same cable. Then suddenly her eyes leaped forward. "FRANCE HAS BEEN MY COUNTRY FOR YEARS I AM OFF TO FIGHT FOR HER. TAKE CARE OF COUSIN SARAH FOR ME. YOURS FOREVER. SAM."

Chapter XXXV

THE sensation that she was perpetually waiting and listening, which had been so strong from the night when David had brought her word that Austria had declared war on Servia, did not end on the afternoon when the cables from Rudolf and Sam reached Faith simultaneously; instead it gradually increased until it became almost an obsession. If she had not constantly struggled against it, it would have overwhelmed her completely.

As August advanced, there was nothing on which she could lay her finger to account for her feeling of impending and inescapable disaster. The letter which Rudolf wrote almost immediately after he had despatched his cable, and which came through with unusual celerity, was calmly matter-of-fact in tone. It went into few details about himself, but none of those supplied sounded ominous; and it revealed meticulous interest in her own welfare.

"We all expect that the war will be over before Christmas," he stated with a confidence which carried conviction, "but since winter will probably be well along before the situation is really tranquil again here, it would reassure me if you would let me know whether you can remain in Hamstead through the cold weather without inconvenience. In the spring it might be possible for me to join you in Hamstead and stay for a time—I should like to see something of America myself, and we might come back to Germany by way of the Orient. Now that I have resigned from the Service there is no reason why I should not have a vacation after the war is over, and you and I have never taken a trip of any consequence together. Would it amuse you, *liebe* Faith, to go to Japan and India, for example?"

Sam's scribbled communications were as different from Rudolf's in tone as they were in penmanship, but they were no more alarming. Apparently he was very happy himself, and certainly he was not worrying about her. He was taking it for granted that she was having the "time of her life" in Hamstead, after hankering for it so many years. And it was a relief to know that Cousin Sarah had given up the idea of going to Salem for the present, and that she was going to make Faith a long visit. He would like to see the old house she had got her claws into, and he would, when the little scrap he had taken on was over—probably his next picture of her would be "The New England Housewife." Meanwhile he certainly was enjoying himself in the Foreign Legion—there were men from ten different countries in his company, and say. . . .

Faith smiled as she read this letter, but the smile did not last except on the surface. She wrote reassuringly to Rudolf: she was very comfortable in Hamstead, she told him, and everyone was very kind to her. Though her life was quiet, it was extremely pleasant—now that David and Jacqueline were back at the Big House there were even a few festivities in Hamstead. She would be glad to remain where she was until he could join her, and then they would have a wonderful trip together. In a way, it would be like a second honeymoon.

To Sam she wrote even more gaily, enclosing snapshots of the old house she had "got her claws into," and of herself as a "New England Housewife"—rather disheveled and beaming broadly, with a broom in one hand and a pail in the other. Cousin Sarah's rheumatism was much better, she told him—David, who was a perfect wonder, was helping her a great deal. Faith had always heard the Foreign Legion was disreputable, and she had no doubt it was more so than ever, now that Sam had joined it; but she loved his stories about it just the same. Would he please write her some more, and illustrate them with sketches? And she was as always. . . .

Hansel and Moses Manning, who had been swimming together, took her letters to the Post Office; and Faith sat down on the stone doorsteps, gazing out toward the mountains, and feeling, now that these were written, that she had nothing of much consequence to do. It was becoming increasingly clear to her that there was not enough to do in Hamstead to fill her time or stimulate her mind. The house, which had temporarily done both, though still a source of satisfaction to her, was ceasing to be one of occupation and excitement; and her friends and neighbors were agreeable rather than thrilling. Her close comradeship with Hansel had been a godsend to her, but she realized that as the friendships he had formed became more and more absorbing, she would see less and less of him herself. Decidedly, Hansel's days of dependence upon her were numbered. Yet her dependence upon him had never been so great.

If time had not been hanging so heavily on her hands, her unformulated fears would have haunted her less; but now that she was no longer preoccupied, her feeling of impending disaster became more and more intense. Her days she managed to fill somehow, by one expedient or another, but the nights became increasingly dreadful. They stretched out before her in endless succession, black, hideous, vacant and interminable. And not alone because terrors which could be stilled in the friendly daylight reared menacingly before her in the darkness: her precipitate fall from the emotional heights which had culminated at Radensholm had been as agonizing as it was swift; and she could not drug or kill the starved passion for Sebastian which had been so close to consummation. David, whose brief and casual visits had become an established custom, watched her solicitously as the weeks went on. At last, with unaccustomed bluntness, the doctor made a challenging statement.

"Look here, Faith, you can't go on indefinitely like this, you know. In fact, you can't go on much longer. You've got to find some outlet for all this pent-up force of yours."

"I know. I'm trying, David, really I am. But there doesn't seem to be anything to do here, beyond what I'm doing already. And I don't know where else to go. Besides, I don't believe going away would help. I seem to be faced with something that is—inescapable."

"Nothing is inescapable," said David still more brusquely. "Work out your own salvation. I told you, when I first got home, that you'd come into your heritage here, even though you didn't realize it yet. Do something with your legacy."

"What?"

"I don't know. If I had, I'd have told you long ago. But do something."

. . . . .

It was with this recommendation that David had left her, somewhat abruptly; and while she sat idly on the doorstep, watching the sun as it sank toward the western hills, and waiting for Hansel to come home, Faith turned his counsel over in her mind, as she had done many times already. She did not doubt the wisdom of his advice; but she was profoundly puzzled as to how she could profit by it. At last, acting, as she so often did, on a sudden impulse, she went into the house and called Caleb Hawks on the telephone.

He was not in, Mrs. Mead informed her, and Faith detected a note of concern in the trusty housekeeper's voice. What with one thing and another, he was "druv almost to death." But of course she would tell him that Mrs. Lowe had "foamed." Was there something special?

"I hoped that he would motor over and have supper

with me. I want very much to see him. Yes, really it is rather special."

"I'll tell him the minute he comes in," Mrs. Mead promised.

It was about half an hour later when Caleb called her back himself. He was plumb tuckered out, he said; but take it all in all, he didn't know but what he'd be glad to get out of Hinsboro for an hour or two even if he was. No one would know where to find him and pester him to death. He guessed maybe he'd better shave and put on a clean shirt—he looked like something the cat brung in; but after that he'd be right along.

He arrived within an hour, shining with heat and cleanliness; but it was plain, as Faith had already gathered, that he was beset with worries. It appeared that there had been a demand for increase of wages at the pencil factory, the second in four months; and though Ted Jenkins, the General Manager and he thought the trade in pencils brisk enough to justify this, there was no telling how long business would continue at its present high pitch; it wasn't prudent to be too optimistic. The contractor for a new pavement on Main Street had reneged on his agreement, and the city stood to lose a good deal of money by his default. But this did not mark the end of his perplexities: the School Board had had its first meeting of the season, and some darn fool had insisted that Spanish should now be added to the High School curriculum. *Spanish!* Just as if the pupils weren't studying enough languages already! There was no one he could find to *teach* Spanish now anyway, not with school opening in three days, unless some marblecutter could be persuaded to give up good wages for a starvation salary. But Sebastian Perez didn't think any of them would. In fact, he didn't even think it would be a good plan to suggest such a thing, with the threatened strike just called off, so——

"I could teach Spanish at the Hinsboro High School," said Faith suddenly. "I—I should be very glad to. Do you think the School Board would consider me? I have never had any experience, of course, but then I wouldn't care about the salary either. Perhaps——"

Caleb, demolishing his fourth ear of sweet corn, dropped it on the table edge, where it balanced precariously for a moment, and then fell to the floor.

"You!" he exclaimed, "teach a parcel of young hoodlums in the Hinsboro High School! Faith, I guess you've took leave of your senses, and that's a fact."

"No, I haven't. Really, Uncle Caleb, I think I would make a very good teacher. Won't you let me try?"

He continued to stare at her in stupefaction, absent-mindedly picking up the breadcrumbs which were scattered about his plate and making them into a little pile.

"It ain't that," he said at last. "Of course you'd make a good teacher. Land o' Goshen, you'd be good at anything! Don't I know it! But you ain't got no idea what you'd be lettin' yourself in for. It'd be hard work for you. The School Board wants there should be at least three of these dumb-fangled classes a week, and it'd be freezing cold driving back and forth between here and Hinsboro every other day. And papers to correct evenin's and order to keep in the schoolroom an' 'neverything. No, it ain't to be thought of. Not but what I appreciate your offerin'."

"Uncle Caleb, you don't understand. I—I want something to do."

"You want something to do!" he said explosively. "Land sakes, ain't you got enough to do as 'tis! You do about three times as much as any woman I was ever acquainted with and here you are clamorin' for more trouble! Well, if you really want it, I'll give you some. Not in the High School though. In the Day Nursery. I tell you, Faith, that Day Nursery is the straw that's broke this camel's back. On top of the new wage scale at the factory, and that rascally contractor that's tryin' to swindle the city, and this high-falutin' idea that boys and girls that's goin' to sell ribbons and dig ditches for a livin' has got to learn some elegant furrin language instead of speakin' the King's English same as the rest of us, what do you think I got on my hands at the Day Nursery? An epidemic of whooping-cough! An' the matron's sick herself, and all the help so druv already, and all the lady visitors so scared of contagion, I don't know whose goin' to take care of them poor young 'uns, and that's a fact!"

"I do," said Faith calmly, "I am."

Chapter XXXVI

THREE weeks later, when Faith began her duties as teacher of Spanish at the Hinsboro High School, the worst of the epidemic of whooping-cough at the Day Nursery was over.

"You couldda knocked me over with a feather," Caleb Hawks told Mrs. Mead, though he had added another twenty pounds to his ponderous weight since he had annoyed Rudolf with this expression, "when I see she weren't jokin' or triflin' or nothin', but dead in earnest. She *wanted* to go to the Day Nursery and look after them poor sick young 'uns. She said Hansel had had whooping-cough anyway, so there warn't no danger to contagion. To make a long story short, there warn't a single objection I c'd raise she didn't brush off like a fly; and she's ben on hand ever since. There ain't nothin' she ain't willin' to do, and some of the work's been kinda nasty, and that's a fact. Them children is awful sick to their stomachs at times, when they cough. And the place warn't none too clean anyway. She was right down on her knees scrubbin' floors before I c'd stop her. Well, with that new matron David Noble helped her to find, and the extra hired girl she dug up somewhere out in West Hamstead herself, I guess things is goin' to run smoother from now on. I told her so, and she laughed and said she aimed to keep her finger on the trigger hereafter, or words to that effect. The kids is all crazy about her, and she sure has got a way with them; and I guess the Lady Governors is goin' to make her a member of the Board. They couldn't very well help it after what she's done, and the office of treasurer is kinda goin' beggin'. Likely, they'll elect her to that."

Mr. Hawks' prediction was fulfilled: three different ladies, separately and cajolingly importuned to take over the thankless task of acting as treasurer for the Hinsboro Day Nursery had declined to do so; but when as a last resort the Board appealed to Faith, she accepted the position with alacrity. She had become deeply interested in the Day Nursery. The situation there had not only roused her sympathies; it had challenged her efficiency; and the hard grueling work she had done there, instead of exhausting her, had acted on her as a tonic and a panacea. She had been up at six every morning, and had given competent and comprehensive directions for the day to Hilda and the still swarming mechanics, before hurling herself into her Dodge, and compelling it to eat up the miles between Hamstead and Hinsboro. Sometimes she took Hansel with her, to spend the day with Caleb and Mrs. Mead or with Junior Conrad; more frequently she left him at home, in charge of Hilda and Cousin Sarah, who was now duly established in the spare chamber; and she was always home again in time to read to him after supper and see him tucked into his trundle bed. When she finally sank down on her great four-poster, and reached for his hand, sleep did not always elude and mock her as it had been doing. The "white nights" of anguish persisted intermittently; but they no longer dominated her or tortured her past the limit of her endurance.

The Hinsboro School Board held another meeting as the epidemic was beginning to subside; and Faith persuaded Caleb Hawks to permit her to accompany him to this, and to state her own case before its members. Several of them had met her already, and the others had heard her achievements heralded. Far from encountering opposition, she found that her services were unanimously solicited; and she was even asked whether, since she would be coming to the school to teach Spanish in any case, she would consider "taking over" a few other classes: there was an incipient course in Fine Arts as well as the one in Spanish, and Mr. Hawks had revealed the fact that she "knew all the furrin picture galleries like a book"; while the director of Home Economics felt sure she would have some suggestions about European recipes which could be tried out to advantage. In short, if she would consider coming five times a week, instead of three, it would be deeply appreciated.

"It'll be ungodly cold by an' by, same as I told you," Caleb cautioned her warningly, as he thought she appeared to hesitate. "And there's an awful crowd of roughnecks among them scholars. 'Tain't as if they wuz pure-breds, same as me and you is—a lot of 'em is furriners, Canucks and Poles and Eye-talians, and Lord knows what."

"I'm goin' to buy a coonskin coat," Faith said briefly. "I won't be cold. And I'm not afraid of foreigners—why Uncle Caleb, haven't I lived with foreigners for nearly twenty years? I'm much more used to them than I am to Amercans! Besides, if I were in Hinsboro every day except Saturday and Sunday, I could keep on going to the Day Nursery regularly, and I want to do that—my idea of a Lady Visitor is someone who *visits!*" she added with a slight touch of scorn, "and if I'm going to take charge of funds, I want to know exactly how money's being apportioned and spent.— But I was thinking of Hansel. It was all right to leave him in an emergency like this one we've just been through, but I shouldn't like to do it all winter. If he would be willing to go to school in Hinsboro instead of Hamstead, though I could arrange for the teaching and the welfare work too; and I don't see why he shouldn't be—it would be fun for both of us, driving back and forth together. I'll talk it over with him when I get home this evening."

"Land sakes, Faith! I never see anyone *organize* the way you do, never in my life, and that's a fact."

"You mustn't pay me such extravagant compliments, Uncle Caleb. The Board will think you're prejudiced," she said glancing about her with a comprehensive and disarming smile. "Will it be all right if I let you know my decision in the morning?" she went on agreeably. "I feel quite sure I can arrange to take over all the classes you have in mind. But I must confer with my son before I promise."

As she left the Board Meeting, and walked back toward Caleb Hawks' house with him, he reiterated his expressions of admiration concerning her executive ability. At the same time, he questioned her rather awkwardly.

"If you'd only ben a man, Faith," he told her, "you'd a ben in the State Legislature by now—in fact, I wouldn't be a mite surprised if you'd a ben Lieutenant Governor! Your grandpa would certainly a ben proud of you—and as for your poor pa, my my! You got all the guts that was left out of him—beg pardon, Faith, that slipped out without my noticing.—Just the same, you still look kinda peaked to me. Are you sure you feel real well?"

"I feel very well. Except that I—I had bad news this morning. It was a good deal of a shock."

"You don't say! Well now, I'm just as sorry as I ken be. What happened?"

"I had another cable," she said in a low voice. "I—I keep expecting them all the time, since the first two came. I—I listen for the knocker in the night. I can't seem to help it. And Sol Daniels seems actually pleased, every time he comes up to the house with another message. This was from Rudolf again. It told me that my brother-in-law, Hans von Hohenlohe, who was a colonel in the German army, was killed at the battle of the Marne—the one that has been going on for nearly a week. Hans was Rudolf's favorite brother. I have heard him say that he 'loved him with his very soul.' And I know he did. This will be a terrible blow to Rudolf, and I do not know whether he is near anyone who —who can comfort him. I am afraid he is not—and that troubles me—very much. Besides, I was very fond of Hans myself. The first time I went to Schönplatz, the von Hohenlohes' country place, he was so kind and cordial to me that I have never forgotten. He was very gentle and affectionate, and he had a voice like an angel. At Christmas time it was always he who led the carol-singing. And now he has been killed—in a war—where men murder each other."

Caleb gave an exclamation of sympathy. Faith turned toward him, and he saw that she was making a supreme effort to keep her lips and voice steady.

"David Noble came in last evening and said that he had been expecting this battle, that it would repulse the German forces, and keep them from getting to Paris," she said. "He told me whole regiments were sent to the front in taxi cabs, the German advance was so close. Of course the French have fought with desperate bravery, and I do not wonder that he admires them for defending their capital so superbly. But the Marne will never mean the place where Paris was saved to me. It will always mean the place where Hans was slaughtered and Rudolf was bereft."

"Now look here, Faith——"

"I know. I won't.... I think David would like to go to France himself. And I told you that Sam Dudley, the best friend I have in the world—has enlisted in the French Foreign Legion. I suppose he'll be fighting soon, if he hasn't already begun. I'm terrified for fear the next cable I get——"

"Like as not you won't get no more cables, Faith. Anyways, don't you go listenin' for 'em in the night. It ain't healthy. It'll wear you down. I'm goin' to say a few words to Sol Daniels myself."

The few words spoken by Caleb were so forceful that when the next cable came, Sol was bewildered as to what to do with it. Certainly he could not withhold it. But neither, in the light of Caleb's remarks, did he dare to deliver it. He finally decided to telephone Mr. Hawks and confer with him.

The idea was not without well-meaning merit; but it chanced that the moment he chose could hardly have been more unfortunate. It had finally been decided, after the discussion of numerous divergent plans, that Faith and Hansel should take their daily dinner with Caleb. Faith's classes at the Hinsboro High School all came in the morning and in the afternoon, while Hansel was at the second session, she went to the Day Nursery for two hours. The noon-time interval was one of relaxation and pleasure; and the little group which was becoming more and more closely knit together had just seated itself at table, when the bell on the dining-room wall jangled, and Caleb Hawks rose to answer it.

"Hello," he said, hastily swallowing a generous portion of Hamburg steak. "Yep, Caleb Hawks, speakin'. Oh—hello, Sol! What's that? What's that you say?"

Instantly, he felt Faith's hand on his arm, and saw her white face close to his.

"Is it Rudolf? she whispered. "Or Sam?"

"It ain't either of 'em," he said quickly. "But it *is* a cable, Faith, *from* Rudolf. Mebbe I better let you take it yourself. There's something about Wipers and a man who was hurt there—I don't reccernize the name. Here's the receiver."

He put his arm around her, and felt her slim body growing more and more rigid as she slowly repeated the words which Sol Daniels was painfully spelling out to her.

"Heinrich — has — died — from — wounds — received — at Ypres," she said tonelessly. "Mother—has—now lost—all—her—sons.—but me. Rudolf."—"Yes—yes—I understand. Yes—I should like a copy of it. Yes—I will come in with an answer this afternoon. Thank you, Sol, good-bye."

She sank down where she had been standing, covering her face with her hands. Caleb tried to wedge a supporting hand under one of her elbows.

"You come upstairs and lay down on the spare-room bed," he said, "till you kinda get hold of yourself. You're not goin' to the Day Nursery this afternoon, not except over my dead body.—All her sons but Rudolf! *All*—why, how many more was there, Faith?"

"There were three," she said in a smothered voice. "The first one—Otto—was a son by another marriage. But he—died violently too. I never told you about that, but some day I will. Oh, Uncle Caleb,—it's too dreadful. Heinrich was like *Tante* Luise—dark and brilliant and charming, full of life and high spirits. It seems impossible that any wound could be deep enough to kill him, his vitality was so dazzling. *Tante* Luise will feel that part of herself has gone this time."

For a moment Faith continued to sit where she was, bowed and shaking, her face still hidden. Then she rose slowly, dried her eyes, and smoothed back her hair, and walking out into the little front entry, reached for her hat and coat.

"What are you aimin' to do, Faith?" Caleb called after her. She turned toward him with a determined, though pitiful attempt at a smile.

"Did you ever read Tolstoy's story about the peasant?" she said. "The one who was out in his field ploughing, and was asked by someone what he would do if he knew he were going to die the next day?—No, I suppose not.—Well, he said he would go on ploughing. I think he had the right idea. I'm going back to the Nursery."

.   .   .   .   .

The long cold winter progressed slowly. There was not as much snow as usual, and there were only a few days when the Dodge could not nose its way somehow through the rutted and frozen roads between Hamstead and Hinsboro; so there were almost no interruptions to the teaching and nursery work with which Faith went doggedly on. The schedule which she had systematized so skillfully was saved from monotony by the approach of the Christmas holidays with their attendant diversified activities: she agreed to teach the school play; and she financed and organized a celebration at the Day Nursery, drilling the children to sing Christmas carols and cajoling Caleb into acting as Santa Claus. All the parents of Faith's charges had come to this celebration; and by the time "refreshments" were being served and the distribution of presents had begun, the very walls were resounding with the hearty merriment of the factory hands and marblecutters and their families. Then next day there was a glorious feast at "Marlowe Manor": Caleb Hawks and his daughter Myra, and her husband, Ted Jenkins, the manager of the pencil factory, and their children all came to it; so did Uncle Ephraim and Aunt Emmeline, and David and Jacqueline Noble. And when the last guest had gone, Hansel looked up joyfully from the new electric train that was already chugging its way over the neatly laid track on the library floor, and asked Faith a question which she realized concealed no disappointment beyond that which he frankly voiced.

"It was a lovely Christmas, wasn't it, mother? As nice as a German Christmas except for not having father and grandmother and the others here. I'm afraid they're missing us too, aren't you? But next year we will all be together again, in Berlin, won't we?"

"I hope so, Hansel. Yes—of course we will."

"Except, I suppose you are thinking, Uncle Hans and Uncle Heinrich won't be there? When we sing 'Heilige Nacht,' it won't seem quite the same without Uncle Hans, will it? But then, perhaps he is singing it in heaven now— just think how that would please all the other angels!"

"I will think of it Hansel. It is a lovely thought."

She walked over to the secretary, and taking out the letter which had come in from Rudolf two days earlier, sat down in the wing chair by the fire to re-read it. He was purposely not sending her a cable, he said, since he feared that by now she might have come to regard the arrival of one with dread (it was strange how separation from her had given him the intuition which intimacy had never evoked!) but he wanted her and Hansel to know that he would be thinking of them both constantly on Christmas Day. He was happy to say that he had been fortunate enough to secure the promise of holiday leave, and General Von Hohenlohe also hoped to get away from the Eastern Front for a few days. So there would be a family gathering in Berlin, and they would make it as cheerful a one as they could, looking forward to next year when everything would be different. But perhaps it would be best for her not to count too confidently on his being with her in the spring—the war might be somewhat more protracted than he had forseen at first. However, as soon as it was over, he would hasten to join her, and they would travel anywhere she chose together. Meanwhile, he sent her his devoted love.

The unfailing regularity with which Rudolf's letters continued to arrive, as well as their loyal and affectionate tone, reminded Faith of those he had sent her immediately after their betrothal, when she and Sarah Atkinson had been visiting the hill cities of Italy together. The exigencies of life at the front seemed to present no more obstacles to uninterrupted correspondence now than her indefinite method of traveling had done with him years earlier. Occasionally, he was even adroit enough to avoid the censor, and to send communications to her through some indirect channel. When this was the case, he wrote her fully and freely, and the pages covered with his clear and forceful handwriting were absorbingly interesting to her, entirely apart from their personal element. He made the intricacy of the trenches and the horrors of No Man's Land clear to her long before anyone else in either Hinsboro or Hamstead had grasped that all time-honored methods of warfare had been revolutionized. The eyes of everyone else she knew seemed focused exclusively on the Western Front, but she understood that the impregnable line which stretched from East Prussia to the Carpathian Mountains, had begun to assume proportions of immeasurable importance to the Central Powers. Reading between the lines in Sam's infrequent and lighthearted letters, casually despatched from the headquarters of the "Stepsons of France," she could understand his optimistic point of view. But it was in Rudolf's analyses rather than in Sam's persiflage that she placed real reliance.

She had learned, early in the previous autumn, to keep her own counsel; and though she was conscious that the United States had been neutral in letter rather than in spirit, almost from the beginning of the war, she seldom detected signs of personal antagonism in the atmosphere about her. She was aware that she was regarded less as the wife of a German officer—entirely unknown in the valley—who was fighting against the Allies, than as the daughter of an American Senator—whose memory was greatly respected and revered—who had opportunely found her way to her ancestral home. She had every reason to feel secure in her enjoyment of popular approval and popular affection.

This feeling of security became solidified as time went on and nothing happened to perturb her. Her emotions were under control at last, even though they were not subdued; the dreadful forebodings which had haunted her for so long became more and more dim as her worst fears remained unrealized; and her driving preoccupations did much to ward off introspection. In addition to everything else she was doing, she had embarked upon a scheme of landscape gardening which would engage her attention through the evenings and weekends during the spring, and engross her intensively after the closing of school during the summer. Now that the house was completely restored to its former beauty, her mind had turned eagerly toward the improving of its surroundings: she had begun to visualize a vegetable garden and orchard stretching out behind a garage and a tennis court; and best of all, extending between her own house and Uncle Ephraim's, paths and plots bordered with flowers, and sweet with summer scent.

It was while she was vigorously spading up earth for her pansy bed one Saturday afternoon early in May that she heard Hansel calling her so loudly and intensely that she realized, even before he came running out to find her, that her new-found sense of peace was shattered; and as she rose hastily, and went toward him with quick alarm, she saw that there was an expression of horror in his eyes which had suddenly robbed them of all childishness.

"What has happened, darling? What is the matter?" she asked, trying to speak calmly.

"It is something about a big ship that has been sunk by the Germans—a passenger ship. Uncle Caleb is on the telephone. He wants to tell you about it before anyone else talks to you. He says he will drive over after supper anyway, but this is so very dreadful that he must speak to you at once. You don't think it can be true, do you—"

"No, darling, of course I don't. Of course it can't be true."

But she knew that it was. If Caleb Hawks were calling her, when he intended, in any case, to come and see her within a few hours, it could be only to soften the deadliness of some terrific shock from which he could not save her; and late that night, when she went up to her room with leadened feet, she found that Hansel was still awake, sobbing in his trundle bed. She gathered him into her arms, and they lay closely locked together while she tried to comfort him. But nothing she could say assuaged his horror and his grief.

"When father's next letter comes, perhaps he will explain, Hansel. There must be something that we do not understand. The *Lusitania* was warned not to sail——"

"But mother, the seas have to be free—America has always said that the seas must be free. I have been learning about it in History. And there were babies on the *Lusitania*, little babies!"

It was not only Hansel's anguished thoughts that were haunted by the dead babies. Everywhere Faith turned, she felt as if she were seeing them herself, floating white and lifeless above the blue waters off the Irish Coast. And everyone she encountered was, she knew, obsessed with the same troubled vision. A sudden strain and silence shadowed all the relationships in which she had been so happy—she was conscious that her neighbors were avoiding her, that her pupils confided in her less freely, that even the mothers of the little charges at the Day Nursery shrank away from her as they came to fetch their children home. The hostile wave of rage and resentment against Germany which had swelled, almost overnight, to gigantic proportions, had engulfed her. She did not know how to struggle against its crushing and devastating force.

Chapter XXXVII

As the spring and summer moved heavily forward, Faith was increasingly thankful both for the intensive labor which her garden exacted from her, and for the sense of solace and escape which its unfolding beauty brought her. She made no aggressive effort to repel the wave of antagonism which had engulfed her. Instead, she went quietly on with her accustomed tasks as if oblivious of encompassing enmity, and withdrew, when these were finished, among her flowers. Sarah Atkinson and Caleb Hawks, watching her anxiously during this crucial period, marveled at her extraordinary wisdom and patience. It was not like Faith, they said to themselves and to each other, to bow her head before a storm and wait for it to pass. But while they marveled, they gave thanks: no other attitude, they knew, could have been so effective in the super-charged atmosphere.

Until school closed, she continued her daily supervision of the Nursery; then she calmly announced that since everything was going well there, she felt that bi-weekly visits from her would be sufficient to insure its continued efficacy and progress, and disappeared from the foreground of its direction. Her fellow members on the Board of Lady Managers, some of whom had been her hostile critics, professed themselves as thankful that she had had the grace to vanish from the picture. But with the advent of dog-days, and their attendant discomforts and ailments, these ladies began to change their minds. None of them cared to give up the outings they had planned to the "shore," or the ease of their own screened piazzas, in order to minister to small wretched victims of "summer complaint"; and eventually a delegation, succumbing to the importunities of the distraught matron, called upon Faith and begged her not only to resume control of the situation immediately, but also to take over the office of President of the Board.

They found her in her garden, which by now had begun to give beautiful evidence of the care lavished upon it, seated on a rustic bench, reading to Hansel. She received them with the utmost courtesy, ordered iced drinks served to them, and listened gravely while they stated their case. But when they had done this, she told them that it would be necessary for her to think the matter over.

By the time she had finally been induced to return to the scene of action, not only the Lady Visitors, but the parents of nearly all her former charges, had been obliged to seek her out in her garden and beseech her continued coöperation. When at last she took up her former duties, it was with the knowledge that she had been thankfully welcomed back to the Nursery, and that the security of her position there would never again be challenged. Fortified by the consciousness of this she composed a letter to the School Board, suggesting, without the least hint of rancor or resentment, that it would perhaps be well if she should resign from the faculty. This Board, having observed with alarm the course of events at the Nursery during her absence, hastened to send her its unanimous assurance that such a withdrawal on her part would be regarded in the light of a calamity. She was entrenched at the High School no less advantageously than she was at the Day Nursery.

With the resumption of daily commuting between Hinsboro and Hamstead, her limited leisure necessarily curtailed the time she could spend in her garden; but she still managed to wedge in a surprising number of hours there. And it was while she was setting out autumn bulbs one windy day in late October, that David Noble came to tell her of the birth of Sebastian's son.

For a moment she closed her eyes, to shut out the blurred vision of earth and sky which rocked around her; and David, looking down at her stricken face, saw that her pallor was startling.

285

"Just let the world roll by for a moment," he said quietly, brushing the fluttering leaves from the rustic bench and seating himself beside her. "And keep saying to yourself, 'I didn't lose Sebastian. I never shall lose him now. I renounced him; and this is the reward of my renunciation.'" Then as Faith did not answer, David added gently, "You hoped all the time that Doña Dolores would some day have a child, didn't you, Faith?"

"Yes—yes, of course. But not—not so soon. It is such a little while since—since Sebastian and I——"

"I know, Faith. But you must try to see the other side— to look at this whole situation squarely and sanely. Don Sebastian talked it over with me very frankly. He asked me how soon I thought it would be safe—and I told him any time, after Doña Dolores had recovered her strength. Remember that she—isn't young. If this hadn't happened soon, it couldn't have happened at all. And then you would have felt—perhaps—that your great sacrifice had been in vain. But now——"

He saw that a faint color was coming back to her ashen lips. Again he spoke very gently.

"Would you like to see Sebastian's letter Faith? I think it was really written as much for you as for me. It is filled with joy and thanksgiving——"

"No, please—please——"

Faith," David said abruptly, "do you know how wonderful I think you are—how wonderful everyone thinks you are? I never saw anyone so unconquerable! You've had enough to contend against, in this last year and a half, to send the average woman into her grave—or an insane asylum! And you've become steadily more magnificent! I shall never forget how you played up to me the night I got here—it was superb! Or how you flung yourself into the breach during that epidemic at the Day Nursery—or how you took the news that Hans and Heinrich von Hohenlohe had been killed—and most of all how you acted those weeks after the *Lusitania* was sunk when you didn't know how far people would turn against you, and when one false step on your part would have made them turn pretty far. You've 'kept on ploughing,' as you put it yourself, through all that. Can't you keep on through this?"

"Yes, David. I can. I'm going to. But for just a moment I think I must—'let the world go by.'"

He continued to watch her, sympathetically and searchingly, but he did not immediately speak to her again. It was she who finally broke the silence.

"Tell me something about your own plans—and Jacque-

286

line's," she said, so calmly that he knew her struggle for self-mastery was almost won.

"You're really interested—and not sensitive? We're all for France, you know."

"Yes, I know. And I am really interested—and not sensitive. Don't forget Sam's all for France, too!"

"Of course he is!" David agreed instantly, seizing upon the opening offered him. "Do you hear from him regularly, Faith?"

"No, very irregularly. Sam is never methodical like—like Rudolf. His letters are delightful when they do come, but they don't come often. It must be six or eight weeks now since I've had one."

There was no apprehension in her voice. David, resolutely closing his mind to the grim foreboding which crossed it, answered the question from which he had been momentarily diverted.

"Jacqueline's planning to do some nursing at a base hospital or convalescent home—the fact that she's had practical experience already, and that she's half French, has helped cut a lot of red tape. I think she'll get off before long. And I'm going over with one of the Harvard Medical Units —I've been waiting for Sylvia's baby to come before making definite arrangements. Austin's terribly worried about her, and to tell you the truth, I am too. She wasn't strong enough for this—yet. But there's something about that marriage that foils interference. If any two human beings ever achieved perfect happiness together, Austin and Sylvia Gray have."

"I've realized that. And I'm glad you haven't interfered, David, whatever happens. Sylvia would rather die, bringing Austin's child into the world, than——"

"Perhaps!" he said quickly, following the drift of her unspoken thought. "But think of Austin afterwards! And think of all the rest of us!"

.   .   .   .   .

In the desolate months that followed, Faith had tragic cause to think of Austin and "all the rest"; for the birth of her twin daughters cost Sylvia Gray her life, and the overwhelming grief of the bereft husband found reflection in the mourning of the entire countryside. When Austin finally found courage to face the world again, it was not through quiet occupations in the peaceful valley where he had lived all his life, but through driving an ambulance over the shell-shot roads of France; and within a week of his desperate departure, David and Jacqueline came to say good-bye to Faith, one bound for a field hospital directly behind the firing-line, the other for a convalescents' home in Brittany. The little brick cottage, and the Big House both stood dark and empty through the long cold winter; and Faith, deprived of these havens of hospitality and friendliness, threw herself, with redoubled intensity, into her chosen work.

It was not until late in June that the summons for which she had listened so long, and for which at last she had almost ceased to listen finally came. She was even more preoccupied than usual, for graduation day of the Hinsboro High School was imminent, and besides teaching her own classes, she was drilling many of the students who were to take an outstanding part in the graduation exercises. Hardly a day went by when she did not find it necessary, toward the end of the morning assembly, to leave her faculty seat and come forward to read general notices, make general requests, and impart general information. She was always able to command immediate attention; even though final examinations and final rehearsals had reduced the entire student body to a state of nervous irritability, her voice and her manner seemed to have a hypnotizing effect upon the pupils. They stopped shuffling their feet the instant she rose to hers. They strained their ears to listen to an announcement that a fraternity pin had been lost and that she would keep it on her desk until the owner claimed it, or a request that the members of the class of 1916 should meet in her room at the end of the morning session, thought similar announcements and requests, coming from other sources, made no dent whatsoever in their consciousness. Mr. Alonzo Markam, the principal, had observed this phenomenon with feelings of mingled envy and relief: it was humiliating to be obliged to admit that any subordinate teacher had more powers of control and attraction than he himself possessed; yet it was reassuring to be certain that as long as Faith Marlowe continued her domination, the lawless young forces under him could always be checked by her charm.

It was with the reluctant knowledge of this that he appealed to her in the crowning emergencies of the school year: Neal Conrad, now Food Administrator for the state, had agreed to make the "principal address" on graduation day; he was without doubt the leading citizen of Hinsboro, and Mr. Alonzo Markam had congratulated himself on his good fortune in securing so desirable an orator. But Neal, with the ruthlessness that characterized his political progress, had telephoned from Belford to say that he was taking a night train to Washington for a conference with the President; he was sorry, of course, if this sudden change of plan would inconvenience Mr. Markam; he was sure, however, that some other speaker, much more eloquent, could easily be found.

"But Mr. Conrad," the distraught principal had protested, "the exercises are *to-morrow evening*. I don't know where to turn, really I don't! Couldn't you possibly——"

"No," Neal had called back crisply. "A Presidential summons is a command.—Surely you know that, Mr. Markam. Well, if you can't do better, ask Faith Marlowe to step into the breach. Tell her I'd appreciate it very much if she'd pinch hit for me. I don't know whether she's ever made a speech in her life or not, but I'm sure she can. Good-bye, Mr. Markam, good-bye, I'm sorry to seem abrupt, but I'm late for my train already!"

For a moment after he had hung up the receiver, Mr. Markam hesitated. But only for a moment. The few well-chosen words which he had prepared to speak during the distribution of diplomas had already cost him hours of anguish; he could not possibly enlarge on them without prostration. The male quartet from the First Congregational Church was to render two choice selections; but these could not be dragged out to consume more than ten minutes. Mr. Caleb Hawks, as mayor of the city, always appeared on the platform on great occasions; but it was unthinkable that he should be permitted, even if he could be persuaded, to air his "King's English" before the large assembly that would attend the graduation. There was nothing to do but telephone Faith Marlowe, who had already returned to Hamstead for the night, and give her Neal Conrad's message.

There was an instant's hesitation on her part also, though this, Mr. Markam almost immediately realized, was not caused by any lack of willingness to coöperate with him. But she had never made a speech, she said—that is, not a real address—she had just talked casually to the pupils now and then. And for a graduation, of course, he would want something much more formal in character. She really didn't know whether—what subject did he have in mind, what sort of a slant would he want her to give it?

"Oh, I'll leave all that to you," Mr. Markam said airily. "Something inspirational, of course—some kind of a special uplift message. I know you'll handle it beautifully. I can't tell you how relieved I am."

.   .   .   .   .

As Faith advanced toward the center of the platform the

following evening, the students gathered before her were conscious that there was something unusually arresting in her looks and manner. She had detached herself quietly from the side of Caleb Hawks, who had accompanied her when she came into the hall; and now she was standing and speaking as she always stood and spoke. Yet there was a subtle change in her poignant voice, an exalted expression on her face, of which her pupils had never been aware before. They watched her breathlessly, as if in the presence of a phenomenon unaccountably appearing upon a familiar scene.

"Last night, when our principal asked me if I would speak to you in the place of our Food Administrator, Mr. Neal Conrad, who has been called to Washington for a conference with the President of the United States," she said vibrantly, "I told him that I feared I might not be able to do so adequately. And since then something has happened which has made it—absolutely impossible for me to prepare the sort of address to which you are entitled to listen on such a great occasion as this. But in order that I might not seem to fail you entirely, when I should be glad to do anything for you that I could, I am going to try to tell you a—a sort of story."

Again there was an instant of silence so tense that the atmosphere seemed to throb.

"When I came here two years ago, I did not expect to stay very long," she continued. "I had lived in Hamstead when I was a little girl, and for years I had been hoping to come back for a visit—this had always seemed to me like the place where I really belonged. But my husband, Rudolf von Hohenlohe, had not been willing to have me leave him, or able to leave his own work and come here with me. So I was very much surprised when he suddenly consented to my wish. But after I reached here I began to understand why he had done so: it was because he knew there was going to be a great and terrible war, and he feared that soon there would be no part of Europe where I could be comfortable or happy or even safe. And so, because he loved me, he sent me away from him to this lovely peaceful valley, which is like the Valley of Avalon that you have read about with me, lying

'Deep-meadowed, happy, fair with orchard lawns,
And bowery hollows crowned with summer seas.' "

"Lord Almighty!" exclaimed Caleb Hawks hoarsely, leaning over and tapping the principal on the shoulder. "She's got 'em all spellbound—them hoodlums! Land, if I could get her to talk in a *campaign!* . . ."

"But of course we expected that when the war was over, he would come and take my little boy and me back to Germany," the clear voice went on. "We had even planned that we would take a long journey together, all the way around the world, stopping in beautiful countries which none of us had ever seen, on our way between my country and his. But now he has gone on a long journey to a strange country—all alone. And he has left me to go on a still longer journey—here among you. I want you to help me make my journey as bravely as I know he has made his. For his was the journey of death, which is very glorious and triumphant. But mine is the journey of life, which is very hard to make without purpose—and courage—and a singing heart."

"Spellbound!" whispered the principal leaning over toward Mr. Hawks. "She has them all crying—those tough foreigners! *Crying!* But how she could have come.—How she can stand up there and——"

"You don't know her same as I do," Caleb whispered back. "She'll stand up under *anything*. Listen! . . ."

"My husband went to the war, you see," Faith was saying. "He was appointed to serve on the Staff of the Crown Prince, under whose leadership the German army has been attacking the great French fortress of Verdun for months. The French have made watchword of their desperate cry for self-preservation. They have proclaimed that Germany should not pass. It has not passed. It will not pass. It—cannot pass. But while thousands of brave men have been giving their lives to defend this fortress, thousands of others, equally brave, have given theirs in the attempt to annihilate it. My husband was one of those men.

"Many years ago I told his mother, whom I love very dearly, that I felt as if there was something glistening about his spirit. It still seems this way to me. I feel as if I could see his spirit shining now—while I am talking to you! I feel as if I could see my husband as he looked at me when I first saw him—like a radiant Saint Michael! Driving away dragons! Bringing salvation and strength! Surrounded by All Angels!"

"Lord Almighty!" exclaimed Caleb Hawks again, passing the back of his hand over his eyes, "if she says anything more about angels I shall be crying myself. Her husband did look sort o' glorious, the first time I seen him. I know what she means. It's a mercy she can think of him that way, stead of like—carrion."

"We were very young then, and we—loved each other.

Afterwards, after we were married, we misunderstood each other sometimes. I was an American, you see, and he was a German—it is often hard for Germans and Americans to interpret each other's thoughts and feelings and—standards. Besides, I believe in almost every marriage there must be misunderstandings, there must be divisions. But husbands and wives must not be discouraged by these—I am very much ashamed to remember now that sometimes I was, and I hope none of you will be ashamed for the same reason. Because these misunderstandings and divisions do not last, if there is respect, and confidence, and tenderness, to draw husbands and wives together again. It is like St. Paul's experience of seeing through a glass—first darkly and then face to face. In these last two years, Rudolf and I have understood each other perfectly and completely and we have seemed close together, though he has been in the war and I have been here with you. But now I have lost him. I know he is near to his fellow angels, but I do not feel that he is near to me. And I am going to be very lonely. Unless —unless you will all go with me—on the journey Rudolf has left me to make without him. If you make me feel you need and want me here at school—that will give my journey purpose! If you promise me that from now on, whatever happens, your people shall be my people—that will give me courage for my journey! If you tell me that you trust and love me—that will give me back in time my singing heart! If you can do all this, tell me so to-day—and let us all start forward—onward—upward—on this journey of life together!"

Almost imperceptibly a subtle and portentous change had been taking place in the supercharged atmosphere. There was still a tense vibrancy in the air; but it was no longer the vibrancy of profound silence, but of pent-up emotion seeking release. As Faith finished speaking, she stretched out her arms, her head held high, her face illumined. And from her audience surged an answering cry that seemed torn from the hearts of every one of her listeners. They were on their feet, they were out of their seats, they were crowding the corridors, they were hurling themselves upon the platform, they were closing in around Faith. A lame ugly boy pushing his way painfully against the throbbing mass, slipped and stumbled his way until he had fought his way to the piano. His soiled powerful fingers closed down over the keys with a sound of crashing chords. Then resonantly he struck the first bars of a hymn that Faith had taught him and his classmates. The next instant the school was singing it in unison:

"The Son of God goes forth to war,
  A kingly crown to gain;
His blood-red banner streams afar:
  Who follows in his train?
Who best can drink his cup of woe,
  Triumphant over pain;
Who patient bears his cross below,
  He follows in his train.

    .   .   .

A noble army, men and boys,
  The matron and the maid,
Around the Saviour's throne rejoice,
  In robes of light arrayed.
They climbed the steep ascent to heaven
  Through peril, toil, and pain:
O God, to us may grace be given
  To follow in their train."

The song rose and swelled through the hall like a triumphant pæan. It had become a processional, for the students were marching now, marching with a verve and buoyancy that gave the effect of victorious troops gloriously returning to a city from which they had long before set forth to an unknown destiny. Someone had caught up the American flag and the school standards: the Stars and Stripes streamed away ahead of the class banners. But someone else—an undersized scrubby girl who could dart about unperceived—had shot out the door and down the street. Nobody saw her go. Nobody cared whether she went or not. Everyone was singing and marching. But when this scrubby girl came panting back into the hall again, she was bearing another flag—a flag bearing broad bands of red and white and black; and burrowing her way to Faith's side, she thrust it into her hands.

"This once!" she gasped. "This once, Faith, we must have Rudolf's flag too whatever happens afterwards! I got it out of Jacob Heine's saloon—I knew he had it in his back room with his own steins—he brought it with him when he came from Hamburg. You take 'em *both*—the 'Merican one and this one too—and lead us, see?—And we'll all come along after you!"

Faith's fingers closed swiftly around the German flag. She raised it, dipped it as if in salute, and raised it again. Then stretching forth her free hand for the other flag, which, just then, went floating past her, she took her place among the standard-bearers.

Caleb Hawks was still standing on the platform, passing first one hand and then the other surreptitiously across his eyes. He suddenly seized the principal's arm and pointed toward the advancing columns.

"Come on!" he said breathlessly. "Let's me and you get into this too! Lord Almighty! It's the biggest thing's ever happened in Hinsboro! But there's goin' to be bigger things happenin' from now on! Faith is goin' to keep on leadin' us, and the rest of us is goin' to follow!"

PART VIII

Sarah Atkinson

Chapter XXXVIII

SARAH ATKINSON'S standards had altered with passing years and changing conditions. She still wore taffeta dresses and did her full duty as she understood this. But the dresses were not quite so steely in color as they once had been, and they did not crackle quite so much; and she interpreted her obligations to God and her fellow men less rigidly than when she had left Salem as a bride. Her years of association with Sam had mellowed her nature and broadened her outlook. It was true that she had brought order and decorum to the helter-skelter studio apartment in the Latin Quarter when she took over its direction; but it was also true that she had gained as much as she had given. The constant ebb and flow of celebrities and strugglers, critics and promoters, wastrels and geniuses, through the spacious shabby rooms which she cleared of clutter and redeemed from dirt, and over which she learned to preside with grace as well as dignity, had left an unmistakable imprint upon her. She came to love her motley throng of visitors, to regard their shortcomings with indulgence, and to rejoice in all their triumphs as if these had been her own.

She had not been able to define the reason for the indefinite but persistent feeling that the time had come for her to wrench herself away from her familiar and congenial surroundings and return to the austerities of Salem, Massachusetts. It had not sprung from fear that the increasing helplessness with which she was so painfully handicapped by rheumatism, would make her a burden to him, Sam was wealthy, in spite of the prodigality with which he had shared his own earnings with fellow artists less fortunate than himself. And certainly it did not spring from discontent, for never had the creative vitality of the atmosphere in which she lived been more agreeable to her. Nevertheless, she instinctively knew that her days in Sam's studio were numbered, and had been determined to take her departure before this was mysteriously forced upon her. When Sam had brought her the intelligence of the murder at Sarajevo, she had instantly read in his face the response to her foreboding; and when David and Jacqueline had offered to give her safe conduct on her voyage across the Atlantic, she had seen the hand of fate in their opportune departure.

As she and Sam sat together before the long window of their *salon*, the evening before she sailed, looking silently down on the lights of Montmartre, flung out in the darkness like jeweled chains, she became aware that he was even more deeply troubled than he confessed. Not wishing to force his confidence, she waited tranquilly for him to unburden himself of his own accord; and when at last, almost overcome with pain and weariness, she was beginning to feel she could not endure the suspense of the charged silence any longer, he suddenly spoke with poignant vehemence.

"Cousin Sarah—I haven't known whether to say anything to you or not—but I am darned worried."

"About me, Sam? But I shall get along splendidly! I'm sure that David and Jacqueline will take the best of care of me. And after I reach home, I shall be among friends."

"No, not about you," he said almost brusquely. "I'll miss you a lot, but you'll be all right. I know that."

"Then you really think there is going to be a war?" she asked, searching for the next eventuality which might cause him distress.

"Yup. I guess so. Any day now. You'll be out of here in the nick of time."

The cheerfulness with which he said this was unmistakable. Again Sarah Atkinson waited.

"It's Faith," he burst out at last. "I'd like to know who the gentleman of color is among her firewood. I'm not so sure it's a *colored* gentleman at that.—Didn't you think, Cousin Sarah, there was something darned fishy about the way she lit out?"

"She had been longing to go home for years, Sam. And Rudolf's letter was perfectly clear and logical. I thought it was very thoughtful of him to write us as he did, explaining that Faith had not had time to do so herself, and that he——"

"Good God, Cousin Sarah, you're not such a damn fool as to believe Rudolf von Hohenlohe didn't write that letter with his tongue in his cheek! He's a gentleman—and a diplomat—and Faith's husband. If he hadn't been, he'd have sent me a missive that read something like this: "Dear Sam: Sebastian de Cerreno has been in Denmark raising

296

nell. He's raised good and plenty. Now there's been a show-down and Faith's got across the river before the ice cracked underneath her, but it's been pretty thin in places, and she's all in. So I've helped her make a quick getaway. It's just as well anyhow, because though *Gott ist mit uns* and all that, you never know, and maybe there'll be quite a war. If I should happen to be pushing up daisies in a year or two, Faith will be better off in the U. S. A. And in case S. de C. decides to leap lightly across the Atlantic in the meantime, I'd rather like to know that Don Juan would encounter a dueña. Thanking you for the same, I'm ever yours truly, R. von H.' "

"Sam! Really!"

"Well, that's the way things are, Cousin Sarah, and you're it."

"I'm what, Sam?"

"The dueña. Give up the idea of Salem, won't you? I always thought it was a damn poor idea anyway. Go and settle down on Faith, and sit tight till I can get there, like a good sport. I'll be along after awhile, honest I will. But just for now—You could feature yourself in Hamstead, couldn't you?"

"My dear Sam——"

"Don't you think Rudolf has that much coming his way? He's had a tough break—mostly his own fault, I know, but he's had it. It seems to me——"

" 'Why don't you speak for yourself, John?' "

Sam, who had begun to pace up and down the room, stopped suddenly in his tracks.

"Why don't I—*Cousin Sarah!*"

"If we are going to speak without reserve, we might as well be thorough in the process," said Sarah Atkinson imperturbably. "But you know I shall be very glad to go to Hamstead—for Faith's sake as well as for Rudolf's. As for 'featuring' myself there, I shall be extremely happy. I will go and wait—for you to rejoin me."

.   .   .   .   .

She had not overestimated her prospective contentment in the quiet village. During the two years since she had gone there to live, she had not known a restless day. She found a deep and peaceful satisfaction in the performance of light household tasks, for she excelled in the homely arts, though she had never practised these since her girlhood; and as she went industriously about the paneled house in Hamstead, on the days when her rheumatism did not trouble her too much, she felt she was recapturing half-forgotten but treasured memories of her youth in Salem. Moreover, she adored Faith and Hansel, and she found all her neighbors congenial. The integrity and simplicity of Uncle Ephraim and Aunt Emmeline appealed to her strongly; she did not find it hard to be "sociable" with them; she found it agreeable. She was always pleased when the grim Miss Manning, or the gossipy Mrs. Elliot came to "pass the afternoon," bringing her sewing; and when Caleb Hawks, who was also a fairly frequent visitor, appeared, puffing and panting before her, the pleasure she took in his company was evident.

As he climbed ponderously upon the piazza, mopping his brow, one sultry afternoon in late August, she was instantly aware that he had not sought her out, this time, for the sole purpose of being "sociable." He "meant business" as he himself was wont to express it. And he came straight to the point.

"I want me and you should have a little talk together," he said. "Quiet."

"It is always quiet in Hamstead, isn't it, Mr. Hawks?" Sarah asked smilingly.

"Well, yes. In a manner of speakin'. But I don't want no interruptions. Where's Hansel? Down to the swimmin' hole?"

"Yes. I'm sure he won't be back a minute before suppertime.—Of course you'll stay for supper with us, Mr. Hawks?"

"Thank you kindly.—And where's Faith? Most generally, when I come over, I see her workin' in that gardin of hers. She ain't took sick has she?"

"No, indeed! She's very well. In fact, though she isn't working in her garden, she's gone to a meeting of the Garden Club, at Mrs. Low's lovely place near Belford. You know Faith was invited to join the club last year—Mrs. Castle is one of the most prominent members and I believe it was she who suggested it. I think Faith has taken a great deal of pleasure in the meetings. Mrs. Conrad came for her early this morning. I imagine they'll be rather late getting back."

"Good!" said Mr. Hawks heartily. "What I mean is, I'm real pleased Faith is gettin' acquainted with these nice women all over the state, and that's a fact. Low and Conrad is runnin' about neck to neck politically these days—I look to see Low go faster and Conrad go further. M-mebbe I'm mistaken, but that's the way I figger it out.—I guess Cal Castle is pleased enough to be back in his shoe factory in Belford, 'stead of in Berlin these days, and he'll stage a come-back to public life when his party comes back into power again. I always thought his wife was a kinda hatchet-faced woman, but she's fond o' Faith and I don't deny she's ben real kind to her. I sortta think Faith mighter broke down if it hadn't ben for that fortnight she spent at the beach with the Castles right after graduation.—But Faith ain't got no airs and graces, no matter how stylish society she's took out in. She mingles considerable right here in the village, don't she?"

"Oh, yes! She and I have both joined the Daughters of the American Revolution and the Home Missionary Society, and we go to church regularly."

"You ain't got no suspicions Faith's got leanin's toward being a Catholic, have you?"

"Why, Mr. Hawks, I never thought of such a thing! Certainly she's never intimated.—What made you ask?"

"Well, I dunno. Now and again she goes off with the Perez? I never give the matter much thought 'til just lately. But my son-in-law, Ted Jenkins, you know, that's manager of the factory, tells me he's heard some talk about her bein' seen in the Catholic Church real frequent. Odd times. Week days."

"It is probably because Faith is feeling the need—and the comfort—of prayer and meditation more urgently than ever before in her life," said Sarah Atkinson, with a candor which once would have been impossible to her. "When that sense of need overwhelms us, it doesn't always conveniently come at half-past ten on Sunday morning, Mr. Hawks. The Catholic Church realizes this, and no desperate soul yearning to enter it is ever turned away from locked doors."

"Well now, that's a thought," said Caleb Hawks looking relieved. "I guess I'll take it up with Mr. Sleeper, my pastor at the First Congregational. Mebbe we could keep our church open too. But be that as it may, I'm glad you don't think Faith's goin' to take any rash steps. I've got considerable respect for your judgment, ma'm. There's another matter, though, that's troublin' me that I think ought to be took up and took up quick."

"Yes," said Sarah encouragingly.

"I want Faith should be naturalized. Without waitin' a day."

"You want her to resume her American citizenship?"

"Yes, I do, Miss Atkinson, and that's a fact. An' I want she should do it before it's too late."

He spoke with extreme earnestness, leaning forward and pointing one large pudgy forefinger at Sarah Atkinson. She could see the carbuncle in his ring gleaming.

"It won't be many months now before the U. S. A. is drew into this damn war," he said with conviction. "And

299

unless we can get them naturalization papers fixed before it is, Faith is going to be an enemy alien. Right here in her own home. Folks could make it pretty unpleasant for her. Some of 'em did the time the *Lusitania* wuz sank. But that warn't a circumstance to what it 'ud be now. Faith ain't rose the way she has in this community without makin' some enemies along with some friends. I want to spike the guns of them skunks that's aimin' to hurt her and me through her! I guess I can steal a march on 'em before they oust me outta office, like they think they're goin' to! That mayoralty ain't much in itself, but I aim to make it a pretty powerful lever!"

He paused for a moment, completely out of breath. Then he went on relentlessly.

"You talk to her," he said, "this very night. And listen— while you're talkin' to her about them papers—talk to her about her name too, will you?"

"Her name!"

"Any woman with your judgment can see that Faith can't call herself the Baroness von Hohenlohe," said Mr. Hawks, pronouncing the words slowly and painfully. "Not in a state like this, even if Germany and the U. S. A. warn't on the point of springin' at each other's throats, which they are. I called Rudolf Mr. Lowe myself when I met him, as a sort o' compromise for—Hohenlohe. An' them young hoodlums that feeds out o' Faith's hands at the High School and the Day Nursery, call her Mrs. Lowe for the same reason. It's a pretty good compromise, seein' as how 'lowe is the last part of her own name too! But now she's gettin' intimate with the wife of the Lieutenant Governor—over to her Belford place to-day you tell me!—and I don't want no confusion between Low and Lowe, not for the world. It's taken less than that to defeat a ticket a good many times, and that's a fact! I want she should come right out and call herself Faith Marlowe, and that fine kid of hers Christian Marlowe III. I tell you, if we're goin' to have the first Christian Marlowe spirit marchin' on—an' we are—his name's goin' to be a powerful help to us."

Sarah Atkinson hesitated. "I'm not sure that I follow you completely," she said at length. "But in any case, don't you think it is perhaps too soon—to bring up the question of changing Faith's name? She has a great deal of reverence for Rudolf's memory. And I think she reproaches herself— because her marriage was not altogether harmonious—more than she ought to, all things considered. I think she kept hoping against hope for a second chance to make it a success—after the war was over, you know. And now that she's been robbed of that hope—I think she's very sensitive—to anything she thinks might reflect on Rudolf."

Mr. Hawks rose restlessly, and began to lumber up and down the piazza.

"Well now, you know best," he said uneasily. "But if there wuz some ways we could manage, it 'ud take a load offen me, and that's a fact.—And there's another thing on my mind mebbe you can help with. It's about that nice hired girl o' yours. I took a likin' to her the minute she set foot in my kitchen, and so did Mrs. Mead and Myra, who ain't easy to please. I'd hate to think she's in trouble!"

"In trouble!" exclaimed Sarah Atkinson with displeased astonishment. "Why, Mr. Hawks, Hilda is not only respectable, she's much more than that. She——" .

"I didn't mean what you think," said Mr. Hawks looking very red and confused. "Course she's respectable—she's a real good girl and that's why I'm worried about her. I should hate like anythin' to have her get into trouble as a —spy."

"A spy!" said Sarah Atkinson, recoiling. "Hilda!"

Hilda's mild and humble face, illumined by honest blue eyes and framed with tightly wound flaxen braids, rose before Sarah's startled vision. It was almost fantastic to suppose that anyone could accuse so simple and sweet a soul with perfidy. Yet if Mr. Hawks dreaded this contingency, his fears must be well-grounded.

"I don't suppose we c'd coax her into bein' an American citizen, too," he said anxiously. "'Twouldn't be so easy in her case, to rush things through. I'm feelin' druv and worried, ma'm, and that's a fact. I guess I won't stay for supper tonight after all, if you'll excuse me. I ain't got no appetite. I could hardly swallow my dinner this noon, and Mrs. Mead's feelins wuz hurt considerable. I guess I'll go back to my office and work for a spell. The Lord knows I got a sight o' things to do there. I guess I'll bid you good-evenin'. But I'm bankin' on your help, ma'm, more'n you know."

. . . . . .

Mr. Hawks spent a troubled night. The more he dwelt upon the many complications in which he had become involved through his affection for Faith, and his belief in her destiny, the less he was able to rest. And he did his breakfast even less justice than he had done his dinner the day before. This time Mrs. Mead remonstrated with him, her mouth looking unusually grim, and her small nose quivering. But he escaped from her, pausing for a moment as he reached the stone deer, in an effort to decide whether he had better go first to the factory, as usual, or whether he should follow the impulse which seemed to propel him in the direction of City Hall instead. He finally decided upon the latter course; and as he opened the door of his outer office, he was amazed to find himself confronted by Faith, who greeted him affectionately.

"Well, well," he said brightening at once. "Come right in, Faith, and set down. Did you have a nice time yesterday? I was real pleased to hear you went down to the Lows' place with Anne Conrad. It's downright handsome, as you might say, now ain't it?"

"It's a lovely place. And I had a beautiful time. I don't know just what there is about women who work in gardens that makes them appeal to me, but they always do. I suppose association with flowers puts a sort of fragrance into their lives."

"Well that's a sweet pretty thought, Faith. You have such thoughts frequent, don't you? And put 'em into words too, smart and quick. Lord Almighty I won't forget that talk you made to the school, not to my dyin' day. St. Michael! Surrounded by All Angels! Lord Al——"

"It was about Rudolf that I wanted to speak to you—that is indirectly," said Faith. "I have decided to build a memorial to him."

Caleb Hawks hitched around in his seat, and swallowed hard several times in swift succession. Considering his firm conviction that all Faith's affiliations with Germany and the Germans should be severed as soon as possible, and all traces of them removed, her suggestion was extremely distasteful to him.

"What kind of a memorial?" he said uneasily. "You mean a handsome monument, or the like of that, in the Hamstead cemetery? Sebastian Perez could help you with that, mebbe, better'n I could. He carves real natural-lookin' urns and wreaths an'——"

"Sebastian Perez is going to help me," said Faith. "I've been to see him already. But I need your help too.—No. I don't want to put up a monument to Rudolf in the Hamstead cemetery. Why should I? He isn't buried there. He's buried in France. I said a memorial, anyway, not a monument."

"Well?" said Caleb, still uneasily.

"As soon as the United States goes into the war, we're going to need more room at the Day Nursery," said Faith. "The factory hands and marblecutters will have to go off and fight, won't they? Well, that will mean that lot's of

302

women who aren't working now will have to begin. And they'll have to leave their children with us. I think you ought to have an architect draw plans for wings on either side of the present building—that could be the central unit in the new plant. I think you ought to get started on it right away too, before the price of construction goes up—you've land enough."

"Well I don't know but what I have," said Caleb. "I don't know but what it 'ud be a good idea, come to think of it. I dunno as women can chip up marble, but they can make pencils. I had orter of thought of that myself, Faith, without your remindin' me that I may be dependent upon 'em. They've all got parcels of young 'uns, and if their husbands gets drew into this war, same as you say, why they couldn't come and work in my factory unless they cud park them kids somewhere. And then what would happen to any factory, I'd like to know?"

An expression of alarm came into his bulging eyes, and he half rose, as if to start out in immediate search of an architect. Faith laid a detaining hand on his arm.

"Nothing is going to happen to your factory," she said soothingly. "It's output will probably be doubled and trebled —and possibly changed in character. Are your contracts for supplies in the most advantageous condition?"

Caleb Hawks' jaw suddenly dropped. He stared at Faith in amazement. As if oblivious of his looks, she went calmly on.

"So we must be prepared to meet the changed situation at the Nursery," she said. "And besides the new wings, which you will naturally wish to add yourself, we shall need a playground. Not just an open place on the street, bleak and bare, with a few swings and some sandboxes; but a secluded garden with plenty of room for the children to romp, and trees and grass and flowers too. So I came here to get your advice about buying the land back of the Nursery, where Mr. Emery has his garage and repair-shop, and where those tenements of his are. You know he is going to move his business into new quarters, because those he has aren't large enough any more; and of course you know too that the tenements have been condemned by the Board of Health, because you had a hand in that. So he is willing to sell me the property at a very fair price. At least it seems to me a very fair price. I talked it over with him Wednesday when I went to see him about turning in my Dodge for a Packard—the poor Dodge has taken an awful punishing on the roads between Hamstead and Hinsboro these two winters, and I need a larger car now anyway."

"Look here, Faith," gasped Caleb, "you're goin' ahead so fast I can't follow you. Emery has ben threatenin' to get me ousted from office, on account of them stinkin' tenements of his—beg pardon, that slipped out before I noticed—and now you have bought a new car, and made him an offer for his land and——"

"I think it will all work out very nicely," Faith said smoothly. "Especially if you should deed him some land in the suburbs for his new tenements—you have lots of it out there that isn't doing any particular good to anyone. Well, then we would have plenty of space back of *your* memorial for *my* memorial."

She came and sat down on the arm of his chair, picking up a pad and pencil that lay on his desk and beginning to sketch.

"It would be something like this," she said, "the swings and sandboxes would be over here, and a croquet ground and poles for volley ball; and this would be an open run for any kind of games. But here we would have gravel walks, with borders of flowers between them and the grass-plots; and we would have a lily pool here, and trellises with rambler roses here. And there would be a high brick wall around the entire enclosure, which would be covered with ivy by and by. And against this wall, in the center, a fountain——"

Caleb Hawks, following her fingers as they flew rapidly over the paper, nodded intently.

"A white marble fountain, with a bas-relief representing angels—multitudes of angels. And stepping out from among them, a full-sized figure of St. Michael. With his sword uplifted and his foot resting on a dragon. Sebastian Perez has made me a drawing of the model. I want you to look at it. Don't you think that is beautiful, Uncle Caleb?"

She drew a piece of heavy white paper from her handbag and held it out to him. Caleb swallowed hard.

"It's sweet pretty, an' that's a fact," he said rather huskily.

"Of course the whole garden will be a memorial to Rudolf, but this figure will—guard over it," Faith said simply. "You see, there will be an inscription on the base of the statue; just the letters and numerals—R. von H.—1880-1916 —'Dulce et Decorum Pro Patria Mori': that is a Latin proverb which means, 'It is sweet and fitting to die for one's country.' "

Caleb blew his nose. "Well, I guess Rudolf thought it was," he said with visible emotion. "I dunno as you could do better than to put them words on that statue. An' I guess if there's anyone goin' to object to a memorial like this, he'd be a pretty mean skunk."

"No one is going to object to it," said Faith, in the same soothing voice that she had used before. "Uncle Caleb, after I got home last night, Cousin Sarah told me about your visit yesterday. I am sorry that you and she should have worried—about my naturalization, and my name, I mean. Because I had been on the point of talking to you on those two subjects myself."

Again Caleb's jaw dropped.

"You see," Faith said softly, "Rudolf thought of all that. He told me the night I went away that he had always been glad we named our son for both his grandfathers, because some time Hansel might want to choose—between his two names. So as soon as you can arrange for the necessary formalities—I will be Faith Marlowe again, and Hansel will be Christian Marlowe III. And we will both be American citizens."

Faith rose. It was evident that she considered the interview over and the question settled. Caleb rose too, and clapped her affectionately on the shoulder.

"Well, this is a big relief to me, an' that's a fact," he said heartily. "You sure have taken a pile o' worries off my chest, and give me some real smart ideas besides. Them raw materials! Them tenements! Them wings! That garding! I guess Will Emery's guns is spiked all right, and his crowd's too. I guess I won't hear no more gossip about not wantin' 'a pro-German mayor in Hinsboro.' I guess me and you is goin' to sail right along without any monkey wrenches being thrown into our works!" He paused, panting, and mopped his brow. "Well, I guess I can make out to eat some dinner after all. I guess Mrs. Mead's mind will be relieved. You'll stay and have a bite with me, won't you, Faith? Nothin' fancy of course."

Again he stopped, this time as if struck by a sudden thought. "Speakin' o' meals and such, Faith, reminds me of Hilda," he said anxiously. "The only thing's botherin' me now is what's goin' to become o' that poor girl, liable to arrest, like she is, as a German spy. It won't be so easy, takin' out naturalization papers for her. I guess we're stumped there."

For the first time since she had come into his office, Faith laughed. "I guess we're not," she said. "Hilda doesn't need any naturalization papers. After next Wednesday, she'll be an American citizen anyway."

For the third time that morning, Caleb Hawks' jaw dropped.

"What's that you're saying?" he gasped.

"Hilda and Perley Stubbs are going to be married," Faith said tranquilly. "At Marlowe Manor. Will you come to the wedding Uncle Caleb?"

Chapter XXXIX

ON Thanksgiving Day a gala dinner was served in the new right wing of the Myra Higgs Hawks Memorial Day Nursery. This wing, like its twin, the left wing, was still incompletely equipped; but the families of the children who came to the Nursery regularly could easily be entertained there, and they and the numerous distinguished visitors who had come from various parts of the state were able to get a general impression of the improvements and innovations.

These impressions were highly favorable: even Mrs. Carolus Cavendish Castle, who was still prone to damning with faint praise everything she regarded through her clicking lorgnette, drew Sarah Atkinson aside with a purposeful gleam in her eye which certainly did not spring from disapproval.

"Suppose we sit down for a moment," she said impellingly. "I should like to have a quiet word with you. I am very much impressed with all this—really very much impressed. It occurs to me that it might be well for me to undertake the erection of a similar plant for my own employees in Belford—on a larger and more elaborate scale. If I did, do you think Faith would coöperate with me?"

"Faith is very busy," Sarah Atkinson said cautiously. "You know she has just taken over the management of the Marlowe Farm, with Perley Stubbs as foreman. Her Uncle Ephraim did not feel equal to the responsibility of it any longer—and there was no reason why he should have it, since Faith feels equal to anything! She has joined the Grange and the Holstein Friesian Association, and has spent every week-end lately going about looking at cattle. But it would do no harm, of course, to tell her what you have in mind and see what her reaction is. Here she is now, coming toward us. Will you excuse me, Mrs. Castle? I promised Mrs. Low to take her through the clinic, and I am afraid she is waiting for me."

Through her lorgnette, Mrs. Castle watched Sarah Atkinson's slow departure and Faith's rapid advance simultaneously. Her new victim had one arm linked through Hansel's, who had shot-up unbelievingly during the last year, and the other through that of Angelico Mendoza's son, Serafino. She greeted Mrs. Castle gaily.

"Don't you want to come out to the garden with me and the boys, Aunt Annabelle?" she asked. "It is such a lovely warm day for November that lots of people are looking it over. When you consider that it is only three months since we began work there, I think you'll agree with me that we've made wonderful progress."

"Suppose Hansel and—his friend preceded us," suggested Mrs. Castle, acknowledging the existence of Serafino reluctantly. "A little later we might rejoin them. But I should like to have a few words with you in private first, my dear, if I may."

"How fortunate! I was just wondering when I could wedge in a few words with *you!—Tante* Luise is sending me all my things, and I am expecting notice from the Port of New York any day saying that they are here. She went over to Copenhagen herself and supervised the packing, taking cases and cases from Schönplatz and Berlin to ship from Denmark with the rest of my possessions. I—I was very much moved. But it is exactly what I should have known she would do. Really, there is no one in the world like her. She and Father Hans have insisted that I should have not only everything that I—have acquired, but everything that was Rudolf's besides—his share of the heirlooms and all."

Mrs. Castle murmured something vaguely appreciative of such princely generosity.

"Of course most of it is Hansel's," Faith continued, "and he may wish to take it back to Germany sometime, since he may eventually inherit Schönplatz. All his cousins are at military training camps already." She shivered slightly, and looked out toward the garden where Hansel and Serafino were now vigorously attacking a volley ball and shouting at each other. "But at present it is better that all of it should be in the United States. And the part which is mine personally—some very beautiful Spanish things for instance, would never be sent back to Europe in any case. And I have no room for them in my house, even if they would be appropriate there. So I was just on the point of asking you if you wouldn't help me arrange for a loan exhibition at the Belford Museum of Fine Arts. We would call it a loan exhibition to protect Hansel's interest. But naturally much of it would be in the nature of a permanent contribution."

"My dear Faith! What a wonderful inspiration! We never could have acquired such masterpieces as you can offer us."

"I know," said Faith a little wearily. "There are paintings and tapestries and quantities of wrought silver and furniture. I might want to save out a few for myself or for—personal gifts. But not many. Most of them are really museum pieces. There is one of those gold beds, for instance, that is so very rare——"

"I should like to make quite an occasion of such an acquisition," said Mrs. Castle eagerly. "Before the exhibition is thrown open to the public we should have a pre-view sponsored by the Governor and Mrs. Warren and other public officials. Could I count on you to speak, Faith? You do it so remarkably well."

"Of course," said Faith almost listlessly. "Shall we go out to the garden now, Aunt Annabelle?"

Mrs. Castle rose, gathering her sables about her. She was already picturing herself presiding over the glittering gathering assembled in the Trustees' Room of the Belford Museum of Fine Arts. She had completely forgotten the Day Nursery which was to so far outshine the one she had come to Hinsboro to see.

.   .   .   .   .

Later on, she remembered it again. But for the moment her mind was agreeably and completely engrossed with the thought of the Loan Collection and Permanent Exhibit which she had persuaded Faith to give to the Belford Museum—for she was already convinced that the idea had been wholly hers, and was planning to present it as emanating from her resourceful brain when she next met the Trustees. She was so pleased that she graciously unbent and admired everything that had been accomplished in the Marlowe garden. And she was forced to admit that a great deal had been achieved in an unbelievably short time. Mr. Emery's garage and workshops and tenements had been razed; the ground had been leveled, resoiled and planted; the high wall of brick already shut out all unsightly surroundings; and from the center of the south side, the glistening statue of St. Michael shone white and splendid in the autumn sunshine against the background of angels.

Mrs. Castle moved toward it impressively, apparently oblivious of the groups clustered admiringly around it, though Faith was hailed by these with enthusiasm, and was soon conversing with them in a variety of tongues. Indeed she permitted herself to be detained so long and so often that Mrs. Castle finally felt forced to turn an impelling glance upon her. Faith gently detached herself from Mrs. Sokovitski and her baby, and rejoined the ex-Ambassadress.

"It is beautiful, isn't it?" she asked, with her eyes on the shining statue.

"It is really very creditable work. I was concerned when I heard you had entrusted it to an unknown marblecutter. I should have been delighted to approach some sculptor of real standing for you."

"But I didn't want a sculptor of standing to do it. I wanted Sebastian Perez. I went to him almost immediately after —after Rudolf was killed and told him about the memorial I had in mind. He worked on the figure secretly all summer. Otherwise it wouldn't have been ready for to-day, and I had my heart set on a Thanksgiving dedication."

"But there have been no dedication exercises!"

"Yes, there have," said Faith swiftly. "Everything that has happened to-day has been a part of them. You can have a dedication without prayers and programs, Aunt Annabelle."

Mrs. Castle glanced at Faith covertly, as if suspecting a veiled allusion to her own rapidly maturing plans for the opening of the Marlowe Permanent Collection and Loan Exhibit. But Faith's face was entirely bland, and Mrs. Castle decided it would be wiser not to charge her with thoughts that had possibly never entered her head.

"It is getting late," she said rearranging her sables again. "I must find the Ambassador and go back to Belford. The last time I saw him he was sitting in a corner with that horrid Caleb Hawks, apparently telling ribald stories. And you call this a dedication!"

"Uncle Carolus tells funnier stories than any man I ever knew," Faith said enthusiastically. "That one about the plumber and his helper, for instance, is simply side-splitting."

"I'm surprised at you, Faith," said Mrs. Castle icily. "It verges on the obscene. I have repeatedly told the Ambassador that his stories will ruin his future and now when it is so important that he should reënter official life——"

"I think his stories are going to be almost as famous in this war as Lincoln's were in the Civil War," Faith said with conviction. "In drives, you know, and so on. If he thought up a really good slogan, he might even get into the next cabinet."

"I do not agree with you," said Mrs. Castle sharply. Nevertheless she looked at Faith covertly again, this time with redoubled attention. "Why not motor back to Belford with the Ambassador and myself for a late supper?" she asked. "I will send you home afterwards—unless you can spend the night, which would really be the better plan. Then we would have ample opportunity to discuss the Loan Collection."

"It is ever so kind of you, Aunt Annabelle, and I should love to. But I have promised to go and spend the evening with Señora Perez. She has not been at all well lately, and I am very troubled about her."

Mrs. Castle glanced carefully about her. None of the importunate and obnoxious groups was very close to her at the moment, although many of them were still lingering in the garden, far past the time, in her opinion, when they might reasonably have been expected to go home. She spoke to Faith in a metallic whisper.

"I don't often interfere in your affairs, Faith," she said in a tone that indicated she felt that she had been commendably forebearing. "But I really do feel I must speak to you about this Señora Perez, as she calls herself—of course that is equivalent to have an American woman call herself Smith or Jones or Brown. I really don't believe it is her name at all. I have only seen her once or twice, but I can't help feeling she isn't respectable. In fact—I dislike enormously to mention such a contingency, but we all have to face the facts of life occasionally, especially in connection with Europeans, though any woman of refinement shrinks from doing so—I can't help feeling that perhaps her son is—illegitimate. He has a great deal more talent than you would expect to find in an ordinary stone-cutter. And there is a certain distinction about his looks which is very arresting—I keep having the uneasy sensation of having seen him somewhere before. It makes me very uncomfortable to have you associate with him so much."

"Why?" asked Faith calmly. "Illegitimacy isn't contagious, is it?—Oh, Cousin Sarah! I was just going to look for you!"

Sarah Atkinson came forward with her usual slow and painful steps. She had on a new winter hat with a stiff turned-back brim, and a neat sealskin coat which nearly covered her gray taffeta dress, though the crackle of this could still be heard. Never had she seemed more completely the embodiment of all Puritan proprieties.

"Sebastian had had his Ford at the door for some time," she said without preamble. "So I think if Mrs. Castle will excuse you——"

"Of course she will! But what do you think she has been saying to me, Cousin Sarah? She has been telling me that she thinks Señora Perez is a lady with a past! Isn't that exciting? And that Sebastian Perez is a ba——"

"Faith!" exclaimed Mrs. Castle cuttingly.

"Well you did! That is you said you thought he was illegitimate. It means the same thing doesn't it? I always get mixed up on terms like that, because I have never heard them very often, except when silly little boys call to each other in the street, but I feel sure an illegitimate son is the same as a——"

"Faith!" exclaimed Mrs. Castle again still more cuttingly.

The corners of Sarah Atkinson's mouth suddenly twitched. She looked from Mrs. Castle to Faith with a gleam of curbed amusement in her fine faded eyes.

"Mrs. Castle is probably right, as usual," she said soberly. "But even if she is, we can hardly depend on the bar sinister to keep Sebastian warm, and he is sitting outside in the cold. Besides, I have the feeling that his mother wants to see you very much." She hesitated for a moment, and then laid her hand on Faith's arm. "I think she wants to talk to you confidentially," Sarah Atkinson added softly. "I know you will be very gentle with her, Faith, no matter what she tells you —very gentle and very sympathetic. And I really think you had better go to her as soon as possible."

"I am going," Faith said steadily, "and I will be very gentle with her, no matter what she tells me."

Mrs. Castle had moved majestically forward—she was preoccupied with a further arrangement of sables. Faith looked straight into Sarah Atkinson's eyes.

"And I shall not be surprised—or too much hurt, no matter what she tells me," she added unflinchingly. "Don't worry about me either, Cousin Sarah."

.   .   .   .   .

When Sebastian Perez had taken Faith to his mother, and placed a chair for her beside the great bed, draped with coarse spotless linen, he went quietly away. The bare whitewashed room was full of shadows. But as Faith looked down at the wasted figure lying motionless beneath the great crucifix, she knew, even though she saw the expression of the drawn gaunt face so dimly, that the dark silent woman who had kept her own counsel for nearly thirty years would indeed now unburden her heart.

"*Sea Usted bienvenida, Doña Fidelidad!*" she exclaimed almost joyfully, the smoldering light in her sunken eyes suddenly kindled. "You do me infinite honor in coming to see me—the one that I do not deserve."

"If it is an honor, I'm sure you do deserve it," Faith answered, trying to speak lightly. She had leaned over and kissed the sick woman on both cheeks, and as she did so, she had felt tears against her lips. Now, as she seated herself, Señora Perez clung to her hand as if she were grasping for salvation and strength.

"If I had known you were so ill I should have come in to see you every day," Faith went on. "Sebastian has excused himself for not telling me by saying he did not want to trouble me when I was busy with preparations for the dedication. But I am really very angry with him. I might have left Hinsboro without seeing you at all."

"The Baronesa is going away!" Señora Perez exclaimed with a note of questioning alarm.

"Only for a fortnight or so," Faith said soothingly. "Hansel and Mrs. Atkinson and Mr. Hawks and I are going to take a holiday trip to New York. We all want a change, for various reasons. So we are making an excuse of the fact that my mother-in-law was sent me a large shipment of household belongings. I think I really ought to see them through the customs myself, especially as I am planning to have most of them sent to the museum in Belford, and I must give orders for their direct despatch. There are only a few pieces about which I have some special sentiment that I am reserving for myself." She hesitated for a moment, pierced with poignant pain. Then, conscious of the sense of deep mystic kinship which bound her to the prostrate woman before her, she added without betraying the effort the words cost her, "There are also a few that I should like to give to you, if you will let me."

"That you would like to give me!" Señora Perez echoed in stupefaction. "But why should you wish to do that, Doña Fidelidad?"

"Because they were given to me by Sebastian de Cerreno," Faith said steadily.

The invalid gasped and turned away her head, hiding her face. She did not loosen her grasp on Faith's fingers.

"Then you knew! You have known—all the time!"

"Yes, I have known all the time," Faith answered quietly, "from the moment that I saw—your son—and his. May I talk to you a little about him, and tell you how he happened to make me the gifts I wish to share with you? The first time I ever met him was in Madrid, at the home of his *Tia* Carlota, when I went there as a bride. He told me, rather satirically, that he supposed I would feel I was not really seeing Spain until I went to the Prado and stood in front of Murillo's 'Inmaculada' pretending to be spellbound. I was annoyed with him for jesting on such a subject, and I asked him if he would not take me to see it himself. He declined on the ground that he had an assignation with a little dancer named Felicidad. But afterwards he felt sorry he had hurt

312

my feelings. So he sent me, with a very tender and delicate message, one of the sketches Murillo made while he was trying to put his vision of the Virgin in definite form. And from that time on, Don Sebastian made me many similar gifts. I think it is characteristic of him, Señora, that he is always sorry afterwards when he has been in the wrong, and has been eager to make atonement."

The Spaniard suddenly lifted her head. "It is true!" she said vibrantly. "He has the gift of repentance, as his brother has the gift of saintliness! He never guessed that I needed a protector! If he had, he would have given me protection."

"I know he would have," Faith said reassuringly.

"But he was only a young boy!" the woman cried impetuously. "A boy so beautiful that when he went along the streets of Granada every girl watched from her window or balcony till he had passed. He was an *hombre de amor*, even then, upon whom no woman of any age could look unmoved. But he was still so young himself that love was a mystery to him, and when it was offered him, he hardly knew what it was that he grasped for so hotly. He told me, Señora, that I was the first to—lie in his arms."

"If he told you so, you may be sure it is the truth," Faith said steadily.

"When I say I offered him my love, you must not think this was my practice, Señora," the sick woman went on imploringly. "He was my first and only lover—I swear it by the Holy Virgin! But from the moment I first saw him, I knew I could not live without him. I was a little older than he, and I made it very easy.—Can you understand what I'm trying to tell you, Señora?"

"Yes—yes—I understand," Faith said in a low voice.

"He gave me many presents, but he never offered me money—he had fine feeling, he knew that all he had had of me had been as freely given as it was freely taken. And then—when he had gone on his joyful careless way again, he would have come back—willingly—impetuously—if I had told him how it was with me. He might even have married me, for he was chivalrous as well as careless, Señora—he would not have looked prudently toward the future as a man of meaner spirit would have done. And I was tempted —greatly tempted. I love him so that my heart pounded in my ears if I so much as heard his step, and I was carrying his child, his eldest son. And I was the daughter of an *hidalgo*, of a poor gentle family which would have been raised to glory and distinction by such a marriage.—Do you still understand, Doña Fidelidad?"

"Yes, I still understand. I—I shall understand everything

313

you tell me. I have been even wondering if you would not tell me your real name, and whether you would not speak to me in English, which I know you must have learned at the convent to which you went as a girl."

"My name is Elena de la Barra, Señora," the Spaniard said slowly and distinctly.

"And what happened, Doña Elena, to deliver you from temptation?"

"I saw the child, Dolores de Romera, coming out of the Cathedral after her first communion," Elena de la Barra whispered. "She was all in white, and she carried lilies in her hand, and her face, beneath her veil and her garland, was the face of an angel. I knew that almost in her cradle she had been betrothed to Don Sebastian. And when I saw —what she could give him——"

"Many years later I saw her picture, taken on her wedding day," Faith whispered back. "Again she was all in white, carrying lilies in her hand, and her face was that of an angel. I know, Doña Elena, how you felt——"

"But afterwards—when tragedy came—I wondered whether I had done right. For Don Sebastian, who loves children as much as women love him, believed himself childless; and he was the father of my son. But how could I tell him the truth? I had fled from Granada, Doña Fidelidad, after seeing that vision at the church door. I took a ship in Malaga which brought me to New York, and then I found my way to Hinsboro, where an aunt and uncle now dead were then living. They befriended me. But they wrote my parents, when my baby was born, that we had died together. And then came the long years——"

"They must have been very long," Faith said slowly, gazing straight in front of her with unseeing eyes.

"They were endless! And through them all, I have been consumed with a burning flame. The fires of a woman's one passion are almost unquenchable."

"Yes," said Faith, still more slowly, "I know—that they are unquenchable."

"Even now, sometimes. . . . And added to the burden of loss has been this burden of futility. Since I have been so ill—it has seemed more than I could bear."

"If—if you knew that Don Sebastian was happy—after all —in the way that you had hoped to give him joy—would the burden be any lighter?"

"If I knew—*Sanctissima Maria*, what are you trying to tell me, Señora?"

Faith freed her hand gently, and walked slowly across the room. As she opened the door, Sebastian rose gravely from the deep chair in which he had been sunk, and looked at her hopefully.

"Have you any champagne in the house?" she asked surprisingly. "I think it would do your mother good to have some. Besides, I have learned to-day that I have a namesake, and it would make me very happy if you and the Señora would drink to her health with me."

"There is champagne, Doña Fidelidad. Sebastian will put a bottle on the ice at once. Will you tell us about the *niña* while it cools?"

Doña Elena's voice was breathless with excitement. She sat up in bed, her dark eyes glowing. Faith looked at her smilingly as she resumed her own seat.

"I used to hope that some day I would have a little girl of my own," she said. "But when my husband died, I thought I should have to wait until Hansel married, before I had a namesake. But now I have the good news of which I spoke. Shall I read you the letter which contains this? I have brought it with me."

"If that would be your pleasure, Doña Fidelidad."

Sebastian had come back into the room, carrying a cooler into which he had plunged a bottle of champagne. He sat down between Faith and his mother, his dark face glowing and expectant. As Faith opened her handbag, she noticed that the light in the shadowy room fell across his hair much as she had seen the light fall across the hair of a man sitting opposite her in a patio near Granada years before.

"My letter comes from Spain," she said unfolding it, and spreading out the sheets covered with delicate handwriting, "From a very great and beautiful lady. Her name is Doña Dolores de Cerreno."

Sebastian gave a smothered exclamation, and half rose, glancing with distress toward his mother. She continued to gaze at Faith without moving, and Faith laid a restraining hand on Sebastian's arm.

"There is nothing in this letter that will cause any of us grief," she said reassuringly. "Listen! *'Excelentissima Señora:* Although I have never had the privilege of meeting you, I have long felt that you were my friend. My husband did not fail to tell me that had it not been for your firm faith in my recovery, our reunion could never have taken place, for he would not have permitted the great American surgeon to operate upon me. A year or more ago, when our son was born, my husband wrote to Dr. Noble, who in replying said, that he had shared the felicitous tidings with you; but now that he has left the peaceful valley of your habitation in order to extend his services to the suffering soldiers of France,

315

I am venturing to communicate with you directly, to inform you that on All Saints' Day, I was safely and joyfully delivered of a daughter.' "

"Madre de Dios!" exclaimed Sebastian, half rising again. It was his mother who laid a detaining hand on his arm now.

" 'When my husband entered my apartment to salute me after my *accouchement,*' " Faith went on reading , " 'his first exclamation took the form of an impetuous question: Had I thought of a name for the child? My reply was immediate. "If it meets with thy pleasure, *alma de mi alma,* it is my wish that she should be called Fidelidad, since but for the lovely and courageous lady by that name, we could not have been accorded the bliss of bringing this precious infant into being."—"That was my thought also," my husband answered, in accents of unbounded happiness. We then embraced each other with ecstasy. . . .' "

The delicate sheets of paper fluttered in Faith's hands. Doña Elena leaned over and touched her.

"Doña Fidelidad!" she said imploringly.

" 'We then embraced each other with ecstasy,' " repeated Faith more firmly, searching for the place where she had left off. " 'And parted for the time being in order that I might maintain the tranquillity necessary for the welfare of my child. Owing to the injunction for early baptism laid upon us by our Holy Church, we were not able to defer this ceremony until after conferring with you, and therefore ventured to take your gracious consent to the name for granted; and on November the eighth our baby was baptized by Gabriel in the Capilla Real. To the name of Fidelidad was added that of Cristina, this being, as I believe you know, the name of my husband's sainted mother, who now rests with God. As if under the protection of her heavenly spirit and your beneficent influence, my daughter grows stronger and more beautiful every day; and it is my earnest hope that in the happy future you will do us the honor of coming to see her yourself. Meanwhile, I beg you to believe that I am, with expressions of the most exalted consideration, Dolores Antonio Maria de Cerreno y Romera.' "

"Madre de Dios!" exclaimed Sebastian de Perez once more.

This time neither Faith nor his mother sought to prevent him when he rose. They were gazing silently at each other, and he saw that the eyes of both were full of tears. And yet there was no grief in either woman's face. On one was an expression of infinite relief, as if from release from endless and unendurable strain; on the other was one of exaltation. It was Faith's voice which fell on the stillness like music.

"A secret shared is never so heavy a burden as one that is born in loneliness," she said. "May you and I not share ours, Señora? Shall we make a covenant together? I will reveal the hidden chambers of my heart to you, and you will do the same to me. Shall it be so?" She put her arms around Sebastian Perez' mother, and drew her closely to her breast. For a long moment they clasped each other. Then Faith turned and held out her hand to Sebastian Perez himself.

"We are going to drink to my namesake, are we not?" she asked, "to whom Don Sebastian gave my name because she is the child of my spirit, though I never bore him a child in the flesh. That great privilege has not been mine. But to a woman who has had it, I know it must have been the compensation for loneliness and exile and even shame, as the world, which understands so little, interprets shame.— Surely you will join with your mother and me, Sebastian, in our toast to your little sister!"

Chapter XL

FAITH was very tired. For two days after she reached New York, she did not get up at all, but lay listlessly in her brass bed at the Waldorf-Astoria, watching the comings and goings of the rest of the little group, in which, for the first time, she took only an inactive part. Sarah Atkinson went shopping while Hansel and Caleb stayed with Faith; then Caleb and Hansel went to the docks to make sure that the shipment from Denmark was all right while Sarah Atkinson stayed with her. When they came back with the report that it was, she was relieved, primarily for the reason that this meant she could stay in bed at least another day before she went down and looked it over herself.

"See here, Faith," Caleb said assertively, when for the third successive evening she dismissed the suggestion of getting dressed for dinner and going out to the theater with the brevity of complete exhaustion, "I'm going to get a doctor in to look at you if you ain't perked up by mornin'. You're plumb tuckered out. You need some good peppery tonic to build you up. I'm goin' to call the floor clerk and see——"

"Honestly, Uncle Caleb, I don't need a good peppery tonic! I was—rather exhausted, but I don't need anything except a good rest, and I'm having it. I'm enjoying it."

"Well, I've seen you when you looked to me as if you were enjoyin' yourself more," he said still doubtfully. "You ain't one of them women that favors layin' in bed. Some do. Now I seen one to-day that I bet my bottom dollar would delight in it. She was down to the dock pesterin' the officers there to tell her when some boat that's overdue would be in. She appeared to blame it upon them because there'd been a storm at sea. 'It's very inconvenient for me to keep comin' down here,' says she, lookin' as if she might burst right out cryin'. 'But I s'pose everyone would think I wuz heartless if I wasn't here when the boat come in, even if I froze to death waitin' for it.' And with that she turned to me and asked if *I* couldn't help her—in one o' them whinin' kind of voices. If there's anything I despise it's a woman that whines when she talks to you. Lord Almighty! As if I could tell her when the damned old boat would be in."

Caleb Hawks drew a large purple handkerchief from his pocket and blew his nose with a loud snort. Faith propped herself up on her pillows and looked at him with amusement.

"This woman seems to have annoyed you very much, Uncle Caleb," she remarked.

"Annoyed me! Say, Faith, she made me so mad I could of choked her. 'There isn't a soul in New York to help me,' she kept saying. 'It's pretty forlorn for a woman in my situation not to have someone to help her.' "

"Uncle Caleb, I believe she was trying to pick you up."

"Pick me up!" he roared indignantly. "Faith, you had otter seen her. Sixty years old if she wuz a day, and one of that type that's so skinny you can't tell whether they're comin' or goin' unless you look at them close. And stringy hair falling all around her face that didn't look like it had been combed in a week. And somethin' fishy about the eyes. Ugh! She give me the creeps!"

"Did she tell you whom she was waiting for, Uncle Caleb? Is it a long lost lover whom she hasn't seen since she was young and charming?"

"Now then, Faith, you quit your kiddin'—not but what I'm relieved to have you act a little more like yourself. Yes, she did. And that simply capped the climax. It's her son, her only son. 'He would go an' enlist in the French Army,' says she, 'though why he shouldda done such a crazy thing, I can't imagine. And now he's bein' sent back blind for me to take care of all the rest of his life. I'm not equal to it,' says she, 'what I need is someone to take care of me.' "

"Oh, Uncle Caleb, how horrible!"

"It wuz horrible, Faith, and that's a fact. Think o' that

318

poor man bein' brought back blind and left at the mercy of a spineless specimen like that!"

As Caleb Hawks mentally reviewed this conversation during the night, he began to regret having told Faith about the episode. He had discovered that she had a way of regarding every case of perplexity and misery that came within the range of her observation as her personal responsibility. If she had not, she would never have stepped into the breach at the Hinsboro High School, or taken over the direction of the Day Nursery, or involved herself—as she evidently had—with the mysterious tragedy which had darkened the life of the Señora Perez. That he guessed, blindly but shrewdly, had somehow been the last straw—He had been anticipating her present collapse ever since Thanksgiving Day, when she had come into his house so silently, with the strange sacrificial look on her face, after leaving the Spaniards' house. She was carrying a self-assumed load of burdens too heavy for her strength. Yet he felt uneasily certain that in the morning, she would tentatively suggest the assumption of another.

He was not mistaken. She knocked at his door before he had finished shaving, and confronted him, completely dressed for the street, while he stood staring at her with tufts of lather dropping from his ruddy double chin.

"I am sorry to be so inopportune," she said apologetically. "But I was afraid you would escape me. I would like to have breakfast with you and afterwards I think we had better go down to the docks. It is really time those cases were cleared, and on their way to the Belford Museum."

It was not until they were bumping along over the cobblestones of lower New York that she said anything to cause him uneasiness, and he had begun to be hopeful that he had worried unnecessarily, when she slipped her hand quietly into his.

"I have been thinking over what you told me about that futile woman," she said. "If she is on the wharf again when we get there, I think I will talk to her a little. If she really isn't able to take care of her blind son, and dosen't know anyone who can do it for her, don't you think perhaps——"

"Now, Faith! I ben kickin' myself all night for tellin' you that. I don't see how I ever come to be so dumb. You gone way beyond your strength already, and the Lord knows I'm so druv I don't know what to do, with a war comin' on an' all——"

"I know. But we could manage somehow. I've been thinking of building a little cottage for Perley and Hilda anyway, and that would give me plenty of room——"

"Land sakes, Faith! You can't take this fellow into your house! He may be a regular scalawag for all you know. A man ain't moral just because he's blind."

"I don't like men that are too moral," retorted Faith. "No woman does, really. She only pretends she does, when she thinks she ought to. And I don't think I ought to."

"Faith, you'll get into trouble some day, the crazy things you say. And the crazy things you *do!*"

"I'm not going to get into trouble this time."

After they had spent nearly two hours on the wharf without seeing anything of a docking ship, or of the latest disturber of Caleb Hawks' peace of mind, he thankfully decided that this might be true. But as he and Faith were preparing to leave, after giving every necessary direction in regard to the shipment of her cases, he suddenly caught sight of the whining woman charging rapidly in his direction.

"It's just coming in!" she gasped. "The boat, I mean. It'll be tied up before noon, and the passengers let off. You were so sympathetic with me yesterday when I told you about my terrible trouble, that I couldn't help wondering whether you and your daughter wouldn't stay with me now and see me through my ordeal."

"I warn't at all sympathetic with you," Caleb said shortly. "An' my daughter ain't well. She's had a tirin' mornin'. I want she should go home and rest."

"Oh, but it would detain you such a short time, and I haven't anyone else to help me! Otherwise I wouldn't think of appealing to a stranger!—Won't *you* try to persuade your father?" the woman insisted, turning to Faith, who was looking at her with veiled aversion.

Certainly Caleb Hawks had not given her an exaggerated description of this obnoxious creature. She was all that he had said and more. Nevertheless, Faith answered her courteously.

"I'm really not tired at all. If you think we can help you, we shall be glad to stay. That must be the boat, just turning around now, isn't it?—I was distressed to hear that such a tragedy had overtaken your son."

"Yes," the woman said impatiently. "It is sad, but as far as he's concerned, of course it's his own fault. He didn't have to go to war. It wasn't as if he'd been French. Though he'd lived in France so long, he'd got into all sorts of loose ways." She lowered her voice, and drew Faith a little away from Caleb. "The last time he came home, almost ten years ago," she said querulously, "he shocked the people in my home town almost to death. He kept talking about men's mistresses and nude models and things like that just the way

320

you'd talk about the weather. He'd refer to friends of his who were dope fiends and degenerates without any more shame than if they'd been clergymen and merchants. It'll be the same now—perfectly disgusting. I don't know how I'm going to put up with it, because this time, I won't be able to look forward to having him leave. There isn't a soul I can ask to help me with him. I'm a widow and he's my only son. He went away from me voluntarily when he was hardly more than a boy, and he's only been home two or three times since. I feel as if I scarcely knew him. And I haven't got a lot of useful cousins and aunts, the way most women have. And think how helpless he's going to be!"

"Yes," said Faith slowly, "I am thinking—how helpless he's going to be. Are you sure you can't think of anyone who would take care of him?"

"Oh, I'm positive! I've tried to find someone—*anyone*—and I can't. I've cried all night long, every night, since I gave up hope of relief." She began to cry now, hysterically. Then, after a few moments of senseless sobbing, she dabbed at her eyes, rolled her handkerchief into a wet ball, and looked searchingly at Faith. "Haven't I met you somewhere before?" she asked curiously. "I can't remember that I have, but somehow you look familiar to me."

"No," said Faith still more slowly. "I don't think we've met before. I don't remember you, and yet I usually remember people very well—even people I haven't seen since I was a child. But it's strange—even though I can't remember seeing you, it seems as if I could remember hearing you cry. Do you—cry a good deal?"

"I guess you'd cry a good deal if you had as much to bear as I have!" the stranger sobbed plaintively, raising her handkerchief again.

"The boat's starting to swing in ma'm," Caleb said brusquely. "Mebbe we better walk over to where they're puttin' the gangplank, if we're goin' to meet this son of yours. He won't be lookin' for you, the way things are."

"No, he won't be looking for me," the woman agreed, crying more violently than ever. "I'll have all the responsibility to bear. In fact I don't even know that he'll be able to walk off with someone leading him. He's been injured in other ways besides his eyes. He may be a permanent cripple. Oh, it's perfectly awful! You don't know how helpless I feel!"

Caleb, aware that Faith was trying to meet his eyes, looked uncomfortably away.

"Well, I guess we do at that," he said scornfully. "But if you go on cryin' like that, you'll strangle.—Not but what it would be much of a loss," he added under his breath. "I guess Faith's right as usual. I guess mebbe we'll have to look after this poor blind feller whether he's a scalawag or not. It 'ud be murder to leave him to the mercies of a woman like that. Why, she'd drown him, just cryin' over him.—If I could find you a glass of water somewheres, would you drink it?" he added aloud.

"Oh, I couldn't possibly swallow anything! Oh, I think the gangplank is going to be put down! Oh, I simply can't bear it!"

The usual crowd of porters and visitors had begun to collect. There was the confused sound of shouted greetings, creaking ropes, lowered boards, and rushing feet. A stream of people carrying small but multitudinous pieces of precious hand baggage, began to come down the gangplank, squirming and wedging their way along. The tumult of voices rose higher.

"Look, there's Mae! Hello there, Mae, it was great of you to come and meet us! . . . You just wait 'til you see what I brought home for you! It's the peachiest little. . . . Oh, any time now! All the Americans that could left Europe long ago. . . . How's mother, Jim? I said, *how's mother?* Gee, isn't it great to get home before Christmas after all? The worst storm in twenty years, the captain said. Yes, but this time he meant it. . . . There, there, for God's sake don't cry so. . . ."

Something suddenly snapped in Faith's subconscious mind. She seemed to be lying again, for the first time, in a narrow berth on an ocean liner, listening to the voices of men and women who had come to see their friends off, and the voices of men and women who were going away, as these resounded through the corridor outside the little cabin where she lay, lonely and frightened.

"Hello there, Tom! Are you with Jack and Mabel? No I haven't been able to locate them anywhere. . . . Well, I did mean to bring some flowers, but I couldn't seem to get around to buying any, and I thought oranges would taste pretty good, they're such a rarity at this time of year. . . . *For God's sake don't cry so, Helen, it isn't as though the boy were in his grave. Most mothers would be pretty proud to have their sons win a prize that would give them two years in Paris free——*"

Faith gave a quick gasp of horror. Then she put her hands on the sobbing woman's shoulders and shook her.

"Listen!" she said. "I think I remember where I heard you crying before! On a boat, the night your son started for

France to study art. Do you live in Jonesville, Ohio? Is your name Helen Dudley?"

The woman gulped, dropping her handkerchief. Before she had time to reply, Faith had read her answer in her face, and had given an exclamation that cut through to Caleb's heart.

"You're Sam Dudley's mother!" she cried. *"Sam Dudley's mother!* And Sam—Sam is being brought home—*blind!"* She threw back her head, as if to shake away the tears which blurred her own vision. Then she held out her hands and rushed forward.

She was just in time. A stretcher, carried by four men, was being carefully borne down the gangplank, and on it was extended a motionless form, so emaciated that the blankets which enshrouded it were hardly lifted by its outline. Two transparent hands lay nervously over the coverings which concealed the long figure. Above these was a bandaged head, of which only the stubbly chin, the blue lips, and the shrunken nostrils were visible. Faith clove through the crowd, and flung herself down beside the stretcher as its bearers lowered it to the platform.

"Sam! My darling Sam!" she cried. "You're safe! You've come back to me! *Oh, thank God, I've got you anyhow!"*

PART IX

Sam

Chapter XLI

"WELL sir, as I've been sayin' to my daughter Myra all winter, it was fortunate you come home just when you did. If you hadn't, Faith wouldda broke down. She was plumb tuckered out, and that's a fact."

"And since my return, of course she's had a complete rest," Sam answered rather dryly.

The two men were extended in easy chairs on the deep piazza overlooking the meadows and mountains at the rear of Marlowe Manor. Iced drinks, sandwiches, and smoking supplies were laid out on a small wicker table that stood between them; and at their feet lay a young police dog, which turned gleaming and watchful eyes on Sam every time he so much as shifted his position. Now and then Caleb refilled Sam's glass, measuring off whisky and ginger ale with the sure touch of one who is in no doubt of another's tastes; but Sam reached for his sandwiches and cigarettes himself, his long slim fingers closing quickly over them, without fumbling or hesitation. He smoked slowly, tilting his head back as if to watch the blue rings floating off into the quiet air; but he often lighted one cigarette from another, while Caleb, on the other hand, sat indefinitely chewing one huge black cigar, to which he apparently had no throught of applying a match.

For a long time an unembarrassed silence, permeated with comfort and congeliality, reigned undisturbed. Then Mr. Hawks broke in upon it with a continuation of his satisfied reminiscence.

"You couldda knocked me over with a feather," he said, though he now tipped the scales at two hundred and seventy-three pounds, "when Faith went down on her knees in front of that stretcher on the wharf. I certainly did think she had suddenly took leave of her senses. She'd ben lookin' pretty peaked for quite a spell, specially after Thanksgiv-

324

ing, when that sick Spaniard I told you about seemed to suck the strength right out of her—and I was considerable worried about her. But land! I never hope to see a woman act more level-headed than she did, after them first few minutes. I didn't know what had happened, hardly, before she had you to bed in Hansel's room, and a good doctor there, and everythin' runnin' on velvet as you might say. And she never once forgot to be civil to that lily-livered old bi—beg pardon, Sam. That slipped out before I noticed."

"Nice of you to speak for me, Caleb," Sam said reassuringly, waving the slim hand that held the cigarette, and taking another long drink from his highball.

"An' you settin' propped up on pillows, eatin' a real Christmas dinner a week later," Caleb went on, "when you looked as if you'd pass away any minute that morning we brung you up to the Waldorf. I know it don't depress you none to hear this, Sam, or I wouldn't tell you, but if I ever seen a livin' man appear like a corpse, you wuz it.—And Faith telegraphin' Sunnora Perez to find out would she take over Faith's Spanish classes for the rest of the year, and Sunnora Perez telegraphin' back that she *would!* An' Faith fixin' up her attic for you because an artist oughtta feel more to home in an attic than anywhere else, and making it look downright handsome, as you might say—'course I don't care much for that gloomy picture you got over your bed, but that's a matter of taste. The rest is certainly fine. An' you helpin' to arrange that exhibit down to the Belford Museum, and sayin' just where everythin' ought to go, same as if you had your sight, so's 'twould be just right when 'twas finished. An' since then, fittin' into everythin' easy and natural, givin' talks to the Fine Arts Class at the High School, and tellin' that gang o' young hoodlums that calls themselves Boy Scouts all about the Foreign Legion, wearin' your uniform with that funny bunnit on your head, and explainin' to the Persian Panthers how it was that Russia come to fall——"

Mr. Hawks paused for breath, spat out some fragments of his cigar which he had reduced to mere shreds, and refilled his own glass. As he did so, he turned his carbuncle ring around so that he could enjoy the color of the stone as he proceeded.

"If you hadn't done all that," he said gratefully, "I think it might have been a mite awkward for Faith, when war was declared, between Germany and the U. S. A., 'spite of everythin' we could do. Course folks are crazy about her—that is, most folks—an' all that, but feelin' runs awful high in war time, especially at the beginnin'. It made all the difference in the world, Sam, when you come here, just in the nick o' time, because you'd fought with the Allies, right from the start, and was a wounded hero and all that. Your condition has ben a real Godsend, and that's a fact."

Caleb Hawks rose and stretched himself. There was a slight, but ominous sound of ripping.

"Lord Almighty, I guess I've bust somethin' again," he said feeling around uneasily. "Sometimes I'm afraid I may be gettin' a mite too fleshy. But, land! If we go in for all them meatless, wheatless, sweetless days, they're talkin' about, I guess I'll reduce whether I want to or not. I guess Faith has got the right idea with all this plantin' of hers, and say, them farmerettes o' hers is real cute. I never wouldda believed I'd live to see the day that Emmeline Marlowe would let a parcel of High School girls overrun that house o' hers, but there they are, spry as can be.—Well, I guess I better go along and have Hilda look me over to see where that rip was. I hope I ain't seatless as well as eatless. See you soon again, Sam."

"You betcha," Sam answered, laughing.

He lit another cigarette, and leaning back in his long chair, reached for the smooth ears of the dog lying beside him. He felt these prick under his touch, and then, after a brief responsive quiver of joy, relax with contentment. The dog, whose registered name was Cerberus, but who was familiarly known as Russie, had been Faith's first gift to him after his return. She had brought it into his room on Christmas morning, and folded his thin arms around the warm, squirming puppy body, as she bent over to kiss his forehead.

"Here's a present for you, Sam!" she had said buoyantly. "It's name is Cerberus, and it's going to guard the entrance of the infernal regions for you—I mean so that you can't get into them, when you're feeling blue. A dog is so satisfying, don't you think so? It's always there, no matter who else goes off and leaves you. You don't mind if he licks your face, do you, Sam?"

No, he had told her a little huskily, he didn't mind. He wondered how she had realized instantaneously that he had been hungrily longing for a dog. Cerberus had never left him since then, except reluctantly and briefly, to be fed and exercised. The puppy was friendly to Caleb and Sarah, and fond of Hansel and Faith; but it was Sam whom he worshipped with all the intensity of canine devotion. Now, blissful under the soothing caress of his master's hand, he sank into the watchful doze which was his nearest approach to sound slumber.

Sam continued to stroke his dog's head, as he waited,

326

without impatience and without restlessness, for Faith to come home. She was devoting much of her time to the farm these days, going over to the Nursery only two or three times a week, unless her presence there was urgently required. School was over for the summer, and even before it closed, she had not resumed the intensive work there that she had done before Sam's arrival. Señora Perez had proved entirely adequate as a Spanish teacher, and Miss Wilkins, Faith's assistant in the Home Economics Department, had been promoted. The Arts Class had remained under Faith's supervision, but Sam had actually done most of the teaching in it for her, from the time he was on his feet.

The transformation of the attic had absorbed them both during the period of his convalescence. Faith had conferred with him about every detail of its adornment and equipment. It was natural enough for her to ask whether he would rather have a tub or a shower in the tiny bathroom that was being wedged in between the eaves, and whether he wouldn't like the fireplace unbricked, and whether he didn't think it wouldn't be airier with more dormer windows. But that she should consult him about colors and fabrics exactly as if he could see them showed a sensibility of which only Faith, among all the women Sam had ever known, would have been capable. She did even more than this: she spoke to him about the pictures and furnishings which were originally destined for the Belford Art Museum, and asked him if he would not like to live surrounded by some of these.

"Of course I would, Faith," Sam said gratefully. "What are there for pictures?"

"There is one tiny Dürer—wonderful!—and two rather good Holbeins in the German art collection—nothing else you'd care for. It was surfeited with baroque that Rudolf's grandfather bought on his first trip to Italy—Carlo Dolce, Guido Reni, Sassoferrato—you know, all that. Belford would simply gloat and gasp over it. Don't rob Mrs. Castle of her triumph."

"I won't," Sam said laughing. Then added, "Nothing Spanish?"

"Oh, yes. The Goya must go to Belford—inevitably—like Carlo Dolce's simpering saints. And I've kept out two little Murillos—a Mater Dolorosa for Doña Elena, and an Inmaculada for myself. Then there is a St. Sebastian by El Greco, and a portrait of Cecilia de Cerreno by Velasquez, and a Crucifixion by Ribera."

"Belford can have St. Sebastian for all of me," Sam said grimly. "And Cecilia de Cerreno too, as far as that goes.

327

But if you think the Crucifixion wouldn't be missed, Faith —good God—what a picture!"

"I'm not sure that's a polite way to talk about God," she said teasingly, quoting the old reproof of her childhood. "Of course Belford won't miss it. I'll hang it over your bed, shall I? There's just the bed for you——"

"Not that gilded cage you had in Copenhagen?"

"Certainly not. That is the chief treasure of the Belford collection. Mrs. Castle and all the other virtuous ladies in the state will go and look at it every now and then, and think how wonderful it would have been to be wicked."

"Is that what you used to think when you slept in it, Faith?"

"Not exactly. . . . Well, anyway, the bed I started to tell you about before you forced all this ribaldry on me, is Portuguese, with big twisted columns—a wonderful carved headboard—not that you deserve it after the way you have talked——"

As soon as Sam was strong enough, he and Cousin Sarah and Russie went to Washington, so that he could consult Dr. Wilmer about his eyes—there was just the hundredth chance, Faith insisted, that the case might not be hopeless, and until the great specialist said it was, she would not believe it. She did not go with the little devoted group—she wanted, she said, to finish her work in the attic without interference! And when Sam returned to Hamstead, their worse fears confirmed, she led him straight to his new quarters, where he could hear the fire crackling and feel the cheerful warmth of its glow; and having installed him in a deep luxurious chair, drawn up beside his own hearthstone, she sat down on the floor in front of him, her head resting against his knees.

How long it was before either of them moved again, Sam never knew. Faith did not speak a single word of commiseration. There were many things, she said, which she had been waiting for just the right chance to tell him about. Now that everyone else had gone to bed, would he care to listen? She reached caressingly for his hands, and drew them down until he clasped them around her neck, his arms resting on her shoulders. Then without reservation or explanation, she opened her heart to him. She was not seeking for pity, she was not anticipating censure; but she poured out her story as if silence had become intolerable to her, and as if she had found the one confessor in all the world who had the wisdom and the power to sustain and comfort her. Every latent misgiving with which Sam had been tortured lest his infirmity might be another load with which he had no right to burden her, every hideous fear lest he might be the one to crush and break her at last, was swept away as his consciousness of her need of him and of her dependence on him crystalized into conviction. What, after all, did his blindness matter, since, in spite of it, she still turned to him for sympathy and strength?

Unremittingly, unfalteringly, he kept assuring himself that it did not matter at all; and still the enormity of his deprivation rose relentlessly before him. He could never ask anything of Faith now beyond that which she gave him so freely, he reflected rebelliously, in the long nights that followed the salvaging revelation which merged his shattered destiny, with mystic fusion, into hers. There could be no reciprocity in their relationship, as there would have been if he had come back to her, whole and triumphant, at the end of the war. That, as Sarah Atkinson had so shrewdly divined, had been his hope and intention. He would have brought her understanding and companionship; but in return he would have claimed his reward for his years of undemanding devotion. If she had said to him then that she had shut love out of her life forever, he would have laughed at her—tenderly and comprehendingly, to be sure, but still he would have laughed; and eventually he would have taught her to laugh with him at the fantastic idea that a normal and beautiful woman could be through with love at twenty-five. Rudolf —he would have told her—had been a young girl's vision of a glittering saint, whose tarnished splendor had been brightened to new radiance by the delusive glory of death. And Sebastian had been a fairy prince waking a sleeping beauty, and then vanished into an enchanted castle of his own, leaving 'her stirred but desolate. The portraits were not entirely accurate, but they would have served his purpose. And then he would have painted another picture: a picture of marriage as she had never visualized it before, lightened with laughter, brightened with congeniality, stabilized with sympathy, cemented with children—not one charming, lonely, supersensitive little boy, but half a dozen lusty youngsters, tumbling and tearing about. He would have convinced her, holding her firmly in his arms at last, that it was not love that she was done with; it was star-gazing, it was moon-reaching, it was glamour, it was high romance. But now he would show her, before it was too late, what strong healthy passion between men and women really was.

Prostrate in the perpetual darkness which engulfed him, and which during the terrible endless night was unassuaged by the manufactured activities of the day, he ground his teeth at the thought of the wastefulness as well as the cruelty of the fate which had deprived him of Faith. He did not underestimate the value and the beauty of the work she was doing; but how incomplete this chaste and consecrated life was! What freedom and fulfillment she should have found in a marriage of maturity! How fair and fruitful she would have been! Often the vision of this became so unendurable that Sam wondered if, after all, he would not be justified in making a mirage a reality. If, as Faith had sat at his feet in front of the fire, resting her head against his knees, he had suddenly leaned over and gathered her against his hammering heart, what would have happened? Why should he sit listening to her faltering confession that only an accident had prevented her from giving herself to another man, without telling her that there was no accident, not even blindness, which would prevent him from claiming her for his own? He knew that she would not have resisted him—her compassion for his mutilation, her own crying need for confidential communion, would have delivered her into his arms twice over. But what would he have gained by so treacherous a victory? If she yielded herself to him through pity and loneliness alone, he would grasp nothing but the shell of the spirit which he longed to possess as completely as he longed to possess the entirety of her lovely flesh. Rudolf had had such a shell, and what Rudolf had had was not enough for him; while the loyalty which Rudolf had accepted with such composure, would have been gall and wormwood to him. To know that he had fettered her forever to a worthless wreck, would have been to redouble the weight of his own heavy chain, which shackled him in the prison house of blindness.

* * * * *

It was already late, judging from the pleasant perfume of cooking wafted to him from the kitchen, before he heard Faith's footsteps. And when he did, they turned first toward the pantry, from which the clink of china and silver were coming. She had gone, evidently, to confer with Hilda; and since she did not lower her voice, which, for all its melody, carried much further than many which were harsher and higher, everything she said was audible to him.

"Mrs. Atkinson and Hansel are going to have supper with the Mannings, Hilda. Oh—I'm glad they didn't forget to tell you themselves. It's such a lovely evening, that I thought I would try to persuade Mr. Dudley to walk down the lane with me and have a picnic supper by the river, if it wouldn't be too much trouble for you to change everything around now. Oh, you are a jewel, Hilda!—Well, in about twenty minutes, I think."

The swinging door to the piazza opened and closed swiftly. There was the soft rustle of a dress. Then Faith sank down on the edge of the long chair where Sam lay extended, and reached for his hand, locking her fingers in his.

"I'm tired," she said without preamble. "I've been way up beyond Whitewater buying cows—I've bought ten. I think this farm can carry twice as many as we've got now, if we manage right. Anyway, I'm going to try, and this is the beginning of the trial. I may have to go over into New York State next week to look for more. I thought it might interest you to go along—we could all go. I feel like taking a trip—somehow when I'm driving a motor I forget for a few minutes, every now and then, about the war."

"Good God! Don't you ever forget about it except when you're driving a motor?"

"Well, sometimes—not often. But I thought I might try to, for a little while to-night. It's going to be a lovely evening—a sunset and a moonrise both together. Silver and rose. You know."

"Sure, I know. So then——"

"So then I thought we might take a hamper and go off. Just you and I. If you would like to, that is."

Sam disengaged his fingers and rose slowly. As he did so, Russie, roused from his torpor, hammered expectantly with his tail. Sam smiled.

"I wouldn't consider it for a minute," he said whimsically. "Not just you and I. It wouldn't do. The proprieties must be observed. What do you say we take Russie with us?"

Chapter XLII

PANSY PERKINS, who guarded the door to the inner office in the Mayor's suite in the Hinsboro City Hall, had a new bob and a new permanent, to both of which, as well as to the transfiguration of her complexion, she devoted careful and constant attention. But underneath the thatch of frizzled hair and behind the plucked eyebrows and powder-coated face, there was a good deal of solid gray matter; and with the first swift glance with which she looked up from her typewriter at the click of the entrance door, she intuitively knew whether it had been opened by some troublesome intruder who should be told that Mr. Hawks had gone to Belford for an indefinite period, or by some welcome guests for whose benefit drinks and cigars should immediately be forthcoming.

Besides the clerks, the manufacturers, and the politicians who were constantly coming and going, there were two women, both of whom Pansy Perkins liked, who smiled their greetings to her, and then went on, unhesitating and unimpeded, to the inner office. One of these was Mr. Hawks' daughter, Myra Jenkins, who with each passing year resembled her father more and more closely. In spite of an active life and agonizing, though spasmodic, attempts at dieting, she had two double chins, and a figure which even the amplest "stylish stouts" were too small to fit. But she was the soul of good nature, and she never forgot to ask after Pansy's boy friends or to send her an enormous box of chocolates on her birthday; and she chuckled with relish at all Pansy's small witticisms.

The other woman—well, she was a lady—was that wonderful Mrs. Marlowe from Hanstead. It was nearly six years now since Pansy had first admitted her to Mr. Hawks' sanctum, and she had changed a good deal. Of course she had always been a "looker" and always would be. But at first there had been something about her that, honest, made you feel as if you would burst right out crying if you noticed the expression in her eyes. And she was so thin and so pale, that made you feel bad too. Though, mercy, her eyes and hair just burnt you up! But now she had gained a little, just enough to take away that starved look, and there was lots of color in her face, which didn't come out of a box either, Pansy reflected regretfully, adding another touch to her own cheeks. And though her clothes were so plain, they had an air about them—Pansy would have liked to know where they came from, only she didn't quite dare ask. But she didn't believe it was from any store in Hinsboro.

The entrance door clicked open. As if her thoughts had conjured up a reality out of a vision, Pansy saw that Mrs. Marlowe had come into the office. It was early spring, and wherever the visitor had done her shopping, she had evidently just been doing it. Pansy laid down her lipstick, and permitted her gaze to rest upon the attractive figure before her.

"Good morning, Pansy, how is everything?"

"Just fine, Mrs. Marlowe. You're looking swell."

"I treated my son to a trip during his spring vacation, so I thought I better treat myself to a few clothes at the same time. I brought this little compact back for you—I do hope you'll like it.—Is Mr. Hawks here? May I go right in?"

"Oh *thanks*, Mrs. Marlowe, it's simply stunning, and *just* what I need. Yes, he's in. He'll be awfully glad to see you."

Pansy rose and held the door open to Mr. Hawks' retreat. It was not often that she did this for a visitor, but something always impelled her to do it for Mrs. Marlowe. She wished she had not had her mouth so full of gum when the visitor came in. But it couldn't be helped now.

．　．　．　．　．　．

As Pansy had predicted, Mr. Hawks was delighted to see Faith, even though she had come to beg, and also scolded him a little before stating the real object of her visit.

"Uncle Caleb, are the front stairs of this building ever cleaned?"

"Why of course, Faith. They're mopped up regular every day or two."

"I don't mean *mopped*, I mean *scrubbed*. Because they need it. They're simply filthy. Besides, you'd think with all the cuspidors around—do you have to have cuspidors, Uncle Caleb?"

"Why, yes," Caleb Hawks answered uneasily, taking his half-chewed cigar out of his mouth and laying it carefully down on the desk in front of him. "Yes, we do . . . Faith, I do hope you ain't gettin' too poison neat to let folks be comfortable, the way my poor wife was. Did you come here this sweet pretty spring mornin' just to tell me to have the stairs in City Hall scrubbed and to throw away the spittoons?"

"No," Faith answered with a little laugh. "I didn't. I wish it hadn't been for anything more serious than that, Uncle Caleb. I came to tell that poor Feodor Sokovitsky has been put in jail again."

"That scalawag! I guess there ain't nothin' that'll ever learn him to run straight. And you with your 'poor'!"

"Well, he never had much chance in Russia, did he? Or much here, for that matter, until the harm was all done. Anyway, it isn't his wife's fault that he's a scalawag."

Caleb snorted, recaptured his cigar, and begun to regard the carbuncle in his ring.

"The eldest girl's doing awfully well at school," Faith went on. "She's at the head of her class—it would be a crime to take her out and make a little drudge of her. Then there are two little boys who are smart as steel traps too. The younger girls—both perfect darlings—are at the Memorial, but Mrs.

Sokovitsky still nurses the baby—not that I believe she'll be able to keep on. She's—she's hungry, and a woman who's hungry can't nurse a baby long, Uncle Caleb."

"I bet she warn't hungry when you left her stinkin' little house!" he barked. "Beg pardon, Faith, that slipped out 'fore I noticed it. But just the same, I bet there was a sizeable basket of provisions a settin' right on her dirty kitchen table! It beats me why you raise a hullabaloo about a few spittoons in City Hall and then put up with all these filthy foreigners. I wouldn't even put it past Sunnora Perez to skimp on her sweepin' now and then, though I don't deny her house is sweet pretty, 'specially now it has all them elegant fittin's you give her in it.—But what I started to say is, you won't hev anythin' put by for your old age, the way you go on. You give beyond your means all the time."

"Well then, if you're worried about that, you ought to be willing to have the city help Mrs. Sokovitsky out. Because if it doesn't, I'll have to."

"All right, all right!" shouted Caleb, pounding on the table in front of him. "I knew I wuz licked, the minute you come inside that door. Ten dollars a week will be ample, I presume?"

"It won't be so very ample. But it will help. Thanks a lot, Uncle Caleb."

She rose and smiled at him with affection. He looked up at her indignantly.

"You ain't leavin', are you, Faith, now you got what you want offen me?" he asked.

"I didn't want to wear out my welcome, Uncle Caleb, that's all. I know you're awfully busy."

"I ain't so busy as all that. Locate, Faith, can't you? It makes me uneasy having you movin' 'round. I want to talk to you. I've got this and that and the other thing on my mind I want to say."

Faith reseated herself quietly. For a moment Caleb chewed his cigar and studied his carbuncle reflectively. Then, without apparent rhyme or reason, he made an unexpected remark.

"Women is goin' to be votin' this next fall, Faith," he said portentously.

"Why so they are! I'd almost forgotten. Well, I'm glad—for the sake of the suffragists, I mean. They've worked hard for it."

Caleb Hawks snorted again.

"Yes, and most of them think politics and suffrage is the same thing. The pore ignorant fools, I'm kinda sorry for 'em. But the harm's done now an' it ain't no use cryin' over spilt milk. What we got to look out for is to see that some woman who does know somethin' about politics gets shoved forward. If we don't, we're liable to have someone like that crazy sister of Neal Conrad's meddlin' around and stickin' her long snoopin' nose into everythin'. Well, I ben talkin' things over with some of the crowd, and we've kinda decided that it would be a good thing to have a woman appointed on the State Committee. Some's agin it, and I don't deny but what it's kinda a startlin' idea, but—Mercy, Faith, but it's gettin' hot already, ain't it? It ain't often we get weather like this in Hinsboro, not so early in the spring. I look to see it followed by a hard frost."

"Did you and your friends have some woman in mind, Uncle Caleb, for the appointment to the State Committee?"

"Well, yes, Faith, we did, and that's a fact. We thought if you would serve on that Committee——"

He was interrupted by an exclamation of such utter amazement that he himself was startled. He jumped in his seat.

"Land sakes, Faith, you give me a turn! I ain't never heard you let out a noise like that before!"

"But, Uncle Caleb, you gave me a turn! Of course you're joking, but you're too ridiculous! I haven't been interested in suffrage at all! That is, I've been interested in a general way, but I've been so busy with the Nursery, and the school, and the farm, and the family, and everything, I mean, that . . . . Why I don't *know* anything about politics!"

She had risen again, and was staring at him in stupefaction. He shoved her gently back into her seat, and stood over her, pointing at her with his large pudgy forefinger.

"You listen here," he said authoritatively. "You know just about all there is to know, except a few details I can learn you easy. Why you was weaned on campaign whisky, as one may say. I don't mean that just literal, Faith, but it comes pretty near to bein' a fact. Before your mother ever lit out on your poor father, you knew more'n lots o' grown men ever learn. Smart like you are, it hadn't oughta be necessary I should point that out to you, but I guess even the smartest women's got a blind spot—that's why we don't want 'em around any blinder than we have to have them. You think you ain't dabbled any in politics, do you? Why you hadn't ben in this town twenty-four hours before you'd settled a strike! I'd call that a pretty good job as a starter, if anyone should ask me! An' then you took over a sickly institution an' all of a sudden it started growin', and now it's doin' the best kind o' work in this part of the country. An' who was the first to think that it 'ud need to be bigger when men wuz drafted and women had to take their place in factories—who wuz it figgered all that out, and acted according? You tell me that, Faith Marlowe, 'stead of sittin' there wringin' your hands!"

"I'm not wringing my hands," Faith protested, ceasing to lock and unlock her fingers. "I suppose I have some executive ability, but——"

"*Some!*" barked Caleb. "I'll say you got some when you can run a nursery, and teach school, and manage a farm, and take care of a blind man, all to oncet! Not to mention always havin' time to set down and read aloud to a kid for an hour every night. That's what we gotta have in politics, someone with executive ability, not just a parcel of women gettin' up on a platform and screechin' about the worthlessness of men folks. That ain't politics, Faith, that's slander! Not but what you can make speeches all right, when it comes to that, and now and agin it does, tho' speeches in politics is kinda like windowdressin' in a store—just bait, not the real goods. Land! I ain't never heard such a speech in my life as the one you made in the High School after you heard Rudolf had ben killed. First you had them young hoodlums cryin' like babies, and then you had them marchin' like soldiers, and that's the way you got to handle any kind of a crowd when you want to swing it. You got the gift of gab and you got the right kind o' voice, and then you're so downright handsome, Faith, as one might say, that it ain't easy to keep from lookin' at you, not for a man, anyways. And women has got to keep on caterin' to men for a while yet, in spite of them being depraved like the suffragists says."

"Well I never said they were depraved," Faith interrupted. "I *like* men, Uncle Caleb, you know that, but——"

"And I'll say they like you too!" Caleb Hawks interrupted in his turn. You got lowbrows like Sebastian Perez and his crowd, and you got highbrows, like Cal Castle and his crowd, all on the run. And all them young hoodlums you hypnotized at the High School with that first speech of yours is voting now. Besides you got women folks on your side strong as men folks, and that ain't usual or even natural, not when a woman's goodlooking as you are. You couldn't a done it if you hadn't kinda a cute way with you, either, no matter how smart you wuz nor how handsome—it takes a cute way to get ahead in politics, an' you've got it. An' when it comes to bein' a joiner, you've shown a lot o' sense in the organizations you've picked. All that's goin' to come in mighty handy now. The next meetin' of the State Committee is going' to be in Belford on the twentieth, and I want you should——"

"But, Uncle Caleb!" Faith exclaimed aghast. "You talk as if this were all settled. I can't decide to join the State Committee just because you snap your fingers at me! I've got to think it over! I've got to see what Cousin Sarah would——"

"This ain't goin' to be no surprise to your Cousin Sarah, Faith. She's known what I wuz hopin' for an' aimin' for since a long while back—ever since I talked to her that day about gettin' naturalized. I threw out some pretty broad hints about some other things then and she caught 'em all. She ain't a stupid woman, Sarah Atkinson ain't."

"Well then, if you and Cousin Sarah have been plotting behind my back all this time, you might at least give me a chance to talk to Sam."

"Sam!" chuckled Caleb Hawks. "Land sakes, Faith, you don't suppose I ain't talked to Sam too, do you? I don't know that there's a more level-headed man anywhere in the state, or one whose judgment I'd sooner rely on. It's peculiar, seein' that the poor fellow is an artist, that he should have so much sense, but he has, an' that's a fact. He looks to see you go far, Faith, same as I do. But all I want you should do to-day is to say I can bring up your name before the State Committee on the twentieth."

Faith rose. There was, Caleb observed, with anxiety, an air of determination about her that might mean almost anything. She walked over to the door with composure. Then she turned.

"In the course of all this surreptitious discussion," she asked, the corners of her mouth twitching a little, "have you asked Pansy Perkins what she thinks?"

Caleb Hawks' jaw dropped. So did his cigar.

"Of course I ain't!" he said almost irritably. "I wouldn't athought o' askin' Pansy Perkins any more'n I'd thought o 'askin' one of Myra's young 'uns."

"Well, I'm going to ask her. And if she thinks it's a good idea I'll do it. There are lots more women in this state like Pansy Perkins than like Cousin Sarah. You ought to have thought of that yourself, Uncle Caleb."

Faith opened the door. Pansy Perkins sat with one hand fluffing up her back hair, and the other busily etching a carmine bow over her pink lips. She started guiltily to her feet.

"Don't get up, Pansy," Faith said pleasantly. "I don't want to interrupt your work, not really. I just want to ask your advice. Mr. Hawks thinks there ought to be a woman on the State Committee, now that women are going to vote, and he believes I could fill the position. What do you think?"

"What do I think?" gasped Pansy. *"Oh lady!"*

She had swallowed her gum. But her meaning was unmistakable.

Chapter XLIII

AFTER Neal Conrad of Hinsboro, who had served with great distinction in the United States Senate for several years, was nominated President of the United States, there was hardly one delegate in a hundred, who did not seize his grip and rush for the first train home. The national convention had been deadlocked for nearly four weeks, and by the time a compromise candidate had been finally chosen and put over, the hoarse and frenzied gathering had reached such a high pitch of nervous fatigue that even the thought of further immediate effort was abhorrent. Its members dispersed, in various stages of collapse, to all parts of the country, to sleep off their exhaustion and recover their enthusiasm, before mapping out the most elementary of campaign plans.

There were, of course, a few exceptions to this general rule, and Caleb Hawks was one of the exceptions. Like Carolus Cavendish Castle, who was almost certain to be an outstanding figure in the next cabinet—the press of the country was practically unanimous in this opinion—he had remained on the scene to confer with the Presidential nominee on various pressing questions. Caleb Hawks was now National Committeeman for his state and Faith Marlowe was National Committeewoman. As Town Representative from Hamstead to the State Legislature, she was doing extremely well, and Caleb had every reason to be satisfied with her progress; but as National Committeewoman, a position to which she had risen without much effort, she was doing still better. Caleb found her coöperation invaluable. There wasn't another National committeeman in the country, he was fond of saying, who could count on such certain, steady and capable help from the Committeewoman working with him. Faith was a Marlowe all right, and she was a marvel too. The phrase tickled him. He used it constantly.

The conference which was to take place in Neal Conrad's suite, was set for six o'clock, and Faith was to go to it with Caleb. But he wanted to have a word or two with her alone first, so he called her up to ask when it would be convenient for her to see him. Pansy Perkins, who answered the telephone, said that Mrs. Marlowe was asleep, and that nothing would induce her, Pansy, to wake the poor tired lady—it was a shame the way she had been overworked all through the convention! But Pansy thought if Mr. Hawks would come around about five-thirty, Mrs. Marlowe would be getting up by that time anyway for the Conrad conference, so probably——

Mr. Hawks smiled as he hung up the receiver. He was constantly accusing Faith of having stolen Pansy from him, and insisting that the City Hall had never been the same since she left him. But actually it was he who had suggested that she should serve as Faith's secretary when it became inescapably obvious that Faith would be obliged to have one. He knew that Pansy would eat up work almost as comprehensively as Faith herself, and that her loyalty and devotion would be unswerving and incorruptible. Not that he distrusted secretaries in general; but when so much was at stake, it was impossible to be too careful.

Pansy opened the door for him when he presented himself at Faith's suite two hours later. He could not have told what had caused the subtle change in Pansy's appearance. He did not know, for instance, that she did not chew gum any longer, or that her fresh pleasant face was unpainted, or that her hair was not frizzed and fluffed, but parted softly away from her pretty forehead and gathered into a smooth knot at the nape of her neck. But he knew she looked different—different and better; and he knew that the change and improvement were both due to Faith.

Faith herself, seated in front of a big desk, signing letters, looked up with a quick smile as Caleb Hawks entered the room. The desk was piled high with papers and correspondence of all sorts; but these were arranged in such neat stacks that there was no sign of confusion or clutter. The blotting pad was spotless, the silver desk set was polished, and a slender cyrstal vase containing three exquisite roses stood near the inkwell.

"And if you will acknowledge these telegrams as I have just indicated on the margins," Faith said, affixing her signature to the last letter which Pansy laid down before her, "and telephone Mrs. James that I shall probably be late for the Committeewomen's dinner because of the Conrad conference, that will be all, Pansy, for the moment. . . . Yes, Uncle Caleb? What is it?"

She turned toward him briskly, the personification of

competence. Never, he considered, had she looked cooler or prettier than she did on this sweltering night. And how she had kept her youth! She was nearly thirty-five now, if he wasn't mistaken, and there wasn't a line in her face or a gray hair in her head. Again, if he had been capable of analysis, he would have realized that a little of the softness, a little of the bloom, of her beauty, had gone. She had presence now, rather than gentleness; but in spite of all her crispness, she still emanated charm.

"I'm very pleased about the Vice-President, aren't you?" she went on, still crisply, as he did not answer immediately. "Of course it was essential that he should come from the South this time, and Harvey Hurlbut has made a splendid record as Governor, besides fulfilling all the geographical requisites. I was terrified for fear the convention would simply dissolve without nominating any Vice-President at all, let alone a suitable one, considering the state it was in after Neal was finally put over——"

"Neal's goin' to tell us, when we get to the conference, whether he's goin' to resign from the Senate or not," cut in Mr. Hawks, fumbling for a cigar.

"Yes?—Unless that's very important, Pansy, take the message please!—Sorry, Uncle Caleb, but this telephone is simply inescapable.—Well, there's precedent for whichever course he prefers. If he shouldn't be elected, it would be too bad if——"

"He's goin' to be elected," Caleb shouted. "And he's goin' to resign from the Senate. To-night. Me and Cal and Warren have talked it all over, and it's as good as done already. He can't afford not to. He's got to have your support, Faith, and——"

"But of course he'll have my support, Uncle Caleb!"

"You bet your bottom dollar he will!" bellowed Caleb Hawks. " 'Cause he's goin' to have you on the ticket with him, see? You make that clear to him from the minute you set foot in that parlor of his. I like Neal Conrad and always have, though I'm inclined to think in that family the gray mare's the better horse of the two. But he's a mite too cautious when it comes to his own interests, and if he thinks he can run with the hare and hunt with the hounds, he's mistaken. We're goin' to have a President *and* a Cabinet Officer *and* the first woman Senator from our state this year, and the rest of the country can like it or lump it. The mornin' papers is goin' to carry headlines a mile high—'CONRAD RESIGNS FROM SENATE, FAITH MARLOWE TO RUN FOR HIS SEAT.' There won't be a bigger story break, not in the whole campaign! This is the day I've

340

waited for and schemed for and, God damn it all—beg pardon, Faith, that slipped out before I thought—prayed for too! You're goin' to take your father's place in the Senate the same day Neal Conrad's inaugurated President, or there won't be no inauguration, so help me God!"

He brought his fist down on her desk with a thundering crash. The neat piles of papers flew off, scattering in every direction, and Pansy, getting down on her knees, began to gather them up again. Caleb saw that her hands were trembling. But this was no moment to waste on Pansy. He faced Faith compellingly.

"Faith," he said almost beseechingly now, "you know I can't never hold no high office myself, and I know it too! Lord, *don't* I know it! I know I ain't never gone so far from the pore little mongrel cur I used to be, that I can't rekkernize him in me still, good an' plenty. An' I never *will* go so far I can't. But *you* will, with me behind you. I can put you in the seats of the mighty anyway. You're more to me than anyone else in the world, Faith, more'n my daughter even—it's the same as if you wuz myself, the way I'd a been, if I'd had a chance.—You ain't goin' to let me down, are you, Faith?"

"No!" she cried impetuously. "No, Uncle Caleb—never in the world!"

The desk was no longer between them. She had risen and going swiftly toward him, had laid her hands on his shoulders. He could see the tears in her eyes, and knew that there were tears in his own. But after her first reassuring cry, she answered him calmly and steadily. She even managed to smile a little.

"You didn't take me quite so much by surprise this time as you did four years ago," she said. "Really, I'm not half so much startled as the thought of being the first woman to run for the Senate as I was at the thought of serving on the State Committee—that's due to your training, Uncle Caleb! Of course I realized you were fitting me for something—but I didn't think of the Senate until Neal was nominated for the Presidency. Then I began to wonder—and still not believe it could be true. . . . 'Something no woman ever was before!'—So that was what the gypsy meant!"

"What's that you're saying', Faith?"

He had worked himself up to such a supreme pitch of excitement and anxiety that he felt curiously let down. He had expected that Faith would be stupefied, and that she would offer objections against which he would have to struggle. Now that he found he had no fight on his hands, he was naturally conscious of embarrassment, as a young lover who

341

has feared to disclose his feelings to his sweetheart might have been if she had suddenly told him she would be glad to marry him. He looked at Faith almost shamefacedly, while he waited for her to explain her cryptic remark.

"Don't you remember, Uncle Caleb, the day we went to the Sacro Monte in Granada? And the pretty gypsy, Chiquita, who told fortunes said,——"

Caleb slapped her heartily on the shoulder. "That's so!" he exclaimed. "Lord Almighty, I hadn't thought of it for years! We went up that hill where the prickly pears was with that good-lookin' brother of the Bishop's, what wuz his name now——"

"It was Sebastian de Cerreno," Faith answered slowly.

"So it was, and that's a fact. I recall him well, now you speak of him. I took to him from the first, and it's real peculiar, but I remember thinkin' there wuz a look about him reminded me of Sebastian Perez.—Say, that's a break for you, Perez just bein' elected president of the Marblecutters' Union. You'll have the furrin vote of the state delivered to you on a silver platter, Faith."

"Yes, I suppose I will," she said, still very slowly. "But it was bought at a great price." She was not looking at him any more, and there was something in her voice vaguely disturbing to Caleb. He clapped her on the shoulder again.

"It warn't bought at all," he said indignantly—"you ain't never resorted to graft, an' you know it. But land sakes, we ain't got time to talk that over this afternoon," he said.

"You better get your bunnit, Faith. Now don't you forget; you put your cards on the table and make Neal Conrad do the same. When he sees he's pressed, he'll give in. Warren's back of you, and Castle's back of you, and I'm back of you. Brown may or may not help—him and Conrad ain't pulled any too well together in the Senate—it's just possible he'll throw his strength to you, and then again he may not. Fletcher, who ran against Conrad in the last campaign, will probably be your opponent on the other ticket. He's a mean skunk, he don't fight fair, I wouldn't put anythin' past 'im. I wish you didn't have the mud he'll sling to face, but it can't be helped. Now, you do like I told you, Faith, and——"

Pansy Perkins emerged from Faith's bedroom, carrying a wide sheer hat, some long white gloves, and a small handbag, all of which she handed to Faith.

"It's two minutes of six," she said, her voice as well as her hands trembling a little now. "I know you don't want to be late to the Conrad conference—Senator Marlowe."

Ex-Governor Warren had come to the convention in his private car, bringing a party of friends with him; and though the personnel of this group was the same going home as it had been going away, it was hard to realize this: Neal Conrad was no longer the Junior Senator from a small state; he was a Presidential nominee. Carolus Cavendish Castle was no longer a submerged private citizen; he was a presumptive Cabinet Officer. And Faith Marlowe was no longer one of forty-eight National Committeewomen; she was the first woman candidate for the Senate.

The car was decorated with streamers, flags, and banners; enormous bouquets of flowers, boxes of candy, and baskets of fruit, filled every rack and corner, and telegrams were constantly being delivered in stacks inches thick. A press delegation traveled in the next Pullman; "prominent citizens" from Belford and Hinsoboro and outstanding politicians from all over the country augmented the original number of Governor Warren's original guests. Cheering and curious crowds thronged every station at which the train stopped, brass bands played, committees of welcome orated, and journalists and photographers darted about. Neal and Ann Conrad appeared on the back platform together, smiling and bowing, and the mob broke into yells. Faith consented to say, "just a few words," and the yells redoubled.

By the time Hinsboro had finally been reached, everyone was almost frantic with fatigue. But at Hinsboro was still to be faced the largest crowd of all, the noisiest band of all, the most enthusiastic delegation of welcome. The Conrads made their way to their house through streets so jammed that the motor in which Caleb and Faith rode with them could hardly wedge its way along; and when they arrived at their destination in the pouring rain, they found small boys swarming over the roof, a packed piazza, and a force of police belligerently endeavoring to maintain some show of order.

It was two o'clock in the morning when Faith resolutely struggled into the coat closet, drawing Hansel after her, and locked the door. He had taken his entrance examinations for Harvard that year, and when these were over, he had joined her at the national convention; but he had wearied of the endless days of balloting and had gone back to his books and music in Hamstead; and he had not left these again until he motored over to Hinsboro that night to meet her. He had shot up into a slim graceful boy, with a sensitive serious face, taller and paler than his mother, and with far less animation and endurance. She saw that there were dark circles under his eyes, and realized that he was wearied to the point of exhaustion.

"You're tired, aren't you, darling?" she said sympathetically, pressing his hand. "I am too—I feel as if I had had as much of this as I can stand for to-night. I wondered if we couldn't possibly slip out of the back door together without being noticed. I thought I'd steal a cap and raincoat from here for disguise, and keep my head down and run. Do you think we could manage it? How far away is the car?"

"Just in the next block. We could try it anyway. But won't Uncle Caleb be worried if you disappear like that?"

Hansel's intuitive sensitiveness to the feelings of others had become more and more intensified as he grew older. Faith sometimes found it necessary to brush this aside.

"He'll guess what's happened, and we'll telephone as soon as we get home. I'm desperate, Hansel—you don't know what it's been like these last few days."

"No, I suppose I don't, mother. Well, are you ready?"

Their dash for freedom was not unimpeded, but it was finally successful; and as the motor swung away from the crowds and shot out toward the country, Faith felt her taut nerves and muscles gradually relaxing. She slipped down comfortably in the seat, and laid her head against Hansel's shoulder.

"You haven't congratulated me yet, darling," she reminded him, looking up at him lovingly.

"I'm sorry. There hasn't been much time though, has there? Of course I do congratulate you, mother."

"You're pleased, aren't you, Hansel?"

"I'm very proud. And I'm glad for Uncle Caleb's sake—this means everything in the world to him. But I don't think I'm exactly pleased myself."

"Why Hansel!" she exclaimed, sitting upright again in her amazement. "I thought you'd be delighted! Why aren't you pleased?"

"Well, you know you promised to go to Germany with me this summer, and I've been looking forward to it a good deal. You see every spring you've said, *this* year you thought we could go, and then when summer came you've always been too busy. I'd sort of like to see my grandmother and grandfather von Hohenlohe; you know I haven't since I was seven years old. I've been thinking about them a lot lately. I'd like to see Schönplatz and Berlin and Bonn, and I'd like to go to the musical festivals at Munich, and Nuremburg and Bayreuth."

"But darling," interrupted Faith eagerly, "I couldn't take you to Germany while the war was going on, or until feeling had died down afterwards! And since then I *have* been too busy! But you can do all that some other summer—next summer! I promise! This summer I want you to give to me. I've got a wonderful plan I'm counting on you to help me with. I'm going to talk to Mr. Emery the first thing in the morning, and see if he can't find or build me a sort of glorified gypsy wagon to do my campaigning in. It would be almost like a little house on wheels. I thought you and I would go about in it together, and I'd make speeches from the back platform wherever we stopped, and you would play the piano for me, and we would take turns driving. Don't you think it would be fun, Hansel?"

"Yes, I guess so."

"Why Hansel, I thought you'd jump at the idea! I know you'll like it after we get started with it! And you'll be simply invaluable to me. There's nothing on earth the public likes to have held up to it more than family devotion. We'll have our pictures taken together, and I'll talk about the stories we've always read together, and—don't you see, Hansel?"

"Yes, mother, I see. All right. Of course I want to help you all I can." There was a subdued note of wistfulness in his voice that Faith could not help but notice. "You haven't asked whether I've heard from Harvard about my entrance examinations," he added hesitatingly. "I did yesterday. I got honors in everything. And Junior Conrad and I have decided to room together."

"Splendid!" Faith exclaimed. But she said it abstractedly, and she went on, "I suppose that means I'll have to part with you the end of September, and I hate to, because I really need you six weeks longer. Of course, Pansy can go with me in the caravan after you leave for college, but it won't be half so effective."

"No, I suppose not," Hansel answered. And his voice was so very tired that Faith did not try to talk to him any more.

The car purred in and out of the peacefully sleeping village of Hamstead, swung up the river road, and passed the Big House, shrouded in darkness. As Marlowe Manor came into view, Faith saw that it was lighted from garret to cellar.

"Why Hansel!" she said again. "What do you think has happened? It's after three o'clock! You don't suppose that Cousin Sarah——"

"Oh, she's all right!" Hansel said reassuringly. "I'd have told you if she hadn't been. But Sam said, right along, that you'd come home to-night. I guess he's having an illumination in your honor. I guess he's waiting up for you."

Chapter XLIV

NEVER, in the annals of American politics, had any candidate waged a more effective campaign than Faith Marlowe did in running for the United States Senate.

In the first place, Marlowe Manor, from which her grandfather and her father had both stepped into public life, was as nearly perfect a stage setting as any that could have been devised. The rotogravure sections of the Sunday papers throughout the country were adorned with pictures of Faith standing under the portrait of the Cabinet Officer which hung above her library mantel, and holding a miniature of the Senator. They were also adorned with Faith (a) working in her garden, (b) walking in her garden, (c) entertaining visiting celebrities in her garden. She was shown standing beside a prize bull, and scattering poultry feed to prize chickens. She was shown, as she had predicted, with her arm through Hansel's, and her face turned adoringly toward his. Naturally, she was also shown at her desk in the Hinsboro High School, among her antiques in the Marlowe Loan Collection, surrounded by the small dark children of the Myra Higgs Hawks Memorial Nursery, and in deep conference with Caleb Hawks and Neal Conrad. But it was the photographs taken in Hamstead that had the widest appeal. On the strength of one that was especially attractive and successful, a large motion picture concern wired offering her a contract, in case she were defeated for the Senate.

Journalistically, as well as pictorially, her background was ideal. The interviews she gave out were always first-page news; and she wrote an article herself about her activities in Hamstead and Hinsboro for a woman's magazine with a circulation of over two million. Reprints of it, in pamphlet form, were distributed from one end of the state to the other. Incidentally, the check she received as an "honorarium" for this article was almost large enough to pay for her caravan, which Will Emery let her have at cost. And of course the caravan capped the dramatic climax for which Faith was striving. Her nomination was opposed by an antagonist representing the more conservative elements of the party—a hotelkeeper from the western part of the state; but it was evident, almost from the beginning, that he did not have a "tinker's chance" against her. The voting public was enthralled by the novel and arresting spectacle of a candidate who traversed the countryside in a huge apple-green motor vehicle with white lace curtains looped back from tiny spotless windows, and a little open platform at the back. If she traveled alone in that, that would have been just a shade too daring—after all, she was a lovely-looking woman, even if she was not quite so young as she appeared. But she always had that fine boy of hers with her, driving the caravan for her, playing the piano at her out-of-door meetings, distributing campaign literature for her, mingling in the crowds with her. Yes, decidedly, Hansel added immeasurably to Faith's inescapable allure.

Hamstead, as soon as it had recovered from the staggering shock of her candidacy, had rallied around her excitedly. Marlowe Manor, in spite of its elasticity, could not begin to hold all the visiting celebrities who had to be entertained; but Aunt Emmeline, the Mannings, the Grays and the Nobles, all opened their doors hospitably. Indeed, Jacqueline went so far as to forestall many emergencies, by telling Faith, at the beginning of the summer, that she would undertake to look after representatives of the press at the Big House. Faith could dismiss every concern for their comfort from her mind, once and for all.

David, seconding his wife's invitation, turned the scrutinizing gaze which Faith had almost forgotten upon the Senatorial candidate. He had been very little in Hamstead in the course of the last eight years. During the war he had invented a new anæsthetic, which had brought him such international acclaim that he had found it impossible to maintain any longer the fiction—already shaken by his brain-surgery—that he was "just a family doctor." This summer he was taking a long and much-needed vacation; and as he asked Faith if he might walk home with her from the Big House, where she had been dining, he realized that he had not had a talk alone with her since he had brought her the news of the birth of Sebastian's eldest son. His mind reverted to the conversation as he strolled along beside her in the moonlight.

"You did find your solution, didn't you, Faith?" he asked admiringly. "In fact, almost more solutions than you had problems! There was just one problem, really—how to keep yourself from thinking too much about a man with whom you were in love and whom you couldn't marry. And how magnificently you've answered it! You're still 'the gallant lady,' Faith."

"Thank you," she said so quietly that he found her reticence provocative.

"So all your solutions have been the compensations 'that do not quite compensate, have they?" he asked searchingly.

"Yes."

"You haven't forgotten—after all these years?"

"No. You told me I never would."

"I remember. But I hoped I might be mistaken."

"You weren't," she said, still more quietly than she had spoken before.

"Have you ever heard from him?"

"Never directly. I've played fair, David. It was a clean break. But I have had strange reminders of him—even here —that have—hurt a good deal. I can't talk about those even to you. And his wife wrote me when his little girl was born, and has occasionally since then. Probably you know that baby was named for me."

"Yes. I've seen her. She's a beautiful child. Jacqueline and I spent a month this last spring with the Cerrenos at the Castello Viejo. They're very happy. They have two younger boys now too, you know."

"Yes, I know. Sebastian has his 'heritage' trebly assured. It ought to be safe. I hope it is—I'm not the only woman who's crucified herself to make it so——"

"Faith," David said suddenly, "I hate to hear you talk this way—to know you feel this way. It couldn't have been different, could it? You wouldn't want it to be different if you reasoned it out. And don't forget that no woman ever rose to fame without tragedy for her stepping-stone."

"Exactly," Faith answered gravely.

But afterwards, she reflected that the next time she had a chance to talk confidentially to David, she would confess to him that though she had never forgotten Sebastian and never would, the thought of him did not dominate her any longer. She had gone through a burning fiery furnace to rescue Señora Perez from torment, but after she had recovered from the shock of this ordeal she discovered that, miraculously, her own anguish had become less unbearable. She would admit, with less bitterness than she had previously revealed, that she realized that the tragedy which had transfigured her life had also enabled her to fulfill her destiny, as David had foretold. Even if her compensations for the loss of Sebastian, "did not quite compensate," they crowded her horizon and proved her powers and stimulated her spirit. And it was exactly because this was true that she did not have another opportunity for an intimate conversation with him before she had emerged triumphantly from the test of the primaries, and was intensively preparing to face the far harder trial of the election. Fletcher, the millionaire owner of the largest newspaper in the state, who had given Neal Conrad the fight of his life when Neal had run for the Senate himself, was her opponent now; and in him she had a far more formidable antagonist than in the conservative hotelkeeper who had been crushed—figuratively speaking—underneath the wheels of her apple-green caravan. The caravan itself would lose some of its effectiveness, now that Hansel was about to start for college; and her best of the glorious autumn weather, which had made her modern gypsying so delightful, would soon be over. She must count up her other assets without losing sight of any of them, and make the most of every one; and at the same time she must count up her liabilities.

She considered all of these meticulously. She was allied with the Presidential candidate, and since many citizens voted the straight ticket—to save trouble, if for no more intelligent reason,—she might be swept in on that, especially as the state was thrilled at the thought of supplying the nation with a Chief Executive for the first time. But she could not reckon without the possibility that the "Conrad crowd might cut her"—it had more than once hinted to her that she was too spectacular, that she stole Neal's curtain calls. The state normally went for the party which she aspired to represent, and that was a great advantage. But it was possible that the conservative wing, which had supported the hotelkeeper in the primaries, might swing to Fletcher. He had made enemies among the foreign population by indiscreet and disparaging references to "Canucks," "Wops," and "Dagos" in the columns of his paper before he had aspired to public life, and these had not been forgotten. Moreover, the intolerance which was his substitute for religion had aligned the Catholic vote against him. But on the other hand, the bulk of the Anglo-Saxons shared his horror of the Papacy, and suspected, though could not prove, that Faith had leanings toward it. This disadvantage was partially offset by her strength with the agricultural element, and her inherited prestige—"Put another Marlowe in the Senate!"—was a powerful plea. But she was just beginning to gauge the ugliness and might of bigotry, and to recognize that it could not be underestimated. The small weekly newspapers were nearly all behind her. But their joint circulation was not much greater than that of Fletcher's *Clarion-Herald,* and publicity released once in seven days could hardly compete with daily propaganda. She could count on generous financial support from Caleb Hawks, from the Castles, and from the Nobles.

But with the principal of the money she had inherited from her father tightly tied up, and the necessity of keeping Hansel's legacy intact, she had a comparatively modest sum of her own at her disposal; and Fletcher was the richest man in the state.

If Sam would have voluntarily come forward with a substantial sum, it would have helped her enormously. But Sam had made no such offer. Indeed, for the first time in his life, he had disappointed her. Aside from welcoming her home when she returned to Hamstead when she announced her candidacy, he had not made a single spontaneous gesture. He listened attentively enough when she talked to him; but she had no more leisure nowadays to talk to Sam than she had to talk to David. She was touring the state in her caravan the greater part of every week. And when she was at home, she dictated to Pansy half the night in order to keep abreast of the mountains of correspondence to which she could give no attention when she was traveling, or as long as the ceaseless stream of guests and reporters sat at her table and overflowed her house.

The day after Hansel's departure for Harvard, a sense of loneliness and loss which she could not shake off seemed to overwhelm her; and though she stuck resolutely to her dictation until nearly midnight, she at last put her hand to her throbbing forehead and pushed back her chair.

"It's no use, Pansy," she said desparingly, "my brain just doesn't seem to function any longer. We'll have to give it up."

"Just write your autograph on these little cards that are to be inclosed with handkerchiefs and dolls for church fairs," Pansy said soothingly. "There are only fifty of them, and you can do it almost automatically. And the galley for your *Delineator* article has to go off the first mail to-morrow. I'll proof-read it for you if you say so, but you told me there were one or two little changes you wanted to make yourself."

The fine type of her printed views on "Careers and Homemaking—Which or Both?" seemed to zig-zag back and forth before Faith's tired eyes, the long sheets of galley kept slipping from her weary fingers. But she persevered, and finally, with a few scribbled notes on the margins, she handed them wearily back to Pansy.

"Well, that's done. Now I'm going——"

"You promised to send a night letter to the Forestville Woman's Club saying definitely whether you would make that speech on 'Consecrated Motherhood and its Relation to Politics' on October fourteenth."

"Well, did you check up on that with Mr. Hawks? Did he think the group was large and influential enough to be worth the effort?"

"He said yes, it was. And Mrs. Trent, the President, hopes you'll come to Forestville in the caravan, because the last time you were there a good many of the club women didn't see it, and they'd like to look it over."

"All right. Send the night letter."

"And Mr. Conrad telephoned late this afternoon to say he feels you must prepare a statement for immediate release about your stand on prohibition. He says there's a feeling in some quarters that you're pussyfooting. He thinks, in a dry state like this——"

"A dry state like this! Now Pansy!"

"Well, you know it is dry, politically, except for the foreign element. He knows you're trying to keep that placated, but still——"

"Keep that placated! I'm trying not to be a self-confessed hypocrite."

"Just as you say of course, Mrs. Marlowe. I can tell Miss Letts, Mr. Conrad's secretary, the first thing in the morning, and say you feel you can't possibly——"

"No—no—I mustn't let you do that. It would be Senatorial suicide for me—it might even jeopardize the ticket in this state. Telephone Miss Letts, and say I'll have a statement ready for release this Saturday, and that I promise it will be satisfactory.—Now that is all, isn't it?"

"I think these bills must be okayed, Mrs. Marlowe, so that I can get the checks out."

"How much can we draw on from the national fund?"

"Well, not *any* more, Mr. Castle said, before the first of the month."

Faith gave a nervous little laugh. "Pansy, that settles it! You'll have to let me go and talk to Mr. Dudley. You know as well as I do that I've just sixty-five dollars and thirty cents left in my personal account to last until the end of the month!"

She rose slowly, stretching her arms above her head with a gesture of complete weariness. Pansy thought, as she watched her go out of the room, that she had never seen her act so tired or so depressed. She hoped that Mr. Dudley, if he were still awake, would be able to cheer her up.

Mr. Dudley had retired for the night, he called to Faith through his door, in response to her knock. But if it were really imperative that she should invade his chaste seclusion, she might come in. She managed to smile a little at his never-failing whimsicality, and as he switched on the light at his elbow, she smiled again. Lying in his Portuguese bed under the somber Ribera which hung above it, his long fingers resting on Russie's sleek head, his dull-blue sleeping jacket open at the throat, there was a certain medieval splendor about his figure which never failed to give her pleasure. The extreme thinness, bordering on emaciation, which he had never lost since his long period of hospitalization, revealed the beautiful bones of his face which youthful flesh had obscured, and gave him an aspect of asceticism; his prematurely white hair crowned his head with a dignity which his shock of sandy locks had never possessed. He might have been the Abbot of some princely order, relaxing after the cares and austerities of the day.

"You are growing handsomer every minute, Sam, do you know it?" Faith asked with admiring tenderness, as she sat down on the edge of his bed.

"Sure I know it," he retorted instantly. "I wouldn't have a lovely lady stealing into my room at midnight if I wasn't, would I?—Or is it just that you have given in at last about that statement Conrad has been hounding you for, and you instinctively turn to the place where the best drinks in the house are kept to buck you up again?—That's sherry in the decanter, Faith, and the cheese sandwiches are good."

"I did give in," she said a little ruefully, as she poured the rich amber liquid into a wine glass and picked up a delicately cut square of bread. "What else could I do?—And I do feel the need of getting bucked up.—But what I really came for was to ask if you could let me have some money?"

She saw a swift flickering change in Sam's expression, almost like that which might have passed over the face of a hopeful boy who had suffered a sharp disappointment. But he answered instantly.

"Why yes, of course. How much?"

"I need five hundred dollars, Sam, to pay bills that must be met at once. And next month I may need more.

"All right. Shall we say two thousand? I'd suggest three, but I don't like to use principal, considering that I'll never earn anything more. And I need a little extra cash myself just now. Cousin Sarah and I have decided to take a short trip to Europe."

"A short trip to Europe!" echoed Faith in stupefaction.

"Sure. On a boat, you know. It's being done all the time."

"But you're not doing it all the time!" Faith protested vehemently. "You've never even suggested such a thing before. And now—in the middle of a campaign———"

"I thought perhaps you'd suggest it, if I waited long enough. But you didn't, and when this senatorial racket

352

came along, I knew you never would. But there isn't any reason why I should stay here. You don't need me—and you don't need Cousin Sarah as much as I do. She agrees with me about that. So she and Russie and I are off on the *France* next week. Russie is going to be a sea-dog, aren't you, Russie? Well, don't upset the lamp in your excitement —I'll promise there won't be any hitch. I'm sorry Hansel couldn't go with us, but of course you *did* need him as long as you could have him, and now college has opened so—"

"Sam, you're hurting my feelings terribly! How can you say I don't need you? I do need you! I can't bear to have you go off and leave me! Just because I haven't time, in this nightmare of a campaign, to sit around for hours talking with you. . . . Why, I don't have time to talk to *anyone*. I've tried for weeks to have a quiet talk with David——"

She attempted, unsuccessfully, to control the trembling in her voice. But Sam seemed unaware that it was trembling.

"Well, by the time 'this nightmare of a campaign' is over, I'll be back," he said unfeelingly. "I agree with you. It is a nightmare. But I don't see why I should keep on having bad dreams for ever just because you—I won't have 'em in Paris. It's gorgeous there at this time of year!—Hold on, Faith, don't go off the handle like that! Good God, you are all shot to pieces!"

He thrust his hand out suddenly, intending to force her to sit down. But she eluded him, and rushed out of the attic, overwhelmed with anger and resentment now as well as fatigue. She did not seek him out again, and she did not discuss the impending departure even with Sarah Atkinson, whom she treated with coolness. When the travelers left, the following week, she laid her cheek briefly against Sarah's, but she did not kiss Sam good-bye. She was stung to the quick by his desertion.

Chapter XLV

FAITH's thoughts were diverted from Sam's departure—on which she had dwelt far more intensively than she could afford, considering the number of other pressing matters demanding her attention—by the receipt of a letter which came in soon after he left, and which she perused with startled pleasure. It was years since she had seen the exquisite, yet virile, handwriting which covered the pages; but she knew instantly, without turning to the stately signature, who had written them.

"My dear Faith——" she read delightedly——

"Since the Eucharistic Congress, to which, as perhaps you know, I was a delegate, I have been making a tour of the old Spanish missions in the United States, accompanied by Father Constantino. (He is now a very old man, but still vigorous, and sends his best regards to you.) We are returning to Spain via Cuba on the *Manuel Calvo* in about a fortnight, but you have been much in my thoughts lately, and I am longing to see you. Would it be convenient and agreeable for you to receive me as a visitor, in the old homestead which you described so vividly to me the first time I ever met you? Or, if there is not room for Father Constantino and me there—I remember you told me the beloved house was small—perhaps we could stay with the Nobles, who are, I understand, neighbors of yours, and to whom my family is now bound with ties of everlasting gratitude. I am writing to them by this same mail. Let me know your pleasure concerning these tentative suggestions, and I will endeavor to conform my plans with yours. I know that in your brilliant new undertaking, which I am following through the press with pride and prayer, your days must be sadly overcrowded already. But I should like to give you my personal blessing once more, and it is now so long since you have come to Spain that I have begun to fear that you will never do so again. Therefore, my dear child, I feel that I must come to you.

"Remember me with affection to Doña Sarah and too the inspired artist, and believe me, *in corde Jesu,* ever faithfully and devotedly your kinsman, Gabriel de Cerreno, Cardinal Archbishop of Granada."

"Pansy!" Faith exclaimed, looking up with an expression of unalloyed pleasure, "who do you think is coming to see us? The Cardinal Archbishop of Granada! He is the most wonderful person in all the world! Get Mrs. Noble on the telephone right away, please! Do you think the Cardinal would rather stay here or at the Big House? Now that Mr. Dudley has gone away, just at the wrong moment, I have no host here, and I rather think that when a Cardinal is your guest, it is more suitable—Oh, Jacqueline! You *did?* Well, what do you think? Yes, I agree with you, but of course you will all come here to dinner with me. We'll both wire, shall we?"

For the next two days she was entirely preoccupied with arrangements for the reception and entertainment of Gabriel. She cancelled a speaking engagement in the western part of the state—the stronghold of the conservative wing of the party—giving illness as her excuse, though she was well aware that a political candidate, like an actor, should never indulge in the luxury of ill health even when this is real. She turned a deaf ear to Pansy's signaled suggestion that she should invite a prominent merchant and his wife who had come up from Belford to remain for luncheon; she even cut short a long distance call from Ex-Governor Warren. And when Caleb Hawks came bursting into her library, on his way back from the important meeting she had failed to address, her guilty conscience smote her as she met his indignant gaze. She was, however, totally unprepared for the accusation he hurled at her.

"Sick, are you?" he thundered in a voice she had never heard him use before. "You know as well as I do, Faith Marlowe, that even if youdda had bubonic plague, you'd otta had made that speech! What do you want to do, let Shaw and all his stinking outfit in for another four years? Or do you want the Pope of Rome moving into the White House instead of Neal Conrad? Or have you just suddenly gone crazy? God damn it all, I want you should tell me?"

He had not even remembered to say, "Beg pardon, that slipped out before I noticed." Faith, angry in her turn, and as puzzled as she was angry, retorted with an indignation that matched his own.

"If I wasn't sick before, I shall be, if you shout at me like that! And I have no idea what else you were talking about!"

"Well, it's true, ain't it, that you got a coupla Catholic priests coming here to stay? Have you seen the extra the *Clarion-Herald* got out at one P.M.? Just take a look at that, and tell me whether you ain't got no idea what I'm talking about!"

He flung the cheap flimsy sheet down in front of her. Heavy black headlines, four inches high swept ominously across it. Beneath them were staggering captions and under all two columns in large print:

"FAITH MARLOWE CONVERT TO ROME

"POPE'S EMISSARY HASTENING IN STATE TO HAMSTEAD

"SPANISH CARDINAL DUE TUESDAY

"DOOM OF WOMAN CANDIDATE'S SENATORIAL HOPES SEEN IN RASH MOVE

355

"It was learned by reliable authority late this morning that Faith Marlow's failure to keep her speaking engagement yesterday was not due, as recorded, to sudden indisposition, but to the formalities attendant upon the impending abandonment of the noble religion of her forefathers. Gabriel de Cerreno, Cardinal Archbishop of Granada, Spain, the cruel land of the Inquisition, is hastening from San Antonio to Hamstead on a specially chartered train. It is well known that this bigoted despot comes from the Vatican under sealed orders. Though it has been given out that his visit is purely personal in character, this attempt to throw dust in the eyes of a watchful public has been thwarted, and a confession has been wrung from Faith Marlowe which will be given to the press in the morning. A further attempt at duplicity was made by using Mrs. David Noble, the wife of a well known surgeon, as a blind in the plot of this Scarlet Woman. Mrs. Noble is to be commiserated upon having permitted herself to be used as a tool, and it is to be hoped that she herself will see her way clear to renouncing a dogma to which she owes only nominal allegiance. Astute politicians have no difficulty in discerning in this rash move the doom of—"

Faith suddenly crumpled the paper between her hands and flung it into the fire. Then she confronted Caleb with blazing eyes.

"You know as well as I do that this silly story is made out of the whole cloth!" she said hotly. "It is true that Gabriel de Cerreno is coming to visit me. But he's no more an emissary of the Pope than you are. He's a cousin of mine! You know he is, and you know he's a saint too! You said so yourself in Granada! And this is the way you repay his kindness to you! Slandering him! Slandering Jacqueline! Slandering me!"

"Look here, Faith, I don't print that paper. Fletcher prints it. I told you he'd fight dirty. Mebbe I wuz a little too hasty, the way I spoke. But you'll never make the voters of this state believe this is just a friendly visit of the Bishop's, never in the world. Most of 'em don't know you ever *wuz* in Spain. Lord Almighty, ain't we sweated blood, to make 'em *forget* how much time you spent in Europe! I've always ben a mite uneasy about your leanin's ever since I see you goin' to Mass with the Perezes, and that's a fact. I spoke to Sarah Atkinson at the time, and——"

"Why, I never had any leanings! I went to church with the Perezes just because it seemed natural! But there's a limit to what I can stand, and I'll ask Gabriel, the instant he gets here, what you *do* to join the Catholic Church! And if it's possible, I *will* join it, right away! This is a country of religious freedom, isn't it? I suppose I can be a Catholic if I want to! And I think I *do* want to!"

She was weeping hysterically. Caleb, aghast at the imminent wreckage of all his hopes, was still staring at her helplessly, when Pansy Perkins, impassive, collected and tranquil, came silently into the room.

"San Antonio is calling you on the telephone, Mrs. Marlowe," she said imperturbably. "Will it be convenient for you to accept the call now, or would you rather have it repeated in an hour?"

Faith snatched up the receiver. "Yes!" she said, still hysterically. *"Yes—*YES—This is Mrs. Marlowe. Oh—oh—of course I will!" The tension in her voice snapped suddenly. The next words she pronounced were so different in tone that Caleb could hardly believe they were uttered by the same woman. A stream of musical liquid Spanish followed, and Caleb, staring open-mouthed at her, saw that she was not crying any more, that she was drying her eyes with her free hand, that she was smiling a little. She hung up the receiver, and turned to him with composure.

"Gabriel's plans have been changed. He's going from San Antonio to Mexico," she said. "He isn't going to sail for Spain until just after Christmas. He asked if I usually spent that here, and I told him always. We will feel very close to Christ, having him with us then."

Her face had softened almost unbelievably. Caleb felt both smitten and touched; but he was immeasurably relieved. By Christmas time the election, for good or evil, would be a thing of the past.

"Incidentally, he suggested to me," Faith went on, her expression hardening again, "that I shouldn't take the trouble to deny Mr. Fletcher's announcement, reports of which had just come to him over the wire with a request for a statement. He has wired back that he was dumbfounded at the rumors which had reached him, as he was just leaving San Antonio to visit a cousin of his in Mexico—it's too funny, Uncle Caleb, these Cerrenos have cousins everywhere!—And much as he would feel honored to pay his respects to the first woman Senator, it would be impossible for him to do so. I should hate to be in Mr. Fletcher's shoes when he finds out that there isn't any Cardinal coming to Hamstead, that there isn't any conversion, that the Pope is still in Rome!"

She actually laughed out loud. Caleb, conscious that it was the "bigoted despot" who, in the course of three minutes' conversation, carried on at the distance of several thousand miles, had wrought this change in her, became increasingly bewildered.

"I won't let you down again," she promised. "I'll make all the speeches you say, even if I do have bubonic plague. But Uncle Caleb—if I'm ever awarded the Golden Rose, we won't let Fletcher have the scoop story, will we?"

"I ain't got no idea what you mean," Caleb said shortly. "But you snuck out of trouble by the skin of your teeth again, and I hope you can keep on doin' it six weeks more. But I ain't any too certain. Ned Fletcher ain't through with you yet, and that's a fact. The madder he gets the dirtier he'll fight. And he's going to be mad, good and plenty."

.   .   .   .   .

If there was one person in the state who was angrier than Mr. Edward Fletcher, it was David Noble. His adoration for his wife amounted almost to an obsession; and the slurs cast upon her made him see red with rage. Up to that time his interest in Faith's campaign had not been intensive. He secretly shared the regret which Sam and Hansel felt at her increasing absorption in political life; while as her physician he deplored the already apparent wreckage of the perfect nervous balance which she had built up slowly. He would have resented the unfairness of Fletcher's attack upon her in any case; but if Jacqueline had not been drawn into it, he might have regarded it as a blessing in disguise, had it been instrumental in bringing about Faith's defeat. Considering the turn it had taken, however, his resentment swelled to vengeful fury; and from the day the scurrilous story made its appearance, he became a militant partisan to Faith's cause.

His latent power in the state, overlooked because of his long and frequent absences, and the fact that he had never taken any active part in politics, began to make itself felt. His own fortune, though not as large as his wife's, was substantial; and he had both the leisure and the means to go about putting in quiet but effective work. There was no part of the state in which his personality and his skill had not been leaving their stamp for nearly twenty years: he had grateful patients everywhere, many of them almost fanatically devoted to him; and they had been eagerly awaiting an opportunity to bear testimony to their thankfulness for the miracles of healing he had wrought. He needed to do no more than make a casual suggestion that it would be gratifying to him if they and their families could see their way clear to supporting Faith's candidacy, to have this support assured. Inside of a fortnight, the number of adherents upon whom Faith could absolutely rely, had been increased by hundreds.

She herself was only vaguely conscious of how much David was doing for her, and when he tried to tell her, in order to reasure her of the brightness of the political outlook, he was shocked to see how ravaged she looked. That the tell-tale evidences of fatigue and strain should be evident by now, was to be expected. She had been under pitiless pressure for more than three months. But that she should look haunted as well as exhausted was distressing to him.

"Don't worry any more about that fantastic story of Fletcher's, Faith," he said kindly. "I've got the snake pretty well scotched now I think."

"Scotched but not killed!" she quoted with a wan smile. "David—I keep waiting for something dreadful to happen, the way I did during the first part of the war. I'm sure Fletcher's going to get out another story. In fact, there was an item in the *Clarion-Herald* yesterday, stating that, 'Further startling revelations concerning the true character of the unwomanly aspirant of Senatorial honors will soon be released.'"

"Well, suppose there are more startling revelations? You know perfectly that there isn't anything that can be said any more convincing than that other story was. People are laughing at Fletcher everywhere for printing such a far-fetched yarn."

"He might print something about—about Sebastian and me. If he found out about that—"

"But good Lord, Faith, how could he find out about that?"

"I don't know. But I'm terrorized for fear that he may. And if he did, Uncle Caleb would be—stricken. His compromises don't extend to—sexual shortcomings."

"Well, if you're going in for hyperboles!" David exclaimed sharply. Then more gently he added, "Don't talk like that Faith. You were never guilty of any sexual shortcomings, and you know it—or would, if you weren't letting yourself get morbid."

"And Hansel!" she went on, almost as if she had not heard him. "You know how a boy feels about his mother —when she is involved in anything like that!"

"Faith, you never were involved in anything! Do look at all this sensibly. As a matter of fact, Hansel isn't thinking half so much about this campaign of yours as he is about his own little personal triumphs. He's done well to stick on the football squad as long as this, because he's underweight—if he gets his letter, it'll be a triumph of grit over sensitiveness. And the fact that he's already been taken into the Instrumental Club is real recognition of some very real talent. Did you know he'd been working on the score of a musical pantomime for nearly a year, Faith?"

"No," acknowledged Faith in astonishment. "I wonder why he never told me?"

"You haven't had much time to devote to Hansel lately, have you, Faith?"

She admitted that she had not, but added that she was planning to give up a week-end entirely to him very soon. She did not realize, when she spoke, how soon this would be. Fletcher's second broadside was discharged the following Friday, and as Pansy brought in the paper and laid it down, with the calm manner and trembling lip characteristic, with her, of supreme emotion, Faith's desperate thoughts leaped forward to the frenzied certainty that the disclosure she had so long been dreading, had at last been made. Her conviction of this was so strong, that she did not once visualize the black headlines towering before her accurately. When she did, their unexpectedness staggered her as much as their calumny:

"DIABOLICAL MACHINATIONS REVEALED
"FAITH MARLOWE'S WAR RECORD DISCLOSED IN
HIDDEN DOCUMENTS
"SERVED AS SPY THROUGHOUT WORLD WAR
"ATTILA THE HUN WALKS AGAIN IN HIS FOL-
LOWERS' FOOTSTEPS

"SHALL WE SEND A TRAITOR TO THE SENATE?
"Belford, Oct. 15.

"After painstaking research, carried on in spite of almost insuperable obstacles, the *Clarion-Herald* is able to give its readers the true story of the woman calling herself Faith Marlowe, whose name is actually Faith von Hohenlohe. As a young girl, renouncing her American heritage for a mess of red pottage, she married a Prussian officer; and she served as his confederate in casting the diabolically widespread net which later was to snare the fine flower of America to its doom. When the conflict for which Germany, the pariah nation, had set the stage with fiendish glee became imminent, Rudolf von Hohenlohe sent his wife to act as his agent in the United States. Trespassing on the sacred soil of the forefathers to whom she had played false, she sent him constant communications in code. The frequency with which cabled messages were received in Hamstead and sent from there is attested. How great a burden of responsibility for wholesale murder rests on the shoulders of this woman and her husband. it is still impossible to say, though later disclosures will doubtless reveal all. Far from repenting of her distardly deeds, she has caused them to be perpetuated by erecting a statue to her partner in crime which commemorates his blood guiltiness. Thus the atrocities committed by men like Rudolf von Hohenlohe and women like his wife can never be forgotten by the people of this state."

"Mrs. Marlowe, don't—don't look like that! *No one* will believe this—The other was fantastic—but this is chimerical! Oh, I can't bear to have you feel so!"

Pansy was weeping so bitterly she could hardly speak. Faith, her face ashen, looked past her without seeming to see or hear her. So this ghoul had not even spared the great and honorable dead, slain for the fatherland—

The telephone had begun to ring clamorously. Outside, someone was hammering importunately on the knocker. There was a sound of motors whirring up the driveway. As if oblivious of every sight and sound, Faith walked out of the library and up the stairs, and locking herself in the deserted attic, flung herself on her knees under the great Crucifixion.

When at last she stirred from her agonized lethargy, it was to realize that the one voice that she could not disregard was calling to her, and that frenzied hands were battering at the door. She drew herself up slowly by the heavy bedpost, and walked across the room with dragging feet. As she turned the latch, Hansel pitched forward against her.

"Why wouldn't you let me in?" he cried agonizingly. "Didn't you know I had to see you—had to—had to! When I came off the football field the newsboys were all screaming extra—and then I heard—I saw.... I jumped in my car and drove straight through here! Mother—do you see what you've given them a chance to say about my father, who died for his country? That he was a criminal, that his hands were stained with blood! *My father!*—I'll never forgive you, never as long as I live!"

He wrenched himself free from the hands with which she strove to clasp him. Then he fell at her feet in a dead faint.

. . . . . .

"No, Faith, it isn't a concussion—that is I hope it isn't. But I *am* afraid of chill as well as shock. Be patient, and try to be as quiet as you can. For the boy's sake, my dear."

Hansel lay, still unconscious, on Sam's bed under the somber hovering picture. Faith sat on one side of him, her body

361

shaken with sobs, her head hidden in her hands. On the other side David was standing, his dexterous fingers at Hansel's inert wrists, his searching eyes on the boy's pallid face. Pansy and Jacqueline were moving noiselessly about the room. Suddenly Faith looked up.

"Pansy," she said in a harsh whisper. "Go and get Mr. Hawks on the telephone. You know what you are to tell him."

"Just a minute," David interrupted impellingly. His gaze did not wander by a hair's breadth from the motionless form in front of him. But he spoke with such intensity that Faith suddenly looked up, swayed by the certainty that he was facing her, and that he was forcing her to face him.

"Listen to me," he commanded, "This isn't just your fight any more—just a case of pretending you're not beaten when you know you are. You've got to vindicate Rudolf's name now as well as your own, for the sake of your son —and his. This boy's. If he convicts you as a coward, you'll never lift your head again as long as you live."

Chapter XLVI

"Mother, Sam didn't ever tell you why he wanted to go to Europe, did he?"

"No, darling, never."

"Didn't you ask him?"

"I don't remember. No, I don't believe I did. Why? Does it matter?"

"I don't know. I just happened to wonder, because I thought, perhaps he hoped you would ask him, perhaps he hoped you'd be interested in knowing. Instead of just being interested in the campaign, I mean."

Faith, locking and unlocking her fingers, pressed her lips together to keep them from quivering. Hansel was sitting up in bed now, with a high pile of snowy pillows behind his shining head, and there was a faint color in the young face, which, during the last year, had rapidly been losing its childish softness. A mass of periodicals lay in front of him, and he was turning the pages of these with desultory attention. Decidedly, in the past day or two, he had gained with surprising rapidity. But there had been a hideous interval, of which Faith knew she would never be able to think without shuddering, when she had been almost certain that Hansel was slipping away from her, that the scope of the tragedy through which she had risen to fame had been widened to embrace her child as well as her lover.

In attacking Faith through her dead husband, Edward Fletcher had been guilty of an error in judgment even far more serious than that he had committed in charging Jacqueline Noble with complicity in a plot with Faith. In the first instance, he had indirectly rallied hundreds to Faith's support through David, whose power he had underestimated; in the second he had indirectly rallied hundreds of others to her support through Hansel, whose power he had entirely overlooked. The news of the boy's collapse and the cause of it had spread like wildfire among an indignant and outraged people. There was not a village in the state where Hansel's shy, charming smile, his pleasant appealing voice, and the unaggressive grace of his manner had not made a deep impression. Even the way he had always brought the green caravan to a stop, leaning nonchalantly forward to put on the brake and shut off the engine, and then glancing toward his mother, as if to be certain of her unspoken approval, before turning with his wide disarming smile of friendliness toward the crowd, had been an entering wedge toward cordial relations. The music that rippled from under his slim fingers was permeated with elfin magic; the greetings which he gave so naturally as he mingled unostentatiously with audiences after meetings and welcomed guests before gatherings, had a fascination which was the more inescapable because it was utterly innocent of self-consciousness and sophistication. There was an almost spiritual quality to it, which his youthfulness and his ingenuousness enhanced. When the word went out that his life and reason were hanging on a thread, Caleb Hawks' declaration that if the boy died, lynching would be too good for Edward Fletcher, found a response so universal that it echoed not only through the state but through the country. When the word went out that he was really better, people laughed and cried for joy when they met together.

Neal Conrad, taking an extra campaign burden upon his capable shoulders, made an announcement whenever he rose to speak which never failed to crystalize the attention and cement the sympathies of his audience. "I know that you were all hoping with me that my friend, Faith Marlowe, the first woman candidate for the United States Senate, would be on the platform with me to-night. Since I resigned from the Senate myself, in order to facilitate her candidacy, I do not need to tell you that she represents my own choice for this high position. In my opinion, she will reflect fresh honors on the name which has already stood for so much that is noble and great in the annals of our country. 'Let us have another Marlowe in the Senate,' should be more than a slogan. It should be a watchword." Here he always paused impressively, in response to a storm of applause. "Naturally, it was Mrs. Marlowe's intention to greet you herself on this auspicious occasion, and to present to you in her own words the policies of the great party to which we confidentially expect you will entrust the destinies of this nation. But she is prevented from being with you for a tragic reason: her only son, the namesake of his grandfather and his great-grandfather, Christian Marlowe III, is lying at death's door. He is the room-mate of my own son at college, and like many of you, I have known him well from childhood. I know you are hoping with me that he may be spared to the state and the nation—and to his mother." Here Neal paused again, with a break in his voice, while a tense silence gripped his audience. "A dastardly attack made upon the boy's dead father, a brave and gallant soldier, came as a terrific shock to this boy when he was not physically or mentally prepared to meet it. He rushed from the football field, and drove for hours through the bitter cold of a windy night to get to his mother, after a newsboy, with careless cruelty, had shouted the slanderous story in his ears. Shock and pneumonia were the result. Pray with me for his recovery—and to his distraught mother, watching at his bedside, give such comfort as lies in your power—the comfort of knowing that, in spirit, you are sharing her vigil, and that she may count on your loyalty to her during her ordeal!"

•   •   •   •   •

Even the indefatigable Pansy could not keep abreast of the avalanche of telegrams of sympathy under which Faith's desk lay buried; and the offerings of flowers, fruit and miscellaneous delicacies, which poured in upon Hansel would have supplied all the patients in a small hospital. But Faith, though she yielded to the importunities with which Caleb Hawks and Cavendish Castle reënforced David's stern admonition that she must not withdraw from her candidacy, steadfastly declined to take any further active part in the campaign. This was her compromise, she stated unequivocally; if an attempt were made to coerce her, she would retire altogether. Her attitude admitted of no doubt that she meant what she said; and aware that for the moment her very absence from the arena had its own peculiar and poignant appeal, the campaign managers allowed her to remain unmolested by Hansel's bedside, hopefully confident that by the time the last rousing rallies were being held, he would be well on the road to recovery, and that she would voluntarily emerge from seclusion.

As Hansel made his ingenuous reference to her preoccupation, Faith's heart contracted. She had missed Sam hideously in the ordeal through which she had been passing; and the ever-deepening feeling of bereavement which his absence gave him, intensified her conscience-stricken sense of having failed him. The inactivity and isolation of his life were largely unrelieved when she was not beside him; its darkness was unillumined. She was aware of this and still she had neglected him. While her need of him had been dominant, she had found it easy enough to spend endless hours with him, no matter how multitudinous the occupations which crowded in upon her had been; but when the urgency of her dependency on him had passed, she had disregarded, with cruel carelessness, the urgency of his dependence upon her.

"You see," Hansel went on after a moment's pause," "he did tell me why he was going. He told me the French Government was going to confer the Cross of the Legion of Honor upon him. I happened to think about it just now because there is an article on it in the number of *L'Illustration* which I have here."

Faith's heart contracted again. Sam had known that this great honor was to be bestowed upon him. And it was in Hansel, instead of her, that he had confided. It was to Sarah, instead of her, that he had turned for help.

She stretched out her hand, almost mechanically, to take the magazine and read the story of Sam's triumph. But Hansel, drawing back a little, held it tightly between the thumb and forefinger which marked the place where he had been reading.

"Perhaps I'd better tell you what the article says," he remarked hesitatingly. "It—it might be too much of a shock to you if you read it all by yourself. You see, it seems that when Sam was sure there was going to be a war, after he had seen Cousin Sarah safely off with Jacqueline and David, he shut himself up in his studio and painted and painted and painted. He began to work as soon as it was light in the morning, and worked until it grew dark at night. And of course, in Europe, the days are very long in the middle of the summer, aren't they? So it wasn't long before he finished his picture. And after he finished it, he locked it up in his studio, and went off and left it."

"Did he forget he had left it there, Hansel?"

"No, he didn't forget. He waited for the right time to go back and get it. I think he hoped that when he did you would go with him. He never gave up the studio. He paid rent on it every year—Cousin Sarah attended to that for him. But early this last summer there was a bad fire in the building, and when the fireman broke into the studio, they found the picture, and rescued it. And—and it was hailed immediately as a great masterpiece."

"What kind of a picture was it, Hansel?" Faith asked chokingly. But she knew.

"It was a picture of you, mother, a picture of 'Faith.' "

He still held the copy of *L'Illustration* firmly beyond her reach. But now he leaned toward her.

"Don't cry, mother," he said tenderly. "There's nothing to cry about. I'm going to tell you a lovely story, much lovelier and more wonderful really than any fairy story you ever told me. You see, the picture was put on exhibition, and thousands of people went to see it. They felt as if it was almost a—miraculous picture, because of the way it had been painted and hidden, and then found and saved and all. And because it—well, it represents so much. It isn't just a picture of a beautiful woman—it's a picture of a woman who is the incarnation of faith. She symbolizes what faith means to everyone in the world. No one has ever interpreted that before as marvelously as Sam has now."

"Hansel, you must let me see it."

"I'm going to, mother. But not until you've listened to me."

Through her tears, Faith looked at him in astonishment. He was speaking to her in a voice of authority, which was not his voice, as she recognized this, but a voice she had not heard in years—his father's voice. For the first time, as she faced him, she realized that she was not only confronted by her own son, but by the son of Rudolf von Hohenlohe. Though half of his heritage had been so long submerged, he was still essentially the child of a dual tradition, and now the part he had almost forgotten was clamoring for acknowledgment.

"When Sam comes home," Hansel went on, compellingly, "he'll bring this picture with him. It'll be put in the museum at Bedford. I don't believe he'll give it to the museum, but he'll lend it. I think he wants to keep it himself, the way he kept the one he painted of you just before you and father were engaged—that was saved too. The French Government has offered him every inducement to part with 'Faith,' and he won't. I think probably he'll put it up in the attic by and by. You know how he feels about having things like that around, even though he can't see them. He

366

told me once you'd been wonderful about realizing that. It seems strange to me, mother, when you guessed how Sam felt about being surrounded by beautiful things, that you shouldn't have guessed how much he wanted to have you with him. Cousin Sarah does all she can for him, I know, and he appreciates it. But of course he doesn't love Cousin Sarah the way he loves you."

"Hansel, you don't know what you're saying."

"Yes, I do. I know just what I'm saying. I know Sam has loved you ever since you were a little girl, and I know he doesn't dare let you see how much, because he thinks it wouldn't be fair, now that he is blind and you are famous It isn't because of my father. He knows my father told you that he was thankful to feel you could count on Sam's devotion whatever happened, and that he hoped some day Sam would be rewarded."

"Hansel—Sam can't—can't possibly know that your father said that."

"But he does. I've heard father say it, and I told Sam so myself."

"Oh, Hansel! *You didn't!*"

"Yes, I did. I'm glad of it too. But I can't argue about that now. It's bothersome getting tired so easily——"

"Darling, I don't think you ought to talk more anyway. Just let me see the picture, and then——"

"I'm going to let you see the picture in a minute, And I won't be half so tired if I tell you what I want to before I rest, as I will be if I lie here thinking that I haven't told you what I started out to say about the picture. Sam will be home with it next week and put it in the museum at Belford. And of course there will be copies of it in all the rotogravure sections and stories about it in all the newspapers. It is wonderful, isn't it, mother, that Sam should have painted it the way he did and that it should have been found the way it was and that it should mean so much to the people who look at it?—Of course that's because it meant so much to Sam, and because he has the genius to show how he feels. I think you're wonderful too, mother, but I can't prove it to the whole world the way Sam does."

He smiled suddenly, his illusive irresistible smile. As she had recognized Rudolf's voice in his for the first time, so Faith now recognized Victoria Luise's expression. She had always taken it for granted that Hansel looked exactly like her. Now she saw that except for his coloring, he looked very much as the Archduchess must have looked when she was seventeen.

"You understand, don't you, mother, that everyone who

sees the picture and copies of it, and reads stories about it, will get the feeling that they didn't realize before how wonderful you were? Because of course a woman who is *very wonderful* would make a man feel that he had to paint a picture like that. I'm not saying this very well, because I'm getting sort of tired, but what I mean is, lots people will be thinking about this pretty hard just about the first of November, and—and——"

He broke off, groping for words. Faith found that she was powerless to help him go on.

"You know those big rallies, in Hinsboro and Belford, the two nights before election, mother? Well, if you ask Sam, don't you think he'd go to them with you? And then you see, when you came out with Sam, on the platform, wearing a dress something like this in the picture, and started to speak, and—and everything—Oh, mother, won't you do it, just to please me? You see I'm so awfully sorry I said what I did to you about never forgiving you because people had slandered my father, of course I know it wasn't your fault at all, that you've always been loyal to father. It's marvelous for a boy to be able to feel that his mother's been so loyal to his father, only really, I don't want you to be *too* loyal, that is—But if you're not elected now, I'll feel it's my fault, because you've had to stay at home with me while I've been sick and everything, and if you do what I say at those rallies, I know you will be elected, and so, oh mother, won't you *please?* Won't you *promise?*"

The voice of authority had vanished, and with it the illusion of all that it represented. Faith saw only a fragile boy, exhausted by illness and emotion, leaning forward to clasp his arms around her neck, and hiding his face on her shoulder so that she would not see that he was crying. The magazine he had been holding slipped to the floor, falling open at a full-page picture. As she turned to look at it, Faith found herself gazing at a vision of such mystic splendor that she caught her breath. Unsullied and undefeated by the world wreckage which formed the shadowy background of the painting, the radiant figure of a woman emerged puissant and victorious from the carnage with which she was surrounded. She seemed to transcend sin and suffering, disaster and death. Her bearing was triumphant; her face was exalted. The golden scroll with which the picture was bound was illuminated, as a priceless missal might have been. Half-blinded with tears as she was, Faith knew that it was inscribed with the immortal words of the Apostle Paul, which Sam had first heard from her lips years before on a dark and stormy night at sea:

"Stand therefore . . . having on the breastplate of righteousness, and your feet shod with the preparation of the gospel of peace; above all, taking the *shield of faith,* wherewith ye shall be able to quench all the fiery darts of the wicked."

Faith, clasping her son in her arms, bent her head until it rested against his. Their tears mingled together. But when at last she spoke to him, her voice was strong and joyous.

"My precious treasure," she said vibrantly, "of course I will! Of course I promise!"

Chapter XLVII

THE President of the United States and Mrs. Conrad were saying good-bye to the guests who had lunched with them after the inauguration, pausing for a moment, as they made the round of the circle which had formed in the Red Room, for a personal word with each in turn.

"This is the same sort of a chain that the diplomats used to make at the Royal Receptions in Copenhagen, isn't it, mother?" Christian Marlowe III asked in an interested whisper, his attentive-gaze shifting for a moment from the lovely lady in fawn-colored lace who was advancing toward them at the President's side, and resting, with even more admiration, on his mother.

"The circle is formed in something the same way; but everything else is different, and it seems to me much pleasanter!" Faith Marlowe whispered back.

Her own smiling glance wandered from the tall graceful boy beside her to the wood fire glowing under the white mantel banked with flowers, and the south window where the warm spring sunshine streamed generously into the room. The rich crimson walls and hangings, the austere Presidential portraits in their massive frames, the furniture, the decorations, even the guests, seemed transfigured in its mellow warmth. The apartment had all the dignity and elegance befitting the drawing-room in the residence of the Chief Executive of a great nation. But there was nothing forbiddingly formal about it. It emanated a festive friendliness.

"Junior tells me that you went on the Dean's List at midyear's, Christian, and that this means you can stay over for the inaugural ball to-night."

The lovely lady in fawn color and the distinguished-looking man with the firm chin and square shoulders had stopped in front of Hansel. They were both regarding him with cordiality and affection.

"Yes, Mr. President. I'm awfully pleased."

"We're pleased too—and we'll look for you there. And Christian, when you come to Washington for your Easter vacation, we shall expect you for dinner. The new moving picture machine will be all ready for use then. If your mother can spare you, perhaps you'll stay overnight with Junior, just for the fun of sleeping in the White House."

"Thank you, Mrs. Conrad, you know I'd love to."

The Presidential pair had gone forward another step. Hansel watched them excitedly as they paused before his mother.

"Well, Senator Marlowe, I know I can count on your support in every one of the measures I'm hoping to put through in the extra session."

"Absolutely, Mr. President. I won't desert you for a day, even if the thermometer goes up to a hundred and fifty!"

"Aren't you too ceremonious, with your 'Senator Marlowe,' and your 'Mr. President'! I hope it's going to be Anne and Neal and Faith, just as it has been all the years we've been neighbors."

"Absolutely again! And we're still going to be neighbors! I have a surprise for you! I'll telephone to-morrow and find out when I may come and talk to you about it."

Anne Conrad had passed along beside her husband, her laces flowing about her. Hansel turned to his mother with enthusiasm.

"They haven't changed at all, have they, mother? Somehow, I couldn't help being afraid they would, after this morning—Can we go over to Sam and Cousin Sarah now?"

"In just a minute, darling. We must wait until the President and Mrs. Conrad have gone out of the room and upstairs—at White House parties, it's the host and hostess who leave first. But next time we come here, nothing will be so formal."

The folding doors leading into the great entrance hall opened and closed impressively. Immediately afterwards, the circle broke, and the guests, converging into small congenial groups, moved forward, talking with animation. Faith and Hansel, crossing the room quickly, joined Sam and Sarah Atkinson, who had stopped to congratulate Carolus Cavendish Castle on his appointment as Secretary of the Navy.

Mrs. Castle, armored with satisfaction and importance, was competently appropriating these congratulations.

"You'll let us take you over to the hotel, won't you, Faith?" she asked, when she felt that enough had been said on this paramount question. "We have room for Mrs. Atkinson and Mr. Dudley, too. The new official car is very spacious."

"It's ever so kind of you. But after all, it's only a step to the Willard. And it's such a perfect afternoon, I thought we might walk around Lafayette Square, before we went back to the hotel. I think we can do it and still be in time for the parade."

"My dear Faith, *nobody* bothers with parades any more! And why should you want to walk around Lafayette Square?"

"To see the house where my grandfather and father lived—the house where I'm going to live too! I've bought it back.—And Hansel adores parades. All boys do. And so does Uncle Caleb. We're going to meet him."

Mrs. Castle gave an expression of horror. "But my dear Faith, you can't live on Lafayette Square! It's changed tremendously since your grandfather's day, even since your father's. There's actually a tea-shop on it, and I'm told that the club which has its headquarters in the old Randall House is communistic! You won't have any suitable neighbors."

"Well, after all, I'll have Neal and Anne. They're suitable. Don't feel so upset, Aunt Annabelle. It's all settled anyway. What I need to do now is to take my family to see the house, and get a consensus of views on remodeling. I want to get started on the work right away, especially as I'll have to be here all summer, now that Neal's going to call an extra session. Do you mind terribly if I go out of the door in front of you? I know it's contrary to all precedent—I may start a new controversy, Senate versus Cabinet, but I must get started!"

She laughed lightly, stopped to shake hands with Mr. Cooper, the head usher, who stood, formal and vigilant, near the front door, bowed, passed out of the portico. Hansel, placing his hand protectingly under her elbow as they went down the steps, began to talk excitedly.

"The moving-picture men will be just outside the gate, mother—don't you want Sam and me to walk on either side of you, so we can push right by them? And Pennsylvania Avenue is roped off for the parade—I'm afraid we can't get through. Why didn't you tell me before about the house? Have you bought it really?"

371

"Yes, really. I always said I was coming back to begin again where my father left off, and I wanted his house as well as his seat in the Senate—I didn't tell you about it because I was keeping it for a surprise—I think we can cross all right if we go up the Avenue a little further. And of course I want Sam and you beside me. I think we might almost walk four abreast, don't you? Then Cousin Sarah and I could be in the middle and you and Sam——"

In spite of their combined perseverance, their progress was slow. The barrage of cameras and moving-picture machines was almost impassable; and the crowd, already gathering for the parade, was surging through the streets. Faith finally appealed to a policeman.

"I'm Senator Marlowe," she said swiftly, "and I want very much to take my son and my—my cousins across the street to see my grandfather's house. We're going to live there ourselves. Do you think you could help us?"

She glanced from the policeman toward Sam, and the officer, following her look, saw what she had not wished to say. He was galvanized into immediate action.

"Stand back there!" he shouted belligerently, addressing the multitude. "Come right along, Senator Marlowe.—Now if you'll just take this gentleman's arm—"

"There!" Faith exclaimed five minutes later. "It wasn't hard after all, was it? We're almost opposite the house now, Sam. It *is* a gloomy gaunt old-looking structure. But I *wanted* it."

"Of course you did!" Sam agreed instantly. He had been rather silent through the inaugural exercises and the luncheon, but now he spoke with evident interest. "I suppose it will need a great deal of repairing and remodeling. But then, you enjoy that sort of thing."

"Yes, I do. And I knew I could count on you to help me. I thought I would have a basement entrance, to do away with the long flight of steps, and make more room on the first floor. The front and back parlors can be thrown into one long drawing-room, I think, with a large dining room behind. The library will still be on the floor above, just as my father and grandfather had it, and I'll have the small study and big bedroom in the rear that were theirs too. That still leaves two stories above with all kinds of space for the rest of you. Would you like the room that used to be mine, Hansel?—Cousin Sarah, you and Sam can have a private sitting-room, and I thought I'd see about putting in an elevator.—Of course the plumbing will all have to be done over—there used to be just *one* bathroom, with a huge funny tin tub enclosed in a rectangular wooden box—and the service quarters must have been terrible, though I don't remember them distinctly.—Oh, we're *here!* I think that black walnut front door is rather impressive-looking, don't you, Cousin Sarah, even if it is dark? I don't believe I'll change that! Shall we go in? Here's the key, Hansel, darling!"

There were tears in her eyes as she stepped inside the door, out of which she had been thrust so precipitously and acrimoniously a quarter of a century before. For a moment she stood still, almost expecting to hear Lily and Ella clattering about in the kitchen, or her mother's shrill voice rising above her father's unhappy protests in the library. Then she linked her arm through Sam's again, and spoke with attempted lightness.

"I'm superstitious about a house," she said. "I always feel as if the people who had lived in it had left their imprint on it, no matter how far away from it they've gone, no matter how long they've been dead. Shall we go upstairs? I want to see my father's library first of all—and then I'm going to look out of the rear windows and try to plan for a little backyard garden. It'll be such a godsend during the summer. I'd like to build a very high wall, to shut out all the unsightly surroundings, and have trellises and a fountain and—can't you visualize just how it would look, Sam?"

"Yes, exactly. You'd have brick walks as well as brick walls, wouldn't you? And borders of pansies? Ramblers on the trellises, and perhaps a bush of old-fashioned yellow roses in the corner? That's the idea, isn't it?"

They all made helpful suggestions. As they went from room to room, Faith felt that their interest and enthusiasm had taken fire from her own; and it was not until they had all returned to the Willard that her sense of abundant joy was shadowed. They were to dine with the Nobles and Caleb Hawks, and go on to the charity ball afterwards. But meanwhile there was a welcome interval for rest and relaxation. And Faith, after slipping into a negligee and ordering tea came back into the pleasant parlor of her suite to find that Sarah, Sam, and Hansel had already gathered there. Sarah had spoken of lying down for a little while, and realizing that she was very tired, Faith was astonished to see that she had changed her mind. She was also astonished at the sudden hush that fell on the little group, almost as if some subject had been under discussion, a continuation of which her presence precluded. She looked from one to the other, smiling.

"What are you doing, plotting?" she asked gaily. And as

no one answered immediately, she went on, "Really, you all act as if I had caught you conspiring against me!"

"Perhaps you might call it that, Faith," Sarah Atkinson said slowly.

"Why, what have I done to deserve such shabby treatment?"

"You have done nothing to deserve shabby treatment, my dear. And I hope you will not feel that any one of us is treating you shabbily. But now that you have surprised us by your fortunate purchase of your old home, we feel that perhaps we should speak to you about our own plans, before we allow you to proceed any further without knowing what these are. We were just considering the question in its various aspects when you came in."

"I see. I'm very sorry that I interrupted. Shall I go away again?"

She spoke with slight sarcasm. After all, this was the greatest day of her life, and instead of permitting her to enjoy it in unalloyed triumph, those who were nearest and dearest to her were apparently preparing to pour drops of bitter into her cup of sweet. She half turned toward her room. But as she did so, Hansel sprang to her side, and put his arm around her waist.

"Don't go, mother," he said imperatively. "Come and sit down beside me on the sofa, won't you? There's nothing we mind telling you, nothing at all. It's just that we hadn't planned to tell you *to-day*. But as Cousin Sarah says, if you're going to start fixing over the house immediately, we thought perhaps you'd do it a little differently, if you realized we wouldn't all be there with you."

Faith looked at him in consternation. The clear direct gaze with which he confronted her did not waver.

"Suppose you explain, Hansel," she said trying to speak quietly.

"Well, mother, you know I was terribly disappointed that we didn't go to Germany last year. But I knew you couldn't, with the campaign and all, and I knew you needed me to help you. So when you promised, absolutely promised, that we should go this year instead, I tried to pretend it really didn't matter very much; and I've been counting off the days on my calendar all winter, and I got sailing schedules and found the *Deutschland* leaves the day after college closes——"

"But Hansel, darling, be reasonable! When I made that promise I had no idea Neal would call an extra session! I've got to stay in Washington."

"Yes, mother, I know you've got to. But I haven't. So I

374

think I'll start for Germany the day after college closes, even if you can't go with me."

There was a knock at the door, and a waiter entered noisily bearing tea. Sarah Atkinson rose, supervised the arrangement of the table with a vain attempt to prevent the rattle of dishes, bestowed a liberal tip, and murmured hasty assurances, designed to check a flow of volubility, to the effect that she would ring if more hot water were needed, and that she really didn't think that any of them cared for cinnamon toast. When she resumed her seat, without reference to the inopportune interruption, she saw that Sam's expression was inscrutable, and heard Hansel calmly continuing his declaration of independence.

"I want to see my grandfather and grandmother," he was saying with succinctness. "I want to spend at least a month with them at Schönplatz. I want to do that every summer from now on. I'm going to be the next Baron von Hohenlohe, and it's disgraceful that I shouldn't know anything about the management of the estate. It must be very sad for my grandparents, now that they are growing old, to keep thinking that all their sons were killed in the war, and that the only Hohenlohe grandson who wasn't killed too, hasn't even seen the place that will be his property some day, since he was seven years old. I should think it would make them wish they could give it to one of the von Mitfelds, one of Aunt Rita's children. But they can't. It's entailed. They have to give it to me."

"But Hansel," Faith said faintly, "I never thought of you as the next Baron von Hohenlohe. I've thought of you for nearly ten years as Christian Marlowe III. Your father said he was perfectly willing you should choose——"

"I know he did, mother. And I have chosen. I like Hamstead, and I love you, and I'm very proud of the Marlowe tradition. But I don't feel, inside, like an American myself. I feel like a German. I am a German. I want to go home, just as much as you wanted to come home."

Faith gave a little cry of anguish. Sam, rising suddenly, walked over with uncanny directness, to the sofa where she and Hansel were, and sat down beside her.

"Let the boy go on, Faith," he said in a low voice. "All this has been bottled up inside of him for a long time."

"I want to go to Bonn," Hansel continued inexorably. "I want to find the rooms my father had when he was there at the University, and try to reserve them for myself. I'm willing to go through Harvard, if I can spend every summer vacation in Germany, but after I've graduated at Harvard, I want to take a post-graduate course at Bonn. I want to

375

study music, too. I want to have a boat on the Rhine, and go camping in the Black Forest, and see the picture galleries in Munich and Dresden and go to the Musical Festivals at Bayreuth. Of course I'll be very pleased to have you come with me, mother, whenever you can, and stay with me as much as you can, and I'm sure grandfather and grandmother will too. They've always loved you dearly, you know that. But I'm going home this summer, even though you can't come with me, and by and by I'm going home to stay. This isn't any time for Germans to be living in some foreign country. They're needed in their own."

He put his arms around her again, and kissed her on her rigid cheek. "I'm sorry, mother," he said more gently. "Really, I didn't mean to tell you this to-day. But when you began talking about fixing up that room that used to be yours for me, I thought you'd feel much worse, if I let you go ahead and do it, and then told you, than——".

"You're altogether too young to make a decision like this," Faith exclaimed suddenly. "I shan't allow it. When you're twenty-one, if you still feel this way, I suppose I can't stop you from going to Germany. But I can now. I shan't let you go."

"Faith, you were just Hansel's age, when Rudolf first declined to let you come home," Sam cut in. "Have you forgotten how you felt?"

"That was different."

"It wasn't different. It was the same—essentially. If you don't let the boy go, Faith, you'll lose him—in the same way Rudolf lost you. If you do let him go, you may keep him."

The telephone jangled. Sarah Atkinson rose, and walking past the table where the tea still stood cooling, picked up the receiver.

"Yes, this is Senator Marlowe's apartment," she said crisply, "but the Senator is in conference. She cannot accept any calls this afternoon. No, not from anyone. When she is at leisure again, I will advise you."

Again she resumed her place in the easy chair beside the sofa, her gray taffeta dress rustling as she disposed it about her. Faith had not answered Sam, and the moment seemed to Sarah opportune for speaking herself.

"I think Sam is right, my dear," she said composedly, "and when you have reflected a little, I believe you will see that he is yourself. Perhaps it would be well not to try to cross too many bridges at once. But at least you can give your consent ungrudgingly to the trip this summer. If Congress should adjourn by August, which is quite possible, you

376

could still join Hansel in Germany for a few weeks. And meanwhile you would have the satisfaction of knowing that instead of being cooped up in Washington, sweltering, he would be cool and comfortable at Schönplatz."

"He can always go to Hamstead, if it get too hot here."

"Do you think Hansel would be contented in Hamstead, alone?"

"Of course not!" Faith said almost sharply. "I supposed, all the time, that through the worst of the heat you would prefer to be in the country, and so——"

"My dear, I dislike to disappoint you, if you were depending upon me. But I have been waiting for the proper moment to ask you whether you did not feel the time had come at last when I might suitably suggest that I should like to go to Salem."

"To Salem!" echoed Faith, more and more aghast.

"Why, yes. That was my plan, you know, when I first thought of coming back to the United States. I abandoned it temporarily, because Sam asked me if I would not go to Hamstead and wait there for him. It was six years ago in December, Faith, that Sam joined me, and I have tried to be very patient. But now that you have entered the Senate, now that the tenor of your life has changed entirely, I feel that you do not need me as much as you did. I feel I have a right to spend my declining years in my own home. I feel, as Hansel does, that before permitting you to remodel your house with a view to my needs, I should tell you that I shall be there only as an occasional guest. Naturally, my dear, I shall not leave you until it is convenient for you to have me do so. But when it is——"

Faith rose in her turn. "I think," she said slowly and scathingly, "that I had better go into my own room—before Sam begins to tell me what his plans are. I've heard the one woman who's stood by me ever since I was a deserted, frightened little girl, say she's going off to leave me, and I've heard my son—my only child—explain that he's not an American but a German. And though I don't see how I'm going to bear all this, I suppose I shall somehow. But I think I won't listen to any more."

She moved majestically away from them, and went into her room without looking back. But as she tried to turn the key in her latch, the door was flung wide open again and slammed shut; and Sam, with his back against it, stood before her.

"Look here, Faith Marlowe!" he exclaimed vehemently, you have no right to speak about me that way and you

377

know it! If you think you can walk out on me, like a tragedy queen, just because you are now the first woman member of the Senate, you have made a great mistake. One of your greatest. And you've made a good many. Good God, I——"

"Sam, will you please go out of my room? At once? I want to be alone."

"No," he said, still more vehemently. "I will not go out of your room. I won't go at once, and I don't know when I shall go. Perhaps not at all. You don't want to be alone. It's the last thing on earth you want. You're like most people who've climbed to the top of the world. You're appalled to find out what a solitary desolate place it is. But I don't intend that you should be any lonelier there than you have to be. Certainly, I don't intend to let you luxuriate in loneliness. If you deliberately choose to be deserted, perhaps I can't help it. But I think I can. Anyway, before you do choose, I'm going to be damn sure you know what you're doing."

He stepped suddenly forward, and before she could draw back, seized both her hands, holding her at arms' length, but still fettered. She struggled ineffectually to free herself.

"Let me go, Sam! How dare you! You must be out of your mind!"

"I must have *been* out of my mind, to let you get in a state like this before I nipped your heroics in the bud. Stand still, Faith, and stop trying to behave like Sarah Bernhardt, will you? You're a lot nicer when you behave like yourself. You can save your oratory for your maiden speech in the Senate. It'll make a lot bigger hit there than it will with me." Then, as he heard a dry convulsive sob, he added more gently, "And don't do that either. Not until you've listened to me. Isn't there a chair in here where we could sit down and talk?"

"*A* chair?"

"Yes. Sure. A great big one. They have them, even in hotels. Where I could hold you in my lap, the way I used to do in my messy old studio when you were a little girl. I'm positive, Faith, that there's a big chair somewhere in this room, and I think it's awfully unfair of you not to tell me, when—Don't, Faith, don't! I didn't mean to be cross, but you were so damn stagey! You've been playing to galleries so long that you've half forgotten—Faith—darling——"

Her ineffectual struggle against him had ended abruptly. She had ceased trying to wrench herself free, but now he could hear her weeping. He drew a deep breath, and releasing one of her hands, but still holding the other, he groped his way across the room. As his questing fingers closed over a high padded chair back, he stopped, swung it swiftly around, and drew her down into his arms.

"Now then," he said comfortingly, but compellingly, "what do you say we forget that you are famous and I am blind? What do you say we forget that your career is beginning and mine is over? What do you say we forget everything in the world, this next hour, except that I love you and what that means?"

"What—what does it mean?"

"It means that Cousin Sarah is going to Salem and Hans Christian is going to Schönplatz, but that I'm *staying*. With you."

"But, Sam," Faith murmured in a muffled voice, "if you stayed, when Cousin Sarah and Hansel were both gone——"

"It would make a scandal in the Senate? Perish the thought! Whoever heard of such a thing? I'm afraid I shall be driven into making an honest woman of you, Faith. Do you suppose there is a parson in the hotel?"

"Sam! How can you—joke?"

"Faith! How can I be serious? You never let me."

"If—if I did let you—what would you do?"

"Just the same thing I should do if you didn't. I'd marry you. I don't mind in the least being called, 'Senator Marlowe's husband.' Not if I *am*."

She gave a little startled gasp. Sam tightened the clasp in which he held her.

"Listen, darling," he said, and there was no levity in his voice now, "I've stood back and let you go your own way for nearly thirty years. Part of the time I couldn't help it. Part of the time I thought I ought not to try to help it. But now I'm just as sure I ought to make you marry me as I was that I ought to save you from drowning. I know what lies ahead of you better than you do. You're thinking just of making good your childish pledge of coming back to Washington, of taking your father's place, of carrying on his work and his name. I believe you can. I believe you will. But if you try to do it all alone, it'll be a rough road. You saw a little of how rough, this last summer, during the campaign. But that wasn't a circumstance to what it will be later on. Wouldn't it comfort you, Faith, wouldn't it help you, if you knew you didn't have to go over that road alone, that I'd always be near you, making it just as smooth for you as I could?"

"You know it would," she answered softly, "but——"

379

"I know what all the buts are, darling, just as well as you do, and they don't frighten me, not even the biggest one of all—the but that you got married once without being in love with your husband, and that though you're ready to shut your eyes and jump, when it comes to anything else, you don't dare do that again. You got badly burnt, and you're afraid of fire. Aren't you?"

"Yes. Terribly."

He felt her wince as she said it. But he only drew her closer to him.

"I know how much you loved Sebastian," he said gently. "But you don't love him any more. You think you do, but you don't. He set his mark on you and it made a pretty deep wound—you'll carry the scar of it to your grave. But it doesn't hurt you any more. You're still thinking of Sebastian as a vital force that changed the current of your life, and he was. But you haven't thought of him as a man in a long time. You haven't thought of any man—in the sense I mean —for a long time. You made up your mind that you couldn't and that you wouldn't, because of Sebastian. But you could. You can. You're going to."

"Sam!" gasped Faith.

"It's a waste," Sam said cheerfully, "this craze of yours for celibacy. You ought to have a half dozen children. Four anyway. If there ever was a modern woman who was meant to be a fruitful vine, like the one in the Bible, it's you. You were made for maternity. I hope you'll have a baby every year or so. You can have them when the other Senators are off on junkets—they're always ranging around, at government expense, to the Panama Canal and Hawaii and the Philippine Islands. Well, while they're doing that you can have babies. You needn't tell me they would interfere with your public activities, because any woman who can do as many different kinds of things at once as you have in the last few years, can more or less take babies in her stride. There's lots of space for them in that house on Lafayette Square. The big front room on the third floor, for instance, that you meant to give Cousin Sarah would make an ideal nursery. Let's see, this is March. Well, by next Christmas we will certainly have a big bouncing baby in that nursery. We will have a tree for him and Hansel will be crazy about him."

This time Faith was beyond gasping.

"You're all through treating me as if I were an elder brother, or a youngish uncle or someone like that," Sam went on serenely, "kissing me casually on the forehead, and perching on the side of my bed, and sitting in front of the fire with your head against my knees. I don't see why I ever let you get away with it. I'm not your elder brother or your young-ish uncle, and I never felt as if I were. But that doesn't matter any more. We won't waste a minute discussing it. Because from now on, you're going to treat me like a man—a man who's head over heels in love with you and always has been. And pretty soon you're going to treat me like a man you're head over heels in love with yourself."

"But I never could be—head over heels in love again, Sam. I had to stamp—all that out of my life, or I'd have gone insane. It wouldn't be fair to you to——"

"It *hasn't* been fair to me," he amended quietly. "But it's going to be. And it hasn't been wholly fair to you either. I know you've tried to 'stamp all that out of your life,' Faith, and I know why you felt you ought to. But you oughtn't to any longer. You mustn't forget that a woman who cheats nature, pays the penalty for it. No matter how much she gains in other ways—and you've gained a good deal—she loses something too: Gentleness. Sweetness. Bloom. Fecundity. Almost everything we mean when we say femininity. She grows hard or she grows bitter; she grows defensive or she grows aggressive. I haven't seen you, Faith, in ten years, but I know how much you've changed. I know you're beautiful, and still I know that—I wouldn't want to paint you now if I could. Not because you're older—you ought to be magnificent in maturity! But because you press your lips together in a hard line, because the outline of your face is sharper, because the softness has gone from your eyes."

He lifted his hands, and with a lightness that had in it the quality of a caress, touched her hair, her features, her throat, her breast. Then, cupping her face between his fingers, he lifted it to his.

"I want to change all that," he whispered. "I want to as an artist—and I want to as a man. I want the Eve and the Lorelei I painted back again—and the Mary—and the Faith too! I want her for myself—and I want her for the world!"

As he spoke, he drew her face closer and closer to his own. When he finished, their lips were already touching. He pressed his against hers, so gently that instinctively she returned the pressure. Then, almost subconsciously, she realized that the gentleness had fused with urgency, that her head was thrown back and his bent forward, that the embrace in which he now held her locked was as passionate as it was tender. A swift stab of pain, fiery and exquisite, shot through her body. But as it pierced her, all her rigidity, all her resistance, seemed to stream away from her. When at last he lifted his head, her own sank down on his shoulder, and she nestled against him, almost as if she were afraid he might let her go, and that with her release, her new-found sense of ecstasy would be shattered. He put his arms around her again.

"You see," he said exultantly. "But suppose I kiss you again, Faith—just to make sure!"

From Avon  The New Leader in Paperbacks!

Frances Parkinson Keyes

Her rich and colorful novels are set in the most exciting locales in the world, and reflect the whole range of this glittering world's adventures, emotions, mysteries, joys, and tragedies. All the fascinating people of the great cities of the Western Hemisphere and Europe are brought vividly to life by this master talespinner and world traveller. Available now:

ALSO THE HILLS	W150	**$1.25**
CRESCENT CARNIVAL	W141	**$1.25**
HONOR BRIGHT	N194	**95¢**
BLUE CAMELLIA	N177	**95¢**
DINNER AT ANTOINE'S	N174	**95¢**
CAME A CAVALIER	W124	**$1.25**
THE SAFE BRIDGE	N310	**95¢**
SENATOR MARLOWE'S DAUGHTER	V2213	**75¢**
ALL THAT GLITTERS	N176	**95¢**
ROSES IN DECEMBER	N288	**95¢**
FIELDING'S FOLLY	N274	**95¢**
THE CAREER OF DAVID NOBLE	N246	**95¢**
PARTS UNKNOWN	N265	**95¢**
STEAMBOAT GOTHIC	N178	**95¢**
JOY STREET	N182	**95¢**
THE ROYAL BOX	N193	**95¢**
QUEEN ANNE'S LACE	N252	**95¢**
VICTORINE	N231	**95¢**
ONCE ON ESPLANADE	V3261	**75¢**

Include 10¢ per copy for handling; allow 3 weeks for delivery.